LEAVING GREEN ISLAND

a novel

Em Barrett

Published in the United States of America.

First Publishing, 2012

ISBN 978-0-9886163-0-1

www.embarrett.com

For Dan…HH

PART I
SPRING OF 2009

Chapter 1

As Stan Dillingham walks into my office, my only real concern is clicking out of Facebook quickly enough to make it appear as though I am in the midst of doing actual legal work. With all my energy focused on trying to nonchalantly close the browser while I greet my boss, I don't think much of it when he asks if I have plans for the evening.

"No big plans," I say, realizing as the words fall out of my mouth that I have probably just inadvertently walked into a night of searching for non-existent case law on some mundane topic. Unfortunately, the reason for his visit is even worse.

"Oh great!" Stan replies, stepping farther into my office and flashing me a toothy smile. "I'm glad you're free. I wound up with an extra opera ticket for this evening and immediately thought of you since I know you're a big fan of live music. It'll be with a group of people, should be a wonderful performance."

"Oh wow, opera, huh," I say, as I frantically search for an excuse to get out of attending the opera on a Monday night with my skeazy boss and his friends. "I don't think I've ever been to the opera actually..."

"Never been to the opera? You're kidding? Well, it's *Parsifal*, and you'll love it. I have to grab my coat from my office but I'll be right back, and then we can walk over together."

With that, he is out the door, and my fate for the evening is apparently sealed. I close my office door and call my best friend as I slump in my chair. I swear I can see my will to live seeping out onto the floor as

he phone to my ear. Thankfully, Lizzy
ı the first ring.

ou see Andrew Wells's pictures? Can you
believe it?" she starts in without so much as a
greeting.

"I haven't gotten to them yet," I reply, realizing
that my despondent state is making my voice
unattractively whiny. "I got your email and was
pulling up Facebook when I got myself into the most
annoying situation..."

"Oh no, I want to hear about it, but you need to
look at those pictures right now."

"I can't – I have to go to the opera with Stan
Dillingham and his friends tonight, and we're leaving
in literally one minute," I explain, wondering why she
is so desperate for me to look at photos of some old
acquaintance of ours anyway. I quickly start to fill her
in on how it is that I unintentionally agreed to spend
my Monday night at the opera with my boss and a
group that will most likely consist of his gang of
fellow pseudo-intellectual divorcee yuppies when she
cuts me off.

"Brecken!" She accentuates both syllables in my
name. "Are you sure it's *Parsifal*? I think that opera is
like six hours long! Literally, six hours. Google it. You
poor thing." Count on Lizzy to know the length of
some random opera. "But, more importantly, you *need*
to look at Andrew's new photos right now, before
you go. Breck, they're pictures of Reed," she says with
a quiet urgency.

My physical reaction to this simple sentence is
surprising, even to me. I'm hit with an overwhelming
sense of nausea and feel incredibly lightheaded. For a
moment I am pretty sure that I might faint for the

first time in my life, and I cannot move or respond or breathe or do anything. My heart is racing. Truly, racing.

"Reed Whalen?" I stutter, when I catch my breath, even though the answer is clearly obvious.

"Yeah..." Lizzy says gently. "He's in a couple of pictures that Andrew posted earlier today. And, they were taken in Chicago."

As I struggle to process the implications of what Lizzy has just told me, Stan opens my office door and pops his head in.

"All set?" he asks cheerily.

"Um, yeah..." I stammer. "I just need one second."

"Liz, I have to go right now, we'll talk tonight." I hang up before she can protest and grab my coat to head out with Stan.

I spend our short walk through Chicago's downtown Loop to the Lyric opera house struggling to engage in conversation with Stan while pushing thoughts of Reed Whalen out of my mind. As Stan chats me up about his favorite opera singers, I give myself a mental pep talk about the potential pluses of spending the evening at the opera with him – unfortunately, it is not a lengthy list. Next to the opera house is a drugstore that Stan suggests we stop in to pick up some snacks for the show.

"We get a boxed dinner at one of the intermissions," he informs me, only then adding, "this is a six-hour performance including the breaks – I hope that doesn't make you want to go home!" He briefly chuckles at the hilarity of the notion that someone could not want to experience a six-hour opera with him as a companion. He then starts prattling on about how the candy is just so overpriced in the opera house that he always stops in the drugstore beforehand to pick up some "goodies" (yes, that is actually the word he used) to eat during the show. This helpful little lesson in frugality is coming from a guy who owns not one, but two, Porsches. Stan is a decent looking guy for someone in, I would guess, his mid-fifties, with a full head of blackish-gray hair and a nice enough face, although his wide nose keeps him from falling in the category of handsome. He's quite tall, with a dark complexion and impeccable clothing.

I'm poking around the snack aisle absentmindedly, trying very hard not to focus on how badly I want to see these photos of the long-lost Reed Whalen, when a middle-aged woman taps Stan on the shoulder and says hello.

"Brecken Pereira, this is Sylvia Dillingham," Stan says simply as the woman now identified as Sylvia extends her arm for a halfhearted handshake and looks me up and down in an interested, slightly critical way. She has wavy dark hair, streaked with gray, which is loosely pulled back with a flowered scarf. While her face is not particularly pretty, she does have a certain attractive presence about her. As I am sizing up her appearance, her last name registers. Sylvia Dillingham. Stan Dillingham... Is this his sister? Cousin? Friend who happens to have the same last name? My curiosity is officially piqued, and I attempt to stealthily tune into their conversation as I pretend to busy myself with checking out the varieties of Starburst and Skittles available.

"Shaina needs your signature to renew her car insurance," Sylvia is saying matter-of-factly, as she pulls some paperwork out of her worn leather satchel.

Stan takes the papers, asking Sylvia whether Andrea has booked her flight into town for Fourth of July weekend yet.

Shaina? Andrea? Those are Stan's daughters' names. Good lord. Is it possible that Sylvia is Stan's ex-wife? Can it be that we have coincidentally run into his ex-wife in a random drugstore in Chicago and that she happened to be conveniently carrying their daughter's car insurance information on her person at that time? It seems distressingly unlikely.

Sylvia soon mumbles that it was nice to meet me and skirts down a different aisle a moment later. As I turn to Stan, my eyes must ask the question.

"My ex-wife," he says with a shrug. "We had six opera tickets when we were married, so in the divorce she got four and I took two." Suddenly my head hurts. A lot. It's beginning to sound like the so-called "group" going to the opera with us consists of me, Stan, his ex-wife and whomever she has invited with her three other tickets. I need to clear this up.

"So, um, who else is coming with us tonight?" I ask, seeing no sense in beating around the bush.

"Well," he stretches out the word as if he is sighing while saying it, "Sylvia, our daughter Shaina, Shaina's boyfriend, and Sylvia's mother." And, there you have it. I am apparently going to be spending the next six hours watching an opera with Stan and his ex-family. Perfect...

When Stan and I get to our row in the theater, Sylvia and an elderly woman, who I presume to be her mother, are whispering to each other conspiratorially and nod acknowledgment as we take the two seats on the other end of the six seat block. It's clear what they are thinking: who is that gold-digging girl with my ex-husband/ex-son-in-law? When Shaina, who I learn is twenty-five, only one year my junior, arrives with her boyfriend a few minutes later, her father once again fails to introduce me as a co-worker or a first year associate in his practice group, and it is clear from Shaina's cold, hard look as she says hello and then turns away immediately, that she shares her mother's and grandmother's misconception regarding my relationship with Stan.

The night continues to go downhill after the performance begins. Truthfully, the opera is pretty impressive – I especially love the orchestra – and it could have been a relatively enjoyable experience if it had been, say, three, rather than six, hours long, and shared with different company. Stan insists on continually leaning over the armrest between our seats to whisper facts about the various arias in my ear, to hand me his binoculars, to offer me some of his Raisinets, et cetera. I do my best to make these little exchanges as short as possible, feeling the icy stares from Stan's family burning into the side of my face each time he leans my way, not to mention that his lacking concept of personal space is really starting to infuriate me. On top of all this, I am becoming more desperately curious to see the photos of Reed with each slow minute that ticks by.

The dinner intermission comes a cool three hours into the performance, and I am starving, having failed to purchase any snacks in the drugstore due to my panic about the identities of my companions for the evening, and having also repeatedly refused Stan's offers to share his various goodies with me.

I follow Stan as he snakes through the crowd to a table over by the wall where I see his family staked out. He saunters up and asks Sylvia to "scootch" a bit in order to make room for the two of us. I am nothing short of horrified.

I've heard plenty of tales about Stan from the other associates at work. He's known for being a conceited, tough and moody guy when he's in work-mode, but a fun-loving, life-of-the-party type the rest of the time. Based on stories from various firm parties, he's thought to be a little bit lecherous by many of the women at the firm, and it's widely known that he left his wife for a much younger woman rather recently. However, the relationship with that younger woman quickly went south, and he's currently single, as far as I know. Despite his decently good looks and loads of money, I have trouble imagining how anyone could find his mix of clueless arrogance and sleaziness at all attractive. I give Sylvia credit for her civility toward Stan – I certainly would not be caught dead hanging out at the opera with some d-bag who had left me for another woman – and I especially give her credit for her civility toward *me*, who she clearly perceives to be his latest twenty-something lady friend.

As I eat the cold turkey sandwich and carrot sticks from my boxed dinner, I meekly smile at Shaina and ask what kind of work she does.

She pauses to give me a hard look for a moment before curtly responding "finance."

"Oh, finance, great!" I say, with way too much enthusiasm. "Have you been doing that for long? Where do you work?"

"Three years. J.P. Morgan."

I usually don't take well to bitchy girls, but frankly I feel pretty bad for Shaina in this particular situation. If I thought some girl my age was hooking up with my dad, I feel pretty confident that I would be even less friendly to her than Shaina is being to me, and I have empathy for any kid of divorced parents. I decide that this little charade of Stan's has gone on too long, and I need to clear my name.

"My boyfriend is in finance too!" I lie with a smile, emphasizing the word "boyfriend". "Yeah, he's been in real estate finance for a few years now," I exclaim proudly, as if anyone had asked for details. Stan stares down as he takes a bite of a carrot stick. I see Sylvia and her mother exchange quick glances as I chatter on about my boyfriend. I realize that Stan has been thoroughly enjoying their misconception that he and I are an item, and he looks irritated that his cover is blown.

The women warm up to me somewhat from that point on, but I'm stuck standing between Stan and Shaina's boyfriend, Charles, who are aggressively discussing obscure jazz musicians, each of them frighteningly arrogant and determined to one-up the other with his knowledge of the uber-unmainstream. Remembering that Stan is my boss and that I probably just embarrassed him, I feel a need to pipe in to their conversation in an effort to smooth things over. I hear Charles mention the raw musical talent of Jason Mraz and take that to be my window.

I'm not even a big fan of Jason Mraz's music, but that doesn't stop me from jumping headfirst into the conversation. "He's *so* great live," I say idiotically, one second before I have the obvious realization that Stan, always determined to seem more intelligent and cultured than all others, would NEVER praise a pop artist.

"You're a Jason Moran fan?!" Stan asks with awe and surprise.

Jason *Moran*. Not Jason *Mraz*. Shit.

"When did you see him live?" Stan inquires as I feel my face becoming warm with embarrassment. Thankfully, unlike Lizzy, who looks like a tomato when she blushes, my face doesn't give me away.

"Um, it was in undergrad," I respond as I frantically try to think of a way to change the subject.

"He's the greatest jazz musician of our time," Charles cuts in authoritatively.

"Not *the greatest*," Stan retorts, as I nod slightly and noncommittally in an effort to suggest my general agreement as Stan continues. "But, he is certainly up there," Stan concedes. Fortunately, before the hole I am digging for myself with regard to this Jason Moran character gets any deeper, the chimes clang signaling the need to return to our seats for the second three-hour installment of *Parsifal*.

Chapter 2

It's just after midnight when my cab drops me outside my apartment building following the opera debacle. I'm completely exhausted and the fact that it's only Monday does not do much to help my outlook. I wave a quick hello to Craig, the doorman, and head into the elevator, trying to determine what I could have done differently to have avoided spending my precious free time in such a disastrous way.

Just as I hope, my best friend and roommate, Lizzy Sutter, is still awake when I walk into the cozy three-bedroom that has been our home for the past four years.

Lizzy's petite frame is stretched out on our comfy green couch in front of the TV, and she tilts her head up to greet me as I kick off my shoes. She's wearing black yoga pants and a white tank top, her strawberry blonde hair knotted slightly messily on the top of her head, and I'm immediately envious that she was able to spend her evening here instead of the Lyric Opera House.

"Sooo..." she begins in a sing-song voice as soon as I step into the TV room, "how'd it go?"

"Pretty miserable," I say with a groan. "And I was *dying* to see those photos all night but Facebook is blocked on our work BlackBerrys, not that I had any time to look at them anyway. I'm just going to run and change out of my suit, which has been digging into my waist for the past, oh, sixteen hours, and grab my laptop. Where's Nevada?" I ask, referring to our other roommate, as I head down the hall.

"She went out with some people from work and isn't back yet," Lizzy calls after me.

As I quickly pull off my work clothes and step into loose sweatpants and my favorite old, worn Pistons t-shirt, I send Will a text message briefly explaining that I was forced into a work event of sorts and that I'll call him tomorrow. I know that as a surgical resident at Northwestern, he will be tied up at the hospital for another few hours anyway. I'm feeling bad about the fact that didn't even have a break to respond to Will's multiple texts at any point during the evening, since Stan had insisted that we share a cab home. I make a mental note to let Will know that if he ever meets Stan, he has to say that he works in real estate finance, which I know he won't mind.

Carrying my laptop with me, I head into the TV room and plop down next to Lizzy on the couch, relieved to finally be in my comfy clothes and away from Stan and his awkward family.

Lizzy pauses the DVD of *Twilight* that she was watching, and I try to appear outwardly calm, to ignore the fierce churning in my stomach, as my laptop slowly boots up. Although, of course, trying to hide anything from Lizzy is pretty much impossible for me.

She and I met in the second grade, when I was the new kid in our class. We proclaimed that we were best friends during the first week of school when we showed up in exactly the same outfit from Limited Too for the first "casual day" where we got to ditch our usual school uniforms and wear any outfit we wanted (well, any outfit within reason, this was

Catholic school after all). A week later, at our school's fall kick-off event at the roller rink, I barely beat Jill Sciavone for first place in the school-wide roller skating race and, being the good sport that she was, Jill responded to this heart-wrenching defeat by furiously throwing her skate at the back of my head a few minutes after the race. Lizzy saw the skate coming and batted it down just before it would have clocked me in the head, and she has honestly never let me down since. Given that our friendship was formed over matching striped outfits and a roller skating nemesis, it's hard to believe we've remained best friends for the next roughly twenty years. Maybe it's weird that the person who understood me best when I was seven years old is still probably the person who gets me better than anyone else, but it's true just the same.

Even at age seven, Lizzy and I had the kind of connection that is pretty rare to find, although I didn't realize or appreciate that until years later, of course. If seven-year-old girls can spot soulmates, then that is what we found in each other, truly, I can't explain it any other way.

Because of our closeness, it is not at all surprising to me that Lizzy's been so focused on these pictures of Reed Whalen all day. Even though she would probably much prefer if she never had to hear his name again for the rest of her life, she told me about the pictures anyway, knowing how much I would want to see them. I know how lucky I am to have someone who understands. Not that Nevada doesn't know the saga of Reed Whalen, but she could never really, truly *understand*. Because, unlike Lizzy, Nevada wasn't there from the beginning.

Chapter 3

I quickly find my way to Andrew Wells's Facebook page. From there, Lizzy directs me to his new photo album, entitled "Chi-Town." Andrew is exactly the type of fratty guy who constantly uses phrases like "Chi-Town" and describes parties as "chill to quite chill" or "very mellow". I have always been more or less indifferent to him, considering him to be kind of a tool but generally harmless enough. Growing up, both he and Reed spent their summers at their families' respective summer homes on shi-shi Green Island in Northern Michigan, the very same private island where Lizzy's family spent their summers as well. Reed always seemed to give Andrew a pass on his douchebag qualities because they'd known each other their whole lives. Well, at least that used to be the case. It's not as though I exactly know Reed anymore, so I guess he could be completely different now. For all I know, Andrew Wells could be his very best friend these days, although somehow I doubt it.

I click through a few pictures of Andrew and some other guys in collared shirts and worn-in Cubs hats at Wrigley Field, with Lizzy leaning sideways and peering over my shoulder, as if seeing these pictures for the first time. As usual, our internet connection is painfully slow in the TV room, and it feels like forever before I come to a picture of Reed. My chest and throat physically tighten when I see that first picture. His skin is a deep tan, his hair now buzzed, and his arms more muscular. But his face, that is the same. Maybe a touch more angular, with a little more dark scruffy stubble, but it's the same face I knew so well.

Reed is in five pictures total, and Lizzy patiently sits beside me as I look through them multiple times. We can tell that two of them were taken at the Green Mill, a vintage jazz club where Nevada, Lizzy and I often hang out. (Just to clarify, I do like cool old jazz clubs, despite the fact that until earlier tonight I'd never heard of Jason Moran, who is, apparently, the world's greatest jazz musician). If I'd run into Reed there the night these photos were taken, I would have been less surprised to see a ghost.

Lizzy and I barely speak as I scrutinize the photos. Eventually, I've had my fill. I close the laptop, turn to Lizzy and shrug, not sure where to begin.

She looks at me for a minute, then asks what I'm thinking, her lightly freckled forehead wrinkling with concern.

"I just, I don't know what I think," I begin, and I really don't. "I guess I didn't realize how much I had come to think of him as dead or nonexistent at this point. To see pictures of him out and about in Chicago like it's no big deal just seems so surreal and wrong."

"Oh I know," Lizzy agrees. "I thought the same thing when I first saw these. Do you think he lives here or was just visiting or something?"

I merely shake my head in response. Her guess is as good as mine. "I checked to see if he has a Facebook page or anything now – he doesn't," she adds.

We are still discussing Reed – speculating as to where he's been for the past eight years and whether he might actually be living here in Chicago, just miles or even blocks away from us – when we hear keys jingling at our door and Nevada Deague comes bursting in.

"How was your opera date?" Nevada cries loudly as she kicks off her high heels in the front hallway and climbs onto the couch next to me.

"Pretty much the worst Monday night I've had in a while," I say with a smile. "How was your night? Where were you?"

"Oh just out at Sedgwick's with some work people. We went to happy hour at Fulton's on the River and then just kept going out after that... Anyway, tell me more about your night."

I take a deep breath and tell my roommates about the evening from beginning to end, and Nevada nearly falls off the couch in hysterics when I get to the part about Jason Mraz.

"The whole night sounds sooo awful," Lizzy says, after shrieking with laughter upon hearing all the details.

"Brecks, I love it, a night like this would only happen to you!" Nevada says, her eyes tearing up from laughter.

"Yeah, yeah, I know, believe me," I say, smiling as I feel myself beginning to loosen up from my stressful night with the Dillinghams and the shock of seeing Reed Whalen's face once again. Neither Lizzy nor I mention the photos of Reed to Nevada. I'll tell her about them later, but I don't feel like rehashing all that again tonight.

Like me, Nevada is a total night owl and even though it's already nearly 1 A.M., she pleads with me and Lizzy to stay up and watch the rest of *Twilight*, once she learns that Lizzy was in the midst of watching it. She and I always stay up way later than we should, and I always pay the price by oversleeping and being late to work on nearly a daily basis. Lizzy usually tries to resist our bad habits and head to bed early, but we succeed in talking her into staying up with us more often than she would like. Nevada soon convinces us to watch at least part of the movie, which isn't a very tough sell. I haven't read any of the *Twilight* books but they seem to be everywhere, and I'm kind of curious to see what all the hype is about.

By the time the movie ends, it's all I can do to keep my eyes open. The three of us brush our teeth and wash our faces together in the bathroom connected to Lizzy's bedroom, despite the fact that we have a second bathroom, while discussing the movie and agreeing that it was surprisingly entertaining. I head into my room, mumbling good night to them.

In the solitude of my bedroom, I force myself to resist the overwhelming urge to look through the pictures of Reed just one more time before shutting off my lights. I won't allow myself to be that weak. I lie in bed, my mind spinning and my heart gripped by a feeling of nostalgia so strong that I can't imagine it will ever subside. It's hard to believe that it has been nearly eight whole years since I last saw or spoke to Reed Whalen. Eight years and yet merely seeing him in a few photos makes me feel as though it was just yesterday that he caused my world to come crashing down. The mixture of loss, heartache, anger and longing that those five photos have evoked is as potent and visceral as those days when my wounds were raw and fresh, and I'm beyond frustrated that a few simple pictures are impacting me like this. I fall asleep convincing myself that the shock of seeing photos of Reed after all this time would make anyone in my situation feel this way and that my uneasiness will surely pass just as quickly as it came.

Chapter 4

I hit the snooze button on my alarm clock three times the next morning, and even then getting out of my bed and into the shower at 7:30 takes every ounce of energy I possess. The shock of the photos has all but erased the awkward and unfortunate opera experience from the forefront of my mind for the time being. I stumble out of the shower to find my Blackberry flashing, informing me that I missed a text from Will: "Division Red Line @ 8:15?" Smiling to myself, I text him back to let him know that I'll see him at 8:15 and then turn on my blow-dryer.

I dodge into the kitchen to grab a granola bar and then run out the door of the apartment with my suit coat under one arm while tucking my dress shirt into my skirt with my free hand. It's a chilly spring morning in Chicago, still cold enough that I wear my Uggs for the commute to work.

Will is waiting, with a Starbucks latte in hand for me, at the corner of Clark and Division when I arrive breathless at 8:18. I plant a long kiss on his lips as I take my coffee, receiving glares from several of the people waiting impatiently at the bus stop next to us who apparently vehemently disapprove of this modest display of affection. As we head down the stairs to catch the Red Line L, I start regaling him with the tale of my pseudo-date with Stan, which I know he will appreciate. I'm still jabbering on as the L pulls up noisily, with people already pressed up against the door, and we elbow and maneuver our way in, unwilling to wait for the next train, which will undoubtedly be just as crowded. I barely make it through the sliding door before the train begins hurtling toward the next stop, and I have to physically squeeze in between people to find a space where I can actually stand upright. The morning commute always marks one of the worst parts of my day. And, although I do love Will's early morning Starbucks runs, a cup of scalding hot coffee only makes riding a ridiculously overcrowded train an even greater challenge. Will and I are separated by the crowd, so I can only wave goodbye to him as he elbows through the people to jump out at the State and Grand stop.

A few minutes later, I get off the L myself and begin walking the three blocks to my office, feeling relieved that seeing Will was so completely normal. His handsome face had stood out to me as I approached Division Street. His witty quips as I told him about my night with Stan made me laugh. And, as always, his lingering British accent made me melt just a little each time he spoke. I know that deep down I was the slightest bit worried that even the prospect of Reed's return might have drained me of my feelings for Will, afraid that I would realize everything I had built with Will over the past two years had been merely a poor substitute for Reed, and God only knows where that would have left me. Thankfully, instead I feel just as attracted to Will as ever. I assure myself that it was merely the unexpected shock of seeing Reed's picture, of having a brief window into his current life, that had sent me reeling with emotion last night. In the light of day, in the routine of my real life, I feel certain that the return of Reed Whalen is a Pandora's box that will remain forever closed, and that's exactly how I want it. Reed once again seems like a dream from a faraway lifetime. And with that conclusion solidified in my mind, I swipe my security card and head into the elevator for another day of billing hours at Baron & Riehl LLP.

Technically, first year attorneys at Baron & Riehl are not assigned to a particular practice group but are instead encouraged to take work from all the groups in order to determine which area of law they are best suited for, as well as to learn a little about each group's work. This is, at least, the way it works theoretically. In reality, each practice group latches onto particular first year associates and expects them to be readily available at all times for work from that group. This is precisely what the corporate group has done to me. It may be for no reason other than that my office happens to be located on the floor where the corporate attorneys sit, but for one reason or another, the corporate group targeted me as their designated first year associate. I came to Baron wanting to focus on litigation in the hopes of eventually (i.e. once my school loans are paid off) using that experience to help me begin a legal career advocating for social justice, civil rights, or one of the other lofty ideals that made me want to become a lawyer in the first place. But, apparently life had other plans for me, and I quickly found myself in the clutches of corporate law, working for the likes of Stan Dillingham and his cronies, for the foreseeable future.

As has become my routine in the past eight months that I have been working here, after stepping off the elevator on the 38th floor, I walk slightly out of my way en route to my office in order to pass by the row of desks where my secretary and several others sit. When I started work here, I had the general impression (not sure where I picked it up) that "secretary" was no longer PC and that "administrative assistant" or some variation of that title was now the correct term to use. However, on my first day at Baron & Riehl, Debbie Stanzler came into my office and introduced herself as my new secretary. So, from then on I have referred to her as my secretary, and hopefully I haven't been inadvertently promulgating some outdated sexist term in doing so.

Debbie sits in a so-called "squad" of secretaries with Rhoda, Sheryl, Linda and Vickie. Except for Sheryl, who's a bit younger, these women are all in their sixties and have, for the most part, been at Baron & Riehl for at least as long as I have been alive. The women in the squad are all secretaries for various attorneys in the corporate practice group, which is mainly comprised of men in their fifties and sixties.

Although there are several secretarial squads on the 38th floor, I mainly interact with Debbie and her squad since they sit closest to my office. They are a funny little group of grandmotherly figures who have been tending to the demands of angry partners for the majority of their lives. It seems like they find me to be a refreshing change of pace from the gray-haired men with whom they usually deal, and they frequently stop by my office to chat or complain. It quickly became clear that they had nominated themselves as my protectors in the office, which I find pretty endearing.

I chat with Linda and Debbie for a few minutes and am heading to my office as Debbie calls after me that Stan called looking for me a few minutes earlier. I roll my eyes in response, and she chuckles good-naturedly.

I flip on the lights in my office, sit down in my chair, kick off my Uggs and slip on one of the seven or so pairs of heels that are strewn about under my desk. I turn on my computer and so begins another day.

• • • • •

As I dig into my work, the hours pass quickly. I disregard Stan's message, even though ignoring a call from the head of my practice group is probably not the best idea. I'm only working on a few hours of sleep, and I just don't have it in me to gush with him about how much I enjoyed the opera. I figure that when he catches up with me, I will simply tell him that I have been swamped with work, which is every partner's favorite thing to hear coming out of an associate's mouth.

I hurry out of the office at 7:30 that evening to make it to my weekly 8:00 Tuesday night dinner date with Lizzy and Nevada. Although we live together, during the week the three of us rarely have much time to hang out between our various work commitments, boyfriends, my band practices and other things that come up. So, every Tuesday we meet at 8:00 at a little Thai restaurant called Tiparo's, which is just a few blocks from our apartment. Tiparo's has the most amazing yellow curry and pad se euw and also makes pretty good sushi, which keeps Nevada happy.

Lizzy constantly complains about my habit of running late, so I head straight to the restaurant in my work clothes, something I hate to do since I'm much happier in a hoodie than a blazer, in order to avoid getting shit from her. I walk in at 7:58 and am greeted by her impressed smile.

The two of them are sipping on bottles of Singha, and the waiter sits a third bottle down in front of me as I get settled in the booth. Before I can say a word, Lizzy blurts out that she has something to tell us.

Nevada and I wait expectantly, as she pauses after this interesting lead in.

"I got laid off," she says bluntly, and I can see the hurt in her eyes.

"What?" I exclaim incredulously. "What the fuck? Are you kidding me? *How* could they lay *you* off?"

Lizzy just shrugs and takes a big swig of her Singha. "Well, they were making cuts at every level. They let a hundred people go across the country."

"A hundred?! I can't believe I didn't hear about this. Why didn't you call me?" I ask, infuriated that McAllistair would treat her this way and stunned that any employer would voluntarily give up a worker as smart and dedicated as Lizzy.

"I guess I needed to let it sink it. I just walked around the city for a while after they told me. I know lots of the people who were laid off have families to provide for, so I can't feel too sorry for myself," she says, her voice sounding a bit forlorn.

Apparently the two of them already ordered our usual dishes because the food arrives as Nevada asks how exactly the layoff played out. Lizzy walks us through all the details, beginning with the rumors that were buzzing through the office when she arrived that morning. The layoffs included people at all levels and all groups within McAllistair, a large audit and accounting firm, and it wasn't until 3:00 that she received a call from her boss, Genevieve. Although Genevieve can be kind of a bitch at times, subtly condescending and extremely passive-aggressive, Lizzy generally hasn't minded working for her all that much. I give Lizzy a lot of credit; she's had to deal with the same miserable type of bullshit as me at work each day, but she's always seemed to let it roll off her back much more easily than I ever have.

Lizzy started working for McAllistair as an intern at their Manhattan office in between junior and senior year of college. She was majoring in accounting at Dartmouth, and I remember her being thrilled to land the internship. That summer I was studying for the LSAT and working as a bartender at The Brown Jug, a little bar in Ann Arbor, so her nights of clubbing in NYC seemed pretty glamorous to me. At the end of that summer they gave her an offer for a full time position once she graduated, and I still recall feeling so proud that all her years of hard work had paid off. As much fun as she'd had that summer in New York, she really wanted to come back to the Midwest after graduation, and McAllistair had agreed that she could have a position as an associate in their Chicago office instead of New York. So, for the four years since graduation, she has been plugging away as an audit associate. Until now.

Even though I realize that some of the other victims of the layoffs had probably worked at McAllistair much longer than Lizzy, I'm still furious that they would just dismiss all Lizzy's hard work over the past four years. She put up with all Genevieve's crap only to be cut loose with a pretty pathetic severance package. Not that Lizzy Sutter will ever be short on money, but still, it's the principle of it.

"Well," Nevada says, her face suddenly brightening with a smile, "here is what I propose. We stop at Jewel after this and grab some bottles of champagne, go home and get dressed up while we have a few drinks, and then go out on the town. It will be our celebration that Liz is finally done with the evil Genevieve!!"

Nevada has a charisma about her that is fascinating. When she suggests something, anything, it sounds ten times better than if anyone else were to suggest it. When she's in the right mood, she can make any random night amazingly fun. I can see that her idea appeals to Lizzy somewhat, although she still seems genuinely sad about her job, the kind of sadness that a night of binge drinking and dancing isn't going to resolve. However, she starts questioning Nevada about where we would go out, so I know she is at least considering it.

I, on the other hand, am really not in the mood for a so-called night on the town tonight. It was a struggle for me to get to Tiparo's by 8:00 with all the work I have looming over me, and I've done the hung-over work day enough times before to know that it is beyond miserable, not to mention unproductive, when all I want to do the whole day is crawl under my desk and sleep. Plus, tonight Will gets off work at the hospital around 9:00 and doesn't have to be back there until noon tomorrow, so I was planning to hang out with him after dinner tonight.

"You guys, you know I can't have a big drinking night tonight," I start, feeling completely lame even as the words come out of my mouth.

"What the hell, Breck," Nevada interrupts me. "You left work at like 5:00 yesterday to go the opera with that creepy partner. Now your best friend needs you to cheer her up, and you don't have time? I'm not taking no for an answer." She gives me a pleased smile and starts aggressively hugging me in an exaggerated way as I laugh and try to pull her off me. Although Nevada's habit of guilt-tripping to get her way is one of her qualities that really bothers me, I have to admit she can be pretty persuasive.

It's a joke between she and Lizzy that I am the world's biggest pushover when it comes to being irresponsible. In college, I could have a huge paper due the next day but if people tried for more than a minute to convince me to come sledding in the Arb or to play beer pong or to do whatever fun and impulsive thing they were doing, I always gave in without much of a fight. It's a trait that I haven't entirely grown out of yet, despite having a job that's not very conducive to late weeknights of partying.

"OK, calm down, spaz," I say, unlatching Nevada's grasp on me and turning to Lizzy. "Liz, if you want to go out, I'm in. Only because I love you and you had a *really* shitty day," and I turn to jokingly glare at Nevada, "and *not* because of Ney's guilt-tripping."

"Yesss, this is going to be the best night!" Nevada says with confidence as she climbs out of our booth. "I'm going to find the waiter to grab our check."

"I guess this means we're going out," Lizzy concedes with a little smile.

A moment later, Nevada returns with the check and three shots of SoCo and lime, placing one in front of me and one in front of Lizzy. Clearly she is not appreciating that I have to be in the office early tomorrow. She currently works in a pharmaceutical sales job that she hates, so she doesn't seem to much care about showing up late or potentially getting fired these days, from what I can tell. She raises her shot glass into the middle of the table, and I halfheartedly follow her lead, knowing I will regret it in the morning, as she loudly toasts "to Lizzy moving on to bigger and better things than being an effing accountant."

We clink our glasses and drink the shots, which, as far as shots go, taste pretty good. As soon as Lizzy has swallowed hers, she turns to Nevada. "What makes you think I'm not going to do accounting anymore?" she asks, with a surprising level of annoyance in her voice. "Just because I got laid off doesn't mean I'm giving up my career," she says more softly.

"Oh, I know, sweetie," Nevada croons in her soothing voice. "I was just joking around. But who knows, maybe you will find something a little more exciting, or at least a more exciting way to use your accounting skills, and you'll probably look back on this day and realize it was all for the best. That's all I meant. Anyway, come on, let's head home and figure out plans for tonight." With that, she links her arm in Lizzy's, and they lead the way out the door of Tiparo's. I pull out my BlackBerry and call Will, explaining that I can't come over in time to watch *Gran Torino* with him as planned, given Lizzy's need for a girls' night out. I assure him that I'll be over in a few hours and stay at his place for the night. He's understanding, as usual, and tells me to let her know he's sorry about her job and that McAllistair must be

run by total idiots if they would let her go. I couldn't
agree more.

Chapter 5

I wake up in Will's bed the next morning, wanting water so desperately that I think I might die if I don't get a sip in the next four seconds. I groan as I sit up, my head pounding in the way that only excessive champagne drinking can accomplish, and reach over Will to the cup of water on the bedside table. Whimpering aloud, I silently berate myself for once again getting talked into staying out too late and drinking too much in the middle of the week. I gulp down the whole glass of water and look at the clock, which reads 8:25. Shit.

Will stirs with all my movement and sits up beside me in bed, stretching his toned arms over his head.

"Good morning, drunky," he says teasingly.

"I'm late! Again!" I say, feeling beyond annoyed with myself for being in this position. "What time did I get here last night? I don't even remember coming over here."

"I think around 3:00 or so. You called on your way and said you guys had been singing karaoke at Blue Frog and then dancing at The Hangge Uppe," he says, putting his hand on my hair and smoothing it for a minute, which surprisingly succeeds in making me feel slightly less stressed. "Want me to drive you home?"

Like me, Will also lives in Old Town, which is just over a mile north of the Loop, where my office is located. Our apartments are only about five blocks apart, which I love.

"Thanks, but that's OK, I can walk. I have to head out now, though. I'm already gonna be pretty late."

"You sure? I feel bad letting you go out in that walk-of-shame attire," he says, winking at me playfully.

I glance at the black minidress lying on the floor beside the bed (which Nevada forced me to wear) and the pair of red Louboutin heels (on loan from Lizzy) next to it and have to laugh. "Good point. I think I have some sweatpants and flip flops here somewhere though." I climb out of bed and root around in his closet until I find the clothes I had in mind. I throw them on, lean back on the bed for a moment to give Will a kiss and then gather my things to leave.

"Hey, what do you have going on Friday night?" Will asks, as I check to make sure I have my keys and phone in my purse. (I do, thankfully. And, I even have all my credit cards, which, sadly, is only true after about two-thirds of my nights out.)

"Um, nothing really, I don't think. Lizzy mentioned something about dinner at Sushi Samba with Jess and Alexa, but it's nothing I can't miss. Why, what's going on?"

"I just feel like we haven't gotten to see each other much the last few weeks and I have Friday night off, so I thought maybe I'd take you out somewhere nice." He grins his broad smile at me as he suggests this, making me feel thankful once again that I have such an incredible boyfriend.

"That sounds great. Can't wait!" I blow him another kiss then dash out of the apartment.

Chapter 6

"Where are we going?" I prod Will on Friday evening, as he mysteriously makes me wait a few steps behind him while he tells the cab driver the address of our destination.

"It's a surprise, babe. I know that's a hard concept for you to accept, but just try to hang in there, OK?" He always likes to hassle me about my need for instant gratification.

"Fine, fine," I say, grabbing his hand as I scoot into the cab.

"You look beautiful," he says, pulling me over next to him in the backseat of the cab. "I mean, you always do, but you look especially gorgeous tonight."

"Thank you, you're looking pretty good yourself," I say, feeling extremely contented and lucky as I snuggle up against him. Even though Will seems like the complete package from the outside (in my humble opinion at least) – a handsome British medical resident who is kind, smart and incredibly funny – it is really the way he puts me at ease and understands me that made him stand out to me when we'd first started talking after one of my band's shows just over two years earlier. And, OK, the accent didn't exactly hurt either.

"Can you at least tell me the type of food? Asian? Mexican? Just a little hint, please?"

He just grins at me and shakes his head to let me know that my guessing is all in vain. I give up and instead ask him about his day at the hospital. We talk and laugh as I lean up against his charcoal cashmere sweater, inhaling the familiar scent of his faint cologne.

It isn't long before the cab stops on West Fulton Market Street. I look out of the smudged window and see our destination.

"Moto? Are you kidding me?"

Will looks quite pleased with his restaurant choice. "I said it was somewhere special, and I know you've always wanted to try this place."

"It's so expensive though," I say, feeling guilty as he pays the cab driver and we head into the restaurant.

"The whole point of money is to spend it on the people you love. So, don't worry about it, and let's enjoy this."

As a resident, Will doesn't make much money (along with owing a staggering amount in student loans, much like yours truly) and eating at a place like Moto is a huge splurge for him. I squeeze his hand as the host escorts us to our table.

• • • • •

The meal is incredibly delicious and breathtakingly unique from start to finish, with the feel of a five star meal created in Willy Wonka's factory. We eat ten small courses, all of which are such mesmerizing works of art that it pains me slightly to dig into them. Well, truthfully, it pains me only until the food hits my tongue, at which point each course qualifies as one of the best dishes I have ever eaten. The presentation of the food is otherworldly, with the most bizarre combinations of flavors and textures imaginable. We nibble on edible forks and foie gras topped with poached pear and peanut mousse, we devour salads that fit in spoons, with pellets flavored like lettuce and accents of dressing, and we fall in love with bacon infused crème brûlée (who knew?). We eat and laugh and drink two bottles of wine, each course serving as its own version of entertainment. It is, undoubtedly, the most memorable meal of my life.

Soon we're winding down, and Will has me laughing at a story about his brother Jake's most recent girlfriend when the waiter stops by our table and informs us that the chef prepared a special dessert for us. Will and I exchange looks with glee, not wanting the meal to end despite the fact that our stomachs are about to burst. He rubs my leg gently under the table, and I honestly can't remember the last time I felt this purely happy and relaxed.

The waiter presents us with a geometric plate containing a chocolate sphere, which, according to him, is as thin as an eggshell and should be tapped lightly with a spoon in order to crack it open. With these instructions, he leaves us to enjoy.

"Go for it," Will says, gesturing for me to do the honors of cracking the chocolate egg as he brushes a piece of his dark blond hair off his forehead in a way that makes me smile.

I tap gently with the side of my spoon and, sure enough, the egg shatters and falls to pieces. What I see in the center of the egg makes me gasp out loud.

Inside the delicate remains sits a gorgeous, sparkling diamond ring. I turn to Will in my stunned state and find him down on one knee. His mouth is moving, and I hear words including "love" and "best friend" and "wife" but they are all a blur as my pulse races and I fight a brief dizzy sensation.

As my mind clears slightly, I look down to see the ring on my finger and hear Will ask, "Brecken, will you marry me?" I nod as he kisses me. I hear clapping and whistles from Moto's other patrons as our waiter rushes over and uncorks a bottle of champagne.

And just like that, I am engaged.

PART II
SUMMER OF 1999

Chapter 7

While going to an all-girls high school certainly had its shortcomings, it wasn't without its perks as well. One of the greatest benefits was the joy of sleeping in each morning until just moments before I needed to leave for school, rolling out of bed and into my plaid skirt and button down shirt and sprinting out the door in almost one semi-awake motion, never giving a second thought (or a first thought, for that matter) to my appearance.

June 1, 1999 was a day that, like most of mine, started out just this way. Lizzy had been driving me to school since November of that school year when she had turned sixteen, a milestone that her parents had celebrated with the gift of a brand new black Jeep Grand Cherokee. The fact that she drove me to and from school, rather than letting me take the bus, was a testament to what a great friend she was, especially given that she had to go at least ten minutes out of her way to pick me up each morning. Unlike me, Lizzy actually liked waking up early and claimed to enjoy the morning drive from her house in Bloomfield Hills over to the east side of Royal Oak to pick me up and then over to the west side of Royal Oak where our school, St. Lucy's Academy, was located.

On this particular early summer Michigan morning, I heard Lizzy honking in the driveway as I ran around frantically looking for my backpack while shoving my feet into a pair of Doc Marten Mary Jane's that were borrowed from Lizzy. My mom, who had been reading the newspaper at the kitchen table, slipped a granola bar into my hand and said good morning as I wrestled with my shoes. If there was any evidence in her eyes of what was to come that evening, I was too sleepy to pick up on it. I gave her a quick one-armed hug then headed out the door. As I climbed into shotgun, Lizzy turned up The Temptations and handed me one of the two coffees, with tons of cream and sugar, that she had picked up for us, as she often did, from Caribou Coffee in nearby Birmingham. Knowing that I'm the complete opposite of a morning person and that I don't even really like to talk any more than necessary for about an hour after I wake up, she happily carried on most of the conversation herself, quickly starting in with a story about her dad finding cigarettes in her older sister Sarah's coat pocket this morning. Apparently Sarah had steadfastly insisted that she only had them because she had taken them away from a friend in an effort to get her friend to stop smoking and had berated her dad for not having more faith in her. For inexplicable reasons, Mr. Sutter had actually fallen for this B.S. story. Lizzy was infuriated that her sister had once again avoided punishment, and she spent the next five minutes complaining about her sister's ability to manipulate their parents. Soon enough, we rolled into the parking lot of St. Lucy's Academy.

St. Lucy's was a pretty tiny school. Not physically tiny, that is, just tiny in terms of the number of students. It was a first through twelfth grade school and had fewer than six hundred students total. This made the odds that Lizzy and I had most of our classes together pretty good, and in that second semester of tenth grade, we had managed a record six out of seven classes in common.

The school day passed uneventfully. I had a soccer game that night and had planned to go to Lizzy's to do my homework and hang out beforehand. However, when Lizzy and I got to her house, there was a note from Lizzy's mom on the counter saying that my mom was looking for me and wanted me to come home. I quickly dialed the phone number for my house, but there was no answer.

"OK then, back to R.O. it is," Lizzy said, using her abbreviated version of Royal Oak, as we headed back out the door to her car. I knew something out of the ordinary must be going on for my mom to be calling Lizzy's mom and asking that I head home, and an uneasy anxiety had settled on my shoulders in the minutes after I read her note. I mentioned this to Lizzy as we drove.

"I was kind of thinking the same thing," she agreed hesitantly, clearly not wanting to add to my concern. "But, thankfully we lead pretty lame lives," she said with a little smile and a roll of her eyes, trying to lighten the mood, "so it's not like you're in trouble or anything..." she trailed off.

"Yeah, true, but that almost makes me more worried," I said, with my thoughts drifting to my grandpa's recent stroke and my brother Griffin's increasingly severe asthma attacks.

"If she found cigarettes in your coat, apparently you can just say you took them away from an irresponsible friend. Seriously, I still can't believe my parents fell for that."

I managed a little laugh at this despite my increasing distress.

"Anyway, stressing about it won't do any good, you'll be home in a minute," she said, turning up the music on Oldies 104.3, her favorite radio station, and we drove the rest of the way without talking, listening to the good vibrations of The Beach Boys.

• • • • •

Through the kitchen window I spotted my parents, along with my twelve-year-old brother Griffin, out on our back deck. My dad was never home in the afternoons. In fact, he was rarely even able to escape work in the evenings to watch my soccer games. The clench in my throat tightened as I headed to join them in the backyard.

The conversation didn't last long. Just long enough for me to get exactly one piece of information, which was enough, actually too much, for me to absorb: my parents were separating.

I heard the words, but it was as though my mind had lost its ability to process and I just stood there for several seconds, unable to respond. When I finally opened my mouth to ask a question, it occurred to me that there wasn't really any question that mattered. They were separating and that just about said it all.

I guess I would have to chalk it up to good old-fashioned denial that I hadn't seen it coming. They fought often, mostly hushed fights behind closed doors, but the tension could be felt in our house any time they were both home, and often even when they weren't. My mom had become increasingly withdrawn, my dad increasingly absent, but neither divorce, nor separation, nor any breaking up of my family unit had ever really entered my mind. I guess I probably hadn't been willing to let it.

Slowly, I turned and walked back inside, my dad calling after me as I headed upstairs and snuggled into my unmade bed in the middle of my messy bedroom. I put on one of my favorite depressing mix tapes and just laid there in my comforter cocoon for hours, sobbing to the sympathetic voices of The Cranberries, Radiohead and The Samples. My thoughts were consumed with the potential impact of this news, what exactly this so-called separation meant for me. Did I know anyone whose parents had separated and then happily reunited? I felt pretty sure the answer was no. No, separation just seemed like a rest stop en route to divorce, mainly just there for the purpose of easing the adjustment to the new arrangement under the comforting guise that it might be nothing more than a temporary change. I really didn't have many friends with divorced parents. Two girls on my travel soccer team, but most of my school friends' parents were still together. I ended up staying in bed that whole night. At some point I heard my mom open my bedroom door, whispering my name, but I pretended to be asleep and felt the hot tears begin again.

I woke up easily the next morning, probably the result of having gone to bed at about 5 P.M. the night before, and avoided going downstairs until I heard Lizzy honk so that I could dodge conversation with my mom. I knew my dad would already have withdrawn to his painting studio. I bounded down the stairs and found my mom waiting for me. I didn't look at her as I put on my shoes and searched for my backpack.

"Mary Beth called last night," she said gently, referring to my soccer coach, who was undoubtedly wondering why I had been a no-show at our game. "I told her we had a family issue come up." She paused for a moment and I just shrugged. "Lizzy called a few times too," she added. I didn't respond. I didn't mean to be immature, but I just couldn't help feeling horribly betrayed by my parents, especially my mom.

"Honey, when you've had a chance to digest this a little, I would really like it if we could sit down and talk," she said, looking and sounding as though she had been crying quite a bit herself. I just shrugged again, not looking her in the eyes, and walked out the door.

"Breck!" Lizzy exclaimed as I pulled open the car door and hopped in. "What's going on?! You never called and your mom was being really weird on the phone, and you missed the game. You've been crying and-"

"My parents are separating," I cut off her barrage of questions. The urge to cry was gone, replaced with a sickening pit in my stomach. Lizzy was clearly surprised, although she seemed less taken aback by it than I had been. Always one to cry easily (she was barely able to speak without bursting into tears for about four days after we saw *My Girl* in fifth grade), Lizzy actually teared up herself as she told me how sorry she was. She asked me for more details as she gave me a hug, but my one sentence response had actually included all the information I had on the subject. As we backed out of my driveway, I explained how I had stormed out on my parents after hearing the news and essentially didn't know any of the particulars of this sad turn of events.

Lizzy let me babble and pour my heart out the whole way to school and didn't say much. For once I actually felt like talking in the morning.

A few blocks from school, Lizzy's face lit up. "Come to Green Island with me this summer!" she exclaimed, sounding more like she was giving an order than making a request.

I gave her a questioning look in response, as we pulled into her assigned parking spot in the student lot.

"Well, it sounds like your parents have some serious issues to work through, you sound really frustrated with them, like you could use some space, and Griffin will be at camp most of the summer, right?"

"Yeah..." I responded slowly, thinking that perhaps my parents could be convinced to go along with this idea.

"Just think about it, pleeeease," Lizzy continued, squeezing my arm repeatedly in her excitement as I gathered up my backpack from where I had tossed it in her backseat.

"You know I would love to go," I started, as we walked through the parking lot into school, waving to Lauren Plant and Amy Eldon a few cars away from us, "but I'm just not sure if my parents will go for it. I'll definitely ask once things calm down though," I said, the idea of escaping my parents and their issues sounding increasingly appealing with each minute that I considered Lizzy's offer. "Are you sure your parents wouldn't mind?"

"Um, yes, you're practically part of our family. Of course they wouldn't mind," she said reassuringly, as we took our seats in Algebra II.

From the moment Ms. Turnik, our Algebra II teacher, opened her mouth to begin the morning's lesson, my mind left the classroom. Despite the extra hours of sleep, I was drained from a night of focusing on my parents' separation and although I wanted to think about anything other than my unraveling family, algebra was apparently not going to cut it as a quality distraction.

Green Island, however, was something worthy of a daydream. A summer there sounded almost too good to be true. I knew it probably wouldn't work out, but right now I needed something, anything, to be hopeful about, and the prospect of retreating to Green Island for a few months, however remote a possibility, was better than nothing.

The Sutter family had been spending their summers on Green Island for two years now, and surviving the summer without Lizzy had been a hardship that I dreaded each spring. The purchase of their summer home had come in the midst of many major changes for the Sutters.

Lizzy's dad was a software developer who had worked for a large tech company for years before he and several co-workers split off to found a much smaller development company. For years Mr. Sutter's start-up had been working on a new piece of software related to search engine technology, and when Lizzy and I were in seventh grade, her dad's company sold this software to Microsoft for millions and millions of dollars.

More or less overnight, the Sutters had become insanely wealthy, and their lives had changed very quickly. Mrs. Sutter had quit her job as a special needs aid in a nearby public school and the Sutters had sold their house in Royal Oak and moved to a mansion, no exaggeration, we're talking a legitimate, Fresh Prince of Bel Aire mansion here, in neighboring Bloomfield Hills. Lizzy and her sisters were offered the option of going to Detroit Country Day School, an exclusive and expensive co-ed private school that my parents never could in a million years have afforded. Even at a fraction of the cost, the tuition for St. Lucy's was already a stretch for them. Lizzy had opted to stay at our small all-girls Catholic school, but both her sisters, Sarah and Katherine, had transferred.

The Sutters had also purchased their summer home on Green Island the following year. I had never heard of Green Island at that time, but when I mentioned the news of the Sutters' most recent extravagance to my mom, she'd made a clicking noise with her tongue that I knew meant she disapproved, before saying "how nice" very disingenuously. I wasn't sure at the time whether she had a problem with Green Island itself or just with the Sutters' upgraded lifestyle generally, but I hadn't pressed the point with her any further.

Although Lizzy and I had managed to talk on the phone frequently throughout her first summer on Green Island, it wasn't until she returned, a week before ninth grade began, that I got the full rundown on the sheltered and privileged world that was Green Island.

Located in Lake Michigan near larger Beaver Island, Green Island was something akin to a Midwestern version of Martha's Vineyard or Nantucket, and Lizzy had informed me that the islanders referred to it simply as "Green." The island was about thirty miles from the northwestern

Michigan town of Charlevoix, was only accessible by boat, and, get this, only homeowners and their guests (as well as employees of Green Island) were allowed entrance onto the island. No cars (or other motorized vehicles) were permitted on Green Island, but horse and carriages circled the loop around the circumference of the island all day and night, in case people didn't feel like walking or biking.

Lizzy had learned that it was exceedingly rare for a house on Green Island to even be sold, since the homes were typically passed down from one generation to the next. However, uncharacteristically, two Green Island homes had gone on the market around the same time and the Sutters had jumped at chance to become Greenies themselves. (Yes, honest to God, she told me with more than a hint of disdain in her voice, the people who summer on Green proudly call themselves "Greenies." This was also the point at which I learned that "summer" could be and was used as a verb.)

From Lizzy's stories, I knew that the bizarre world of Green Island included gorgeous white sand Lake Michigan beaches, tons of security ensuring that the exclusive enclave was never compromised and the equivalent of a posh country club to which all Greenies (and only Greenies) were granted membership. There was a small, upscale market on the island, but generally the Greenies had to take the ferry over to Charlevoix for most of their groceries and other shopping.

While Lizzy came back from her first summer on Green with plenty of impressive stories and hundreds of freckles (the Sutter version of a tan), she said the Sutters were clearly considered outsiders and hadn't really gotten to know many people until summer was almost over.

I had suggested that Green sounded... perhaps just the slightest bit pretentious, not wanting to offend Lizzy, whose feelings veered on the fragile side. Lizzy had cracked up, much to my relief. "You have no idea!" she'd said, rolling her eyes and laughing. "Honestly, some of the Greenies I met have to be among the most out-of-touch, snotty people in the world."

"Well, you're a Greenie too now, Liz," I had said with a smirk, thankful that my friend had returned to me unchanged. She'd just shaken her head emphatically at me in response.

By the end of her second summer on Green Island, however, Lizzy had seemingly become much more fond of the place. Her sister Sarah, always extremely desperate to fit in, had diligently devoted her days to working her way into the clique of Green's cool teenagers, while Lizzy had focused on enjoying the beaches, learning to sail, and lots of reading. She said that as she'd gotten to know more of the Greenies, it turned out there were actually more than a handful who seemed pretty down-to-earth and normal.

After hearing so many tales of this extravagant and beautiful world, I was curious to experience it firsthand. The thought of gorgeous beaches and lazy days sounded like heaven. Not to mention how appealing it sounded to spend all summer with Lizzy as my roommate and avoid the painful situation going on with my family, even if only temporarily. I had been planning to pass the summer working at the front desk of the local YMCA part-time and teaching guitar lessons a few hours a week as well. While I did need to earn some money, I thought my parents might be persuaded to cut me a break in light of the previous day's developments.

Chapter 8

While it had not been an easy sell, not by any means, my parents had eventually agreed that I could spend the summer on Green Island with the Sutters. When I say my parents agreed, it was really just my mom, as my dad had somewhat checked out in the days since Griffin and I learned the news of the separation. Although my mom had begrudgingly acquiesced to my proposal, she'd made it exceedingly clear that she wasn't too crazy about the idea of me spending the summer on Green Island, which didn't come as a surprise to me in the least. She held a general disdain for country club types, and it had long been apparent that she frowned upon the Sutters' enthusiastic plunge into that world the moment they got the chance. Lizzy's new Jeep had been greeted with an exaggerated eye roll and head shake, and the news of their purchase of their massive Bloomfield Hills mansion had resulted in her mutterings of "nouveau riche" and "pathetic". While she and Mrs. Sutter had never been close friends, my mom made a general effort to avoid anything beyond the briefest small talk with her these days. So, needless to say, the idea of her teenage daughter spending the summer immersed in work-free days of tanning, sailing and lounging with people she wrote off as superficial was not overly appealing to my mom. However, she did love Lizzy, and it was clear to everyone that Lizzy had not been seduced by rubbing elbows with the rich as her parents had. In the end, after a few days of heated debate about Green Island mixed with emotionally draining conversations about the separation, my mom had caved.

"Just promise me that you'll remember Green Island isn't the real world, OK?" she had said gently upon agreeing that I could go. "I know you're not someone who would be too impressed by that place, but just don't come back any different from the way you are now..."

"Mom, you know me better than that. It's not like I'm going to start feeling entitled to a Corvette just because I spent the summer around guys named Chip and Brooks who love pastel Polo shirts and own personal yachts. I just want this summer as a break from things, you know? I have my whole life to work, and spending this summer on Green Island feels like maybe my last chance to be free." It sounded dramatic, but it really was how I felt.

"I know, honey," she agreed. "That's why I said you could go."

My mom had been extraordinarily accommodating since the news of the separation had been dropped on me and Griffin. I guess she probably felt guilty about putting us through this. While I still felt angry with both my parents for not fighting harder for our family, after the passing of a week I also felt somewhat more sympathetic toward them and just generally sad about the situation. My dad, never one to open up to me emotionally, had kept a pretty low profile since they told us about the separation. He hadn't moved out yet — he was looking for an apartment — but he seemed to be away from the house even more than usual. In talking with my mom in-depth about the situation, it became apparent that the separation was largely her idea, and I had to assume my dad was having a pretty tough time with the state of affairs on a lot of levels.

While my mom was skeptical about Green Island in general, I suspected she also may have been a bit relieved to have the house to herself for the summer, free from the obligations of motherhood with the space to figure out the situation with my dad, one way or another. Like I said, she'd always loved Lizzy, and she knew that the Sutters, despite their recent materialistic tendencies, would take good care of me. Lizzy was nothing short of ecstatic when I called her with the news.

The night before we left, I had my dad's old hockey duffel bag open on my bed as I sorted through my summer clothes and decided what to take with me. Although I was about four inches taller than Lizzy, most of her clothes, with the exception of her pants (unless I wanted to wear them all as capris), fit me pretty well. I usually ended up wearing her stuff a lot of the time, so I wasn't too concerned about bringing enough clothes. I was a pretty basic dresser anyway, throwing in my several worn pairs of jean cutoffs, a variety of tank tops, my two favorite hoodies, two J. Crew bikinis and a few other items that I couldn't live without. My feet were exactly the same size as Lizzy's – size 8 – so I packed two pairs of flip flops and my running shoes and figured I could borrow whatever else I needed.

I was winding my headphone cord around my Discman when there was a tapping on my bedroom door as it opened. My dad always did that, opening the door as he knocked, his knock serving as more of a warning that he was coming in rather than a request for permission to enter. It typically irritated me, but this time I was just happy to see him.

"Bag looks familiar," he said with one of his crooked smiles as he sat on my bed next to my piles of items to take with me. He looked tired, with more than a day's worth of stubble on his face and dark circles under his eyes, something I rarely saw settle on his dark complexion.

"Oh, yeah, do you mind that I'm taking it?" I asked, not mentioning that my mom had been the one to suggest I use that bag.

"No, no, of course not," he responded, his familiar Brazilian accent more defined than usual, as it always was when he wasn't sleeping well. He sat quietly on my bed for a minute before clearing his throat. "Breck, I'm sorry I haven't been around much the past few weeks." He paused for another few seconds before continuing. "This family is everything to me. I know it might not always seem obvious to you, but everything I do, all the hours I work, it's all for you and Griff. And for your mom. If that hasn't been clear to you guys, then, I am so sorry." His face looked fragile in a way that I hadn't seen since his mother, whom we had called Vovó, died. My throat and nasal passage started to burn, letting me know that if I tried to talk, I would certainly burst out crying. Instead, I sat down next to him on the bed and wrapped my arms around him. I buried my face in his broad shoulder and could no longer stop the tears. Although my crying usually made my dad uncomfortable, this time he just held me. I wondered if I would ever sit in my bedroom with him again, if I would soon be a child of divorce who slept on a pull-out couch a few nights a week when I visited him. We sat like that for about five minutes, before he stood up and kissed my forehead.

"I hope you have a great summer, querida," he said quietly, adding with a lighthearted wink, "I hope it's kick-ass," using his fingers to make air quotes when he said the word "kick-ass," a phrase he frequently made fun of me for using. I laughed, the exchange pushing our emotional moment into the past. "And don't forget to call," he said with a genuine smile as he pulled my bedroom door shut behind him.

He was a hard man to understand. One part struggling convenience store owner who came home short-tempered and irritable. One part desperate artist who wanted nothing more than to earn his living through his talent as a painter rather than through slaving away at his store. And, of course, one part father and husband who wanted, more than anything, for all of us to be happy. Maybe all my mom needed was to see more of this last part of him, which had seemed all but absent in recent months or maybe even years. Hopefully a summer without the kids could help them reconnect, maybe the separation would scare my dad back into living a life that reflected his claims that our family was what mattered most to him. I could only hope.

In the end, I fit my clothes, books, tapes and CDs easily into the old duffel bag, which I carried downstairs and set by the front door. I picked up my guitar from the table in our den, put it in its case, and set it on top of my duffel bag as well. Through the kitchen window, I noticed my mom sitting out on the back deck. Still feeling emotional from my talk with my dad, I walked through the back door to join her.

It was a chilly early June night, and she had one of our worn den blankets draped over her legs. As I sat down next to her, she threw part of the blanket over my bare legs without saying anything. She was holding a rocks glass, and I could tell from the wafting smell that it was filled with an inch or so of whiskey, which she drank occasionally.

"I'm really going to miss you, honey," she said, apparently also in one of her sweet moods.

"I'll miss you too, Mom. But, I think it will be good for you to have me and Griff out of your hair for the summer," I said, hesitating before adding, "good for you and dad to have some time together."

"Are you all packed?" she asked, not responding to my comment. I nodded.

She held her glass out to me. "Want a sip?"

"Seriously?" This was not my mom's ordinary way. Offering her sixteen-year-old daughter a sip of whiskey was not her norm at all. She wasn't one of those party moms who was still desperate to feel like she was one of the kids. She was way too secure and grounded for that.

"Only because you're with me," she added, handing me the glass. "Don't you dare take this as an approval of you drinking generally. Just this once."

I took a tiny sip. The burning sensation hit my tongue as a warmth traveled down my throat, making me cringe, but kind of in a good way. She took the glass back, and we talked about her summer plans. She was teaching a journalistic writing course at University of Michigan's campus in Dearborn, a satellite to the main Ann Arbor campus, which she seemed ecstatic about. For years she had been writing for a local Detroit newspaper but was always relegated to trivial topics and lifestyle matters – reporting on suburban art festivals or reviewing local plays. She loathed her editor, Bob Trelyse, who never let her cover the criminal cases or compelling issues that interested her – corruption in local government, the questionable murder conviction of a local teenager, the Malice Green beating. My mom was convinced that Bob didn't believe a working mother had the time available to commit to covering the real stories and had kept her off such beats accordingly.

Earlier this year, she had become fed up with this treatment and quit. Now she was figuring out how to jump-start her career and had applied for this adjunct professorship, which she had been thrilled to land. I wondered if all this change had caused her to re-evaluate her marriage as well. I didn't bring it up though, I was too afraid of hearing what she might have to say about her relationship with my dad in her slightly intoxicated state. We passed the glass back and forth a few times before she told me I'd had enough.

"Are you nervous at all about spending the summer there?" she asked gently before I stood up to head inside.

"Not really... I mean, I'll miss you and Dad, and I'm not really thrilled about spending the summer with Sarah Sutter, but mostly I'm excited."

"I wouldn't worry about Sarah at all," she said, pulling the blanket more tightly around her knees. "She's just jealous of you."

"Jealous," I scoffed. "What would she be jealous about?"

"Well, it's pretty obvious that she is completely superficial and insecure, and you are a beautiful girl, so she just views you as competition."

I shake my head. "No way."

"Trust me, Breck, I've known plenty of Sarah Sutters in my life. She's a plain jane who would probably give anything to look like you. Just think how upset she was when that big shot guy from her school took you to their dance. I'm sure she doesn't like the idea of having you to compete with on Green Island either. Not to mention that you're closer with her sister than she is."

Suddenly this conversation made me feel awkward and uncomfortable. I just shrugged in response, said good night and headed inside, thankful that the whiskey had left my mind soft around the edges.

"Hon," my mom called after me as I was opening the door to step inside. I turned my head. "Don't tell your dad that you had a few sips, OK?"

"It's not a big deal," I said, with an unintended tone of hostility in my voice, which I immediately felt guilty about. I walked back over to her and gave her a quick hug. "Sorry, I didn't mean to snap at you. Love you so much, Mom," I added as I walked inside and closed the door behind me.

Chapter 9

Lizzy took the four-hour drive to Charlevoix as an opportunity to give me a complete rundown on every inhabitant of the one hundred forty summer homes located on Green Island. Obviously I couldn't begin to keep them all straight, but I figured I would learn the ones I needed to know once I got there and her stories kept me entertained for much of the ride.

Sarah Sutter, one year older than us and going into her senior year of high school, was riding in the car with us as well. With the exception of their similar looks, it was often hard for me to believe Lizzy and Sarah were related. While Sarah wasn't necessarily a *bad* person, she was the absolute epitome of a stereotypically snotty and spoiled teenage girl. As my mom had been getting at the night before, Sarah was obsessed with how she looked and being popular and seemed to care about pretty much nothing else. As far as I could tell, in Sarah's eyes, she was a Heather and Lizzy and I were lowly Veronicas. Especially me. She was typically cold and catty toward me, taking every opportunity to make a snide comment at my expense, which I had always just chalked up to her thinking she was better than us and certainly not to jealousy. She had been condescending and rude to me and to Lizzy for as long as I could remember, so while it didn't really upset me exactly, she definitely got on my nerves. I tried not to let her bother me though, since she wasn't someone whose opinion I valued at all.

And, since I did love the rest of the Sutter family, I accepted Sarah's presence with a grain of salt and did my best to tolerate her, while more or less disregarding her as well. I had been thrilled when she switched from St. Lucy's to Detroit Country Day, cutting down somewhat on the amount of time I had to be around her.

Sarah was not the least bit happy that she had been forced to drive to Charlevoix with the two of us and made no motions to offer me shotgun for even a portion of the ride. Her parents had recently taken her car away after she was caught sneaking out in the middle of the night, and apparently she had decided riding with the two of us was preferable to riding in the other car with her parents, Katherine, the youngest Sutter sister, and Indy, the Sutters' yorkie.

I knew that Sarah, unsurprisingly, had thrown herself into the Green Island social circuit full-throttle. She'd made it her quest to become friends with the island's "in-crowd", a task that had proven difficult, according to Lizzy, given that people on Green Island weren't all that keen on newbies, especially when they were of the new money variety. By the second year, however, Sarah had somehow managed to become a part of the inner circle, which, I learned during the car ride, was comprised of girls named Dalton Aldridge, Nikki Patton, Shelby Rhode, and now, Sarah Sutter as well.

"You'll die when you see how the people there dress, Brecken," Sarah piped in as Lizzy told me about the various cliques and characters of Green. "Especially when you meet Dalton — she's one of my best friends — she basically looks identical to Elle Macpherson and her mom is one of the heads of

Vogue magazine, so she pretty much dresses better than most celebrities." She paused for a minute, clearly awaiting an envious reaction from me in the backseat. As she should have known to expect by now, however, I was not going to give her any such satisfaction. I shot Lizzy a look in the rear-view mirror and could see her smirking back at me. It kind of bothered me that she wouldn't ever tell her sister that we weren't interested in her social climbing successes, but then that was Lizzy, always wanting to keep the peace.

From both girls' descriptions, Dalton sounded like the leader of the pack on Green Island, with Shelby, Nikki and Sarah as her loyal lackeys. Lizzy was telling me about their next door neighbor on Green, a man named Tom Hooks, who everyone knew was cheating on his wife with Marcy DiMario. Everyone that is, except for Mrs. Hooks. Sarah was looking out the window, seemingly bored because the topic had strewn from her own life, when she cut Lizzy off.

"Oh my God, won't Brecken totally die when she sees Reed Whalen?!" Sarah exclaimed enthusiastically, turning toward her sister for confirmation.

I honestly did not understand how Lizzy could tolerate Sarah day in and day out, but she halfheartedly responded, "yeah, Reed is definitely insanely good looking," knowing that I couldn't care less.

Sarah craned her head around from the front seat, her perfectly made up face looking back at me from next to her headrest. "He is, I'm not exaggerating here, literally the perfect physical specimen. He's gorgeous."

"Sounds like you have a little crush, Sar," I responded with a mock sweetness in my voice, knowing this would get under her skin.

"Crush?! Um, not even close. Dalton and Reed have been on and off dating forever, and they are basically the perfect couple. Like Brad Pitt and Jennifer Aniston, although Dalton is actually way prettier than Jennifer Aniston. Anyway, Dalton is one of my best friends, so no, I don't have a crush on her boyfriend. It's just an indisputable fact that he is one of the best looking human beings I've ever seen, actors and models included."

Clearly Green Island, as well as all the other luxuries her parents' recent wealth had made available to her, were heaven to Sarah. It was so hard for me to comprehend how the same parents could have raised someone as shallow as Sarah and someone as grounded and sweet as Lizzy. If there was a better argument out there for nature trumping nurture, I would have liked to see it.

"Hmmm, cool..." I said, with absolutely no enthusiasm when Sarah finally finished, and she turned back to face the front without further comment.

"Well, I'm going to listen to my Discman for a while," I said, realizing I couldn't stand another minute of Sarah's inane conversation and worshiping of the rich and beautiful. I unzipped my CD case and pulled out *Blonde on Blonde*, slipped it into my Discman and felt instant relief as I drowned out Sarah's chattering. I flipped open *High Fidelity*, a book that my mom had given me for the trip, knowing that Nick Hornby was one of my favorite writers. Glancing at the front seat for a second, I could see Sarah's mouth was still going a mile a minute as her hands flailed about in exaggerated gestures, and I smiled to myself as I turned my full attention to my book.

Chapter 10

We'd gotten a late start and stopped a few times en route to Charlevoix for gas and McDonald's french fries (no, Sarah did not eat any), so it was already almost 7 P.M. by the time we arrived in the heart of Charlevoix, a quaint little town wedged between Lake Charlevoix and Round Lake to the east and vast Lake Michigan to the west. We passed by old fashioned bakeries and charming fudge shops, and Lizzy soon turned off Bridge Street into a large marina area.

"Lots of boats use this marina," Sarah informed me, "but the private parking for the Green Island is around Round Lake a bit, away from all this chaos," she waved her hand toward the small number of people near the various boats, a scene I would hardly have described as chaotic. For the last twenty minutes of our drive, she had been frantically re-applying mascara, blush and lip gloss in the visor mirror above her seat, as well as brushing and fluffing her hair until we pulled up.

I gathered up my Discman, book and hoodie, which were strewn around me in the backseat and hopped out of the car once we'd parked in a covered lot. A man who looked to be in his late fifties and was dressed in a white suit with a green tie hurried over to help with our bags. I soon learned that his name was Patrick, and he was one of the most beloved Green Island staff members. He was manager of the transportation staff and was extremely friendly and charismatic, giving both the Sutter girls big hugs and welcoming me to Green Island. Once he had loaded our bags and my guitar case onto a cart, we followed behind him to the ferry dock.

The ferries, of which there were three currently docked, seated about twenty people comfortably and were large and swanky. The sun was already beginning its descent over the water, and the sky was streaked with pink and purple. I felt contented and peaceful as we bounced over the waves, thankful to be spending my summer in such a beautiful setting, to be having a little adventure, however insubstantial.

For some reason I'd imagined the ferry to Green Island would take about fifteen minutes, but after we departed, Lizzy mentioned that it would be take us about an hour to reach the island, even in the high-speed ferries. (Sarah made sure to inform me that this was half as long as it took the larger Beaver Island ferries to go to the same distance). With the wind whipping through my hair and the waves crashing around me, I wouldn't have minded if the ride took all night.

• • • • •

The ferry coasted into the Green Island marina, which housed mainly sailboats, speed boats and large cruisers, and at which several more identical ferry boats were docked. Ricky, the man operating the ferry, secured the boat and folded down a makeshift walkway from the dock. He held each of our right hands as we descended onto the walkway.

As soon as we stepped off the boat, Sarah and Lizzy were waving to a few nearby people milling around the marina. Ricky and another worker who had appeared, also dressed in a white suit and green tie, loaded our bags onto a horse drawn carriage waiting by the marina entrance. The whole scene was so foreign, and admittedly, more than a little magical, especially with the last lingering light of sunset illuminating the island, that I found myself walking very slowly from the dock to the carriage, taking it all in. This was a place where people stood waiting to carry our bags, to escort us in horse drawn carriages, where I would have a whole summer to do nothing but have fun. While I knew this drew no parallel to the reality of my life, I was just thankful that I had ended up here for a brief time. As we joined our bags in the carriage, I promised myself that I would indulge in the entire experience, make the most of this opportunity, and leave the sadness and troubles of my family behind, just for the next ten weeks.

"Ooh, look at that big smile on Brecken's face," Sarah interrupted my thoughts as we bounced along in the carriage. "Pretty divine here, isn't it?" she boasted.

I nodded, my permanent grin expanding as we passed a charming lighthouse that stretched upward just beyond the marina, and Lizzy squeezed my arm affectionately. The girls pointed out various places to me along our route, Sarah being uncharacteristically nice in her excitement to show off Green Island to a newcomer. Each house was of generally the same style, although the girls assured me that each was unique. The homes had all been designed by the architect Theodore Wilhelm in the 1920's, financed by a group of wealthy businessmen from the Midwest who wanted an exclusive paradise close to home. The sprawling houses were a mixture of light brick and white wood siding, typically with dark shutters and ranging between four and nine bedrooms. They varied between two and three floors, some with grand balconies, others with covered porches that wrapped around the entirety of the house. The lawns faded from meticulous gardens up near the houses to a more natural grass that transitioned naturally into the white beach, (I learned later that gardeners were available to the Greenies and the cost was included in their annual dues) and nearly every person we passed waved cheerily and called out a greeting.

The trees thinned out as we passed the vast Green Island Country Club golf course. The Club property spanned nearly a quarter of the island, and the Club was, based on what the girls were telling me, the social center of Green. The dads and sons golfed, the moms and daughters sunned and played tennis, and everyone dined and drank. The Club was admittedly gorgeous, with an enormous main clubhouse and several smaller buildings, which were also Wilhelm's creations, two large pools, several hot tubs and tennis courts, and the green, lush grounds of the golf course, which, surprise, surprise, was considered one of the best in Michigan – right up there with Oakland Hills.

It was about fifteen minutes before we pulled in front of the Sutter house, Cottage 78. The houses on Green Island had no driveways; I guess without cars they were an unnecessary use of space. Many, including Cottage 78, had worn paths in the grass where it appeared that bikes frequently traveled from the porch to the dirt road that circled the island. Our carriage driver, Marco, carried our bags to the porch and wished us a "lovely" summer. The front door was open and we headed inside. As I would soon realize, houses were absolutely never locked on Green Island. Bikes were left on the front lawn, and children were allowed to run free all day and into the night. At all times, there were no less than twenty security guards dispersed about the island. They ensured that no outsiders attempted to dock there and generally assisted the Greenies in whatever manner was needed. The security and the four heads of staff had access to the only four-wheelers on the island, which were used solely in the event of an emergency.

Mrs. Sutter had left us a note saying that she, Mr. Sutter and Katherine had gone to the Club for dinner and that we were welcome to join them once we had gotten settled in.

Sarah quickly disappeared upstairs, saying she needed to "make herself presentable," which left me wondering what her application of full makeup and the hairstyling that had gone on in the car an hour earlier had constituted.

"So, my room's on the second floor, but my mom suggested that you and I take over the third floor for the summer," Lizzy said to me as we lugged our bags up the first flight of stairs, followed by Indy, who was especially rambunctious and making every effort to trip us on our way up. "Then she'll just use my usual room as a guest room or something, if we need it this summer. I'll give you the full tour later."

"Sounds good to me," I said, focused on not tumbling down the stairs.

We reached the second floor and Lizzy pointed down the hallway. "Sarah's is the first door on the left, then Katherine's is the second, and my parents' is at the end of the hall. This one," she pointed to the doorway on the right, "is usually mine. There are three bedrooms on the third floor, but they're all kind of small, especially one of them, but there is also kind of an open area with a TV and a couch and stuff. I think it's going to be awesome to have it to ourselves for the summer."

"Sounds perfect," I agreed, thinking of my tiny bedroom back home. "Let's see it!"

"Plus," Lizzy added with a smirk, "this way you can keep your messiness in your own bedroom."

"I'm not that messy!" I insisted. "Seriously, I know I can be bad about hanging up clothes but it's an organized mess, you know that."

"Mmhmm, OK," Lizzy said still smiling as she opened the door next to her old bedroom door, which hid another staircase and led the way up to the third floor.

A big part of me wished I was still a little child when I saw the third floor. It was the kind of space that would have been ideal for games of make-believe and escaping from adults. It had oddly shaped random closets all over the place, a cool little bathroom with a slanted ceiling and lots of tiny windows. Even as a sixteen-year-old, the space seemed magical to me, and I was thrilled that Lizzy and I would be taking it over for the summer.

We each chose a little bedroom to call our own. Like Lizzy's, "my" bedroom was already nearly filled by the double bed, cozy chair and dresser that occupied it. Even though we had the whole space of the third floor, I thought it would be nice to have my own little space, from time to time. I never really got annoyed with Lizzy, which was kind of crazy given the fact that we spent insane amounts of time together. But, it was true that my messiness got on her nerves and, truthfully, she snored, so having my own room would have its up sides.

We never made it up to the Club that night. Sarah had come upstairs about an hour after we arrived to say she was heading over there. Although her outfit was casual and simple, a gray cotton skirt and a pale pink Michael Stars shirt with a scoop neck, she had clearly spent time putting on additional makeup and flat-ironing her strawberry blonde hair. I had to admit that she looked pretty. The Hani Mori perfume that both Lizzy and Sarah swore by had wafted into the main room of the third floor as she entered. She asked if we wanted to go with her, but Lizzy and I agreed that we were just going to take it easy, get unpacked and then veg. Sarah rolled her eyes at us, clearly finding it unfathomable that bee-lining for the Club could be anything but our first priority.

Lizzy brought her stereo up from her bedroom downstairs, and we spent the next few hours listening to The Traveling Wilburys, switching furniture with Lizzy's old room and getting our new space all set up. The third floor didn't get much use and apparently therefore did not get much attention from the Sutters' cleaning ladies. At Lizzy's urging, we had dusted and vacuumed, and we had stocked our little refrigerator with items we lifted from the kitchen. One downside to the beautiful old house was that it was built in the days before central air conditioning. This didn't really bother me since my house didn't have AC either, but the third floor did seem to get pretty warm, despite the nice breeze off the lake and the ceiling and window fans in each room.

Once we'd had all we could take of the heat up there, we each took a quick shower and then walked the full loop around the island, stopping at one point to sit on the soft white sand beach for almost an hour. It turned out that Green Island was home to millions of fireflies, and their tiny flickering lights made the breezy summer night seem dream-like. I could definitely see myself getting used to this place, I thought, as I laid on my back in the sand next to Lizzy, admiring the stars.

Chapter 11

My first week on Green was nothing short of heavenly. Most days, Lizzy and I would waste away the hours serenely lying out in the sun at the beach, rising only briefly for lunch at the Club or to explore the lake and other nearby islands in her dad's boat. When the heat of the sun became too much, I would retire to reading or playing my guitar in the shade of the Sutters' covered porch. Our list of relaxing activities went on and on. I had always imagined that I would quickly get bored without my constant barrage of school, homework, soccer, babysitting, and guitar and violin lessons, but I realized immediately that this thought was so incredibly wrong. Instead, I felt like I was on a luxury vacation that I wished would never end, and Royal Oak, Michigan felt a world away.

Most of the other Green Island families arrived throughout our first week there. A few days in, I met Charlotte Monahan and Greta Knox, who were the two girls around our age that Lizzy had become friendly with the past summer. I was pleasantly surprised to realize that I really liked both girls, Greta especially. Both of their families had been "summering" on Green Island for generations, and they seemed to be friendly with most of the other teenagers on the island. While they weren't obsessed with Dalton and her gang in the worshipful way that Sarah was, they seemed to like her and the rest of the party crowd among the Green teens, insisting that they weren't so bad once you got to know them. Greta and Charlotte were easy-going and funny, and they seemed to know and like nearly everyone on Green. I wasn't surprised that Lizzy had clicked so well with them, but at the same time they seemed immersed in Green's world in a way that I couldn't imagine Lizzy would ever be. I'd been enjoying the pleasant distance that Lizzy and I kept from the Green social circles, which intimidated me more than I cared to admit.

The second week after we arrived on Green Island, Lizzy suggested we stop by Greta's house late one afternoon as we were walking home from the marina. We found Greta painting her toenails with baby blue polish on the steps of her front porch, her long, perfectly highlighted blonde hair hanging over one shoulder. She greeted us warmly, saying she had just gotten home from playing beach volleyball. Her mom was over at the Club, as were her brothers. Greta's dad, like most on the island, usually only came to Green on the weekends. She was from a suburb of Chicago called Winnetka, and her dad usually went back there during the week for work. In fact, I had realized that Mr. Sutter was one of a small group of fathers who spent the whole summer on Green, having the luxury of working only when he was offered consulting jobs that appealed to him. Greta was telling us about how she had been at a bonfire party at Nikki Patton's house the night before and had made out with a guy named Andrew Wells, whose summer house was next door to Greta's.

"Yeah, it was kind of weird I guess. I've known Andrew my whole life, and we've definitely always been friends, but I never realized he was interested in me at all. He's such a flirt all the time, you know? So, I never thought anything of it when he would put his arm around me or whatever," Greta explained as she set her nail polish aside and fanned her hands above her toes, going on to give us the play-by-play of her hook up on the beach with Andrew.

I listened attentively to all the details, soaking them up, memorizing them for later consideration. The truth was, I was embarrassingly inexperienced when it came to guys. St. Lucy's didn't even have so much as a brother school, so my contact with guys my age was pathetically minimal. My parents had sent me to St. Lucy's because my mom thought an all-girls school created stronger, more confident females, or at least that's what she claimed. She wasn't even a practicing Catholic, and my dad only went to church on Christmas Eve and Easter, but St. Lucy's was the only affordable option in town if they wanted me guarded from the evils of coed education.

Greta continued with her story of how she and Andrew had gotten pretty wasted playing beer pong (it turns out beer pong is not one of Greta's strongest skills) and then he had suggested they walk home together. They had walked on the beach, rather than the road, to avoid running into as many parents in their drunken state, since it wasn't all that late. Greta stopped mid-story and smiled.

"I know what we need. A few vodka lemonades and some brie and crackers, agreed?" she asked with a mischievous smile. "After all, it *is* 4:00, which means it's cocktail hour on Green!" While I might normally have found a personality like hers to be kind of obnoxious, Greta actually managed to seem

gregarious
her despite

"Uh, (
hesitantly, l
thought of (

"Yeah, w
to help Gret

Boys and
typical subur
virtually no e:
earlier on the
I'd ever had. '
drank weren't
reasons. I had
knew my paren

mostly about music, and th
dance. As I'd said yes
stomach at the pros
school dance, eve
At least it was
placid life.
How
up
so

caught me coming home d_____. And, so, drinking had just never really been on my radar. At least not until now. But this was my summer of freedom after all, so I figured I might as well dive in headfirst.

As far as boys went, my one and only kiss had been more or less a disastrous event a few months earlier with Joe Stafford, one of Sarah Sutter's guy friends who had taken me to a Detroit Country Day dance after we met at the Sutters' house. Sarah had clearly been quite irritated by the fact that he was interested in me, and I hadn't really known what to make of it myself. He was good looking, but in kind of a generic Ken doll way, and although he had seemed nice enough, I think I was more intrigued by the novelty of a guy liking me than I was interested in Joe himself. He'd asked for my phone number at the Sutters' house, which I had awkwardly given him. When he'd called the next night, and again a few nights after that, we'd had decent conversations,

en he had asked me to the
I'd felt a little flutter in my
ect of attending an actual high
if it was with a guy I barely knew.
a change of pace from my otherwise

ver, the whole dance experience had ended
eing pretty miserable. Apparently Joe was
mewhat of a stud among the Detroit Country Day
crowd (which I promise was more a reflection of the
motley crew that made up the rest of the guys at
Country Day than it was a reflection of anything
particularly stellar about Joe) and the other girls in our
group for the dance, including Sarah, had their
territorial claws out from the moment I arrived at the
pre-dance photo party. After the photos, we'd driven
around in a limo for a few hours and everyone had
gotten really drunk. Everyone but me, that is. I wasn't
about to drink for the first time with people I barely
knew and had no reason to think I could rely upon.
So, I had turned down the beers, Zima and
liquor/Coke concoctions that were being passed
around in pop bottles, with my refusal resulting in
laughter from Sarah and the other girls. It was kind of
embarrassing, but I reminded myself that I didn't care
what these bitchy girls thought of me. When we
finally got to the dance, about two hours after it
started, I was already wishing it was time to go home.
As it turned out, we only stayed at the dance for
about half an hour. According to Sarah, the dances
themselves were "totally lame." I considered telling
Sarah that the dance seemed like more fun than
driving around the Detroit suburbs in a crowded limo
listening to people I barely knew brag about how

wasted they were, but I managed to keep that thought to myself.

After our brief stint at the actual dance, the group headed back to our limo and over to the house where a guy named Hayden lived. Apparently Hayden's parents were hosting the after-party in their basement and backyard. Although Joe had been nice enough, I felt completely out of place and wasn't having any fun, so I'd already begun concocting potential excuses for my quick exit once we got to the after-party. The basement at Hayden's house was larger than my entire house, and it was equipped with a pool table, two big screen TVs, and an indoor pool. The backyard was set up with tiki torches and had a bubbling hot tub. Tough life, I thought, wishing I had someone there to feel like an outsider with me.

By the time we arrived at Hayden's, Joe was completely hammered. He could barely handle the walk from the limo to the house without falling over. The whole ride from the dance to the party, he'd been rubbing my shoulders and touching my hair, but I didn't feel the slightest attraction to him. In fact, I was starting to find him pretty annoying, and I felt the urge to smack his hand away each time he touched me. Once we were in Hayden's basement, I tried to play pool with a few of the other guys who were less drunk, thinking I would make the best of the situation for a little while and then get out of there.

Unfortunately, as the pool game was about to start, Joe came over and said he needed to talk to me. I barely knew the guy and doubted he could have anything very crucial to tell me, but I humored him since I was his date and all that. Plus, he usually seemed like a pretty decent guy, so I didn't want to be a total bitch to him. I plopped down next to him on the couch as he was fumbling with the tab to open another can of Miller High Life.

"So, what's up?" I asked, as he finally managed to muster up the coordination to open his beer.

He swayed a little bit and then grabbed onto my right hand with his free hand, which was big and sweaty. Before I could react, he started talking.

"You're so gorgeous," he slurred. "You are honestly the most beautiful girl I've ever seen. And your eyes, they're gold. I've never seen eyes like yours before." He stopped for a minute.

"Umm, Joe, that's really nice but-" I started awkwardly, but he cut in.

"Sorry. Sorry, I'm drunk. Sorry, but I just, it's just that you're so hot. And cool, you're so cool too, and, I just, sorry, I'm drunk."

I waited for a minute, realizing it didn't really matter how I responded, since he was clearly too obliterated to understand or remember what I was saying. I was still debating how to politely get out of the situation when he kissed me. And so it was that right there, in a random basement with an extremely drunk guy whom I barely knew, I had my first kiss.

Other than being startled, I felt nothing. No sparks, no weak stomach, no dreams of a long life together. Nothing, except kind of disgusted as he pressed his thick tongue into my mouth and rubbed it around. At that moment, absolutely all I wanted was for the kiss to end. I started to pull away as my mind raced with ideas of how I could quickly get the hell out of there. From across the room, I heard Sarah yell, "Hey Joe, get a room!" and the cackles of her drunken gaggle of idiot friends. I took that as my window to jump off the couch. I stammered a brief excuse to Joe, along the line that I suddenly felt sick, as I turned and ran upstairs before he had time to respond.

I hurried out of the basement and into the kitchen of Hayden's house, where a woman who I assumed was Hayden's mom was preparing late night food to bring downstairs to all the kids. I told her I didn't feel well and needed to call my mom. She was very sweet and showed me into their study where she said I could use the phone and have some privacy. I punched in Lizzy's number and begged her to pick me up immediately, assuring her that I would give her all the details as soon as she saved me from this awkward night. I then called my mom to say the dance had been awful and that I would be sleeping at Lizzy's. I had known she would still be awake, she always waited up for me when I was coming home late. I didn't have a curfew – sadly, I didn't go out enough to need one – so my mom had just told me to come home from the dance when the other kids did. My mom trusted me to a frightening degree. She clearly never even considered that I could be potentially lying to her on the phone and staying out all night at this ridiculous after-party, sleeping on the couch with my date. Instead, she trusted me, trusted that I was in fact staying at Lizzy's. The fact that she always believed me made me feel horribly guilty whenever I did anything she wouldn't approve of, which truthfully didn't happen very often. Lizzy and I had recently started smoking cigarettes when we drove around in her car at night, just to spice things up a little. Once my mom had noticed the smell and assumed we had been in the smoking section of a restaurant. Sometimes I wished she would trust me a little bit less.

So, that was my first kiss, and clearly, it wasn't the spellbinding experience that I'd hoped it would be. In fact, it made me wonder if maybe I was a lesbian, given that I had felt absolutely nothing in the way of attraction when Joe Stafford had kissed me.

"Well, do you feel attracted to girls?" Lizzy had asked on our drive home from the after-party when I had thrown this idea out there, thankful that I had a friend close enough that I could discuss this kind of thing with her.

"No... but maybe I've just been repressing my true sexuality because I feel like I *should* be attracted to guys."

"Seriously, Breck, I'm pretty sure you're not a lesbian. That guy was just drunk and you weren't into him. I think if you were a lesbian, you would probably know it by now. We're surrounded by nothing but girls in skirts all day, after all. I don't think that's the kind of thing that a person can be oblivious to, especially not one who overanalyzes everything like you do."

"Yeah, you're probably right. But what if I'm asexual, though? I mean, that would be horrible, because I would never be attracted to anyone, so I'd more or less be destined for an utterly sad and lonely existence," I had said, starting to feel a panicked sensation creeping in.

Lizzy had started laughing at this. "I think that we are just very, very deprived of male interaction. And, I think that you should just put the whole Joe kiss and your potential to go through life as a lonely asexual out of your mind. I'm pretty sure it will all make sense when you meet someone you actually *are* really attracted to."

"I hope so," I'd said, feeling doubtful.

Chapter 12

So there we were, a few months after my kissing disaster, drinking lemonade and vodkas on the balcony outside Greta's bedroom, where we had migrated after making our drinks, and Greta was wrapping up the rundown of her rendezvous on the beach with Andrew Wells. Lizzy, being the one sixteen-year-old on earth with even less sexual experience than me, was especially enthralled.

"So you and Andrew have never hooked up before?" I piped in as Greta finished giving us all the details.

"Nah, never. Like I said, I had no idea that he was into me at all. Last summer, he and Nikki Patton were together, so I doubt she's going to be too happy with me when word gets around, which it always does on Green."

"She's one of Sarah's friends, right?" I asked, turning to Lizzy, who nodded in response.

"Yeah, Sarah seems like she's always with Dalton, Nikki and Shelby," Greta agreed. She turned to Lizzy and asked, "You two close?"

"Well, she's my sister, so of course I love her, but no, I guess I wouldn't really say we're that close. I mean, I probably wouldn't be able to stand her if she wasn't related to me. But, she has her really good moments too. I think she's just really insecure." I was surprised to hear Lizzy opening up about her true feelings on her sister to Greta like this. Usually she was hesitant to say a bad word about anyone, especially her family. I noticed her cheeks were turning especially pink and realized the vodka might be starting to hit her. Actually, now that I thought about it, I was feeling kind of relaxed and chatty myself. The warm buzz from the vodka, combined with the afternoon view of the glistening water from Greta's window, left me feeling incredibly peaceful.

"Yeah, she definitely seems kind of, I don't know, in need of approval, or something like that," Greta agreed. "Nikki's the same way, and that kind of girl always seems drawn to Dalton. Probably because of Dalton's confidence, and I'm sure the fact that she's gorgeous and everyone loves her doesn't hurt either. It's like all the follower types think that people will assume they are just like Dalton if they hang out with her, rather than realizing they just come off looking kind of pathetic. The exact same thing happens all the time at New Trier, my high school," Greta said.

"So what's the story with this Dalton girl," I asked. "Why is everyone here so obsessed with her anyway?"

"Well, not *everyone* is obsessed with her, but she's fun to be around and really pretty. And, like I said, she's also really confident and people just seem to gravitate to her I guess," Greta said with a shrug.

"The couple times I met her last summer, she seemed like kind of an idiot," Lizzy said.

"Yeah, she's definitely overrated in my opinion. I don't get what all the hype is about myself... Although, she is the only girl here who has managed to get Reed Whalen's attention, even if it didn't last long, so I guess that's saying something," Greta responded as she tipped her glass, sending the last of her recently replenished vodka lemonade down her throat.

"You know," she said, as she got up and stretched her thin arms, "there's a bonfire at Andrew's house tonight. You guys should come. How come you never hang out with us at night? That needs to change, ASAP," she said with a grin. "Charlotte's coming over here after dinner to have some drinks and get ready beforehand, you guys have to come too!"

Lizzy gave me a questioning look. Whether it was my vodka haze or Greta's enthusiasm rubbing off on me, I couldn't say, but Greta's proposition sounded surprisingly appealing to me. "For sure, we're in," I said, standing up myself.

"Yay!" Greta exclaimed in an exaggerated voice as she wrapped one arm around my shoulder. "It'll be so much fun, plus I could use the moral support tonight...I'm afraid it's gonna be really weird to see Andrew again after last night."

"No way, you'll be fine," I smiled at Greta. "Do you like him? Or was that just a one time thing?" I wanted more details, momentarily living vicariously through Greta, who, unlike me, actually had a life.

"Well, I've actually always had a little crush on him, but I never realized he thought of me as more than a friend. So, I don't know, we'll see how things go tonight I guess!"

"OK, well, Breck, let's head home and shower and get some dinner and stuff," Lizzy said, swaying as she stood up from her chair.

"Easy there, Liz," I said with a laugh, grabbing her arm to steady her.

"Char's coming over around 8:00, but you guys can come over whenever you want," Greta said, leading the way inside and back downstairs. "I'll be here."

Chapter 13

We'd been at the bonfire party on the beach in front of Andrew Wells's house for about an hour, and I was sitting with Greta and Charlotte smoking a cigarette and drinking a Corona by the fire, contentedly rubbing my bare feet in the sand. *If my mom could see me now*, I thought with a pang of guilt, which I quickly pushed out of my head. I was sipping my beer slowly, not completely past my vodka buzz from earlier in the evening. Lizzy was playing beer pong on the other side of the fire with a guy named James Tucker as her partner. A total of about twenty-five or so people were there, and Dave Matthews Band serenaded us from the speakers that the Wellses had wired down to the beach.

I had been telling Charlotte and Greta about the trip I'd taken to Brazil with my dad a couple years earlier to visit all his extended family who still lived there, when Sarah Sutter, who had just shown up at the party, caught my eye and walked over to us.

"Wow, drinking *and* smoking now, Breck?" she said in a syrupy, nasty voice. "Rebel, rebel."

"Fuck off, Sarah," I shot back, surprising myself with my hostility, as I turned back to Charlotte and Greta, who cracked up as Sarah walked away.

"I can't stand that bitch," Charlotte said, as I looked over to see that Sarah had retreated back to the safety of her huddle around a very pretty blonde girl in a baby blue strapless dress. No one needed to tell me that she was Dalton Aldridge.

"Did you hear about what happened with Sarah and Trevor Ollins last summer?" I shook my head excitedly, and Charlotte entertained us with a story involving a drunken Sarah making out with an older guy on Green last summer, only to accidentally puke in his mouth. I felt a twinge of sympathy for Sarah, but it quickly passed when I looked up again to see her glaring at me across the fire.

"You ladies want to play some flip cup?" Andrew Wells asked, walking up behind me with his friend Josh Roister. Andrew and Josh were just two of the many Greenies who Greta and Charlotte had introduced me to already that night.

"Sure," Greta said, smiling, at the same time that I asked what, exactly flip cup was.

"Oh, Brecken, my naïve little friend, watch and learn," Josh said chuckling. He grabbed my hand and pulled me to my feet from the log where I was perched. "It's really simple. Two teams line up on each side of a table and fill their cups up part way with beer. The first person on each team drinks his beer and then he has to flip his cup until it lands upside down on the table, and when he's done that, the next person on his team does the same thing. The first team to finish wins."

"I can probably handle that," I said, hoping I didn't end up pulling a Sarah Sutter myself and puke on someone that night. We walked over to the table where Lizzy had just finished her beer pong game. She and James appeared to have won, and he was wrapping her in a big hug. Interesting. I couldn't remember seeing Lizzy hug a guy our age before. Ever. She then stumbled over to me, her eyes glazed.

"Breck," she said, leaning her arm on mine, "we won!" She then pulled me closer and whispered in my ear. "Isn't he cute? He kept putting his arm around me," she whispered loudly, looking over at James as she talked.

I smiled encouragingly at her. "He's really cute, you guys should go hang out by the fire and talk or something," I suggested, thinking she had probably had enough drinking games for one night.

"Oooh, good idea," she squealed with as much enthusiasm as if I had just come up with a solution to global warming. I laughed and left her to head over to the group at the flip cup table.

The game turned out to be as simple as it sounded and after about six rounds, I realized that I was, for the first time in my life, incredibly drunk. "No more flip cup for me," I mumbled to Greta, who was standing beside me, as I turned around to look for Lizzy.

I found her not far from the fire, lying in the sand with James Tucker. I could not believe it at first, but there, in the light of the moon, I found my best friend making out with a guy!

"Lizzy!" I shouted, being so shocked at the sight that I hadn't even considered that I probably shouldn't interrupt them until after her name had already left my lips.

She and James both shot to a sitting position, looking incredibly startled. "Shit, sorry guys," I said, turning to walk away.

"Are you OK, Breck?" Lizzy called after me, and I just waved my hand at her dismissively as I walked back toward the group and found Greta.

"I think I need to go to bed," I told her, as things continued to become blurrier around me.

Overhearing our conversation, Josh Roister said that he would walk me home. I felt slightly panicked at the thought of what a walk home with Josh might entail. Josh was nice but I wasn't attracted to him at all, and the last thing I wanted was a repeat of the Joe Stafford kiss debacle or something worse. I shot Charlotte and Greta a desperate look, and Charlotte came to my rescue.

"I've gotta head home too," Charlotte said, linking her arm through mine. "I'll make sure Brecken gets to bed safely."

I don't remember much else after that, but Charlotte must have kept her word because I woke up in my bed on the third floor of the Sutter house, and although I felt about as good as if I had been run over by a train, I smiled thinking that it had been a pretty fun night, and definitely an interesting change of pace. I drank the big glass of water that was conveniently next to my bed, probably Charlotte's doing, and fell back asleep until lunchtime.

Chapter 14

The bonfire party had several immediate results. First, Lizzy had a crush, something that had never happened before. Second, Sarah Sutter started to actually hate me, or, probably more accurately, she stopped pretending, even minimally, that she didn't hate me. Third, I no longer felt anxious about drinking in the way that I always had, in fact I thought it was pretty fun, at least in moderation (the moderation part being a lesson learned from the pounding headache and urge to throw up that hounded me the whole following day). In a place like Green, where the parents didn't seem to set any rules and the kids ran free, where there were no cars or sober drivers to worry about, no soccer coaches who would kick me off the team, no police officers to break up the parties, and no mom and dad to disappoint by getting arrested, drinking suddenly seemed like a fun pastime rather than a risk that wasn't worth the potential downside.

And, the most interesting effect of the party was that Lizzy and I seemed to have found friends on Green Island. When we walked on the beach in the morning, Josh Roister would whistle at us from the volleyball court. When we ate lunch at the Club a few days later, James Tucker and Andrew Wells pulled up chairs and asked to join us. It actually felt pretty good to be a part of the Green Island world, and I was realizing that the people on Green weren't nearly as stuck up as I had expected. Well, at least not most of them. And, in fact, a lot of them were pretty interesting and cool. Especially Charlotte and Greta, who I genuinely liked so much that I wished I could take them back to St. Lucy's with me at the end of the summer.

The morning after the party, or I should say the afternoon after, since it was well past 1 P.M. by the time I managed to pull myself out of bed, I looked out my bedroom window and spotted Lizzy lying out at the beach in front of the house. I threw on a bathing suit, filled up a water bottle with ice water in the kitchen and headed down to join her. She was stretched on her back in her beloved yellow halter bikini and tortoise sunglasses. Although she was just as hung-over as me, she had still woken up by 10 A.M., which she considered sleeping in.

I laid down next to her on her humongous blue and white beach towel with "Sutter" embroidered in one corner.

"Good morning. Where should we begin..." I said, smirking. "Oh I know, how about we start with the part of the night where you were getting it on with James Tucker in the sand, shall we?"

The corners of her mouth turned up in a slight smile. "I feel like crap," she said, moaning quietly as she spoke to emphasize her pained state. I handed her my water bottle, which she nearly drained in one long, aggressive gulp.

"Yeah, me too, I barely even remember the end of the night. But, thankfully, I do remember that you were making out with James, so tell me everything!"

She started laughing.

"Elizabeth Jane Sutter, start telling me every single detail right now!"

"All right, all right," she said, still giggling, clearly somewhat giddy. "So, you know, we were playing beer pong, and he randomly ended up as my partner. Well, I thought it was random, but," she broke out in a grin, "I guess he had been trying to figure out a way to talk to me and had asked Josh to put us on the same team. I don't know why he didn't think he could just ask me to be his partner or start talking to me, but whatever, I think it is pretty cute that he arranged to be my partner, don't you?"

"Yeah, that's really sweet," I said enthusiastically, thinking it actually sounded a tiny bit lame to rig a beer pong partnership as a way of talking to a girl, but the fact that Lizzy was touched by it was enough to make me happy. "Tell me more."

"So, I don't know, I guess he was flirting with me while we played. He gave me his baseball cap to wear, saying it would be good luck when it was my turn to throw, and kept brushing against my arm and stuff. But, you know me, I have pretty much no clue if a guy is flirting with me, since it has, um, essentially never happened that I am aware of... So I wasn't really reading too much into how he was acting, but I was pretty attracted to him. I mean, I'm sure the drinking was part of it, but the few times we hung out in a group last summer, I always thought he seemed really interesting and kind of more substantive than most of the other guys. Plus, I think he's so cute."

She kept grinning intermittently as she told the story.

"So, anyway, when you guys started playing flip cup, we, you know, went over by the fire and started talking," she continued. "He was just telling me about La Jolla, California, that's where he's from, and I was telling him about Bloomfield and St. Lucy's, and just random stuff I guess. And, then, he suddenly kissed me. He brushed my hair out of my face a little bit as he did it, and I guess it sounds cheesy now that I'm saying it, but at the time it seemed really sweet. So, anyway, I was completely dreading Sarah seeing us and being her usual annoying self about it, so I suggested we go over closer to the water, away from everyone. He started telling me how he had a crush on me last summer, I mean he didn't use the word crush, I forget how he said it, but anyway, the whole thing was just really... exciting."

"That's awesome. I'm so happy for you," I told her, and I was.

"Yeah, I'm honestly kind of thankful that I was drunk, because otherwise I think I would have been really awkward about the whole situation, since I have never even kissed anyone before. But, for whatever reason, I felt really comfortable, and it just kind of seemed natural."

"Aww, Liz, you're like a secret sex goddess, I love it," I said as she smacked me on the stomach.

"Ummm, hardly! All we did was kiss. He kind of put his hand up my shirt and I panicked and pushed it away. He wasn't like being aggressive about it, but I just kind of felt self-conscious for a minute I guess."

"How come?"

"I'm not sure really. I guess I want to take things slowly since I don't really know him all that well."

I was thinking that over when Katherine Sutter walked up to us with a few of her friends. She sat with us for a while, telling us about a kids' boat race that she was competing in that afternoon. It was too bad that only Sarah seemed to lack the Sutter gene for sweetness.

Chapter 15

Over the next two weeks, Lizzy and I went to a party every few nights, and we spent most of our days lying on the beach and lounging at the Club or hanging out in Charlevoix, checking out kitschy shops and summer movies with Charlotte and Greta when rain or overcast skies hit. My skin quickly darkened, with a faint smattering of little freckles sprouting on my nose, and my light brown hair became streaked with blonde. I'd never spent so many hours in the sun and was more or less in heaven.

I felt refreshed and alive as the days passed, listening to the waves loll lightly onto the beach, and my parents and their problems felt wonderfully far away. I talked to my mom every few days or so, as well as my dad from time to time, but as the weeks rolled on, I spent so little time inside the house that I rarely thought to call them until it was too late at night. My dad had rented an apartment in Royal Oak, which he had moved into a few days after I left for Green Island. However, he had been at the house once when I called, so I took that as a good sign.

It was hard to believe how quickly days filled with pure leisure could fly by and soon we were well into July. The only interruption to our happiness was when John F. Kennedy, Jr.'s plane crashed. I don't how exactly it originated, but all four of the Sutter females had a serious love, bordering on obsession, for the Kennedys – especially John, Jr. – so we all spent two days glued to the TV set once his plane went missing. I think it was probably the most time the whole family spent together all summer. Although I wasn't a Kennedy fanatic like them, I still got pretty caught up in the tragedy of the crash, and it took us all a few days to recover.

By late July, I was fully entrenched in island life. Lizzy and James were still in a limbo stage, where things seemed to be progressing kind of slowly, in my opinion. They never went out together without other people or made specific plans, but instead they just always ended up hanging out and then making out when we went to parties. She was constantly obsessing over what this meant and whether he did, in fact, really like her. Initially I had chalked their lack of progress up to them both being pretty shy, but over time it began to seem a little questionable to me that he wasn't putting in more effort. We were only going to be on Green for about four more weeks and then James would be heading back to California anyway, so maybe it was better overall if she didn't get too attached.

I woke up one morning on the early side and peaked into Lizzy's room to see her sleeping soundly, which was a rare shift from her usual early rising ways. We'd gone into town the night before to see a movie at the quaint Charlevoix Cinema with Greta and Charlotte. After debating, we'd decided to see *The Sixth Sense*. Lizzy had campaigned hard for *Runaway Bride*, but she ended up absolutely loving *The Sixth Sense* – we all did. I'd gone to bed when we'd gotten back, but Lizzy had been desperate to stop by a party at Nikki Patton's house in the hope of seeing James. Greta had agreed to go with her, so I was able to skip out. As much fun as I usually had at the Green parties, the drama and hangovers that accompanied them could wear a little thin at times so I'd been happy to take a night off.

A gentle breeze was blowing in my open bedroom window that morning, and the sun was glittering on the lake, so I threw on my navy bikini, jean cut-offs, green flip flops and a thin white V-neck t-shirt and headed down to the beach. I never got tired of the exquisite views on Green and decided to walk along the shoreline for a while and enjoy the tranquility before most people were out and about.

I waved to Josh Roister's parents as I passed them strolling at the water's edge and encountered a few mothers and au pairs with little children who were out enjoying the morning sun as well. I loved wandering among the beautiful old Green Island homes, observing the intricacies of each house. I couldn't imagine what an extraordinary and fascinating job it would have been to design each unique home for this little isolated paradise.

Not long after I passed by Charlotte's house, I ventured onto the sand bar that jutted out into the water on the northeast side of the island, kicking off my flip flops to enjoy the feel of the soft white sand. I reached my hand into the edge of the cold, clear water upon spotting an elusive Petoskey stone, which I dried off a bit with my shirt and dropped into my pocket, feeling like a little child in doing so. My mom had always loved searching for Petoskey stones on the Michigan beaches, and my mind wandered to my family and my real life as I returned from the sand bar and continued down the beach.

"Hey," a warm and slightly gravelly male voice brought me back to reality. I looked up, startled, to see an unfamiliar, shirtless teenage guy walking down the beach from the direction I was headed.

He had nearly passed me already by the time I responded with "hello," which came out too forcefully and hung awkwardly in the air as we both kept walking in our own directions. I had seen his face for only a few short seconds, but it left me feeling startled. He had been shockingly attractive, with slightly longish dark hair, which was pushed haphazardly behind his ears. His skin was lightly tanned, his body wiry but muscular, from what I saw of it. In the brief second that our eyes had met, I'd seen a flash of his bright blue eyes surrounded by thick dark lashes. I was certain I had never encountered a person, male or female of any age, who was nearly as beautiful as him. Sure there were good looking guys, hot ones even, whose paths I had crossed in my life, but this guy was a different species altogether. And, it wasn't just his face that had struck me. That voice, with its raspy edge, replayed in my head.

I continued walking, feeling too overwhelmed to look behind me for several minutes. By the time I turned my head to glance back casually, he was already out of sight. Who the hell was that? I had to find out. This was a private island, after all, how hard could it be?

Chapter 16

I ended up walking the entire perimeter of Green Island, realizing that by the time I thought about turning back, I was already more than half way around. When I returned, I found Lizzy awake and in her light pink bikini and a cotton skirt, eating Life cereal and watching a re-run of *Party of Five* in our little third-floor den.

"Hey! Where were you? I looked out on the beach but didn't see you," she said instantly as I walked in the room. "I really want to talk to you about last night."

I had grabbed a raisin bagel as I chatted with Mrs. Sutter for a few minutes in the kitchen on my way into the house, and I began eating as I plopped down next to Lizzy on the couch. "I woke up early and went for a walk on the beach, ended up going all the way around the island."

"Nice. I love the morning beach... Too bad I always seem to be out too late to get up in time to enjoy it these days."

"Yeah, it was so pretty out there, and peaceful."

"OK, so about last night," she started right in. "I don't even know where to start."

"What happened?" I asked, trying to be genuinely interested despite the fact that I was becoming more and more convinced that Lizzy deserved someone willing to put in a little (or a lot!) more effort than what I'd been seeing from James.

Lizzy told me the play-by-play of a night which more or less consisted of James kind of blowing her off and spending a fair amount of time talking to Lisa Ciccarelli. She re-played the night in detail for my dissection, giving me exact quotes of their brief conversations and waiting anxiously for my analysis of what I took them to mean.

What I took them to mean was that James was a dickhead who wasn't worthy of Lizzy, but I wasn't sure how to break that to her gently.

"Well, what were Greta's thoughts? Since she was there, she probably has the best take on how he was acting," I suggested, trying to avoid giving my negative opinion as I popped a piece of bagel into my mouth.

"I don't know. I mean, I think she kind of thought he was being an ass but was trying to be diplomatic about it..." Lizzy said, sounding depressed. I hated to see her this way.

"So I'm going to put this out there, and just do me a favor and think about it," I said slowly. "Do you really genuinely think James is that great, or is it just kind of nice to feel like someone likes you? If it's the second option, there's nothing wrong with that, I mean everyone appreciates feeling wanted. But, it doesn't really seem like James is making a big effort, not the kind of effort that a guy should be making for someone as amazing as you, and if he is blowing you off for a ditz like Lisa Ciccarelli, I feel like that pretty much seals the deal that you deserve way better than him."

Lizzy was silent for a minute before I saw tears welling up in her eyes. "I don't know," she muttered, letting her head fall back into the couch.

"Well, it *is* almost the end of July, so in a few weeks you guys are going to be across the country from each other anyway," I said, although I doubted whether this fact really helped matters very much.

"It isn't as if I thought he was the love of my life or something like that," she said. "But, it would be nice to feel like he really, truly liked me, rather than just feeling like he put in a minimal amount of effort to see if he could sleep with me and when that wasn't working out, he just moved onto someone else without even really acknowledging that anything had been going on between us. It just makes me feel like complete crap."

I felt anger boiling up inside me. Who did this asshole think he was to treat Lizzy this way? I wished I knew what to say, how to help her.

"Want to take your dad's speedboat out for the day, get a break from things here?" I suggested, thinking that a little space from the island might help her mindset. "We could go to Harbor Springs and have lunch there."

"Yeah, that could be fun, I guess," she said, without much enthusiasm.

"OK. I'll throw some clothes and snacks and tapes in my bag and you ask your dad if we can take the boat," I directed. "Do you want to invite Greta and Char too?"

"Nah, let's just go the two of us," she said, heading down our stairs to find her dad.

Chapter 17

Just before sunset, Lizzy and I wound down our boating excursion and headed back to Green. We spotted bonfires glowing along the beach and could hear the squeals of children laughing as we approached the marina.

A day on the boat seemed to have eased Lizzy's downtrodden mood. We'd eaten crepes with fresh berries and citrus salads for lunch at a quaint little restaurant that operated on the water in the town of Harbor Springs, not too far from Charlevoix. We'd left the boat docked and taken inflatable rafts out on the nearby sand bar to float in the waves for most of the afternoon, then we'd sped home in the boat, blasting an Oldies mix tape and singing at the top of our lungs. We discussed James a little bit, but most of the day we didn't talk at all and just basked in the sun and waves.

After docking the boat in the marina with assistance from a muscular worker named Jay, we were walking down the dock and I happened to glance to my right, to the area where sailboats over forty feet were docked. I felt my pulse quicken immediately as I spotted a lithe, tanned body with a familiar mop of dark hair covered by an old backward baseball cap. Although I couldn't make out his distant face in the dimming light of dusk, I knew it had to be the guy from my morning beach walk. As we stepped off the docks onto the sand, he disappeared from my line of sight.

I was afraid it might be a little insensitive to bring up my mystery crush in the midst of Lizzy's break up of sorts, but I thought I could probably be stealth about it.

"So, when I was out walking this morning before you were up," I started in as we began our walk back to the Sutters' house, "I saw this guy around our age, or maybe a little older, who I've never seen on Green before."

"Hmm," Lizzy responded, making me wonder if she was even listening.

"Yeah, he had dark hair that was kind of tucked behind his ears, but in a cute way. He was good looking, I mean *really* good looking, and I was surprised that we hadn't noticed him before," I tried again to get her to bite.

"Maybe one of the Anderson brothers. Their family has become really religious lately, they started home-schooling their kids and stuff, and they don't really mix with the other people on Green, but Jack Anderson is really cute. His hair is more of a dirty blond though," she replied.

"No, this guy's hair was definitely really dark. He said hi when I walked past him, and he had this kind of distinctive voice, a little bit raspy."

"Ohhh, it must have been Reed Whalen! I forgot that you hadn't seen him yet. I heard he just got to Green this week because he was doing an internship or something that just ended."

My heart sank. Really original, Brecken, I told myself. Way to have a crush on the same guy who, at the mere mention of his name, practically causes every girl on Green faint from his dreaminess. Ugh! I chided myself silently for even slightly lusting over a guy who hung out with the likes of Dalton Aldridge and her minion Sarah Sutter.

"Oh, yeah, I guess that must have been him," I agreed, trying not to let my voice convey my disappointment.

"Yeah, his voice is so sexy, like Clint Eastwood or something," she said wistfully.

"Clint Eastwood?! Seriously? Where do you come up with this stuff?" I laughed. "You're funny."

She laughed too. "My dad is always watching those old movies, and trust me, Clint Eastwood has a sexy voice," she insisted.

"If you say so..." I said, wishing my mystery guy had turned out to be anybody but the legendary Reed Whalen.

We decided to stay in that night and watch a movie, which I knew would probably end up being *Love Story, Titanic* or *Legends of the Fall,* Lizzy's three favorite depressing movies. I was irritated with myself for being so disappointed about the identity of my beach crush. I mean, he had said all of one word to me, and it wasn't as though I knew the first thing about him, so it made no sense that I would feel so let down. But that didn't change the fact that I barely heard one word Leonardo DiCaprio or Kate Winslet said that night. Instead, I spent the entire movie inside my head, thinking about Lizzy and James, about my parents, about the fact that the one guy I had seen all summer (or ever for that matter) who had made me feel an ounce of excitement was nothing more than another yuppie playboy. I watched Kate and Leo in the steamed up car in the lower decks of the Titanic and wondered if I would ever experience passion like that, if love in real life was ever like love in the movies. If it was, I sure hadn't seen it. Somehow I felt pretty sure I'd never find a guy for whom I'd be willing to stay on a sinking ship because life just wouldn't be worth living without him. And yet, even though I doubted that it would ever happen, I felt incredibly pathetic and lonely when I realized how badly I wished it would all the same.

Chapter 18

In the two weeks after James blew off Lizzy for Lisa Ciccarelli, we pretty much abstained from all social functions on Green. Greta and Charlotte would stop by occasionally and supply me with updates, softened versions of which I would relay to Lizzy, to the effect that James and Lisa unfortunately did seem to have become an item.

However, after our two weeks of self-imposed exile, Lizzy caught me off-guard by suggesting that we attend the lobster bake at the Club that took place in early August each year, known simply as Lobster Day (despite the fact that the festivities took place entirely at night and not during the day at all). Hundreds of fresh lobsters were flown into the nearby East Jordan Airport the morning of Lobster Day and transported over to Green in several loads on the morning ferries.

It was hard to tell whether Mrs. Sutter or Sarah was more excited about Lobster Day. And, for some reason, Lizzy, who had been pretty mopey until Lobster Day arrived, woke up that morning with seemingly a new lease on life.

"I am *not* missing *Lobster Day* because of that loser," she proclaimed when I came downstairs that morning to find her cooking scrambled eggs for both of us. "I really need to find an amazing dress to wear tonight though. Want to go with me to Traverse City to shop? I'll buy you a dress too!"

While I didn't think Lizzy should be going out of her way to prove anything to James, I was in favor of any activity that she seemed excited about after having spent the past two weeks watching sad movies and keeping her company while she wallowed. Although, truthfully, her recent mood had also provided me with a much-needed break from the nights of too much drinking, rampant mosquitoes and come-ons from cheesy guys in popped collars. It had been nice to wake up without a hangover and spend the evenings playing my guitar (which I had been neglecting all summer), reading the books that I had brought with me to Green, and taking on Mrs. Sutter, Lizzy and Katherine in endless games of Monopoly on the screened-in porch.

"Going shopping in Traverse sounds good to me," I agreed enthusiastically. "Although you definitely are not buying me a new dress. I brought my green cotton one with the straps that tie behind my neck."

"Uh uh." Lizzy shook her head as she placed a plate of eggs and toast in front of me and handed me a bowl of the fresh fruit that Mrs. Sutter cut up every few days and kept in the fridge for us to eat. "I told you — everyone has to wear *all* white to Lobster Day," she reminded me. "I don't know why exactly, but it's a tradition. It looks kind of cool in photos though. People get really dressed up for it. Also, everyone drinks only gin drinks for some reason. It's weird, I guess, but that's what they do. It's really a ton of fun, there's live music and they set up tons of torches and twinkle lights all over the beach by the Club and everyone dances and eats and drinks on the beach all night."

Lizzy's description of Lobster Day kind of sounded suspiciously like every single other night on Green except with everyone wearing white, but I kept that thought to myself, not wanting to quash her good mood with any negativity.

After breakfast we took the ferry over to Charlevoix and then headed off in Lizzy's car for Traverse City, home of the best cherries in the world. Traverse was about an hour away and the streets of its little downtown were lined mostly with boutiques. Lizzy already knew the few stores with clothes she liked, so we headed straight for them. The first store we tried was tiny and had only one white dress (which looked like a potato sack when Lizzy tried it on her petite frame), so we headed down the street to a store called Layla, which Lizzy promised was likely to have the perfect dress.

Whoever this Layla character was, I had to give her credit for her ability to play to her audience. In anticipation of wealthy Lobster Day attendees in search of a new ensemble for the festivities, roughly half of her store was filled with gorgeous white dresses of all styles, fabrics and lengths.

We waved to Marcheline Dubois and her daughter Chloe, whose house was two down from the Sutters' on Green. They were modeling white dresses for each other in front of the full length mirrors near the back of the store.

"You just missed your sister, dear! She and Dalton both just bought the loveliest little frocks for tonight!" Mrs. DuBois said to Lizzy, as she motioned for Chloe to hold her stomach in as she zipped her dress.

"Oh, great, can't wait to see them," Lizzy said with fake enthusiasm, turning her head and rolling her eyes at me before smiling back at Mrs. DuBois.

Lizzy and I went through the four substantial racks of white dresses, pulling out each dress for examination and consulting on the ones we liked best. I noticed there was rarely more than one of a particular dress, probably because it was clear that Greenies were not the type of people who found it acceptable to show up to a party and find three other people wearing the same outfit. Lizzy found six dresses to try on, and at her urging, I wound up with two potentials as well. Thankfully, the DuBoises had made their purchases and left the store before we headed into the dressing rooms ourselves, so we avoided getting their unsolicited advice about our picks.

I pulled my tank top over my head and slid my tattered jean cut-offs onto the floor, noticing the drastic tan lines that I had developed. The first dress was strapless and structured, hitting me a few inches above the knees. It was pretty simple but had a funky cream-colored belt made of a silky material with a gorgeous antiquey looking fabric flower slightly off center in the front. It was delicate and feminine and not my usual style, but I had been drawn to it for some reason.

Layla's was one of those unfortunate stores where they refuse to put mirrors in the dressing rooms, so you are forced to come out into the store to see a mirror and have the pushy saleswomen tell you how *just stunning* everything looks on you.

"Lizzy?" I said into the wall that divided our dressing rooms, once I had the dress on.

"I'm almost ready. The first one did not fit at all, so I'm just putting the second one on now. I'll be right out."

I waited another minute until she said she was ready and then headed out.

"Whoa, Liz, you look absolutely gorgeous!"

She was beaming. The bright mid-day sunlight was streaming in the window exactly where she stood, and she looked like a little angel, with her light strawberry blonde hair twisted up in a loose knot, and a white dress that tied behind her neck and then wrapped around her upper body, crossing over at her chest before flowing down to the tops of her knee caps.

"Seriously, I almost don't think you should try on any others. This one is perfect," I encouraged her, thinking how beautiful she looked.

"Really?" Clearly her confidence, which had never been her greatest strength, had been further compromised by worthless James Tucker.

"Yes, really! Definitely. You look stunning, I promise."

"OK," she said excitedly. "I'm not going to try the others then, this is the one. It was my favorite on the hanger anyway."

With that decided, I glanced into the mirror to see my own reflection. The dress was too big on me, with the fabric gapping in a weird way around the top of the dress. "This doesn't fit right," I announced, hoping Lizzy would just permit me to wear a white tank top and shorts to Lobster Day.

"Well try the other one you took in there, and I'll go through the racks one more time to see if there are any good ones we missed the first time."

I shuffled back into the dressing room and tried on the second dress, which was simpler than the first. It had an eyelet lace overlay with very thin straps, and it was fitted on top and then filled out slightly in the skirt, which stopped a few inches above my knees. It fit like a glove.

Lizzy squealed as I came back out of my dressing room. "You look gorgeous!" she said, stretching out the word "gorgeous" for emphasis. "Even more beautiful than you do every day. Take that dress off and give it to me so I can buy it."

I let out an exasperated sigh as I glanced at the price tag, which read "$210."

"I really don't need a white dress that costs over two hundred dollars. You've paid for me all summer, and I don't feel at all right about you buying this for me."

It was a continuing issue we had, and I knew her response before the words came out.

"Breck, please don't start with this again today. I was lucky enough to have my dad make tons of money and my parents couldn't care less if I buy clothes for my friends with it from time to time. I love being able to treat you to stuff, and I know you'd do the same if you were in my position, so just let me buy it. OK? You're my best friend and I know you would be happy wearing an old white t-shirt to Lobster Day but that's not happening and I AM buying that dress for you, so the sooner you accept that, the sooner we can leave."

Lizzy had put her foot down, a rare event, so I knew my protests would be fruitless.

"Well, then thank you," I said, as I handed the dress to her under the dressing room door. "I really appreciate it."

"And I really appreciate having my best friend with me for the summer. Seriously, I can't imagine how much less fun this summer would have been without you. We have to find a way to convince your parents to let you come back next year," Lizzy said as I slid back into my comfortable clothes.

I laughed. "I would love that, believe me. It's just my mom we'll have to sell on the idea..."

After Lizzy paid, we walked to the 7-Eleven at the end of the block and picked up mixed cherry and Coke Big Gulps before we got on the road and headed back to Green.

Chapter 19

Mrs. Sutter set up her camera on a tripod on the lawn in front of the Sutter house to capture us in all our Lobster Day glory before our walk over to the Club.

Sarah had insisted on getting ready for the party with her friends but had begrudgingly agreed to stop by for some family photographs.

After a few photos, I ducked out of the group, suggesting they take a few shots of just the Sutter family. The camera was on a timer and clicked a shot every fifteen seconds, so I stood back behind the tripod while the last several were snapped. The scene was certainly picturesque, with the girls and Mrs. Sutter all cloaked in their adorable white dresses and Mr. Sutter in a white linen suit. After a few minutes, Sarah hurried off to rejoin Dalton and her entourage, and the rest of us meandered along the beach together, taking the long route to the Club. Lizzy linked her arm in mine and continually rubbed her eyebrows, her tell that she was stressed or nervous. Clearly she was anxious about seeing James and Lisa Ciccarelli. I couldn't blame her for feeling that way but I wished I could somehow make her appreciate the degree to which James did not deserve to have any impact on how she felt.

Lobster Day was in full swing by the time we arrived. I had to admit that it was a pretty impressive sight, the whole island population garbed in their white finest and the reflection of the glowing flames from the plentiful torches dancing across the surface of the lake. We were all greeted by our various circles of friends and the Sutter clan rapidly dispersed into the mix. We spotted Greta, who was animatedly chatting with her mom and Mr. and Mrs. DuBois, and she quickly ran over upon seeing us across the crowd.

"Finally!" Greta cried, wrapping an arm around each of us. "It's been soo lonely without you guys around." We exchanged compliments on each other's dresses and headed off to find ourselves a few gin and tonics. At the bar we chatted with a stream of Greenies in white ensembles ranging from simple to quite elaborate (one woman wore a long tunic made completely out of white feathers...seriously!) and ordered three gin and tonics, which Lizzy charged to her parents' Club account. It had shocked me at first that the legal drinking age did not seem to apply whatsoever on Green and no one batted an eye at the sight of teenagers ordering shots at the bar while their parents sat at the next table over. Lizzy said her parents didn't mind if she and Sarah drank on Green because they thought it was a safe environment, provided that they were expected to keep the drinking within moderate levels and act responsibly. I tried to imagine how my mom would react if I proposed such an arrangement to her, but I was quickly learning that Green was a world entirely dislodged from the one where I lived. I guessed that the Sutters probably didn't want to impede their kids' likelihood of fitting in on Green, but it still seemed incredibly strange that they were so much more lax about things here than they were back home.

This was my first time drinking a gin and tonic, and truthfully I wasn't sure whether I was a big fan after my first sip. However, it did have a nice fresh, crisp taste to it that was refreshing in the heat, so after a second sip I could see the appeal. We mingled with the other kids our age, with the Sutters' neighbors, with various parents and random people I'd never met before. It was probably the only time all summer that I'd seen more or less the entire population of Green gathered in one location, and Greta and Lizzy were constantly pointing out faces in the crowd as people they had mentioned to me in one story or another.

Charlotte showed up at the party with her brother Nick after Lizzy and I had been there for about an hour, just in time for dinner. Everyone took seats at the beautiful tables, all of which were decorated with extravagant overflowing vases of fresh white flowers. Lizzy, Charlotte, Greta and I were at a table with six guys we knew, thankfully not including James Tucker.

I'd only eaten lobster once before, which had also been with the Sutters, and I absolutely loved it. So, I was thoroughly focused on enjoying every succulent bite as I half-listened to the guys at our table tell stories about the road trip they had taken together that spring from Detroit to New Orleans. Talking over each other, they entertained us with their ridiculous adventures, and before long I was laughing so hard that I could barely swallow my food without choking. I got into a long conversation about music with a guy named Todd Hamlin, whom I had only met once before, and he was telling me a story about a jazz club they had gone to in New Orleans when

Josh Roister pulled up his chair more or less between us and butted into the conversation.

"Oh yeah, that jazz place was off the hook, for sure," he said. "So, Brecken, where have you and little Lizzy been holed up lately? I haven't seen you chickadees out and about in a while."

I took a deep breath to remind myself not to tell Josh that the reason we had been staying in had been to avoid douchebags like him. "I don't know, just been taking it easy I guess," I said nonchalantly, then attempted to restart my conversation with Todd who unfortunately was already talking across the table with Turner Adams. Desperate to avoid Josh's cheesy come-ons, I grabbed onto Greta's arm next to me and discreetly whispered "save me" into her ear as Josh continued talking my ear off on the other side.

Greta got the picture and immediately pulled me out of my seat. "Time to dance!" she cried, using her other arm to grab Lizzy and then Charlotte as well. The music, which had been mellow during dinner, was beginning to pick up and a few people had already ventured out onto the sandy beach in front of the band to awkwardly begin the dance party.

Greta and I jumped and shook along with the steel drums, dissolving into frequent fits of laughter, while Lizzy and Charlotte stood talking on the outskirts of the dance area.

"Where's Andrew?" I asked Greta as we danced. The two of them had remained a casual item since the beginning of summer, but I hadn't seen him at Lobster Day.

"Oh, he was in a sailing race today, but he should be getting here soon, hopefully!" Greta responded over the music, and I nodded in response as we sang along to the band's rendition of Bob Marley's "Could You Be Loved," gin and tonics in hand. With a mild buzz, the cool night air and festive music enveloped me, and I felt inexplicably light and carefree. I was having a blast as more and more people joined us, kicking off their shoes and swaying along to the music. Well, having a blast, that is, until I glanced over at Lizzy and realized that, first off, she was really drunk, and second, her gaze was fixed on someone across the party at the bar. I didn't even need to follow her line of sight to know that James or Lisa or both would be at the end of it.

Sure enough, James had his arm around Lisa at the bar and I saw Lizzy was pointing over to them and gesturing with drunken exaggeration to Charlotte as she spoke.

I ran over to her, and the tears springing up in her eyes let me know that she was about to fall apart. Charlotte gave me a helpless look.

"How could he possibly like her? I don't understand," Lizzy wailed quietly. She looked as sad as I had ever seen her, and I knew I needed to get her out of there right away.

"I don't know why, probably because he's a fucking idiot who never deserved you in the first place. Let's go home, K?" I suggested assertively, already leaning down to grab our nearby shoes.

"OK... I love you, Breck," she said, leaning on my shoulder as I bent down and tried to slip her wedge sandals on her feet. It took about two seconds for me to realize that this effort to put her shoes on was pointless, so I picked them up to carry.

"I love you too, Liz, you're the best," I said, meaning it. Charlotte gave us each a hug and then left us in search of her brother.

If possible, I wanted to avoid Mr. and Mrs. Sutter seeing Lizzy's drunken state as we made our exit, although they were likely pretty bombed themselves by this point.

I looked across the dance floor and saw Greta. I pointed to Lizzy and then drew my finger back and forth across my neck, trying to let Greta know that I had to get Lizzy out of there ASAP. Greta nodded back at me showing she caught my drift, and only then did I notice that she was standing in between Andrew Wells, who must have just arrived, and none other than Reed Whalen. As much as I hated to acknowledge it, I knew that I had secretly been half keeping an eye out for him all night. It looked like he had probably just arrived at Lobster Day with Andrew.

If only I had stayed on the dance floor a few minutes longer, I could have talked to him. But I pushed that thought out of my slightly drunk mind immediately, reminding myself that I was not about to chase after a guy like that, who would undoubtedly turn out to be some stuck up prick, the type of guy who was into girls like Dalton Aldridge. And, clearly, he was way out of my league anyway.

Greta blew a kiss to me and Lizzy and I waved back, Lizzy nearly falling over into the sand in doing so. I thought it was clear that I was waving at Greta, but I saw that Reed waved back at me, a little smirk of some sort on his face. I felt myself blush as I quickly turned away, wrapping my arm around Lizzy's waist and escorting her off down the beach as I tried with little success to console her.

Chapter 20

After her Lobster Day breakdown, I was concerned Lizzy would fall back into her despondent state of the previous weeks, but instead, the dismissive treatment dished out by James that evening seemed to have had the opposite effect. Whether it gave her some sort of closure or she simply realized he had never been worth the trouble in the first place, I wasn't sure. And, I wasn't about to press her on it. I was just thankful to have Lizzy back to her usual bubbly, happy self.

We went to a few parties here and there over the next week, but just as often we'd skip the nightly social events and sit in the sand with a bottle of wine, Lizzy's stereo and a few cigarettes, admiring the stars. Charlotte would hang out with us from time to time too, since Greta was becoming increasingly occupied by Andrew Wells.

During the days, we would ride bikes or walk around the island, stopping at times to join a game of beach volleyball or meet a group to eat at the Club. It was, in short, blissful.

The updates from home had been mixed and vague but they'd left me hopeful. In talking to my parents more, it became clear that my dad was initially pretty angry and hurt by the separation but in the past month or so, he had apparently been putting a huge effort into repairing their relationship. According to my brother, who had recently gotten home from summer camp, our dad had been coming over to the house for dinner most nights and our parents seemed to be getting along really well, at least from the perspective of a twelve-year-old.

While my mom's response when I asked about the situation was always something in the vein of "we're still working through things," "it's going to be a long process," and "we'll see," I would have been lying to say I hadn't been getting my hopes up about their reconciliation.

And then, the night of August 10th, just two weeks before we would be leaving Green Island and heading back home, my high hopes came rapidly crashing down.

After a dinner of barbecued bratwursts, corn on the cob and a salad with Mrs. Sutter's homemade raspberry vinaigrette, Lizzy and I were playing against Mr. Sutter and Katherine in a game of euchre on the porch with Indy curled at our feet. We had taken a quick break between games to run inside and grab a piece of Mrs. Sutter's cherry pie when the phone rang.

Mr. Sutter answered and quickly handed the phone off to me, letting me know that it was my mom calling. I stepped into the den to find the portable phone so I could escape the bustle in the kitchen and picked up the line.

"Hey, Mom!"

"Brecken," she said simply, and the tone of her voice made it clear that something was off.

"What's going on? You sound upset."

She didn't respond, and I started to panic.

"Mom! Come on, what's going on?" I demanded.

"Well, your dad and I have decided we are getting a divorce. I'm filing the paperwork tomorrow. I wanted you to know that beforehand." Her voice sounded hollow and emotionless.

"What? Are you kidding me? I thought you two were supposedly in the long process of figuring things out! Why would you do this now?" I could hear my voice was becoming hysterical, but I couldn't help it. "Don't file yet, Mom, please. I'll come home early, and we can all try to talk about the situation and give it more time," I pleaded.

"I've realized that it's not a situation that can be resolved. We're getting a divorce, and that's the final word," she paused for a minute. "But, I would appreciate if you could come home early, I could really use your support right now. Griffin and I can drive up to Charlevoix to get you."

I felt enraged and despondent, desperate and empty, and most of all, I felt painfully helpless when it came to stopping the dissolution of my family.

"Why now?" I asked, the question coming out as a sob. "Why can't you give it more time?"

"I'd rather not talk about that right now, but I now know there's no hope of saving this marriage," she said, rather matter-of-factly, her voice still eerily void of emotion.

"I can't just accept that, Mom! What does Dad want? Think of him, think of me and Griff. I can't believe you're acting so impulsively about something this important. It's just so selfish." My angry sadness penetrated my voice, and the phone receiver against my face was slick from my tears. The kitchen had grown silent, and I assumed the Sutters had ventured back out to the porch to give me some space.

"You know what, Brecken," my mom cut in, suddenly coming to life. "I didn't want to have to get into this now, but I found out yesterday that your father *slept* with Mary Ann McClain two days after we separated. While I thought we were trying to repair this family, he was out fucking my so-called friend, so I can't really handle you making this my fault right now," the words poured out of her with a fury that I had never heard in her voice in all the sixteen years of my life. "We are getting divorced, and that's final. I'll call you tomorrow." And with that, she hung up on me. Another first.

I just sat there for a minute, alone in the dark of the den, still holding the phone in my hand, my heart racing. My parents were getting divorced. And, I suddenly had to wonder if I knew my father at all.

After I had regained my composure to a limited extent, I headed upstairs to my bed. I couldn't deal with trying to carry on a game of cards. I just needed to be alone.

Even though it was only 8:00, I laid down in bed in my clothes with no intention of getting up. Eventually I heard Lizzy standing in the doorway, gently asking if I was awake.

"Hey, I'm awake, but I kind of just feel like being alone, if that's OK," I whispered back to her. "I guess my parents are definitely getting a divorce. I'll tell you about it later."

She was quiet for a few seconds. "I am so sorry," she said simply. "You know where to find me if you need anything at all."

"Thanks," I said, as she quietly shut the door behind her and headed back downstairs.

Thoughts of my mom and dad, of Griffin, of Mary Ann the home-wrecker McClain, occupied my thoughts for hours until I eventually drifted off into a fitful sleep.

Chapter 21

After several hours of tossing and turning, I found myself wide awake in the middle of the night, still wearing cut-offs, a tight tank top and an incredibly uncomfortable bra as I lay in my bed. I blinked my dry eyes a few times, realizing I'd forgotten to take out my contact lenses, and was finally able to focus enough to read the tiny illuminated clock numbers across the room, which let me know it was 1:19 A.M. My thoughts returned to my conversation with my mom as I clicked on the bedside lamp. The house was silent as I crept out of my bed, trying to avoid the ear-piercingly squeaky floorboards in my room and the hallway, and slowly opened the door to Lizzy's bedroom. I could see she was in her bed, sound asleep, so I quietly closed the door and slunk back over to my room.

I changed into my comfy old green "Leo's Coney Island" t-shirt and a pair of cotton running shorts. Even in these lightweight clothes, I felt hot and smothered in my tiny room. I tried opening the window, but there was virtually no breeze at all coming in, although the sound of the crickets chirping was kind of soothing. I opened up *The Client*, a John Grisham book that I had found on the Sutters' bookshelves, hoping that reading for a bit would distract me, but I couldn't seem to focus and found myself reading the same sentence over and over.

After about half an hour of this, I grabbed my guitar and the pack of Parliament Lights that were in Lizzy's purse on our shared couch and quietly slipped downstairs.

I paused in the front hallway and turned back toward the kitchen. Feeling a twinge of guilt, I opened the Sutters' liquor cabinet and reached for one of their ten or so bottles of whiskey. I wrapped the bottle in a lavender beach towel that was sitting in a stack next to the washing machine and slowly slipped out of the house.

The night air was heavy but the breeze picked up slightly as I stepped onto the sand, and I took in a deep and refreshing breath as I ventured further into the lonely night. I headed toward the dock, surprised by how quiet and desolate the beach seemed in the light of a nearly full moon.

As I was stepping onto the dock, I heard someone say, "Hello there," in a loud voice.

I turned to see Andy, one of the island guards, walking toward me on the beach. I headed over to say hello. I'd learned not to be worried about the guards — they had strict orders not to involve themselves in the lives of Greenies or to reprimand them in any way. Instead, the guards were merely there in case anyone on Green needed their help.

"Oh, hey, Andy!" I said with a smile, having chatted with him many times before.

"How are you, Brecken? Everything all right?"

I was thankful that the whiskey was hidden by my blanket. Not because Andy would have said anything about it, but because I would have felt like a bit of a degenerate if he had seen me heading out to the dock by myself in the middle of the night with a bottle of whiskey.

"Oh, yeah, everything's good," I responded. "Just couldn't sleep, so I thought I'd come out here for some fresh air and play my guitar a little."

"OK, well just be careful by the water. There's some serious undertow tonight. Holler if you need anything. I won't be too far."

"Thanks a lot, Andy," I said, giving him a wave and heading back over toward the dock as he continued his rounds of the area surrounding the Sutters' house and the other nearby homes.

After unwrapping the whiskey bottle, I folded the fluffy towel in half and spread it out over a portion of the dock, leaving a few inches to drape over the edge and protect my legs from slivers. I sat down and uncorked the bottle, which the label identified as Booker's Bourbon. It was just over half full and there had been a few other identical bottles in the cabinet, so I hoped the few drinks I planned to have wouldn't be missed. I was pretty sure they wouldn't. And, anyway, if the Sutters noticed the missing bourbon and cared, Sarah would probably be the one blamed, and I definitely wouldn't lose any sleep over that miscarriage of justice.

I took a sip and coughed at the powerful burning sensation as it went down. I wished I'd thought to bring a Coke or Vernors or something to mix it with, but it seemed like too much trouble to go back inside now. I waited a minute and took another small swig, which didn't go down any easier than the first.

After putting my guitar strap over my shoulder, I played some gentle melodies, pieces of songs I loved and new strings of notes that I put together as I went along, periodically breaking for a moment here and there for another drink.

It only took about fifteen minutes before I noticed a warmth setting in from the bourbon, which I realized was pretty strong stuff. My mind felt fuzzy yet raw at the same time and the lapping waves, the exaggerated darkness of the water and fresh air of the warm night were soothing. Fireflies flitted around me from time to time, giving the night a dream-like, surreal feel, as they always seemed to do.

After a half hour or so, I set my guitar on my lap and lit a cigarette, which intensified my buzz immediately, making me feel slightly dizzy. I smiled thinking about how I would look right now to a passerby, sitting out here by myself, accessorized with my guitar, a bottle of bourbon and a pack of cigarettes. I sounded like a bad country song. Hopefully Andy wouldn't think less of me if he happened to stroll by again.

I watched the smoke rise from my lips and imagined what it would be like when I got back home. Would we sell our house, the only home I had ever known? Would my parents become vindictive towards one another, using me and Griffin as their pawns, the way I had heard of other divorced parents doing? I couldn't imagine my parents acting that way, but then again, they seemed to be full of surprises lately.

I tried to blow a smoke ring, a skill I had been unsuccessfully attempting to learn all summer. A few of the guys had patiently explained to me about rolling my tongue and puffing out the ring, demonstrating for me and giving me pointers, but I had yet to see a legitimate O come out of my mouth.

Tonight seemed to be no exception, with the smoke simply coming out in awkward puffs.

The cigarette was burning close to my fingertips, so I rubbed the tip in the surface of the water to extinguish it and then sat the butt on a plank of the dock to take in with me later. I hated how some kids on Green threw their cigarettes into the lake. It made me feel incredibly sad, maybe disproportionately so, to see a dirty cigarette butt floating along the surface of the beautiful, pristine water.

I took another large gulp of the bourbon and then began playing chords and melodies more quickly, my fingers dancing gently across the strings. I hoped I wasn't being too loud, but I assumed Andy would probably pay me a visit if I started making too much noise.

As I was working my way through Clapton's "Bell Bottom Blues," quietly singing along, I was startled by a noise at the end of the dock and my head snapped up as I stopped playing.

Standing at the foot of the dock, with his head tipped to the side, watching me intently, was Reed Whalen.

Chapter 22

It seemed like maybe Reed was unsure of what to do now that I had become aware of his presence, and he remained standing at the foot of the dock as I glared at him, feeling extremely exposed by his unexpected appearance. After a moment, he began walking toward me, an expression on his face that I couldn't interpret.

I didn't react to his presence at all, at least not outwardly, feeling surprisingly bold and confident, undoubtedly thanks to my new buddy Booker and his bourbon.

Reed broke the silence as he neared me at the end of the dock.

"Well, this definitely adds to your mystery," he said, now standing next to where I sat. I shrugged in response, not really looking at him.

"Mind if I sit?" he asked, his raspy voice making his ordinary question sound complex and, frankly, pretty sexy.

"Sure, go for it," I said, starting to feel slightly nervous about being in such close proximity to him. I reached for the bottle and took another sip as he lowered himself onto the edge of the dock next to me, his legs long enough that his feet broke the surface of the water. "Want some?" I offered, extending the bottle toward him. I avoided eye contact. I honestly had never seen anyone so unbelievably good looking up close before, and I didn't think I could play it very cool if I looked directly into that face.

He was sitting right next to me, about as close as was physically possible without us actually touching. He accepted the bottle from me and took a long swallow. We sat there without speaking for what must have been about two minutes, both looking out at the water. Again, he broke the silence.

"So, is this a pretty standard Monday night for you?" he asked jokingly, and I couldn't help but laugh.

"Not exactly, just had kind of a crazy day and couldn't sleep. I'm Brecken, by the way," I said. I shot a quick glance in his direction and saw that he was looking right at me. We made eye contact for a second before I looked away. My stomach was in knots.

"Yeah, I know who you are." The combination of his voice and his words made my pulse quicken. "I'm Reed," he quickly added.

"So, Reed, is this a pretty standard Monday night for you? Wandering around the island alone in the middle of the night?"

"Yeah, actually, it kind of is." He gave one of the same quick smiles that I had seen at Lobster Day, briefly flashing a sliver of his perfect teeth. "I like it out here at night, especially when the moon's out. It's so quiet and... peaceful."

I wasn't sure how to respond to that, so I didn't say anything. It was definitely a more thoughtful answer than I had anticipated. I suddenly felt incredibly conscious of my hands and couldn't figure out what to do with them, so I reached for a cigarette to avoid continuously fidgeting.

"Want one?" I offered, tilting the open and slightly crushed pack in his direction. I didn't look up at him as I asked. I felt incapable of carrying on any semblance of a conversation when looking him in the eye.

I saw his fingers reach into the pack and grab a cigarette as well as the blue Bic lighter that was crammed in there. He flicked the lighter and held it out to me. I'd become familiar with this gesture in my time on Green, and I leaned slightly forward and inhaled. Thankfully it lit right away. Reed kept the flame burning and lit his own. He then leaned back so that he was lying flat on my towel, his legs still hanging over the edge of the dock. He had his right hand behind his head and smoked his cigarette with his left.

Afraid that I was missing my chance to get to know him, I searched quickly for a question to ask him, hoping I wasn't coming off as some sort of mute dud. I thought the silences between us felt poignant, as if there was an unspoken connection, but I hoped he wasn't taking them to mean I was a bore. I liked that he didn't blabber on like Josh Roister and Andrew Wells, assuming everyone around them was dying to hear them talking at all times.

"So, where do you live, I mean, when you're not here for the summer?" It was the best I could come up with at the moment, my brain feeling like it was finally beginning to recover from the shock of Reed turning up like this, but still lagging from the stream of bourbon that I'd been sucking down.

"New York. What about you?"

"New York City?" I asked, impressed. Not only had I never been to New York City, I also couldn't think of anyone I'd met who actually lived there.

He shook his head. "An area called Westchester. It's not far from the City though, both my parents commute in there for work."

I nodded as I smoked and reached for another gulp of whiskey. After I took a sip, Reed reached his hand out to ask for the bottle and I passed it to him. He lifted his head a bit to take a sip and then laid back down. Without thinking about it, I lowered myself onto my back next to him, my legs hanging off the end of the dock as well. We lay there side by side, smoking, gazing up at the sky.

"So, you didn't tell me where you're from," he said, turning his head toward me.

"Oh, I'm from Michigan, a suburb of Detroit called Royal Oak. It's not far from where the Sutters live, but, you know, less swanky. It's a cool little place though, I like it."

He didn't respond initially, and I began to have visions that he'd hop up after his cigarette and continue on his nighttime stroll. And, there was nothing I was more sure of than the fact that I wanted him to stay right there next to me for as long as possible.

"I haven't seen you around until recently. What were you up to the rest of the summer, before you got here?" I asked, genuinely curious. I had heard mentions that he had an internship or was at a summer lacrosse program but I wondered if those rumors were accurate.

He sat up to put his cigarette out in the lake before laying the butt on the dock beside mine from earlier in the night. "Well, I was in this writing workshop," he paused and then laid back down beside me, this time the side of his hand brushed my bare arm as he lowered himself back down. His hands were warm, unlike mine, which were eternally cold, and the brief brush of his hand caused my entire body to buzz in a way I had never experienced before. It threw me for a second.

"What kind of writing workshop? I guess I'm not sure exactly what you mean."

"Well... they have a writing workshop at the University of Iowa for pre-college age fiction writers. So, that's where I was the past few weeks."

"That's really cool," I said, intrigued. I noticed that he spoke slowly, deliberately, making even the simplest word seem laden with meaning. "What do you write? Short stories or novels or what?"

"I'm mostly interested in writing novels, I mean, having a novel published someday would be my dream, but who knows if that's realistic. I actually just finished a rough draft of one though. It's the first one I've finished, so I took that with me to the workshop to get input and all that."

"Nice. That's really cool," I said, pretty shocked to be hearing that this was how he'd spent his summer. "Are you proud of it?" I asked.

"Huh?" Reed looked over at me confused for an instant and this time I managed to look him in the eye for a few seconds without feeling the need to look away.

"You know," I said, feeling slightly self-conscious, "are you proud of your book? Sometimes I write songs and end up playing them at a school concert or something, and I guess that's the main thing that I think of as being important – not what other people think, but if I am proud of them," I said, thinking that maybe I was sounding like a weirdo, but I was just being honest.

"I'm pretty sure that no one's ever asked me that before," he said, still looking at me in a way that struck me as pretty intense. I wasn't sure if this was meant as a compliment or was a polite way of telling me I was weird. "Everyone always asks about the plot, which is a drag because I can't really explain it unless they have some time, and no one actually wants to listen for that long. But, anyway, to answer your question, now that I think about it, yeah, I am proud of it."

"That's good," I said, returning his look for an instant. "So, who's your favorite writer," I asked, wanting to keep the conversation going.

He thought for a moment. "I guess Hemingway is my favorite, if I have to pick just one."

"Everyone loves him," I said with a smile. "He's like the Frank Sinatra of literature, eternally cool." In the darkness I could see him smirking at my response, but he didn't say anything. "Didn't he spend his summers near here?" I asked.

"Yeah, he did. Walloon Lake, it's the next big lake east of Lake Charlevoix. I've heard his house is still there." For a second I considered suggesting that we go see it some time, but I bit my tongue, not wanting to scare him off, remembering that this was Reed Whalen I was talking to.

"So, tell me about this guitar playing of yours..." he began, changing the subject as he took the cap off the whiskey once again.

Chapter 23

"Any idea what time it is?" I asked Reed, rubbing my tired eyes, my contact lenses so dry that I was worried they'd fall right out of my eyes as I rubbed.

"No clue," he said, his voice relaxed. "And, I don't want to know," he added with a smile. After what must have been two hours or so of listening to my stomach growl as we lay on the dock talking, he had convinced me to take a walk with him down the beach to his family's boat which had a little kitchen with a stocked fridge. I had agreed and, upon attempting to stand up, had realized just how completely hammered I had managed to get.

I must have stumbled a little as I tried to stand, because Reed grabbed my arm quickly and made me hand over my guitar, which he slung gently over his left shoulder. We'd gone through the remainder of the Sutters' bottle of bourbon, which I was already feeling slightly guilty about, as well as the six or seven cigarettes that had been left in the pack. I'd poured out to him about my parents' impending divorce and he'd listened closely, never interjecting. When I'd stopped talking, he hadn't spoken right away. I liked that. It seemed as though he was still digesting what I'd said. At first, I'd left out the part about my dad's indiscretion, not quite ready to put that out there for Reed or myself to dissect just yet. But his thoughtful pauses and expressive eyes pulled me right in, and before I realized it, I was unloading the whole truth onto him, putting my newly broken home out on the table for perfection's poster child. And yet, it seemed as natural as telling Lizzy, completely effortless.

As the night evolved around us, we had also talked about simple things, our schools, our siblings, our thoughts about Green Island. His dry humor and perspective on the world impressed me, and it quickly became obvious that he was of a nature wholly separate from the Andrew Wellses or Josh Roisters of the world. Not only was he gorgeous, he was also shockingly soulful and grounded for a seventeen-year-old guy, and yet he still managed to fit in amongst the Green Island crowd with ease. I hated to acknowledge that clearly his godlike status among Green Island's teen queens was well deserved. A part of me wished I could have been the one to resist his spell, but from that first morning when our eyes met on the beach, I'd never stood a chance.

It was still dark out as we walked along the deserted beach in what felt to me like a poetic silence, Reed carrying my guitar over his shoulder and the empty whiskey bottle in one hand, me cradling my crumpled towel in both arms, not having taken the effort to fold it up before we departed from the dock.

We arrived at the marina in what seemed like no time and walked over to the boat where I had spotted Reed weeks before. I didn't know the first thing about various types of sailboats, but it was clear even to me that this one was pretty high-end. It contained two bedrooms and a kitchen, as well as a comfortable little living room area below deck. My eye caught the clock in the kitchen, which read 4:17 A.M. Reed tossed the Booker's bottle in the kitchen trash and asked me if I wanted anything else to drink.

"I'll just go for water," I said, my head starting to rapidly spin. I tried leaning back on the couch and closing my eyes, but that only made it much worse.

"Probably a good call," he agreed, filling up two glasses with water from a large jug in the fridge and rustling around through the cupboard.

"How do you feel about grilled cheese? There's not as much food in here as I thought, so that might be the best I can do," he said, pulling butter and several kinds of exotic looking cheeses from the fridge. Apparently this was not going to be a Wonder Bread and Kraft singles kind of sandwich.

"Sounds so good," I mumbled, curling up on the soft couch as much as I could manage without adding to my case of the spins.

A few minutes later, he presented me with a golden brown grilled cheese on a paper plate and refilled the glass of water that I had gulped down. He had made a sandwich for himself as well, and he motioned for me to follow him out to the deck of the boat.

He waited as I began my stumble up the stairs ahead of him and then followed close behind. Even with him carrying my water, I was lucky to make it up the stairs without tripping or dropping my sandwich. We sat on the cushioned boat seats and began to eat.

"Do you have any Worcestershire sauce?" I asked hopefully.

"Any what?"

"Worcestershire sauce..."

He laughed. "Brecken, first of all, this is a boat. We have about fifteen food items total, and, no, one of them is not Worcestershire sauce. Also, who eats that on a grilled cheese?" He seemed amused.

I rolled my eyes at him. "Have you ever even tried it? It tastes unbelievably good."

"Uh, no I haven't tried it, and that's because Worcestershire sauce is for *steak* not *grilled cheese*," he said in a tone that I hoped was flirtatious but may just have been good-natured mocking.

"Your loss," I said with a shrug and went back to enjoying my grilled cheese (which I had to admit was delicious despite the lack of Worcestershire sauce).

Chapter 24

I must have fallen almost immediately asleep after finishing my grilled cheese because some time later I awoke in the same spot where I had been eating. I was stretched out on a bench seat near the back of the boat with a beach towel laid over me like a blanket, which must have been Reed's doing. He was sleeping on another bench seat which connected with mine to form an L. Our feet were touching in the crux when I woke up somewhere between drunk and very hung-over. I quickly swallowed the remaining water in the glass next to me as I got my bearings.

The sky was barely beginning to lighten and I figured it was probably some time around 5:30 A.M., although I couldn't say for sure. The island was not yet stirring. I seized the chance to examine Reed as he slept, happy to have this opportunity after having spent the whole night trying my very best not to awkwardly stare at his flawless face.

He had a red sweatshirt balled up as a pillow and slept on his side with both hands close to his face. His arms were tan and muscled in the lean way typical of athletic teenage boys. His fingernails were cut very short, which only added to my attraction, since something about overgrown fingernails on guys really grossed me out (although I felt like given all his other impressive attributes, I might have been willing to give him a pass on overgrown fingernails). However, that was not even an issue because, big surprise, his nails and hands were, like the rest of him, pretty much perfect.

His thick, dark hair was slightly messy, a few pieces pressed to his forehead by his makeshift pillow, and his long dark lashes curled perfectly away from his face. The angles of his cheekbones and chin, along with the slight shadow of stubble on his jawline, added manliness to the sweetness of his hair and eyes.

I had been looking at him with intrigue for a few minutes when I realized how creepy and *Fatal Attraction*-ish I would probably seem if he awoke to find me staring at him as he slept. In fact, the morning fishing entourage would probably be arriving at the marina soon anyway, so I needed to get out of there and back to the Sutters' house stat.

Leaving him there sleeping felt a little bit rude, but I figured it avoided any awkward goodbye that might spoil the connection I'd felt between us the night before.

When I initially considered leaving a note, the messages that popped into my head — "thanks for a great night" and "thanks for a good time" — not only sounded stupid, they also sounded like we'd had a night of passionate sex, when really he had not even tried to so much as kiss me. I left the lack of kiss analysis for another time and went down the stairs to grab my guitar. A pen was sitting next to a paper napkin on the coffee table, so, with a last minute change of heart, I scribbled *Thanks for the grilled cheese — good talk. Brecken,* and left it lying next to where he slept before I could give it any more thought. I glanced around the marina to confirm that it was still empty before hopping off the boat and onto the dock

with my guitar in hand and speeding off down the
beach toward my bed.

Chapter 25

"Breck, Breck," I heard Lizzy saying my name and felt her lightly shaking me. "Wake up." The shaking grew increasingly less gentle. I opened my eyes a crack and rolled over toward her.

"Can I sleep for a while? I had trouble sleeping last night," I mumbled, desperate for her to leave me in peace.

"Yeah, you smell like alcohol, what were you doing? Drinking alone?"

I shrugged, and began to turn back over toward the wall. She didn't push me on it.

"Well, your mom just called. She said that she and Griffin are in Charlevoix *right now*, and she's coming over on the ferry soon to get you."

Now she had my full attention, and I shot up to a sitting position, my head throbbing. "What? When did she call?"

"Just like two minutes ago. I talked to her and told her you were sleeping. She said to wake you up and tell you that she was taking you back home today."

I rubbed my forehead, trying to collect my still alcohol-saturated thoughts for a second.

"I'm so confused," Lizzy started. "Fill me in."

I put my hands on my pounding temples as I wrapped my head around the fact that my mom would be on Green Island shortly. "I'm confused too. Basically my mom was hysterical when I talked to her last night. She said she found out my dad slept with

Mary Ann McClain..." I saw Lizzy cringe, a sympathetic frown spreading across her face. With Lizzy I didn't even have to ask her not to tell anyone this information, it was a given that I could trust her with my family's dirty laundry. "And basically she said they were absolutely getting a divorce. I was upset with her initially and she kind of snapped at me and then hung up the phone. I thought she said she was going to call me today, but I guess she drove here instead. That's all I know," I was getting out of bed, examining my disheveled appearance in the mirror as I provided Lizzy with this synopsis. "I guess I should shower, I look like shit."

Lizzy's face was pained. "I can't believe all that happened. I'm so sorry that we didn't get to talk about it."

"I wasn't ready to talk right away, just needed a night to process it I guess."

"I wish you could stay. I can't imagine the rest of summer without you here, even if it's only two more weeks."

"Yeah, I want to stay too," *especially after last night*, I thought. "I guess we'll see what's going on when my mom gets here. Does she know how to get here?"

"Yep, I explained it all to her. It sounds like they'll be here in about an hour or around then. I called over to the marina and they'll have a carriage bring them here."

I left Lizzy sitting on my bed and stepped into our shower, letting the scalding water beat down on my scalp. Desperation and sadness washed over me. My parents were getting divorced, my family was falling apart, I'd had one of the most memorable nights of my life with a guy who I was most likely never going to see again, and, I had a killer hangover to top it all off. I knew my mom needed me right now, my family needed me. By the time I stepped out of the shower and downed two Advil, I had pulled myself together, well somewhat at least, and resolved to be as supportive of my mom as I could in a situation that I knew had to be even harder on her than it was on me. I wouldn't even let myself consider how I felt about my dad.

Chapter 26

I left Green Island a few hours after I woke up that morning, heading back to Royal Oak with my mom and Griffin, back to my reality.

"I'm just trying to figure out how to get through this, Breck," my Mom told me gently after apologizing for hanging up on me the night before, and for springing so much on me at once. We had said our goodbyes and thank yous to the Sutters, departed from the ferry, and loaded my stuff into my mom's red Jimmy. "This isn't exactly a motherhood moment I had prepared for or expected."

"I know, Mom. I'm so sorry. Where *is* Dad now anyway?" I asked, slightly concerned about how she would react to me bringing up his name. I knew Griffin was listening to his Discman in the backseat, but I turned up Paul Simon, my mom's favorite, on the car CD player to further drown out our conversation.

"He's moving the rest of his stuff out right now, into the apartment he rented for the summer." She pursed her lips hard after she said this, a face that I knew meant she was holding in tears. She rarely cried, which made it infinitely more heartbreaking on the occasions when she did break down. I reached over and squeezed her arm supportively.

"It'll be OK, Mom, really, I promise," I said, and then we just listened to the music in silence for the next few hours, each lost in our own worlds. I closed my eyes, making a pillow out of my sweatshirt and leaning against the car window, trying to will away my still wretched hangover and all thoughts of my parents, especially my dad. It took all of about three seconds for my mind to race back to the night before, to replay every detail, every minute.

I went through it all, word by word, moment by moment. The shared cigarettes, the jokes, the intriguing layers of Reed Whalen that I would never have expected to find, the nearly suffocating feeling in my chest every time I looked at him.

I let myself remember it all and then was hit with a crushing wave of sadness. Sure, the night with Reed had felt like floating, but in reality, he lived in New York, and I lived in Michigan, and we barely even knew each other. Then there was also the minor detail that Reed Whalen was practically a worshiped deity in the eyes of the girls of Green Island, and likely everywhere else he went. A worshiped deity who had not even so much as tried to kiss me. Maybe it was better this way, never seeing him again, I tried to convince myself. This way I could preserve the night in my mind, never having to face him blowing me off the next day on the beach or seeing him cuddled up with Dalton Aldridge at some bonfire party.

Then and there I decided never to mention the night with Reed to Lizzy or anyone else. I wanted to pack it away in my mind and keep it sacred. Telling Lizzy would mean rehashing all the details of that night, analyzing each of the words we'd exchanged, and, in essence, generally tearing apart what was likely the only night I would ever spend with him. And I wasn't ready to do that, even if it meant keeping a secret from her for pretty much the first time in my life. Plus, it would be clear to anyone listening that Reed would never, ever be into a girl like me. Not that Lizzy would ever admit that, but even I knew it was the truth.

I regretted leaving him that stupid note though. I must have been deliriously tired or still drunk (probably both!) to have thought that was a good idea.

"Can we get Burger King?" Griffin startled me from my daydreams as he popped his head up between the front seats.

"Sure, why not," my mom said, extremely uncharacteristically. She usually went to great lengths to avoid fast food, including packing healthy lunches for car trips, but all rules seemed to be going out the window these days, fast food bans included.

We pulled off the expressway and into a BK lot, Griffin speeding out the car door and inside the second we shifted into "park." My mom and I followed. She reached her arms out in a stretch outside the car, and I slung my arm around her waist. "We'll be all right, Mama," I said, her anxiety apparent as I examined her face sadly.

"Thanks, baby," she said, a name she rarely called me anymore. She wrapped her arm around my shoulder as we walked into the welcoming aroma of golden french fries.

PART III
SPRING OF 2009

Chapter 27

"Engaged?!" Lizzy cries, her exclamation followed by shrieks of congratulations from Nevada as Lizzy switches me to speaker phone. She was my first call as Will and I left Moto. Once their screams die down, both Lizzy and Nevada start rapid-firing questions at me.

"Easy guys," I say, laughing. "I'll tell you *everything* tomorrow, but Will claims he has a few more surprises tonight so I have to go." I smile over at him, sitting next to me in the back of the cab, holding my free hand.

"Can we meet for brunch in the morning then?" Nevada asks.

"Definitely. How about Nookies around noon?"

"Perfect," they both agree in unison, and we quickly hang up. I untwine the fingers of my left hand from Will's grasp and hold my hand out in front of us, tilting it back and forth to let the diamond give off an exaggerated twinkle in the glow of the city lights.

"This is so surreal," I whisper.

"Surreal in a good way, right?" Will asks, lovingly rubbing the palm of my hand with his.

"Wellll," I start jokingly. "Yes, definitely in a good way. I'm incredibly happy," I say, my tone becoming genuine and serious as I look at my future husband.

"I'm incredibly happy too," he says, his voice atypically serious as well, with his usual jesting inflection completely absent.

Our cab stops in front of the Hancock Building, and I scurry out while trying to keep my hair and dress under control despite the violently gusty wind between the street and the doorway. Will follows me after paying for the cab and leads the way to the elevator. We exit on the 96th floor, stepping into the Signature Lounge, a cocktail bar with breathtaking views of the city.

"I thought we could have a bottle of wine and maybe share a little more dessert, if that sounds good to you?" Will says, as we're escorted to a little table and each accept a menu from the host.

"Sounds great," I say, scanning the dessert and wine menus quickly. "How about you pick the wine and I'll pick a dessert for us to share."

Will selects a bottle of Malbec, and I decide on a white and dark chocolate mousse cake.

A cute blonde waitress comes over to take our order, introducing herself as Jen. With amusement I watch her react, as people, especially females, often do to Will's accent.

"You're English!" she exclaims, as if informing him of this fact. She beams at him as though he were Prince William himself.

"That I am," he says, nodding and smiling kindly, as he always does on the several times most days that these exchanges happen.

"An accent is so sexy – I'm jealous," she adds playfully, giving me a once-over and an obligatory smile as she saunters away to place our order.

"I think our friend Jen may have a little crush," I say, giving him a hard time.

"Well, we can't blame her for that, now can we?" he responds, winking at me as he takes my hand across the table. "But, sadly for Jen, I am now a happily engaged man."

"Glad to hear it," I say, smiling myself at the word "engaged".

"Are you sure you're OK waiting until tomorrow to tell your family?" he asks.

"Mmhmm. I feel kind of bad about it, but it's already almost midnight in Michigan and I know my dad and Donna are asleep by now. Same goes for my mom, and I'm sure Griffin's awake but I wouldn't feel right telling him before my mom, you know? I'll just call all of them first thing tomorrow. It's better that way anyway, because talking to all three of them would take such a long time, and I wouldn't get to just enjoy the moment here with you."

"I agree completely, just wanted to make sure you weren't worrying about it," he says.

"Plus, I got to tell Lizzy and Ney, and they're pretty much family but more understanding than my parents when I force them off the phone."

He laughs. "Good point. My mom is going to be through the roof at the thought of finally having another female in the family."

There are so many aspects of the engagement to process. Will's two brothers and his parents will become my in-laws. I will have actual *in-laws*. The thought makes me feel old. I'll be moving out of my apartment, leaving Lizzy and Nevada, I'll be a wife, a Mrs., and if I were to get pregnant, it would be a happy thing, rather than a disaster. It's hard to believe so many changes have been set in motion in just one night. Hard to believe and a little overwhelming.

"I feel like we're going to spend the whole day on the phone tomorrow," I say, thinking out loud.

"I'm sure, but it'll be exciting to tell everyone."

I'm nodding in agreement as Jen reappears with our bottle of wine. She presents it to Will and pours him a taste.

One of the (very) few things that bothers me about Will is his inexplicable view of himself as a wine connoisseur of some sort. Whenever we go to a restaurant, he insists on performing the whole drawn out tasting ritual – the swirling, the sniffing, the sloshing of wine around in his mouth, and then pausing several seconds, apparently to process the full taste, before giving the OK to the waiter or waitress. On two occasions, he actually sent bottles back, something I have never experienced with anyone else. For a while I continually gave him a hard time about it, but he claims that the initial tasting is one of his favorite parts of drinking wine, so eventually I stopped commenting on it, figuring everyone should be allowed a few quirks.

This particular bottle meets with his satisfaction and he tells Jen so. She pours a glass for me and is topping off Will's, when my ring catches her eye.

"You're engaged!" she exclaims, with the same tone she used to announce that Will was British.

I nod with a smile. "We just got engaged tonight," Will says, beaming.

Jen turns to me and says, "lucky you!" She then informs us that our dessert will be arriving shortly.

Will raises his glass as Jen departs. "To my incredibly beautiful fiancée," he says. "I can't wait to spend my life with you."

"Me too," I say, clinking his glass with a smile and taking a sip, pushing thoughts of all the overwhelming changes from my mind and focusing on enjoying my wine with Will.

Chapter 28

"There they are, over to the right in the back," I say, leading Will as we snake through the tables in Nookies to where Lizzy and Nevada are seated, along with our friends Brian Hodgkins, who we pretty much always call "Hodge," and Pete Karaca.

Hodge and Pete live in an apartment in our building, just a few doors down from us, and we've all been friends for years. Back in the summer of 2005, Lizzy (or, more accurately, Lizzy's parents) bought the three-bedroom apartment where we now live, and she, Nevada and I moved in shortly after. I started law school at the University of Chicago that fall, a few weeks after Lizzy started her full time position at McAllistair and Nevada began her first of several pharmaceutical sales jobs, all of which she more or less loathed.

A few weeks into that first year of law school, Nevada, Lizzy and I were coming home from the bar when we heard raucous singing and loud guitars coming from a neighboring apartment as we walked down the hallway. The door to this festive apartment was partially ajar that night, and Nevada had barged right in, in her typical forward fashion. We found Hodge and his friend Sean Brennan playing Oasis songs on the guitar while Pete and a variety of other random drunken people sang along enthusiastically. No one looked particularly startled when we walked in and introduced ourselves as the neighbors. Hodge told us to grab a beer and hang out, which we did.

It only took about ten minutes before Nevada announced to the entire room that everyone needed to hear me play. I shook my head and shot her a threatening look.

"Breck is unbelievable on the guitar. And the violin too actually!" Lizzy had chimed in from across the room where she was chatting with a guy whose name I can't remember.

Hodge had stopped playing. "Who's Breck?" he asked, looking around the room.

"I'm Brecken," I said finally.

"You really play violin?" Sean asked.

"Uh, yeah, but I - "

Hodge cut me off. "Can you go get it? We really need a good violin player for our band. I hadn't thought about a girl... but that could work." I saw him nodding at Sean.

"Oh, that's OK, I'm so busy with school right now and not really looking to join a band," I said, annoyed with Nevada for volunteering me. I wasn't even sure if these guys were being serious about having a band, but I was starting to feel kind of self-conscious and decided it was time to head out. "I have to get to bed anyway, I have a ton of studying to do tomorrow."

"Breck, c'mon, just go get it," Nevada had whined, as all the eyes at this little jam fest fixed on me.

"Sorry guys, go back to playing though, you really sounded good," I'd said, feeling pretty lame. The music had then picked back up, and I told Lizzy that I was heading out to get to bed.

A few days later, Hodge, Pete and Sean had stopped by with another friend and member of the band, Tim Costello, and convinced me to play for them. As I pulled my violin from the case, tuned it, and considered what I should play, they told me about their band. I learned that Hodge, Pete, Sean and Tim had met when they were students at University of Illinois, and they had formed a band their freshman year. Pete wasn't exactly musically inclined, but he was the band manager and never missed a show. Apparently, the band had developed a pretty decent following around Chicago and other parts of the Midwest. They'd added another guitar player, Scott Karam, after moving to Chicago. I had to admit I was kind of excited by the prospect of playing with a band, even if I didn't have much free time to spare.

"So, what's the name of the band?" I'd asked them.

"Ishmael," Sean had responded as I finished up my tuning.

"Ishmael? As in Ishmael from *Moby Dick*?" I'd asked.

"Yeah," Hodge had responded. "Because, he's the narrator of both his own story and the stories of those around him, you know, everyone else on the boat. And that's how we think of our songs."

I wasn't that crazy about the name, honestly, but Hodge's explanation was kind of intriguing, and they'd definitely put more thought into the name than I'd expected.

"Interesting," I had said with a smile in response, as I began to play one Paganini Caprice and then transitioned into another.

When I finished, the guys asked me to play an upcoming show with them at a bar in Lakeview called

Blue Bayou, just as a trial, to see how it went. That night at Blue Bayou turned out to be one of the more exhilarating experiences I'd had in a long time. I was completely hooked, and one show had turned into many.

Ever since, I've been playing with them in about half their shows. It's hard to believe it's already been almost four years. Not only has the band provided me with new friends and a therapeutic break from life as a law student and then lawyer, it was also because of the band that Will and I met.

The summer that Will turned sixteen, his family moved to Whitefish Bay, Wisconsin from Cheltenham, England because his dad was transferred to his company's U.S. office. After graduating from high school in Whitefish, Will had gone on to the University of Wisconsin, and one of his college buddies was also a friend of Hodge's from work. During my second year of law school, Will had come along with this mutual friend to a show at Schubas where Ishmael was one of the two opening bands.

After that night, Will began coming to nearly all our shows and hanging around afterwards to have drinks with us. Although I thought he was objectively pretty hot, there was also something indefinable about him that made him catch my eye. He hadn't come on too strong, and I'd liked that about him. Not long after he'd become an established regular at our shows, I ran into him at the bar and jokingly called him a groupie.

"Groupie?" he had responded, a wry smile on his face, his British accent surprising me. "Don't you become a groupie by sleeping with the band? I'm fairly certain I would remember if I'd slept with you."

"*Fairly* certain?!" I'd responded, hearing the flirtation in my voice and not minding.

"Yeah, you know, I sleep with so many beautiful violin-playing band chicks that sometimes they all run together..."

"I see," I'd said, laughing, and when he had asked if he could buy me a drink, I couldn't think of any reason to say no.

Chapter 29

Will has gotten to know all the guys in the band pretty well over the past two years, so I'm not at all surprised to see that Pete and Hodge have joined us for brunch at Nookies.

The girls both jump up and rush over when they spot us approaching the table.

"Ahh!" Lizzy cries, wrapping me in a hug.

"Lemme see the rock!" Nevada demands, pulling my left hand out of the hug for examination. "Oof, I love it! Nice work buddy," she says, playfully punching Will in the arm.

"Congrats, Breckenridge!" Hodge says, smiling at me. Although I had initially attempted to get Hodge to give up this oh-so-clever nickname for me, my protests only added to his enjoyment, and I let it go a long time ago.

I thank him, giving each of the guys a quick hug. They both look pretty rough this morning, as though they rolled out of bed approximately one minute before leaving to meet us, which I'm guessing is probably the case.

"So, what color bridesmaid dresses are we thinking?" Nevada asks, clearly only half-joking, as we settle into our seats.

"Wow, cutting right to the chase, Nevada, very impressive," Will says, always entertained by my roommates.

"Well, I'll just go ahead and put it out there that green and blue are my best colors, so do with that what you will," Nevada says, as Lizzy jabs her with a look of affectionate annoyance.

"Mmhmm, I'll be sure to keep that in mind," I say. After a few minutes more of wedding talk, during which I assure the girls that we have not so much as discussed the location, date, size or the all-important color of bridesmaid dresses, we move on to other topics, much to the obvious relief of Hodge and Pete, whose eyes have already started to glaze over.

Hodge and I are debating the merits of ketchup on eggs, with the majority of the table taking his side (delicious and crucial) over mine (gross and overpowering), when Lizzy announces that she and Nevada have "big" news for us. We all quiet down.

"So... not to detract from Breck and Will's news..." Lizzy starts, looking briefly to Nevada for support before continuing, "and I know this might sound a little crazy, but Nevada and I are going to open a bar."

Well, I certainly did not see that one coming.

Lizzy continues. "We've always talked about how we would love to own and operate our own bar, and we've had that idea for a stock market-themed bar with fluctuating prices forever. And, anyway, between me getting laid off and Ney hating her job and wanting to quit, we just decided that this was the time to go for it..." Lizzy's self-assured tone dissipates with each word, so Nevada confidently sweeps in as Lizzy trails off.

"It's going to be incredible, you guys," Nevada says enthusiastically, oozing her usual charm. "It will be a really sleek set up, with a huge stock ticker circling the entire place. And, basically, the more of a particular drink that people buy, the lower the price will be. However, they have to keep rapidly buying drinks to keep the price down. We're going to work out all the calculations so that we're always profiting, of course, and once a particular drink price gets really low, to the point where we are just breaking even on that drink, it will instantly rise unless people keep buying."

Lizzy, now seemingly remembering why it is that she's on board with this idea, cuts back in. "Also, it's going to be a perfect way for people to meet, because it makes sense for tables to work together to keep prices of certain drinks down, sending rounds to each other and that kind of thing."

"Exactly," Nevada says, smiling supportively at Lizzy. "We'll be catering to the young, trendy professional scene. We have to find the perfect space for it, but we're definitely thinking River North or Gold Coast area. There'll be different gimmicks and specials different nights of the week. There's nothing like this in Chicago, and there is essentially no way it could fail."

"Wow, how... exciting," I say, caught a little off-guard by all of this. "How are you going to be financing all this?" I ask, thinking I may know the answer.

Nevada shoots me a look, apparently taking this to be an unsupportive comment. "Well we presented our initial rough business plan, which we've been working on all week, to Lizzy's dad yesterday over email and the phone. He agreed to provide half the financing if we can raise the rest from other investors."

They were working on a business plan all week? I feel more than a little out of the loop. "Well, I'm really happy for you guys," I say, curious to hear more details of how all this came to be. "Ney are you going to be quitting your job and doing this full time then?"

"Yep, giving my two weeks notice at the end of the month," she says matter-of-factly. Leave it to Nevada to make that sound like a minor matter. Yep, quitting my career in pharmaceutical sales after four years to open a bar with my friend, no big deal. She left me feeling like I had a seriously underdeveloped sense of whimsy.

"I think the most important question is, can we drink for free there?!" Pete asks, getting a laugh out of everyone.

"We'll see," Nevada responds slyly.

"Well this is a pretty exciting development. Let's hear more," Will says, catching Nevada's vigor. "Is there a name yet? When do you think it'll open?"

Brunch flies by as everyone contributes their two cents about my roommates' new endeavor, which they are tentatively planning to call Crash. I can't help but feel envious of them, a large part of me wishing I was in a position to chuck it all at Baron & Riehl and be a part of their excitement. Must be nice, I think, as I finish the last bites of my omelette.

Chapter 30

"I'd literally do anything right now to come with you!" I tell Will despondently as we pull up at O'Hare Airport in the international departure terminal on Saturday evening. Will's two week break from his residency begins this weekend, and he's heading to England to visit his parents, a few old friends and lots of extended family. The year Will graduated from the University of Wisconsin, his dad's company relocated him back to England. Will and both his brothers had become fully acclimated to life in the U.S. by that point, and they all stayed behind in the U.S. when their parents moved back.

"Aww, I know, babe. I wish you could come too. I would love to show you where I grew up, introduce you to my old school mates and have you away from that horrible law firm for two weeks. Can we be sure to make it happen next time?"

"Definitely next time," I agree, putting the car in park as we reach the curb. Will leans in and kisses me for approximately one second before I hear an aggressive rapping on the car window. I turn to see a stout, stern-faced female cop swinging her arm around at me in a motion that clearly means that I need to keep moving.

"Damn, they don't mess around here, huh?" I say to Will. He gives me another quick kiss and then opens his door.

"Love you so much, *fiancée*," he says, exaggerating the word. We've already had several conversations in the week since we got engaged about how awkward the word fiancé/fiancée is, how it feels so unnatural to say it. I swear it just sounds like you are trying to show off that you are engaged or something every time you say it: this is my fi-ahhhn-sayyy. Plus, I can't help but always think of Beyoncé due to the rhyme, which is just kind of weird. Clearly, being engaged is still taking some adjustment for me. "I'll call you when I land," he says, as the traffic officer shoots us a threatening glare.

"Geez, I better get out of here before we get arrested. Love you too," I say as he quickly pulls his suitcase out of the trunk of Lizzy's Range Rover, which I borrowed for the airport run. He waves as I pull out of the drop off lane and head for I-90, watching him disappear in my rearview mirror.

• • • • •

When I arrive at home, I find Lizzy and Nevada camped out at the dining room table, a mess of papers, folders and charts in front of them, and Jack Johnson playing quietly in the background.

"So is lover boy en route to the homeland?" Nevada asks as I flop down on the green couch in the adjoining TV room.

"Yep," I say, thinking how strange it will be to have him so far away for two weeks. "You guys want to go out tonight?" I ask, thinking that sitting home and listening to them plan Crash for the whole night is not especially appealing and a girls' night out sounds fun.

"We have a reservation for Mercat a la Planxa at 8:30 for three, if you want to come. I thought you might not."

"Yeah, of course, you know I love that place. Why wouldn't I want to go?" I ask, confused by Nevada's comment.

"I don't know," Nevada says, her voice with a clear edge of irritation. "You missed Tuesday dinner at Tiparo's, and you've just seemed really... I don't know, just not into stuff lately," she says, with an accusatory tone.

I see Lizzy's apologetic look, silently telling me not to bite on Nevada's bitchy prodding, but I can't help it.

"What? I told you that I had a closing Wednesday and there was no way I could do dinner Tuesday. I didn't get home from the office until after midnight that night. Why would that mean I wouldn't want to come to dinner tonight? And, how have I been *not into stuff lately?*"

"Guys, stop," Lizzy starts, slipping into her usual peacemaking role.

"I just want to understand why Nevada is making all these comments," I say, realizing that I'm not helping the situation.

"You just haven't seemed that supportive of Crash, for one thing, and you've spent every free minute with Will lately, that's all I meant," Nevada says, no longer looking up and now pretending to be engrossed in the documents in front of her as she speaks to me.

"So sorry, Nevada, how terrible of me to want to spend time with Will before he leaves for two weeks and to not want to get fired from my job, that was so thoughtless of me," I say sarcastically, as I slowly get up and walk to my bedroom, close to exploding with frustration at her unexpected attack.

So much for a fun girls' night. I stretch out on my bed and flip through one of the wedding magazines that Lizzy surprised me with earlier in the week, but all the spreads of elaborately detailed picturesque weddings are not exactly the distraction I need so I pull my BlackBerry off its charger and call my mom. The year after Griffin graduated from high school and headed off to college in Ann Arbor, my mom had been offered a full-time faculty position in the journalism department at CUNY in Manhattan. She'd jumped at the opportunity, sold our house and most of the furniture and moved to a tiny one bedroom apartment in an old walk-up in the West Village. While I had been genuinely happy for her, her move had also felt like the final stage of the loss of my family and sense of home, the loss that had begun with my parents' separation years before. With time, it became clear that my mom was flourishing in academia as well as in New York, and I have even come to enjoy the company of Ted, her boyfriend of several years now, no longer cringing inside when I see them kiss. As usually happens now that she is fully immersed in her new life, my call goes to voicemail, and I leave her a message asking her to give me a call. I flip on my iPod speakers, scroll to the Flaming Lips, and immerse myself in *City of Thieves,* a David Benioff novel that I picked up at Borders on my way home from the office the other day.

An hour or so later, there is a soft tap on my door, and Nevada comes in without waiting for my response. She has a drink in her hand.

"I decided to make mint juleps," she says, with her trademark "I'm sorry" smile plastered across her face. "This is for you," she says as she sits the drink down on my bedstand. I don't respond right away, waiting to see what else she has to say. "You're coming to dinner with us, right?" she asks, as if she had never considered I might not be joining them, as if our earlier conversation had never happened. I've known Nevada long enough to understand that this is her version of an apology. She will almost never *actually apologize* for her hostile moods. Instead, she starts acting extremely sweet and goes out of her way to be exceedingly nice to smooth things over. Truthfully, I'm relieved she came around so quickly tonight because I really do feel like a night out, and I go along with her surge of niceness, not wanting to rock the boat and spend Saturday night sitting home alone.

"Mint juleps? Festive. Is it the Kentucky Derby this weekend or something?" I ask, my friendliness letting her know I accept her apology.

"Nope. But they're so good. It's stupid that people only drink them on Kentucky Derby day. So... I'm changing that trend. They'll be a regular menu item at Crash," she says, flashing me another smile. "Want me to do your makeup tonight?" she offers, continuing to kill me with kindness. Nevada is a makeup junkie and is much more talented in applying it than most of the professionals I've seen in action at the makeup counters. Left to my own devices, I rarely go beyond mascara and a little cover-up, sometimes a few brushes of bronzer, which Nevada introduced me to. I'm pretty certain that if Nevada could take only one thing with her to a desert island, it would be a lifetime supply of bronzer – she is absolutely obsessed with the stuff. Once Lizzy and I hid all seven or so of her bronzer compacts on April Fools Day, and I truly thought she might have a stroke. We were only able to hold out for about three minutes before we took pity on her and returned them.

"OK, that sounds great," I say, smiling at her.

"Perfect. I'm doing Lizzy's too, so come into her room whenever and we can all get ready together. We should probably grab a cab by 8:15 or so. Oh, also, Hodge, Pete and Sean are coming with us. I changed the reservation, hopefully you don't mind?"

"Of course not, sounds like fun." And it did.

"OK, get to work on your julep," she says in a cheerful voice as she heads out of my room.

Following Nevada's orders, I take a sip of my drink, which turns out to be incredibly delicious, and fish around in my closet for a few minutes before sliding on a pair of dark gray skinny jeans and a long, narrow black sweater that Lizzy gave me the previous Christmas. Looking in the mirror, I pull my wavy hair into a loose ponytail and tie a thin blue scarf around my head like a headband to make the outfit a bit less boring. I slip on a pair of low leather strappy heels, and then head down the hall for my makeover.

• • • • •

As always, the food at Mercat a la Planxa is overwhelmingly delicious. It's literally all I can do to refrain from licking my plate. Nevada's hostile attitude of earlier has continued to be replaced by a buoyant, vivacious mood. I know that it's just how she is, high and low, always in the extremes, so I try not to take her lash-outs too personally, although sometimes, today for example, I'm not overly successful in my efforts to be patient with her.

When we've finished the last of our sangria, we're persuaded by Hodge to head to The Map Room in Bucktown because some girl he met at one of our recent shows has been texting him tonight, telling him that he should meet her there. So, we soon find ourselves a van cab and pile in for the ten minute ride to Bucktown.

"Maybe we can find you a sexy Wicker Park hipster boyfriend tonight, Liz," Nevada says in a teasing tone.

"Maybe we can find you one," Lizzy suggests, only mildly amused. Both of my roommates are single but for more or less opposite reasons. Nevada is not all that discerning about who she hooks up with, but she is completely commitment-phobic and typically dates a guy for only a few weeks before she loses interest, while Lizzy is only interested in guys who she sees long-term potential with, and she typically dismisses every guy she meets out at the bar as a sleazy tool. Usually I agree with her on this assessment, but sometimes I worry that she doesn't even give guys a chance to prove her wrong. She is definitely attracted to the preppy, clean-cut types, so we all know the likelihood of her finding a hipster love tonight is clearly minimal. She broke up with a guy named Jason (for the second time, they also dated briefly in college) about a month ago and hasn't shown much interest in dating since then anyway.

"You two better not be mocking hipsters," Hodge says. "In case you haven't noticed, Pete and Sean are rocking the hipster look these days."

"I'm not a fucking hipster, dude," Sean says, unamused by Hodge's heckling.

"Yeah, you guys are more hippies than hipsters," Nevada adds. "There's a big difference."

"Wow, listen to Nevada go here. Ney, can you box the rest of us into a stereotypical classifications as well?" Hodge's tone, as always, is jesting and sarcastic. If he has ever been serious in his life, it certainly hasn't been in my presence.

"Obviously," Nevada says, never one to back down on a challenge, even one that was probably meant to be rhetorical. "Sean and Pete are mainstream casual with hippie influence. Breck is in the same vein, casual trendy with a bohemian influence, although I must say you are drifting more toward trendy sometimes these days, Breck, excluding when you're all hipped out for your shows. Lizard is, of course, high fashion slash prepster," she continues, using her favorite (and Lizzy's least favorite) nickname for Lizzy. "Hodge, you're grunge-prep. And I," she concludes with a faux-dramatic air, "am my own unique combination of styles that simply cannot be defined."

We all start protesting and laughing, although I really have to admit Nevada's descriptions of everyone were pretty accurate. I do wear more of my vintage, funky clothes when I'm playing with Ishmael than when I'm dressing for every day life, but that's probably more a product of the fact that I spend the vast majority of the rest of my time at Baron & Riehl, where, believe it or not, adventurous dressing is not really encouraged. These days, once I get home and out of my dreadful business attire, I mostly just want to wear the most comfortable option, and I'm OK with the fact that my style has apparently suffered as a result.

"I can classify your style, Nevada," Hodge offers, "it's called 'I try too hard to be unique and all my outfits clash'."

"You asshole! As a grunge-prepster, the lamest and least inventive of styles, you are not in a position to critique my style," she says, their tones bordering on flirtatious as the cab pulls up in front of The Map Room. This kind of insulting banter is more or less the basis of their friendship. "Plus, you are a huge fucking dork for being a dude who uses the word 'clash' in any context other than talking about the mind-blowing talents of Mick Jones, Joe Strummer, et cetera. And anyway, for the record, I think clashing looks awesome."

"Well, obviously you do, but unfortunately no one agrees with you," Hodge says, rubbing her hair with his hand to mess it up. She swats at him and tucks her head into my shoulder to avoid his reach.

"Did you call me fucking mainstream casual with a hippie influence?" Pete asks, coming out of the woodwork all of the sudden in his usual fashion, referencing Nevada's earlier classification of his look. "It's actually more like I have been wearing the same old t-shirts since high school, but I guess I'm not in a position to question your fashion expertise," he says, sliding open the van cab door and hopping out. The rest of us follow.

The Map Room is bustling, and we make a beeline for the bar since it's immediately obvious that our odds of getting a table any time soon are slim at best. Lizzy squeezes in between two groups at the bar and a minute later she's passing back glasses to all of us, filled with some Belgian beer that's on tap.

We move away from the chaos of the bar area to stake out a little space when Hodge spots his girl at one of the larger tables.

"There's Shannon," he says, motioning toward a petite blonde girl sitting with a big group. "I'm gonna go say hi," and with that he leaves us. Sean discreetly points out a girl he hooked up with a few months ago and never called again, and Nevada and Lizzy and I do our best to nonchalantly check her out as Sean grumbles about the prospect of her spotting him. A minute later we see Hodge motioning for us to join him at Shannon's table, and we make our way over.

"Hey guys, this is Shannon," he says, resting his hand on her back. "Shannon, these are Sean, Pete, Nevada, Lizzy and Brecken. You might remember Sean and Brecken from the other night, they're in the band too." Shannon nods without showing much interest, as if to say that, yes, she remembers us, and, no, she doesn't really care in the least. "Anyway, a couple of Shannon's friends are heading out now, once they pay, so we can take their chairs and hang out at this table too." This is exactly what we do a few minutes later, mixing in among the four of Shannon's friends who remain, with Nevada quickly grabbing the open seat next to the one attractive guy in Shannon's bunch.

We end up playing quarters for a while and getting pretty drunk. The girl sitting next to me, who I learn is named Courtney, befriends me and tells me she grew up in Birmingham, Michigan, just a few miles away from Royal Oak. Courtney's face is caked with too much foundation and, sitting so close to her, I can't seem to focus on anything other than the orange-ish patches when I look at her face. She seems to be a nice enough girl but when she stands to head to the bathroom, I take the opportunity to swivel the other way and join in a conversation with Lizzy, Sean and Pete for the remainder of the night. At about 1:30, I am officially exhausted and ready to leave, knowing I have to spend a chunk of time in the office the next day. Nevada and Hodge are both still occupied with their respective new *friends,* and Lizzy says she wants to stay out and will take a cab later with Nevada, Sean and Pete (and maybe Hodge too, depending on how his luck goes). I say my goodbyes and head out.

After a few minutes of unavailable cabs speeding past me, I realize that I'm never going to have any luck finding an empty one on Hoyne, so I turn the corner and begin walking down Armitage. I search around in my jam-packed purse for my BlackBerry, wanting to check if I missed a call from Will, who I know is waking up early to golf with his dad.

As I finally locate my phone, I look up and nearly drop to the sidewalk in shock.

Chapter 31

He is about two buildings away from me, approaching quickly, yet I feel like everything is occurring in slow motion. I watch him see me, just a second after I spot him, watch his shock register, watch his face break out in a confused smile. A stick-thin, very pretty girl in a short skirt has her arm hooked in his, is virtually hanging on him.

I panic and look down, my heart racing so fast it is virtually vibrating as I pretend to go back to searching through my purse, utterly unable to think with my long-lost ex-boyfriend just steps away from me. I immediately realize that I am acting like a total freak and look up once again as Reed Whalen arrives just feet away from me and stops.

"Brecken." His deep, raspy voice is exactly the same. Exactly. His voice actually impacts me even more than seeing him did seconds earlier. He is even more attractive now, if that is possible, with a more defined jaw and angled cheekbones. Just as I'd seen in the photos that my stalker of a best friend had found, his floppy hairstyle has been replaced by a longish buzz cut, and his skin is a deep tan. It's actually frightening how gorgeous he is.

"Hi," he tries again, saying it in an intense tone, putting emotion behind the usually trite greeting. He furrows his forehead slightly as he says it, as if narrowing his eyes will allow him to read me. At this point, I realize that I must be staring blankly at him.

His anorexic companion is clearly not liking this exchange and is giving me what can only be described as a death look. I take a deep breath.

"Reed," I say softly as I exhale, feeling like an idiot, unable to think of anything else to say. I can't bring myself to look him in the eye for reasons I am not fully clear about.

"I'm Kelsey," the girl says, sticking her hand out to shake mine in what is clearly a completely disingenuous gesture of friendliness, her voice ridden with false congeniality.

"Brecken," I say, giving her bony arm a quick obligatory shake.

"Yeah, I got that," she says rudely. I feel my distress compounding, rising up in me. For all the times, the millions of times, I have pictured this encounter in my head, I have never imagined it this way. My flight instinct kicks in.

"I'm sorry, I have to go," I sputter, and with that I quickly turn and walk a few steps before stepping between two parked cars at the curb with my hand up in the air. Luck is with me at this instant and a yellow cab instantly swerves over and stops in front of me. I frantically open the door and scoot in, telling the cabbie to head to Old Town. As we speed off, I'm tempted to look back but resist the urge and instead burst into quiet, heavy tears.

My phone rings and I look down to see Will's name lighting up. I ignore it, unable to deal with carrying on a normal conversation. I take a few deep breaths and manage to compose myself by the time we reach my building. I pay the cab driver and wave a quick hello to Craig, not at all in the mood for small talk.

Once in the safety of my apartment, I peel off my clothes, knot my hair up on the top of my head and turn on the water in Lizzy's whirlpool bathtub, which she never minds if I use. It's already just after 2 A.M. and I have to put in a long day of work tomorrow, but I know it would be next to impossible for me to sleep right now, so I decide a hot bath is the way to go. I move my iPod speakers to the bathroom and put on the always soothing Ray LaMontagne, feeling slightly calmer just hearing his voice. I pour some of Lizzy's Sabon bath salts into the tub for good measure before slowly lowering myself into the steaming water as it continues to rise, not turning it off until it reaches my chest.

I try to get my thoughts in order as my drunkenness wears off. Even soaking in the tranquility of the bathtub, I still feel shaky from the encounter. I have no idea what aspect of it is upsetting me the most... Seeing him when I wasn't prepared for it? Seeing him with that Kelsey character? Just seeing him at all? I'm completely unsure. There are so many levels to it, so many angles. For one, he came back to the U.S., to the very city where I live, in fact, and he didn't contact me. For another, he was hanging out with a bitchy, model-y girl who I couldn't have imagined him liking at all, back when I knew him. And then there was that voice of his, that ridiculously perfect face. They still get to me, and I know it. I might as well have been the lonely sixteen-year-old girl on the dock all over again given the way my knees buckled and my stomach lurched when I spotted him tonight. Am I most upset about the realization that I even care about seeing him after all this time? The thoughts stream through my mind rapid-fire, and I know I could go on like this all night. I could make myself crazy. And going crazy over Reed Whalen is a path that I have already traveled. I'm older now, older and much wiser, I remind myself, a slight sense of empowerment returning. I am not about to let him crush me again.

I look down at my left hand through the bathwater, at my beautiful ring. I am engaged to marry a wonderful man, the man I love, no less. The rest is just water under the bridge, a twist in the path that brought me to Will — to Will's kindness, his humor, his love. I'm officially starting to feel better. I take a slow, deep breath, inhaling the steamy air, listening to Ray croon, and actually smile. Anyone would be stunned to unexpectedly see a ghost from their past like that, I reassure myself, and now I have closed the Reed Whalen chapter of my life once and for all. With that, I pull the plug in the tub and wrap myself in a towel as the water gurgles down the drain. Otherwise I hear only silence, which means Nevada and Lizzy are not yet home. I throw on a comfy old gray t-shirt and climb into bed, feeling surprisingly at peace.

Chapter 32

While there is certainly something uniquely depressing about being at the office on a Sunday, there is also a small part of me that enjoys the quiet ability to work without interruption that is only possible on the weekends. No partners barging in with additional assignments, no clients emailing me with frantic needs, no financial planners calling and employing scare tactics to convince me to set up a free estate planning meeting with them. The other benefit, which is pretty significant in my view, is that there is no dress code in the office on the weekends. I always take full advantage of this fact, rolling in wearing my comfiest sweatpants, a worn t-shirt, oversized hoodie and flip flops, determined to maximize my comfort on the days when I can avoid wearing a miserably confining suit and tucked in, fitted, collared shirt.

On this particular Sunday morning, I appreciate the quiet more than ever. In Lizzy's green Dartmouth sweatshirt and my favorite lightweight lululemon sweatpants, I arrive in the office by 10:30, which is pretty impressive for me on a weekend. After my bath, I hadn't exactly fallen right to sleep, but I'd gotten there eventually, and I awoke this morning feeling surprisingly refreshed.

My plan is to devote the day to beginning my due diligence document review for the sale of all the shares of a corporation, a transaction which is still in the final stages of negotiation. It will be a large, complex deal, and the parties involved are referring to it as Project Aristotle, for reasons unknown to me. The investment bankers involved in a particular deal usually select a code name like this, and although I have my doubts as to whether stealth code names are actually necessary for confidentiality purposes, using them is the status quo nonetheless. My billable hours weren't too impressive last month and with whispers of potential layoffs circulating the office for the past several weeks, I feel somewhat comforted to have just been added to the team for Project Aristotle, even if it does mean more time dealing with sleazy Stan Dillingham, who is the senior partner on the deal. It will keep me busy for weeks and give me a chance to get back on track with my hours. Even though I hate the work I do most days, and even though I feel desperately, suffocatingly envious of Nevada and Lizzy spending their days planning and designing Crash, I am definitely not in a financial position where I could handle getting laid off. Not even close. And so, here I am, booting up my computer for a long day in a virtual data room, hoping Stan will not be joining me in the office.

As always, my first move upon sitting down at my desk is to turn on my computer and open Outlook. I click through a few random emails about Project Aristotle and a couple miscellaneous work emails on other issues that I ignored when they arrived on my BlackBerry yesterday. And then there is suddenly one more new email, which arrives a moment after I open Outlook. My heart races, and I double click:

From: reedwhalen22@yahoo.com
To: bpereira@baronriehl.com
Subject: (no subject)

Brecken...

I'm really sorry about last night. I've imagined
seeing you again so many times, but I guess I
didn't know how to react when it actually
happened. I only recently got back to the U.S.
for the first time since 2001 and have been
trying to figure out the right way to get in touch
with you. Obviously last night is not what I had
in mind...

Would you be willing to meet me some time
this week for a drink?

Reed

I read it again and again, stopping only after I've
been through it four times, my mind racing, absorbing
his words, trying to decipher everything that lies
beneath them. I could just delete this, I think,
recalling my contentment of last night, my resolve to
put the Reed Whalen saga behind me permanently. I
pull out my cell and call Lizzy, thinking that the odds
of this being a productive day of due diligence review
probably just went out the window.

My call goes straight to voicemail. Most likely
Lizzy's phone died last night and she didn't remember
to charge it when she got home. I consider calling
Nevada and decide against it. She doesn't quite get
the nuances of the Reed situation in the way that

Lizzy does. I make a mental pact with myself to focus on work until 5:00, at which time I can get Lizzy's advice about how, if at all, I should respond to Reed's email.

With that, I open the electronic data room website and begin poring over the details of the target corporation's capital structure. I tick away the hours, one six minute increment at a time, forcing myself to focus only on board resolutions, financial statements, assignability clauses, and anything but Reed's email. Stan sends me a few emails but blessedly does not come into the office all day.

I run to Potbelly for a quick lunch break but otherwise keep my nose to the grindstone. My cell rings around 2:30, and seeing that it's my mom, I answer.

"Hey, Mom," I say.

"Hi, honey. How are you? Not working I hope?"

I groan. "Yeah, I'm at the office, unfortunately. Hopefully not for too much longer though. How are you?"

"Oh I'm good. Sorry that I missed your call yesterday. I was out with Ted at a benefit dinner and forgot my cell, as usual."

I smile, thinking that my mom will never adjust to the idea of constantly carrying a phone around with her.

"No prob," I tell her. "I was just calling to say hi anyway, nothing important or anything."

"Well, I was planning to call you anyway, because I just found out that I'm going to be in Chicago this Thursday night. I got a last minute spot in a conference at Northwestern that goes all day Friday, so I'm flying in Thursday afternoon. Think you'd be available for dinner Thursday? My treat."

"Oh, I'd love that," I say, thrilled at the thought of seeing my mom for the first time since Christmas. "But I should be treating you! I'll make us a reservation somewhere. Does 8:00 sound good?"

"Sure, sounds great. I'm staying at a Hilton down in the Loop, but I can meet you anywhere."

"OK, I'll find somewhere good for us. I can't wait to see you."

"Me either. I'll let you work now. We'll have lots of time to talk Thursday."

"OK. Love you, Mom."

"Love you too, Breck. Good luck with all the work."

Alone in my office, I smile at the thought of spending a little time with my mom in just a few days, and my mood is noticeably lighter as I force myself to get back to work. Eventually, 5:00 comes, and I am free, having made it to my self-imposed quitting time. I quickly type up my daily time entry and head for the L.

Fifteen minutes later I walk in the door and find Lizzy and Nevada discussing plans for their business venture, as usual.

"Finally! Were you at work?" Lizzy greets me.

"Yesss. So miserable, but I forced myself to stay until 5:00 and I actually got a lot done, so this week should be more manageable now, hopefully." I plop down next to Nevada on the couch, glancing at the various sheets of notes and printed documents that are spread on the coffee table and the couches.

"That's good. We need your advice on some things for Crash," Nevada says, barely looking up.

"We're going a little stir crazy and need an outside opinion." It will definitely take me some adjustment to get used to being considered an "outside opinion" when it comes to Lizzy and Nevada.

"I can't wait to hear all about it, but first I have so much to tell you guys," I say, which comes out sounding more dramatic than I intended. They both look up with interest as I continue. "So, last night after I left Map Room, I was walking up Armitage looking for a cab, kind of not paying attention to the people around me, and when I looked up, I was basically face to face with *Reed*."

The look of shock on Lizzy's face is about the same reaction I would expect if I had just announced to her that I was growing a third arm.

"No fucking way," Nevada says, although she characteristically looks less fazed than Lizzy. "Did you guys talk?"

"Um, not really. He was with some girl too..." I say, shaking my head at the memory of the whole awkward exchange.

"Whoa, hold on," Lizzy says, "you need to start from the beginning of when you saw him and tell us every single detail. *Every* detail."

"OK, so I saw him from a distance and he saw me at about the same time and said my name. And I more or less just stood there awkwardly, totally panicked. Then this girl who he was with, "Kelsey," introduces herself in this kind of obnoxious way, and I said that I had to go just as a cab happened to pull up near us, so I jumped in and that was it..."

I honestly think Lizzy is going to cry out of empathy.

"Well, that doesn't sound all *that* bad," Nevada says.

"Are you kidding me?" Lizzy says. "It sounds horrible. Sorry, Breck, not to make you feel worse. It's just that I know how many times you have pictured seeing him again over the years, and what it would be like, and this is just..." she trails off. "I just know that this must be incredibly hard."

"Yeah, it was just really bizarre more than anything," I say, wanting to downplay the drama as I remind myself that I should be way, way beyond obsessing over Reed at this point in my life. But, given my audience, I know they appreciate that the intensity of this scenario is pretty hard to ignore. "Actually though, there's more. I got an email from him today, at my work email address, so I guess he found it on Google or something."

"What? Let me see it!" Lizzy cries, practically grabbing my BlackBerry out of my hand.

I laugh. "Easy, spaz," I say, handing her my phone. She proceeds to read the email aloud to Nevada and me.

"This is crazy," Nevada says. "I *cannot* believe he's finally resurfaced. I always thought he would eventually, but honestly after, what has it been, seven or eight years? I had pretty much written him off at this point."

"Um, yeah, you and me both," I say, stealing a sip of the fountain Coke that Lizzy has been drinking. Our love of regular Coke and hatred of the so-sweet taste of Diet Coke is just one of our many shared traits.

"Sooo, on to the obvious question..." Nevada says.

"Am I going to meet him?" I complete her thought.

"Exactly," Nevada says, her eyes questioning me.

"Do you really think you might?" Lizzy asks, which surprises me.

"Do you really think you might *not?*" Nevada chimes in, also clearly surprised by Lizzy.

"So does that mean that, Ney, you think I should go and, Liz, you don't?"

"No!" They both emphatically protest in unison, and then burst out laughing.

"Well, what do you think I should do. I honestly have no clue. One second I think, how could I not meet him? How could I not want to hear the truth about where he's been and why he acted the way he did, for the sake of closure and curiosity and everything in between. And then, a second later, I think that maybe he doesn't deserve a chance to be heard by me, and that I already have a great life without him, so what good could possibly come from seeing him, especially given how awkward it was last night? And I just go back and forth..." I look to them helplessly.

"I feel like I need to think about it a little more, there are so many things to consider," Lizzy says thoughtfully. "I'm just worried that maybe meeting him is like playing with fire, not to sound melodramatic, but you know what I mean. Right now, you're in a great relationship, you're getting married, you're totally content with Will. I mean, more than content, you're happy. But I'm afraid that if you see Reed, everything could become...so confusing."

"But if just meeting this guy for a drink will potentially make you *that* confused about your relationship with Will, don't you think you almost owe it to yourself and to Will to see Reed? I mean, if you aren't certain enough about your relationship with Will to feel confident that it can withstand you meeting up with your ex-boyfriend for a few hours, then maybe you guys shouldn't be getting married," Nevada offers bluntly.

"Well, Reed isn't just any old ex-boyfriend," Lizzy says to Nevada. "The whole situation is so charged. I think maybe Breck should just leave well enough alone and not delve into the past."

I lean back on the couch feeling torn. I think Nevada has the stronger argument, but I know Lizzy has a better appreciation for the subtleties of the Reed situation and just wants to protect me.

"I think it just comes down to this. Do you *want* to see him?" Nevada says. "Because, if you do want to see him but you don't go meet him, I think you'll always wonder about him and what it was he wanted to tell you."

Lizzy shrugs and I can see in her expression that she has plenty of qualms about my potential reunion with Reed.

"That makes sense," I say slowly, mulling it all over in my head. "And, if I'm being honest with myself, I do *want* to see him. I think it will help me to put him behind me for good." I say it with finality, happy to have made a decision. Lizzy shifts her position on the couch, and it's clear to me that she's not entirely behind this conclusion.

"What, Liz? You really think it's a big mistake?" I ask, having trouble feeling confident about seeing Reed if my most trusted supporter isn't in my corner.

"Um, it's hard to say," she says quietly. "It's not like I don't understand why you would want to see him. But, if I had what you and Will have, I just know that I wouldn't risk ruining it over some guy who broke my heart and disappeared for almost eight years without so much as a word." This is a pretty opinionated stance for Lizzy, and since I value her insight over anyone else's, I'm not sure what to say.

Silence hangs in the air for a few seconds.

"Yeah, I guess I truly don't believe there is any way that seeing Reed will affect my feelings for Will, but I'm going to give it a night and think about it. I'll just decide tomorrow," I say, suddenly feeling the desperate urge to talk about something else.

"So," I say, taking it upon myself to change the subject, "any excitement after I left Map Room?"

"Not really. There were a surprising number of good looking guys there late night, but Lizard here wouldn't talk to any of them." Nevada's jesting tone is ridden with a layer of loving snarkiness.

"Um, not true, I was hanging out with Sean and Pete all night," Lizzy said, sounding slightly on the defensive.

"Clearly they don't count," Nevada says dismissively.

"Well, I also felt like crap because for some reason we kept taking these warm SoCo shots, which were disgusting," Lizzy says with an exaggerated shiver. "Just the words 'warm SoCo' make me want to vomit."

"Well then stop saying them!" I say with a laugh. "What happened with that guy you were talking to, Ney? Was he cool?"

She crinkles her face. "Uh, he was all right, but I couldn't seem to get past the fact that his name was Krith..."

"Krith?" I ask. "Like Chris but with a 'TH' at the end?"

"Yep..." Nevada says.

"But that just sounds like you're saying Chris with a lisp!" I cry. "That's the worst name I've ever heard!"

"I know!" Nevada agrees. "Who would do that to their child?"

Lizzy looks horrified. "That's like naming a baby Jethica! Or Melitha!"

Nevada nods knowingly. "So, yeah, I know it's not his fault that his name's Krith, but regardless, I don't think we have much of a future together."

It's a full minute before I can stop laughing. "So, what's the latest on Crash?" I ask once I'm able to speak again. "If I have to work as a miserable corporate lawyer while you guys get to design a bar, you at least need to give me all the details so that I can live vicariously."

They both start bubbling immediately at the mention of Crash and bring me up to speed on all the developments. We order pizza delivery from Sarpino's, and although we do not mention the name Reed Whalen again that night, I can't say that he is ever far from my mind.

Chapter 33

I reread my email:

From: bpereira@baronriehl.com
To: reedwhalen22@yahoo.com
Subject: re: (no subject)

Hey Reed,

Thanks for your email. Meeting for a drink works for me. I'm busy tomorrow, Thursday and Friday this week though, so maybe next week would be better. Let me know what works for you.

Brecken

I had decided that less was more when I drafted the email and am feeling good about my approach of keeping it simple and straightforward, not including any inside jokes or snide references to Kelsey. I won't allow myself to re-write it, because, after all, I couldn't care less what Reed thinks of me anyway. I have a meeting with Stan in five minutes and don't want to waste any more time obsessing over whether I am making the right decision, so I bite the bullet and hit send, the email disappearing into cyberspace within an instant.

I gather my working files for Project Aristotle, grab a fresh legal pad from my drawer, and head over to Stan's office on the other side of the floor.

"Good morning future bride!" Debbie says enthusiastically as I approach her desk en route to Stan's office.

"Morning, Deb," I say with a smile, thinking that she is possibly more excited about my engagement than my own mother.

"Any plans yet? Set a date?" Rhoda chimes from the desk next to Debbie.

"Not yet," I say, stopping for a moment by Debbie's desk. "Will just left to visit his family in England for two weeks, so we haven't really had a chance to start thinking about planning that much yet. I'll definitely keep you posted on all the developments though," I say as I continue around the corner.

Stan is on the phone when I arrive at his door but motions for me to come in and sit, which I do. Many of the partners on my floor share this annoying habit of asking associates to come in and sit in their office while they proceed to finish telephone calls. This would be fine for a minute or two, but I am frequently stuck sitting there for fifteen or twenty minutes while a partner finishes a call, even though they fully know that I cannot bill any of that time since I'm not doing any work other than listening to one side of a telephone conversation on a wholly unrelated matter. Thankfully, this time Stan concludes his call within a few minutes.

"I noticed we're sporting a new piece of jewelry," he says, chuckling as though he thinks this is a clever comment.

"Yep. I got engaged last week," I say, not wanting to encourage the conversation.

"Well, congratulations! Or, I suppose I should say best wishes, right? Congratulations is only for men?"

"Oh yeah, I think I've heard something about that," I say noncommittally, "but I think congratulations is OK for females these days, a lot people have said congratulations to me."

"So, I'm pretty outdated, huh?" he says, with a playful tone in his voice, feigning that he is offended. "What, do you think of me as some old guy who is your dad's age or something?"

I resist the temptation to tell him that I am quite sure he is older than my dad and instead just say, "I didn't mean it like that."

"So tell me about the lucky guy," Stan says, as I continue to watch the potential billable minutes slip away from me.

I try to keep my answers as short as possible without sounding curt or bitchy.

"Well, let's see, his name is Will, he's a medical resident at Northwestern, he's from England originally and is just a really great guy all around." As these words come out of my mouth, I immediately realize my mistake, recalling that I told Stan and his family that Will worked in finance in my desperate attempts to incorporate the fact that I had a boyfriend into the conversation at the opera. Hopefully he doesn't remember.

"Medical resident? Hmm. I thought that when we were at the opera you said your boyfriend worked in real estate finance."

Shit.

I give him a confused look and then say, "Oh, no, that's my *brother, Griffin,* who works in real estate finance. Will is a doctor."

"Really?" He pauses for an instant. "I could have sworn that you said boyfriend. I guess my *old* brain must be failing me," he says, giving a creepy laugh, his tone making it clear that he certainly does not think he is misremembering what I said. "In any event, let's talk Project Aristotle, shall we? Where are we on the due diligence?"

And with that, the billable day begins.

• • • • •

A response from Reed is waiting for me when I return from my meeting with Stan, which ended up taking almost an hour. I hate that my pulse quickens when I see it in my Inbox.

From: reedwhalen22@yahoo.com
To: bpereira@baronriehl.com
Subject: re: (no subject)

All business with your emails these days I see... If you're busy later in the week, how about meeting tonight? Would 8:00 at Inner Town Pub in Wicker Park work? Not sure where you live, so let me know if there is a place that's better for you. I can meet you wherever.

Tonight? I haven't been mentally preparing to see him so soon. But, then again, maybe that's a good thing. I could avoid overthinking and obsessing, which I know I shouldn't be doing anyway. I instinctively pick up my work phone to call Lizzy for her input but quickly place it back in the receiver without dialing. Lizzy made her thoughts on the situation pretty clear last night: seeing Reed again was a risk not worth taking. She could be right, but I know I want some finality with respect to what has been a longstanding ellipses in my life. I could call Nevada to get her input about the timing, but then what difference does the timing of when I see him really make anyway? I decide that tonight is as good a time as any, because frankly he isn't worth the thought I have already given him. I draft another brief email saying that I'll see him at 8:00 at Inner Town Pub and then turn my attention back to Project Aristotle.

$$\bullet \; \bullet \; \bullet \; \bullet \; \bullet$$

It's 7:00 as I board the Red Line L for the quick commute home from work. I could easily have stayed at the office until midnight with the amount of work I have left to do, but I want time to change out of my work clothes before heading over to Wicker Park.

I haven't yet told Will about Reed resurfacing. He knows only a very cursory, minimalist version of the Reed story. Essentially I mentioned only that I had a high school boyfriend and that we broke up when I started college – a pretty standard turn of events when it comes to high school relationships, and he has never asked to know more. I hadn't seen any point in filling him in on particulars of my other serious, albeit less emotionally charged, relationship with a guy named Evan, either. And, Will isn't the type who would want to hear all the details anyway. I talked to Will for an hour yesterday before I went to bed but didn't mention running into Reed at all, which undoubtedly makes me a selective truth teller, but hopefully not a straight up liar.

I will meet Reed just this one time, get my answers, and say goodbye to him. Easy-peasy, as Lizzy would say. So trivial that it's not even worth mentioning.

The L stops at Clark and Division, and I climb the dingy stairs up into the evening sunlight. I quickly walk home and find the apartment empty, presumably Nevada and Lizzy are out hunting for start-up financing or checking out potential buildings to house Crash or something like that. Feeling thankful that I will likely be able to sneak off without an interrogation, I pull my work clothes off, tossing the shirt into my dry cleaning hamper and hanging my pants up, deciding they have few enough wrinkles to be worn again. I pull on my favorite J. Brand jeans, a black ribbed tank top and a few long necklaces then examine myself in the mirror. Before I can overthink it, I apply a quick coat of mascara, a dab of foundation and a few strokes of bronzer to my face and shake my hair out of the slightly messy ponytail that it has been in all day. No harm in looking a little less bedraggled. I open the fridge and decide on two Eggo waffles, which I toast, butter, lather in syrup and devour. By this time, it's 7:45. I quickly brush my teeth and grab my purse, slipping on green Old Navy flip flops and heading out the door. Craig flips on the cab light for me, and I'm en route to Wicker Park by 7:55. I'll be a few minutes late, but then again, Reed certainly kept me waiting around for him long enough, once upon a time.

Despite having felt calm and collected during the ride over, a wave of anxiety and panic washes over me as I pay the taxi driver before stepping out on the curb at Inner Town Pub, an appealingly grungy little bar that I have been to only once before.

What am I even doing here? Resisting the sudden urge to hop back in the cab and return to the safety of my apartment, I pull open the door to the bar.

PART IV
SUMMER OF 2000

Chapter 34

"Ooh, turn this up!" Lizzy cried as *December 1963 (Oh What A Night)*, one of her many favorite golden oldies, came on the radio while we whizzed through the fields of central Michigan on our way to Green Island. Finding any song on the radio that was not country was a borderline miracle in this neck of the woods, and with Lizzy's in-car CD player having broken just the day before we left, she was even more excited than usual to locate a beloved oldies song.

I increased the volume as we both sang along loudly. I still couldn't believe I was going back. Once I had informed my parents that a local music studio in Charlevoix had agreed to pay me $20 an hour to teach violin lessons several days a week, they had quickly agreed that I could go back to Green Island for a second summer. One thing I had realized about my post-divorce parents was that neither of them ever wanted to be the bad guy when avoidable, and they were noticeably more accommodating than they used to be. Usually this made me uncomfortable, only serving to highlight how drastically my family had changed in such a short time frame, but in this instance I definitely didn't mind because it meant I was on my way back.

Thankfully, this year Lizzy and I had managed to avoid having Sarah as a passenger for the trip up north. Sarah had received a brand new silver BMW convertible as her high school graduation gift from her parents (because, I mean, clearly a high school graduate could not possibly be expected to continue driving the brand new Lexus SUV she had received a year and a half earlier...), so she had already driven herself to Charlevoix in her new wheels the previous week. This September, Sarah would be leaving to begin her freshman year at Duke, and I was ecstatic that Lizzy and I would be enjoying senior year without being subjected to her snide comments and barrage of insults on a daily basis.

To say that I was anxious about potentially seeing Reed Whalen again would be a drastic understatement. Although he had occupied nearly every daydream I'd had since leaving Green last summer, I had never said a word about our night together to anyone, Lizzy included.

We were heading to Green Island near the end of June, a little later than last year because we'd needed to stay in town for the SATs a week after school got out for the summer. Lizzy had stayed at my house for the week since the rest of her family had already left for Green Island. We'd taken the test just this morning and after a brief stop home to grab our already packed bags and hug my mom, we were on our way at long last.

I felt a hint of guilt about leaving my mom for the summer. The past year had been pretty rough for her. I'm not sure how, but word about my dad and Mary Ann McClain had circulated around Royal Oak pretty quickly, and, needless to say, my mom was humiliated. Mary Ann had been my mom's tennis partner on and off for years, and although she had never been one of her closest friends, my mom certainly hadn't seen her as the type of casual friend who would betray her in this way. At least Griffin would be around this summer to keep her company, and she would be teaching a new summer course at U of M Dearborn, so she'd be occupied with that, I reassured myself.

As to what my dad was feeling, I could only guess, because after an emotional apology to all of us, he had basically withdrawn to his new apartment, his work and his painting. My dad had owned his convenience store since I was a baby, when he'd bought it as a means of making a living while he established himself in the local art community. For as long as I could remember, he'd spent much of his free time painting at the small studio that he rented out just a few blocks away, often working late into the night. While he sold paintings from time to time for a fair chunk of change, he'd never been able to produce a reliable stream of revenue from his art, so he'd never been able to sell the store as planned and rely on painting as his sole means of income. While he told us that he wanted to see me and Griffin as much as possible after he moved out, he also said he was leaving it up to us to reach out to him whenever we felt ready. He posed it as though he was being noble, while I viewed it as him taking the easy way out, leaving it up to us, his teenage children, to reach out to him after he had single-handedly messed up our chances of ever being a family again.

After a month or so had passed without me or my brother contacting him, however, my dad had started calling us, taking us to dinner or a movie, that kind of thing. On these occasions, we didn't really talk about their divorce, instead moving forward as if nothing had happened, as if he had always lived in a separate home from us. It was bizarre and frustrating, but for now we were in a decent place with each other, at least on the surface, and I tried to accept that maybe it would be a while before we could hope for more than that.

It took us just over four hours of driving before we turned onto Bridge Road and zipped into the marina. Lizzy and I smiled excitedly at each other as she pulled the key out of the ignition, eager to begin our summer vacation in the land of white sand, fireflies and bonfires that was Green Island.

We hopped out of the car, my back cracking as I stood up, and popped open the trunk. Just like last year, Patrick rushed over to warmly welcome us, dressed in his dapper standard green and white ensemble. He and a few of the other workers quickly assisted us with our various suitcases and other items, which they wheeled over to the ferry, and we were on board in a matter of minutes.

Once we'd greeted the few miscellaneous familiar faces who would be making the ferry trip with us, Lizzy and I each collapsed into our seats contentedly, settling in for the ride.

"Finally..." she said, looking sublimely happy, "I literally could not be happier to be here. All my stress about the SAT and college applications and all that, it just literally dissolved the moment I stepped on the ferry. And, I just have this feeling that this is going to be the absolute best summer we've ever had."

"I couldn't agree more," I said with a smile, reclining in my seat as Green Island, still tiny in the distance, drew us in once again.

Chapter 35

As Lizzy and I approached the marina in the early morning light on the Fourth of July, people were already busy setting up for the massive fireworks display that Green puts on each year. It was hard to believe it could be Fourth of July already when it had been just over a week since we'd arrived on Green. Lizzy and I had quickly adapted back into the groove of the Green lifestyle. I'd had my first three days of teaching lessons in Charlevoix earlier in the week, and so far I was loving it. Having a little structure and responsibility (not to mention a paycheck!) actually made me enjoy my days of leisure even more.

We spotted Charlotte waiting for us by the nearest marina dock, waving at us and shielding her eyes from the bright morning sun.

"Hey!" she cried as we approached. "Greta's already on the boat, getting a little breakfast spread set up for us and rigging up the fishing poles."

"Any chance the breakfast spread includes coffee?" I asked hopefully, still only about half awake.

"Of course!" Charlotte said with a smile. "Actually, she made some iced vanilla coffee concoction especially for you."

"Aw, she's so sweet," I said, switching my bag from one arm to the other as we followed Charlotte toward the dock.

"I volunteered to come out here and wait for you guys so that I could avoid putting the worms on the hooks," she said, smiling slyly.

"Yeah, I already recruited Breck to bait my hooks and unhook my fish for me," said Lizzy, nudging me affectionately.

"You guys are *such* girls," I said, jokingly shaking my head at them. I'd been fishing with my dad tons of times when I was younger, and slimy worms and their guts didn't really bother me in the least. The only time I got flustered was when a fish swallowed the hook and I could see the desperation in its eyes as I frantically tried to dislodge it before the little guy died. I always liked to throw my fish back, and the few times that I had done so only to have their lifeless bodies remain floating on the surface of the water, I'd nearly felt like crying.

I picked up my pace a little, heading down the dock with more purpose now that I knew there was coffee waiting for me at the end. The other girls were a step behind me, and we all nearly fell into the water when I spun around at the sound of my name. I knew who it was before I saw his face, and suddenly I was very, very awake.

"Brecken!" Reed called again from the shore by the dock, now heading down the dock toward us as I felt Charlotte's and Lizzy's questioning looks burning holes into me from each side.

"Oh, hey Reed," I said, my usual Reed-induced paralysis of the mind setting in instantly. All of the witty lines I had prepared in my daydreams slipped from me the moment I saw his face.

As he approached us, all still rooted in the place we'd been standing when he'd called my name seconds before, he was smirking — that same subtle smile I'd seen last summer.

"You're back," he said, now within a few feet of us, the raspy edge to his voice as mesmerizing as ever. He held my gaze for a second before I looked away, my stomach flipping as though I was on a roller coaster. "Hey Lizzy, hey Charlotte," he added. Both girls mumbled hellos to him, seemingly as flustered as I was by his unexpected presence. I briefly regretted the fact that I hadn't so much as glanced in the mirror after rolling out of bed early this morning, and I self-consciously reached a hand up to smooth my messy ponytail which was sticking out from under my old Detroit Tigers baseball cap. How could I have known that our early morning girls' fishing trip would end up being the day I finally crossed paths with him? Not that lots of makeup and perfectly blow-dried hair were my thing, but I still wished I could have looked a little less unkempt for this encounter.

"Yeah, we just got here a few days ago," I said, relieved to find that I was sounding at least minimally coherent.

"Cool," he said nonchalantly. "You guys heading out fishing?" he asked, looking at the tackle box Lizzy was holding.

"Yeah, that's the plan," I said, sounding about as interesting as a brick wall once again.

"Nice," he said, his blue eyes flashing at me as I found the courage to make eye contact for a second. Somehow he made even the simplest words seem clever and poignant. He seemed to consider something for a second and then spoke again. "I'm having a few people out on my boat to watch the fireworks tonight. Would you want to come?" he asked, looking to the other girls as well when he said this, making it clear the invitation was extended to all of us.

"Yeah, definitely!" Charlotte said, finally unfreezing. She sounded as if she had just been offered a million dollars. "Is it OK if Greta Knox comes too?" she asked. "We all had plans to watch the fireworks together..."

"Yeah, of course. Bring anyone you want," he said, and I could feel that he was looking right at me, so I forced myself to look up again and meet his gaze. I smiled at him, feeling lightheaded as the corners of his mouth again turned up in a slight smile as well. "Well, I'll swing by Lizzy's house around 8:00 or so to pick all of you up on the boat, if that works for you."

"Sounds great," I said, briefly imagining the look on Sarah's face when Reed Whalen arrived to pick up me and Lizzy and our friends.

"Yeah, see you then," Lizzy said, speaking for the first time. I gave a little wave and we turned in silence and headed down the dock, not speaking until we were on the boat.

"Finally!" Greta said. "These iced coffees aren't going to be iced much longer," she complained, handing a large glass to each of us. I took a big swig, feeling the caffeine's effect almost immediately.

"What the hell was that?!" Lizzy demanded, turning to face me now that we were undoubtedly out of earshot of anyone else in the marina.

"Um, yeah, seriously. Not that I'm complaining, but I've been coming here for my whole life and I never even knew that Reed Whalen knew my name until today. How do you know him?" Charlotte asked, as Greta looked on with confusion.

"Wait, what did I miss?!" Greta cried.

"Yeah, how *do* you know him?" Lizzy asked, ignoring Greta, and it was clear she was not at all happy with me.

"Uh, I hung out with him one night last summer," I said timidly, trying to remember why it was exactly that it had seemed like a good idea to keep this information from Lizzy in the first place. "I'm so sorry that I didn't tell you sooner," I sputtered as I saw the hurt in her expression. "Really, Liz, I am. Let's head out and I'll tell you guys every single detail, I promise."

"Yeah, we should head out," Greta said, starting the engine and slowly backing out of the slip into the main lane of the marina. "And maybe someone can also tell me what the F you guys are even talking about, please?"

"Sure. We just ran into Reed Whalen and apparently Brecken is *quite* good buddies with him," Lizzy said.

"Reed Whalen?! Gah! How did I manage to miss the two minutes of this summer when something actually eventful happened," Greta lamented.

Lizzy didn't say anything else as she and Charlotte began filling up plates with the bagels and fruit that Greta had set out for us. I sucked down my coffee as I processed the fact that I would be hanging out with Reed this very night.

As Greta slowly steered us toward one of the small bays formed by the curves of Green Island's western shoreline, Lizzy and Charlotte returned with their plates in hand and began munching.

"All right, time to divulge! Let's hear it," Charlotte said, looking at me expectantly.

And so, I gave them the complete rundown of the last night I was on Green Island the previous summer as they listened intently, with Greta slowly directing the boat toward a weedy spot just offshore where a few other fishing boats were drifting about.

"Why didn't you tell me about this?" Lizzy asked, sounding more than a little hurt.

"I don't know. I guess maybe I felt like a big cliché for having a crush on the same guy as every other girl on this island. And he didn't try to kiss me or anything like that, so I didn't want to seem like some pathetic girl who was trying to imagine that she had something going on with Reed Whalen," I admitted. "I was afraid that analyzing the night would make me realize that I'd made it into a big deal in my head when in actuality it was probably just like every other night in Reed Whalen's life."

"Seriously?" Lizzy asked, sounding appalled. "First of all, I never would have seen it that way, obviously, and I can't believe you thought I would. And second, just because he didn't kiss you doesn't mean he isn't interested. He definitely seemed interested to me back at the marina."

"Uh, yeah! More than just a little interested," Charlotte piped in. "He practically chased you down back there and wants to hang out tonight. I'd say he's definitely into you."

"You guys, come on, I don't want to think like that. I shouldn't let myself, it's just not realistic," I said, hoping Lizzy's irritation with me would pass quickly. "I mean, that's really sweet of you to say and all but this isn't going to be some Molly Ringwald in *Sixteen Candles* scenario where the guy who could have any girl happens, for some inexplicable reason, to want me. That kind of thing doesn't happen in real life, it just doesn't."

"Well, I'm not suggesting this is a *Sixteen Candles* situation. Not even close," Greta said as she turned off the boat's ignition. "I mean, why wouldn't you expect that he'd like you? You're beautiful, and, more importantly, you're an awesome person. On top of the fact that Reed is ridiculously hot, I think he's also a pretty complicated, interesting guy, based on what I know of him. I bet he's intrigued by you."

"Yeah, that's definitely true," Charlotte agreed. "And he was clearly excited to see you this morning."

Lizzy still wasn't saying much, but I could see from her face that she was softening a little bit, a very little bit, as she accepted a fishing pole from Greta.

"So are you guys really up for watching the fireworks from his boat?" I asked hopefully, reaching for a worm and impaling it with Lizzy's hook as it squirmed and she looked away.

"Yeah, for sure," Charlotte said, sounding excited by the prospect.

"Welllll, do you know if Andrew is going to be there?" Greta asked hesitantly. Greta's relationship with Andrew Wells had pretty much fizzled once they both left Green Island at the end of last summer and returned to their respective states. Now that she was dating a new guy, named Ben, who lived back in Winnetka, she had generally been trying to avoid interacting much with Andrew, the whole situation being kind of awkward for her.

"I don't know for sure, but I guess there's probably a good chance that he will be," I said. "If you'd feel weird going, we can just watch the fireworks from the Sutters' boat like we'd planned," I offered, silently praying that she wouldn't take me up on this but also not wanting to put her in an uncomfortable spot.

Greta sighed. "No, it's all right. Watching from Reed's boat sounds fun. It would be stupid to miss it just because Andrew might be there. I have to deal with facing him eventually anyway."

Phew.

I looked over at Lizzy. "Liz, does that sound OK for you tonight?" I asked gently.

"Yeah, sounds good to me," she said, and although she was lacking her usual upbeat enthusiasm, I could tell that she had already somewhat forgiven me for not telling her about my night with Reed.

We all began chattering about the night, speculating as to who else would be on the boat and discussing what to wear as we cast our lines into the water.

Chapter 36

The four of us were sitting on Lizzy's dock a few minutes before 8:00, awaiting Reed's arrival. It had turned into a scorching day and despite my shower just an hour earlier, there was already perspiration forming on my back. Lovely. My nerves certainly weren't helping matters either. I'd been so anxious and jittery just a half hour earlier that Greta had forced me to down a quick glass of white wine to take the edge off.

"Can we move down closer to the end of the dock? I want to sit where it's lower to the water so that I can put my feet in – I'm sweltering," I said. We shifted down about 20 feet and I dipped my toes in the cool water. The refreshing cold felt heavenly, and I could finally take a deep breath despite the suffocating humidity.

"Oh, there they are," Charlotte said with quiet urgency, as all our heads snapped further to the left where Reed's boat was steadily approaching. The calm of an instant earlier immediately left me, replaced by a surge of anxiety as I felt my heart rate quicken.

Lizzy reached over and squeezed my hand, which was surprisingly comforting.

"Just be yourself, Breck," Lizzy said. "Seriously, don't freak out about this. He obviously already likes you."

I wasn't so sure about that, but I smiled back at her nonetheless. Within a few minutes, we could make out some of the various figures standing on deck, and sure enough Andrew Wells was one of them.

"You sure you're gonna be all right hanging out with Andrew?" I asked Greta while the boat was still out of earshot.

"Yeah, no big deal," Greta said confidently, but I could see her eyes were darting about, looking anywhere but at the boat rapidly approaching us with her ex-boyfriend of sorts on board.

I felt paralyzed by awkward trepidation as the boat coasted in next to the Sutters' dock, the people on board greeting us. I forced myself to look at the boat, which was now just feet from the edge of the dock, and found that I was staring right at Reed.

"Hey Brecken," he said, his voice making my body feel electric.

"Hey Reed," I said, trying to convey a calm that I did not feel.

He extended his hand to help me onto the boat as several other people on board held onto the dock posts to steady the boat as we boarded. I placed my hand in his, briefly feeling the warmth radiating from his palm and fingers. I hopped down into the boat and was quickly followed by my three friends.

"Thanks for having us," I said, once we had all boarded and pushed off from the dock, the four of us standing next to Reed for the moment.

"Sure, thanks for coming," he said. "Help yourself to food and everything," he said, gesturing to what appeared to be a catered meal set up downstairs, as well as a fully stocked bar. "Can I get anyone a drink?

My sister's been making margaritas, so I think there's a pitcher of those around somewhere if anyone wants one."

It was quiet for a second. "I guess I'll have a beer, thanks a lot," I said, thinking that starting off with liquor probably wasn't a good idea for me tonight, and the other girls quickly agreed that they, too, would have beers. Reed led the way to a large red cooler filled with a wide variety of beers for us to choose from. I went for a Corona, since it was the first one I spotted that I actually recognized.

As my friends and I filled up our plates with various items from the colorful spread that was laid out in the air conditioned area below deck, I glanced up through the doorway where Reed was standing talking to the girl who was steering the boat. He was barefoot and tan, wearing an old, worn green t-shirt with writing on it and gray shorts. A part of me wished he wasn't so gorgeous, that he wasn't the guy whom every girl on the boat (actually, make that every girl on Green Island) was undoubtedly swooning over. I couldn't resist Reed's pull, but I knew it was for reasons that went beyond his looks. From what I could tell, he seemed to be everything I wanted, somehow packaged in a body that looked like Brad Pitt's dark-haired younger brother and part of a family with more money than they knew how to use.

Greta caught me observing Reed and let out a little laugh. "Looks like someone has a pretty serious case of the Reed Whalens. That's his sister, Stephanie, by the way. She goes to Stanford." She nodded in the direction of the girl Reed was talking with, and I immediately recognized the similarities in their faces, although Stephanie's features didn't gel quite as poetically as Reed's. She was still very pretty though, and she had a friendly, welcoming face that made me think I would like her. I looked enviously at her outfit of cotton shorts and a basic white tank top of the variety that most people call "wife-beaters," a term which my mom had forced me not use with her ardent insistence that it was horribly offensive to her. I regretted that I'd let my friends talk me into wearing a sundress, now feeling certain that I would have been more at ease in my usual, more casual clothes.

By the time we emerged from the lower deck, Reed, his sister and Andrew Wells all appeared to be completely focused on taking down the sails as we neared the marina and prepared to anchor near the deep end of the sand bar. At least thirty other boats were already anchored in this vicinity. It was yet another example of a picturesque Green Island moment – white sailboats and colorful pontoons sprinkled about the sandbar, set to the backdrop of the gorgeous island spotted with old white mansions beneath the painted sunset sky. Sometimes it was hard to believe that this place was real. Well, make that most of the time.

Greta got caught up talking to some super tan, skinny girl I didn't know, so Lizzy, Charlotte and I left her behind and headed to sit with the majority of the party out on the front of the boat. I spotted only a few familiar faces, and Charlotte whispered to me that most of the people were a year or two older than us and she was little more than acquaintances with them. Nonetheless, everyone we met was friendly and talkative, and neighboring boats drifted over to greet us as Ben Harper crooned from the boat speakers. From a distance, I spotted Sarah Sutter and her posse on Shelby Rhode's boat with a small group of people. While, much to my dismay, Sarah hadn't been around this evening to see Reed pick us up on her dock, I had no doubt that she'd caught wind that her little sister and I were hanging out on Reed's boat. I knew she must be seething at the thought and her boat certainly wouldn't be circling by to visit us any time soon.

After four beers, it was getting dark, and I realized I should take a quick trip to the bathroom below deck to pee before the fireworks started. Also, Reed hadn't ventured up to the front of the deck to join us, so I was curious to see what he was up to. I was concerned that my serious case of nerves was making me come off as kind of lame, and I didn't want to let any chance I might have to redeem myself slip away.

I skirted down the relatively narrow space that connected the flat front area of the boat to the main cabin and stepped down. As I turned again to head down the steps to bathroom in the lower cabin, the very same cabin where Reed had cooked me a grilled cheese sandwich less than a year before, I spotted him talking with his sister and another girl near the coolers and bar area. Not wanting to interrupt, I headed downstairs, hoping he would come join everyone else on the front of the boat by the time the fireworks began, if not sooner.

In the dimly lit bathroom mirror, I gave myself a once-over. My forehead was glistening from the heat and the little hairs near my hairline were beginning to curl from the humidity. I tried to smooth them down without much success.

I slid the bathroom door open and as I stepped out, there he was, waiting, just a few feet from me. Unsurprisingly, the heat didn't seem to be compromising his appearance in the slightest, and I could barely keep myself from staring across the hallway at him.

"That was quite a Houdini you pulled on me last summer," he said, his scratchy voice making me feel lightheaded. As I was learning was often the case with him, his face wore a hint of a smile, barely there really, unless you were looking for it.

"Houdini?" I asked, confused.

"Yeah, you know, disappearing act."

"Oh," I said with a nervous laugh. "Yeah, I guess maybe I did. Not intentionally though. My mom showed up the next morning and needed me back home, so I left Green Island that day."

I was praying no one else would venture down to the lower cabin to interrupt my moment alone with him. He was leaning against the wall across from me, and I realized I was still planted just inches beyond the bathroom door. I took a step closer to him, not wanting to seem timid or disinterested, not wanting the fact that my stomach was flip-flopping every second to be evident.

"Yeah, eventually I figured out that you'd left Green." The subtle smirk was gone for the moment. He paused for a few seconds before he continued, seemingly lost in thought for an instant. I liked observing him. I watched him, studied him, with more intrigue than I had anyone or anything else in my life, as though I was going to be quizzed on every detail of him, every mannerism, every motion. I'd never been mesmerized like this before, doubted I ever would be again, and wished I wasn't just one of the many girls whom he affected in this way.

He spoke again. "So, how come you never called?" he asked gently. He paused for another second as I frantically considered his question. "I don't mean to make it weird," he went on, "I was just curious if you had a boyfriend or just didn't feel like calling or what?" The smirk returned then. "I guess I'm just trying to see if I might still have a chance."

Why didn't I *call him*? A *chance*? Huh? Was I drunker than I thought? I had no clue what he was talking about.

"I don't know what you mean," I said slowly. "I didn't even have your phone number."

"I gave it to Sarah Sutter, I asked her to give it to you. I knew she'd see you once she got back home," he said, now sounding slightly agitated as an unfamiliar expression darkened his face and he ran his hand through his hair.

Ah, Sarah Sutter, I should have known. "Sarah more or less hates me. We've never really gotten along. I gave up trying to figure her out a long time ago. Anyway, she never gave me your number," I explained, as the fact that Reed had been trying to get in touch with me began to sink in. I felt dizzy, and it could have just been the rocking of the boat, but I really didn't think so.

He nodded slightly, as if considering this information. "Well that's good to know," he said, just as his sister came bounding down the stairs.

"Oh, hey," Stephanie said, clearly realizing she had burst into our conversation. "I'm just running into the bathroom, don't mind me," she said, flashing me a smile.

I laughed. "No problem, I was just going to head up to watch the fireworks anyway," I said, my usual awkwardness returning. She had already closed the bathroom door by the time the words were out of my mouth.

"Yeah, let's head up there now so we don't miss them," Reed said, stepping back and motioning for me to go first up the stairs, which I did. I grabbed two more beers on the main deck and then walked carefully down the narrow connector to the front of the boat where the party was now in full swing. I could hear that Reed was a few steps behind me as I focused on not losing my balance. By the time I sat down next to Lizzy and glanced back at him, he was already talking with a few guys I didn't recognize across the bow. Our conversation was still occupying my thoughts completely.

"You OK?" Lizzy asked, turning away from the conversation. "I was starting to think you fell overboard."

"I'm fine," I said with a reassuring smile as I half listened to the conversation around me, trying to disguise the fact that I was lost in thought. Lizzy, Charlotte and Greta were engrossed in a debate with Andrew Wells (who, incidentally, was sitting noticeably close to Greta and hanging on her every word), Todd Hamlin and John Cooke regarding what constituted the various "bases" of a hook up. The guys were insisting that kissing was not a base, while the girls, Lizzy especially, insisted that kissing was inarguably first base. I tuned them out and tried to peek casually over to the spot almost directly behind me where Reed had been hanging out when I sat down.

However, as I turned my head to look at Reed, I found myself staring right at his legs, only about a foot away from me. I glanced upward to see his blue eyes looking down at me with amusement.

"Mind if I sit?" he asked.

I patted the spot next to me as an invitation, and he sat down. It reminded me of our night on the dock the year before. I could feel Lizzy, Greta and Charlotte watching us, failing miserably at any efforts they may have been making to be discreet.

Before I could get even one word out, the first thunderous series of fireworks began bursting across the sky, and they were met with a chorus of "oohs" and "ahs" from the people aboard the many boats now docked around us. Corks flew from several bottles of champagne on our boat, including one held by Lizzy, who quickly passed overflowing glasses to both me and Reed. A steady stream of explosions continued as elaborate, colorful patterns of light illuminated the starry night sky. I was always surprised by how strikingly beautiful fireworks could be, regardless of the number of times I had seen them before. I was sipping my glass of champagne, my head tilted toward the sky, when I felt Reed shift, ever so slightly, so that our arms, which had been a few inches apart, were touching. It sounds like it would be such a tiny thing, touching arms, but it wasn't tiny at all. I kept my eyes on the fireworks, trying to seem unaffected, trying not to betray the intensity that I felt from the simple brushing of arms, trying to keep an absurd smile from spreading across my face.

Chapter 37

The fireworks ended with a grand finale that included a continuous barrage of colorful lights and must have lasted at least ten minutes. I had never seen anything like it. As you might expect, Green wasn't a place where they scrimped on the fireworks.

As the finale concluded, I asked Lizzy to pass me the champagne bottle for a refill, which I immediately realized had been a mistake because in order to accept it from her, I was forced to pull my left arm away from Reed's.

"Want more?" I asked him, holding the bottle in his direction, looking at him directly for the first time since he'd sat down next to me.

"I think I'm switching back to beer. Thanks anyway though," he said. "I can't believe it's still so hot out. It must be, what, eleven o'clock by now?"

"We could go swimming," I suggested, desperate to escape the thick coat of sweat that had dampened my entire body over the past several hours. I'd been having visions of plunging into the cool water since I'd stepped onto the boat.

"Really?" he asked.

"Yeah, why not?"

"You going in your clothes?"

"Um..." I hadn't thought this through well, clearly. "Yeah, sure. I think my dress can survive a swim," I said with a smile.

"All right then," he said, now flashing me a full-on smile, making my pulse quicken. The thoughts that should have filled my mind were completely absent. I didn't think about the dangers of swimming drunk or in the dark. I didn't consider the likelihood of getting run over by one of the many nearby boats. The truth was, in that moment, I didn't care about any of it.

He stood up and reached his hand down to pull me up as well. I felt a shiver of happiness shoot down my body as our fingers touched.

"Where are you going?" I heard Lizzy hiss as he pulled me up.

"Swimming..." I said.

"Now? Here?" Lizzy asked with more than a hint of panic in her voice.

I nodded.

"Ooh, I'm coming!" Greta cried, overhearing us. "This heat is torture."

I smiled at her, took a few steps toward the side of the boat and then jumped over the edge. I heard another splash follow close behind me as I plunged into Lake Michigan, the water somewhere between refreshing and numbing. I quickly resurfaced, pushing my hair out of my face as I laughed out loud. I opened my eyes to see Reed, Greta and Charlotte bobbing nearby. Within seconds, we were surrounded by splashes as nearly our entire party jumped overboard. I looked up to see Lizzy still peering over the edge.

"C'mon in Liz! It's soo refreshing!" I yelled to her.

"Yeah, seriously, it's heaven!" Charlotte cried.

I could tell she was considering it.

"Elizabeth Jane Sutter, get in the water!" I insisted.

"Geez, all right, fine," Lizzy said, in response to which Greta, Charlotte and I all exploded in cheers. A moment later, Lizzy's dainty frame flew off the boat, her squeals filling the air. I could see people from a few of the other nearby boats watching us with varying levels of amusement. After a few more dives under the dark water, I began to shiver and my three friends and I climbed up the ladder on the back of the boat. I'd kept my eyes on Reed as we swam, but he'd been busy horsing around with other people in the water.

We all stood dripping near the back of the boat, crossing our arms over our boobs and trying to stay warm as others began climbing up out of the water as well.

"You guys look like you could probably use a few towels," said Stephanie Whalen, emerging from the lower cabin with a stack of fluffy multi-colored towels in hand. She was one of the few who had stayed on the boat. "We won't have enough for everyone, so you were smart to get up here first," she said with a warm smile.

"Thanks so much!" I said, as we pulled towels off the pile and wrapped them around ourselves.

"You're a lifesaver, Stephanie, thanks," said Greta.

We grabbed fresh beers and snuggled together up on the front of the boat as the other kids continued streaming out of the water as well.

"He *loves* you," said Lizzy, stretching out the word "loves" in a joking way.

"Stop," I said, shaking my head. "We've barely even talked all night."

"Yeah, but he's always watching you," said Charlotte. "I had a perfect view of him all night and he was constantly looking over at you. It's so sweet. I mean, it's Reed Whalen! Unreal."

I wanted to believe them. I wanted nothing more than for them to be right. I looked over to the back of the boat where Reed was dripping, his tone, tanned upper body glimmering in the moonlight. He was talking to a few girls, only one of whom I recognized, each of them nearly falling all over him. I looked away, a knot in my stomach as I considered how much credence I should give to his comment about wondering if he had a chance with me. Had he even said that? I was beginning to worry that I was misremembering our conversation. And, for all I knew he said that to all the girls.

"So, what's going on with Andrew?" I asked Greta, eager to change the subject. "He seemed to be snuggling right up to you tonight."

"Shit, did it seem that way to you too? I thought he was being really touchy, but I didn't know if it was all in my head," Greta said.

"Uh no, he was all over you. On the boat and in the water," Charlotte piped in.

"Do you still have feelings for him at all?" Lizzy asked, sounding concerned.

"No, I really don't. I mean, honestly, I guess it's kind of flattering that he still seems interested, but what I have with Ben is so much better than the relationship I had with Andrew. Andrew's just too...I don't know, worried about his image or something. Kind of phony. I mean, he has good sides to him, but we weren't the right match," Greta said, sounding certain.

"Well it must be nice to know for sure that you're over him," I offered, trying to focus on the conversation instead of on Reed's every move on the other side of the boat.

"Yeah, it is," Greta agreed. "And, I'm *soo* excited for Ben to visit next week. I can't wait for you guys to meet him. You'll love him."

We discussed Ben's upcoming visit and the fact that Greta's parents wouldn't even let him stay in a bedroom on the same side of the house as Greta. I managed to keep us off the topic of Reed Whalen as the boat made its way back to the marina. A few people floated in and out of our conversation, asking if we were coming to the after-party at John Cooke's house. We all answered noncommittally – I think that between our early morning fishing, a long day in the sun and an evening of drinking, the four of us were all pretty much ready to call it a night when the boat docked. Well, OK, maybe not me. I was still wide awake, wanting more time with Reed but realizing that I probably wouldn't get it at this point.

My thoughts kept racing back to our conversation in the cabin. I tried to recall what his exact words had been. *I wanted to see if there's any way I have a chance?* Was that it? Something like that. I needed to understand if he meant what I thought he meant. I wasn't ready for the night to end. I wondered if Reed would be going to this after-party. He didn't seem to be very into those types of things, from what I could tell, but it was hard to be sure. And, I didn't want to be chasing him around either. I just wished I could teleport us back to that night last summer, when I had him all to myself and felt like I could actually relax long enough to be myself.

"I'm dying for a shower," Lizzy mumbled as we climbed off the boat.

"Yeah, me too, big time," Greta agreed, her wet sundress clinging to her curvy figure.

We worked our way through the little crowd exiting Reed's boat in order to find him and thank him before we took off. I felt a hint of panic, fear that tonight may have marked my BIG CHANCE with Reed and that I'd blown it.

He was finishing tying up the boat by himself as we approached.

"Thanks for having us tonight, Reed!" Greta said enthusiastically. "We had the best time."

"Yeah, thanks so much," I said, hoping maybe he would hug us goodbye.

He looked up, glancing from Greta to me. "Any time. Really glad you could all make it," he said, his scratchy voice warm and genuine. "So you guys are taking off?" he asked, and I thought (hoped!) he sounded a little disappointed.

"Uh, yeah," I said awkwardly. "I think we're going to pass on the after-party tonight."

He didn't say anything for an instant. I was learning that these thoughtful little pauses were a trait of his. "Can you stay for a little while?" he then asked bluntly, the question clearly directed at me. "I can walk her home in a little bit," he said to Lizzy, as if asking her permission.

I felt four pairs of eyes on me. "OK, sure, I can stay," I said, my heart palpitating once again.

Chapter 38

Once Reed's boat was tied up in the marina, which was now quiet and relatively empty, Reed and I climbed back on as the last of his guests departed down the dock, with several of them giving me quizzical looks as I lingered behind with Reed.

"Thanks for staying," he said. "I feel like we barely got to hang out tonight."

My mind was a jumble of nerves and excitement. This whole situation was so foreign that it was all I could do to try to act remotely normal. "Yeah, I know," was all I could think to say in response, as we worked our way back out to the front of the boat where we sat on the edge, our legs dangling off.

Reed had brought a little cooler up to the front and offered me a beer, which I turned down. I'd definitely had enough to drink already.

"So," I said, thinking I didn't want to miss out on this chance to get to know him better, "if I had gotten your number from Sarah and I had decided to call you, what would you have said?"

He laughed at this. "I don't know really. Anything. Nothing. I'm pretty sure we would have found something to talk about." He cast a sideways glance at me. My hair was finally starting to dry and was devolving into a tangled mess blowing around in the breeze. I tried to smooth it a bit with my hands and pulled it into a damp ponytail. "I just wanted to talk to you more. Get to know you," he said.

"Well, looks like you've got another chance," I said, hearing my voice take on an unfamiliar, flirtatious tone.

He looked at me and smiled, more than a smirk, a genuine smile. I could never ever in a million years have imagined myself using the phrase 'devastatingly handsome' to describe someone — it sounded like a line I would make fun of my mom for using — and yet those words popped into my mind as I watched him smile.

"So, how was your year?" he asked. "How are things with your parents? Any better?"

"Not really. Things with them are pretty bad actually. They're divorced now. My mom's having a pretty tough time, well they both are I guess, in their own ways. Royal Oak — the city where we live — it's a pretty small place. Somehow everyone knows about my dad cheating with my mom's friend. The whole thing is just really humiliating for her. She's this really strong, smart, kind woman, and it's just so unfair and wrong that she has to go through all of this."

"That must be hard," he said slowly, as if really considering each word I had said. "How are things with your dad?"

"Not so good. I've been pretty upset with him about the whole situation, and rather than trying to talk to me or anything, he just kind of withdrew from everything. I've barely even been to his new apartment, and he just consumes himself with his painting and work. I know that he feels embarrassed and like he let me and Griffin — that's my brother — down, but I think the way he's handled the whole thing has been even worse than his cheating. I don't mean to bash him, I love him of course, so much, but it's just that I feel like everything I knew came crashing down around me and he was more worried about himself than he was about me and my brother..." I paused for a minute, wondering if this was more information that Reed had been looking for. "So, anyway, it was a pretty messed up year. It's been really refreshing to get a little break from it all back here."

"Well, you seem like you're handling it better than most people would," Reed said, looking at me intently for a second. "But it sounds like a pretty shitty situation – I'm really sorry."

"Thanks," I said, feeling a little worked up and desperately hoping I wouldn't start crying. "How about you? How was your year?" I asked, shifting the conversation away from my dysfunctional family.

"It was pretty good. You know, except for waiting by the phone for you to call," he winked at me and smirked as he said this.

"Somehow I feel pretty confident that didn't happen," I said with a laugh, my mood lightening. "So you graduated, right? What are your plans for next year?" Of course, I had already heard that he had been offered lacrosse scholarships at Duke, UVA and Harvard, but I wasn't about to admit that I was keeping up on the Reed Whalen gossip around the island. Plus, no one seemed to be certain of what his actual plans were.

"Going to Amherst in the fall. Well, I head there in late August actually, for freshman orientation before classes start."

"Where's Amherst?" I asked, slightly embarrassed that I'd never even heard of it.

"Oh, it's in Massachusetts. It's a pretty small school — only about fifteen hundred students. They have a great writing program, and I have a few friends who go there and really like it. I'm definitely ready for the change of scene." He didn't even mention anything about his lacrosse scholarships, which only made him infinitely more attractive. I didn't know many teenage guys who would skip over mentioning the accolade of scholarship offers from the top lacrosse schools in the country.

"Are you gonna play lacrosse there?" I asked, curious to see if this would prompt him to mention all his scholarships.

"Nah," he said casually. "I thought about it, but I'm pretty ready to be done with lacrosse," he said, and I could tell this was a more complicated issue than he was making it out to be.

Interesting. I hadn't heard anyone on Green even mention that Reed was turning down all his lacrosse offers to attend this college called Amherst. Turns out the gossip mill wasn't quite that reliable, even in a tiny place like Green.

"That's cool," I said. "Well you must be excited about starting college. I can't wait," I said, feeling envious of the incoming freshmen girls at Amherst — imagine showing up at your dorm to find Reed Whalen would be living just down the hall. I felt momentarily ill with jealousy at this mental image.

"Yeah, I'm looking forward to it," he said, kind of nonchalantly. "You're a senior next year, right?" he asked, and I felt nothing short of thrilled that he remembered this detail about me.

I nodded.

"Any plans after that yet?" he asked.

"Nothing for sure yet. I mean, I have to do my college applications this fall and all that, but I'll probably go to an in-state school. So, most likely University of Michigan or Michigan State." I was tempted to tell him about how I'd love to go away somewhere, to New York or California or somewhere exciting... but, since that would never be possible for me financially, I didn't mention it. The last thing I wanted was to be viewed as some sort of pity case in Reed's eyes.

"I have a couple friends going to Michigan," he said. "I hear Ann Arbor is one of the best college towns — my dad and I have been planning to check out a football game there one of these years."

"Yeah, hopefully I'll get in there. It's still a ways off anyway."

He nodded, and as I turned my head toward him to continue talking, he gently grabbed my face with his hand, catching me slightly off-guard once again. An instant later, I felt his lips on mine. His kiss was gentle — I literally felt myself melting away as he continued to kiss me, as I kissed him back. I brushed his face with my hand as well, felt his trace of stubble on his cheek. After a minute, he pulled away slowly, smiling at me.

"Hey, come with me," he said then, pulling me up off the edge of the boat. He kept his fingers intertwined in mine as he led me down into the lower cabin of the boat.

My heart started racing as I wondered what exactly he had in mind. I mean, I couldn't deny that I was pretty smitten, but I hoped he didn't think we were going to be having sex or something. He didn't seem like that type, I hoped he wasn't.

He opened the door to the little fridge and pulled out a dark bottle.

"I bought this after you were over here last time, before I realized you'd left Green," he said, holding it out to me. Worcestershire sauce. I laughed, unable to believe he'd remembered. "So, you want a grilled cheese?" he offered.

"Sure, I'd love one," I said. "That's pretty sweet, that you bought that for me, thanks."

"Well, I had to see what all the hype was about. I tried it out."

"And? You loved it, right?"

"Uh, sort of. Actually no, I thought it tasted like shit," he said, laughing. "And, it's too overpowering, you can't taste the grilled cheese."

"Whaaat? You're crazy," I said, unable to stop smiling.

"Whatever you say."

"Can I help you cook?" I offered.

"Nah, I've got it," he said. "But can you grab some paper plates?"

I returned down the stairs a minute later with the plates he'd requested. He was looking right at me as I stepped down the stairs.

"You're so beautiful," he said, his voice sounding so genuine that he somehow avoided sounding cheesy. "Really, it's..." he trailed off.

I felt myself blush, completely at a loss for how to respond.

"Thanks..." I said, wondering how I'd found myself in this bizarre situation where *Reed* was telling *me* that *I* was beautiful. I wasn't sure what to do or say next, so I reached over and handed the plates to him.

"Thanks," he said as he took the plates from me. "Sorry, I didn't mean to say it like that. It's just, I've never met anyone like you. I haven't been able to stop thinking about you all year. I figured that once I talked to you, you'd just be another shallow beautiful girl, but then, that night we hung out, you were the most interesting and incredible girl I've ever met. Really. And, then you just disappeared, and even after a year, I still thought about you all the time. Now that you're back, it's just, I really don't want to fuck it up." He paused and then continued, seeming actually a little bit flustered, the cool facade I'd always seen gone for the moment. "I know I probably shouldn't be saying this, and I don't want to scare you off or anything, but the summer is so short. I don't want to let the weeks waste away, so I figured I should just put this all out there."

I might as well have been standing with my jaw on the ground for the degree of shock I felt as I heard these words come out of his mouth. How could it be possible that Reed felt this way about me? The very same inexplicable way I felt about him. Things like that really didn't happen – did they? Certainly not to girls like me with guys like Reed Whalen. I couldn't even respond, had no clue where to begin.

He was staring at me, in a way that looked slightly concerned, as if he expected I would turn and run away. "So, you're looking at me like I'm crazy..." he said, cracking a little smile, breaking the silence which was probably awkward to him but which I hadn't even noticed.

"I feel the same way," I said finally. "Honestly, I feel exactly the same way. I thought I was crazy though. Everything you just said, I might as well have been the one talking about how I felt all year about you. About the way I still feel," I said, surprised that I'd been able to express my thoughts. I'd never been good at saying how I felt, but somehow the words had come crashing out.

He turned off the stove, walked the few steps over to me and began kissing me. I mean, really kissing me. He pressed me against the wall and kissed my lips, then my neck, my lips again. I didn't even have time to feel insecure about the fact that these were more or less my first real kisses. Instead, it all just happened kind of instinctively.

Eventually we moved into the bedroom off the kitchen. We only kissed, and it was perfect. We kissed for hours, rolling around on the bed, our bodies pressed against each other. He never tried to reach under my dress, never tried to pressure me to do anything more. When I finally got up to go to the bathroom, the kitchen clock read 3:05 A.M. Hopefully Lizzy wasn't waiting up for me. Our cold uneaten grilled cheeses sat on the counter, and I smiled to myself as I passed them in the dim light of the kitchen.

"I hate to say this," I said reluctantly a few minutes later, walking back into the bedroom, "but I should really get going. It's already three o'clock, and I don't want Lizzy worrying about me."

He shook his head, his trademark smirk on his face, a piece of his now disheveled hair falling into his eye. "Ten more minutes?" he asked, reaching for my hand and pulling me back toward the bed. How could I be expected to say *no* to a face like that?

I curled up beside him, and after what was definitely more than ten minutes, he agreed that he should probably get me home.

We shuffled down the beach in a groggy state, his arm around my shoulder, my lips feeling sweetly raw and chaffed from his stubble.

"So, what are you up to tomorrow?" he asked me, his voice bringing me out of my daze.

"Nothing really planned. I don't have to work, so I'll probably just go to the beach and hang out," I told him.

"Can I take you to dinner?" he asked.

I nodded, unable to contain my smile, as we turned up the pathway to the Sutters' house.

"OK, cool. I'll stop by here around seven, if that works for you."

"Seven sounds good," I told him, as we reached the Sutters' doorway.

He gave me another quick kiss on the lips. "See you tomorrow then," he said, his smirk returning.

I turned in the darkness and pushed open their front door, knowing that despite being completely exhausted, it was going to be a while before I was able to sleep. I crept up the stairs slowly, trying to minimize the creaking of the floor panels. As I reached the second floor, I saw a line of light peering through the doorway to the third floor, letting me know that Lizzy was still awake.

Chapter 39

"I was about to give up on you!" Lizzy said as I excitedly pushed open her bedroom door and flopped onto her bed in a state of bliss. She was snuggled under a thin blanket in the large, comfy arm chair in her little bedroom, with her wispy hair knotted up in a bun and her reading glasses on. "I got sucked into this book though, so I was kind of happy to have an excuse to stay up reading it," she said, holding out a copy of *The Alchemist*, which had been nestled in her lap.

"I'm so sorry for keeping you up," I said lightheartedly from my sprawled out position on my back. "But this night was in-cred-i-ble." I turned onto my stomach and propped my chin up on my hands so that I could see Lizzy better.

"Eee – tell me everything!" she said, climbing over to the bed to lie down next to me. "And I mean *everything*!" she said pointedly, clearly referencing my failure to tell her about my night with Reed last summer.

With that I launched into a detailed retelling of my night, beginning with my initial conversation with Reed down in the cabin. Lizzy was horrified, although not surprised, of course, that her sister had failed to pass Reed's number on to me.

"I can't believe this is happening," Lizzy said wistfully when I finished my story. "What are you thinking?" she asked.

"I don't even know," I said. "I mean, the way he makes me feel is unreal. I never thought I would be the type of person to be all sappy and dramatic, but now I feel like a lovesick idiot."

Lizzy smiled. "It's really cute – like a fairy tale or something. So, I guess this means you're not asexual after all," she said, elbowing me.

"Ha, yeah, I guess not. I'm completely exhausted. I'm gonna head to bed. I really am sorry for keeping you up," I said, giving her a hug as I stood up from the bed.

"'Night Breck. Love you," she said as I headed out of her room and collapsed happily in my bed. I fell right asleep, still wearing my now dry sundress with my hair in a tangled mess and my face unwashed. I wasn't ready to let go of any part of this night just yet.

• • • • •

Given that I had no idea what kind of restaurant Reed and I would be going to for dinner, I hadn't the slightest idea what I should wear.

"Sundress!" Lizzy insisted from her bedroom across the hall as I raked through the minimal wardrobe that had accompanied me to Green. Lizzy essentially wore nothing but sundresses (and bathing suits) in the summer. She would always insist that sundresses were practically as comfortable as wearing nothing at all, but they looked dressy enough to go almost anywhere, and therefore were the perfect outfit for all occasions. I wasn't a big fan of sundresses in general, but since I found myself putting one on for the second night in a row, I couldn't argue that there wasn't at least a little merit to Lizzy's claims about their versatility. I'd borrowed a pair of Lizzy's black leather flat sandals, which looked perfect with the multi-colored paisley Anthropologie sundress I was wearing, a birthday gift from Lizzy. After just a few days in the sun, I had a decent base tan and a few faint freckles were surfacing on my nose and cheeks.

"How do I look?" I asked Lizzy, who was busy getting ready herself for dinner at the Club with Greta, Charlotte and a few other people.

"You look good," Lizzy said, giving me a once-over. "You should put some mascara on though, it'll make your eyes stand out even more."

I frowned in response. "You know I suck at putting on makeup."

"Yeah, yeah, well you have to learn eventually," Lizzy said, without the slightest bit of sympathy. Lizzy loathed her blonde eyelashes and had been an expert in mascara application since late middle school. She handed me a tube of her Chanel mascara. "Here, you can have this one," she said.

"Can you put it on for me?" I asked hopefully.

"Nope. But I'll watch and give you tips. Practice makes perfect," she said with a smile. "Anyway, I can't send you off to college unable to do your own makeup. And based on how bad you are at it, you're going to need a whole year to learn."

"Ha, maybe I just pretend to be bad at it so you'll do it for me," I joked as we headed into our shared bathroom where the lighting was much better. I cringed inside at the thought of being separated from Lizzy the next fall. Although I realized we were probably too dependent on each other and forging our own paths would supposedly be good for us and all that (at least according to my mom), I couldn't imagine my days without my best friend by my side. She was already looking at lots of east coast schools, and I knew there was no chance that she'd stay in-state for college. I certainly couldn't blame her for that, although I knew she felt bad that she'd be leaving me behind in good old Michigan.

It took a few Q-tips to wash off the spots where I'd missed my lashes with the mascara wand and created black streaks on my eyelids, but after a few minutes, Lizzy gave her seal of approval. It was just before seven o'clock, and after a little pep talk from Lizzy, I headed out by the dock to wait for Reed, not wanting him to come to the door and be subjected to making small talk with Mr. and Mrs. Sutter. I hadn't seen Sarah since I'd spotted her on Shelby's boat last night, so I hadn't had the chance to confront her about not giving me Reed's phone number. Truthfully, I didn't even know if it was worth bringing it up to her. It was looking like it hadn't cost me the chance to get to know Reed (which I was sure she would be disappointed to learn), and I knew nothing productive would come from talking to her anyway. She was pretty much a lost cause in my book.

Chapter 40

"So, there's been a change in plans..." Reed said as I stood up from the spot where I'd been sitting to wait for him, near the base of the dock. His dark hair was damp, smelling like he'd just showered. He was wearing a light blue Polo shirt and khaki shorts with a worn pair of gray flip flops, looking generally more preppy than the other times I'd seen him.

He smiled at me and then kissed me quickly on the lips, which caught me off-guard. It was one thing to have a late night makeout session on his boat after hours of drinking, but an evening kiss on the lips on the Sutters' front lawn meant that the whole island would undoubtedly catch word of it before the sun had even set. Apparently he didn't mind who knew about the two of us, and this realization made me so exuberantly happy that I literally thought I might float away.

"Hey," I said, as our faces separated. "So what's the change in plans? No dinner?"

"Welllll, I was planning on taking you to this place called The Rowe Inn – it's one of my favorite restaurants and it's just outside Charlevoix. But it turns out my dad has to head back to New York tomorrow for work, and he'll be gone for at least two weeks. By then my sister is going to be back in Chicago to finish her internship and we won't see her again before she heads back to California for school, so my parents really want us to have a family dinner before he leaves."

I tried to hide my disappointment, the floating sensation dissipating instantly.

"That's totally fine," I said, hoping that I sounded convincing. "We'll just get dinner another time – you can't miss your family dinner."

"Uh, no way. You're not getting out of it that easily. You have to have dinner with my family, seriously, I'm forcing you. My parents are really good cooks, so at least I can promise the food will be better than my grilled cheeses."

"I don't want to intrude..." I said, feeling panicked at the thought of dinner with the whole Whalen family. I was intimidated enough when I thought it was just going to be me and Reed!

"You won't be." He flashed me a smile. "Everyone wants you there."

"All right then... Count me in," I said, not feeling like there was any way around it. He took my hand in his and we started down the beach toward his house, which I knew was located almost directly on the opposite side of Green from the Sutters' house.

"So what's your dad's job, that he's heading back to New York for?" I asked as we walked, curious about how exactly it was that the Whalens were so rich.

"He works at a bank," Reed said quickly.

"You're pretty cryptic," I said with a laugh. "What does he *do* at the bank? I need a little background here before I meet the parents."

"Fair enough," he said, giving me his slight smile. "He's the president of a bank that was founded by my great-grandfather. I guess there's some potential transaction going on with a smaller bank, so he has to be back in New York to deal with it."

"Hmm, so did your grandfather run the bank too?"

"No, actually my grandfather's brother did, but my grandfather was involved, on the board of directors and stuff like that. His brother didn't have kids, and my dad was really into finance and went to business school and all that, so I guess he was the only one who made sense to take over."

"So, is there any pressure then for you to continue the legacy?" I asked, thinking that maybe some rich families actually were like they seemed in the movies, always obsessed with their children following in their footsteps.

"Nah, not at all. They're really supportive of me wanting to be a writer."

"That's good. What about your mom? What's her story?"

"Her story?" He laughed. "You're funny. Well, I'd say her story is that she's a pediatric oncologist at Sloan-Kettering, in the city, and she's really devoted to her work but it's really draining, so she's happy to get a break from it, too. She loves it in northern Michigan. I think Green Island is maybe a little... stuck up, I guess, for her liking, but if it was up to her I think she would seriously consider moving to northern Michigan permanently. She just seems to completely unwind here. She spends tons of time on our gardens, I'm sure she'll give you a tour if you want. She takes two months off from work every summer to be here, although she flies back to New York a fair amount when her patients need her specifically."

Geez. I thought the Whalens were daunting enough based on their money and good looks. Now it turns out they were genius saints too!

He must have sensed my concerns.

"They're really easy-going, seriously. Sorry, this is kind of a shitty first date, I know."

"No, no, I'm excited to meet them," I said, which was true, despite the intimidation factor. "It's just that your family sounds so together and accomplished and all that." Truthfully, I was more than a little worried that they would be underwhelmed by me, but I didn't want to say that and seem insecure. "Oh, listen to this," I said, changing the subject and telling him about how Mrs. Sutter had mentioned at breakfast that she'd heard a group of kids were jumping into the dark, crowded waters near the fireworks after a night of drinking and that she was thankful her kids were too responsible to do anything like that...

"Ha, do you think she knew and was just trying to lay on the guilt?" Reed asked.

"Nah, she's more direct than that. Luckily Sarah never eats breakfast and wasn't around, or she definitely would have jumped at the opportunity to sell us out."

"What's that girl's deal, anyway?" Reed asked. I just shrugged as we turned down the path to the Whalens' mansion among mansions, thinking that I'd been wondering the same thing since I was seven years old.

"Anything else I need to know before I meet them?" I asked, suddenly feeling desperately anxious, as we stood on the Whalens' front porch.

He just smiled his usual smile and shook his head as he pushed open the door. The pungent aroma of herbs and barbecuing meat rushed over me as we stepped into the welcoming front hall. The furniture in the hallway – two benches and a table – had a shabby chic look to them, as did the couch, arm chairs, rug and simple decorative pieces in the room directly to my left. We stood in the hallway for a second and slipped off our shoes. The paisley fabrics in muted tones and the antique-y looking chandelier that hung overhead were just what I would have imagined seeing in the Kennedy cottages in Hyannis Port. (Blame this on spending so much time with the Kennedy-obsessed Sutters, I couldn't help but relate everything back to their beloved Camelot.) It felt like a home the moment I walked in, which was both comforting and distressing given that my own house hadn't even felt like home to me since my dad had moved out.

"Oh good, you're here! Just in time!" exclaimed a woman who had just come cruising into the front hall, presumably Reed's mom. Her dark hair was cut stylishly short, and she wore a fitted knee-length, casual tan dress and minimal makeup. Her skin was a deep tan, her arms were well-toned (probably a benefit of all that gardening Reed was talking about), and I saw immediately where Reed had gotten his bright blue eyes and long dark lashes.

"Hi, Brecken, we're so glad you were able to join us," she said, turning to me giving me possibly the warmest, kindest smile I had ever seen. She looked directly into my eyes as she spoke, and I could just imagine how reassuring she would be as a doctor.

"It's so nice to meet you, Mrs. – I mean, Doctor Whalen," I said, thankful that I'd at least sort of caught my mistake. "Thank you so much for inviting me over for dinner."

"Please, call me Ellen, I insist," she said smiling again.

"C'mon," Reed said, grabbing my hand and gesturing for me to follow him into the kitchen, his mom trailing behind us.

Stephanie Whalen was sitting on a stool at the countertop island in the middle of the expansive kitchen, drinking a glass of white wine and flipping through a magazine. "Table's all set," she said to her mom, who had returned to the stove top where something that smelled delicious was bubbling away. Stephanie's dark hair was scraped back in a messy ponytail, and she wore a loose blue t-shirt and a pair of gray Hardtail sweatpants. For the second time in two days, I was envious of her comfortable outfit. Lizzy and her sundresses, why did I listen?!

"Hey, Brecken. How's it going?" Stephanie asked casually, looking up from her magazine.

"Pretty good, how are you?" I asked. "I heard you're leaving Green Island soon?"

"Yeah," she said, "unfortunately. I have an internship at a hospital in Chicago this summer, and I have a long weekend off for Fourth of July, but I have to head back to Chicago the day after tomorrow and won't have another long weekend, so I don't think I'm gonna have time to get back here again this summer."

"Is this your first summer on Green Island?" Ellen asked me, as she drained pasta over the sink. "Reed mentioned that you're here with the Sutters."

"I was here last summer too. After one summer on Green Island, I was dying to get back though. It's so... magical here," I said.

"Isn't it?" she agreed, flashing her flawless smile at me. "My husband's parents bought this house before he was born, so he grew up spending his summers here. I'd never been to northern Michigan before the first time he brought me here – that was back in 1969, if you can believe it – and I just fell in love with this area. It's such a great escape." She poured an aromatic sauce over the pasta as she talked.

"I couldn't agree more," I said, thinking that despite their vast differences in lifestyle, I could see my mom and Ellen being good friends.

"Hey Pops," Reed said, as a handsome middle-aged man walked through a back entrance balancing what appeared to be two pork tenderloins on a tray in one hand and a variety of barbecue tools in the other.

"Hey guys!" he exclaimed jovially in a booming voice. "Reed, will you take these from me? I have to grab the corn off the grill too." Reed took the tray of meat from his dad, who I expected to turn right around and head back out for the corn. Instead, he extended his newly free hand to me.

"You must be Brecken," he said, his voice filling the room, as I stuck out my hand to shake his. "Great to meet you. Hope you brought your appetite."

"Nice to meet you too, Mr. Whalen," I said. Clearly, Reed's good looks and charm were not the result of chance.

"Please, call me Dan. If you call me Mr. Whalen, you'll make me feel old. With my youngest kid going off to college, I don't need anything else reminding me of my age," he said with a good-natured twinkle in his eye. It was not the least bit surprising that he was a successful businessman. Like his son and wife, Dan Whalen oozed charm yet somehow managed to leave me suspecting that everything he said was completely heartfelt. Seriously, these people missed their calling as politicians. Stephanie came off as a little rougher around the edges, but she seemed really genuine and down-to-earth, and I felt pretty confident that I'd like her if I ever got the chance to know her.

"I'll be right back," Dan said, heading back out to the barbecue. During our exchange, Ellen, Reed and Stephanie had brought a salad, a bowl of pasta covered in what I could now see what a freshly made pesto sauce and a pitcher of lemonade over to the table.

"Please, grab a seat anywhere, Brecken," Ellen said, touching my back gently as she passed behind me.

Reed pulled out a chair for me, and I found myself seated between him and his mom as Dan, who had returned with the corn on the cob, was busy slicing the pork loin.

• • • • •

"I hope you play euchre, Brecken," Dan Whalen said, his deep voice warm and endearing.

"Of course," I said, smiling at him, already kind of in love with the entire Whalen family. "I *am* from Michigan after all."

"Good, let's have a game or two then, before you kids go running off like that daughter of mine," he said good-naturedly. Stephanie had headed out to meet her friends for a bit after we finished off Ellen's blueberry cobbler. The cobbler was perfect, with those little sugar crystals on the crust that make all pastries taste better – seriously, I don't know why they aren't on every dessert ever baked.

"Sounds good to me," I agreed happily. How was it possible that a guy as close to perfection as Reed also happened to have an adorable, loving family? It was like those gorgeous actresses who also turned out to have amazing singing voices. I mean, really, share the wealth! "What are the teams?" I asked.

"I think I'll claim you as my partner, Brecken, if that's all right by you," Ellen said, pulling a deck of cards from a kitchen drawer. "Reed and Dan have beaten me and Steph a few times in the last few days, and I'm in the mood for redemption."

"Great," I agreed with a smile. Both Dan and Ellen were sipping on glasses of wine, but I was interested to notice they hadn't offered any to me or Reed. Maybe they weren't quite on board with the open teen drinking policy that most of the Green Island parents subscribed to, or maybe they just didn't like to directly condone it. I'd have to ask Reed about that later.

"Sounds like we've been issued a challenge, son," Dan said to Reed, leaning back in his chair.

"I'm not worried," Reed said, and his hand quickly brushed my knee affectionately under the table before he reached for the deck and began sorting out the cards needed for euchre. Had my family ever been this happy together? Not that I could remember. If there was such a time, it was so long ago that any memories were now tarnished by the taint of the recent years. I pushed my parents and Griffin out of my mind, instead relishing my moments with Reed and the Norman Rockwell world he called home.

Chapter 41

After a heated five game battle in euchre, from which Ellen and I emerged victorious, Reed and I spent hours walking the circumference of the island, my arm linked through his. Other than Lizzy, I'd never met anyone whom I could talk with as easily and comfortably as I could with Reed. I'd never had an instantaneous click like that with anyone. The most unbelievable part of that night was realizing that for some unknown reason, Reed had the same feeling about me.

Beginning that night, Reed and I became inseparable. Although I tried not to neglect my friendship with Lizzy, the truth was that being with Reed became the only thing I wanted to do. The days melted away, slipping one into another, as I fell ridiculously, hopelessly, madly in love with Reed Whalen. It was the kind of love that seems like bullshit when you see in the movies — a montage of a couple running in the rain, frolicking on the beach, wiping streaks of paint on each other's faces as they repaint an old fence — but this time it was me and it was real. All the clichés that I would have mocked before meeting Reed now seemed completely reasonable. It was the kind of love that made me want to carve our initials in trees and write love songs and stare into his eyes for hours.

After three weeks, he told me he loved me. I knew I loved him long before that, maybe I knew the first time I saw him, even if that sounds insane. We talked about everything, honestly, everything. It was true that I loved his face, his body, his hair, his eyes, which were inarguably beautiful, but that was just the beginning, just the smallest part of what I'd found in him. As I discovered his patience, his kindness, his dry, witty humor, his interest in the world outside his privileged cocoon, I continued to fall deeper as he managed to be my perfect fit in every way. He was my drug, and I could not get enough.

There was just one topic we hadn't discussed, the one that scared me most. I was leaving Green Island on August 14th, going back to my life in Royal Oak, back to St. Lucy's, back to reality. And Reed would be a college freshman over five hundred miles away. It was early August by the time I broached the subject. After a long day of wakeboarding on Greta's boat with a handful of other kids, Reed and I were lounging in the hammock, nestled in a grove of trees in the vast yard in front of his family's house. For weeks I'd been considering how to delicately raise the topic – not wanting to risk ruining the last few weeks we had together on Green.

"Your eyes are the craziest color," Reed said, our faces a few inches apart in the hammock.

"Light brown? Yeah, really crazy," I said mockingly. "How can you even see them anyway, you're like two inches away from me.

"They're not light brown. Seriously, they're gold. I've never seen eyes your color before. No one has said anything to you about them before?"

My mind jumped to my dad, who had called me "Tiger Eyes" when I was a little girl. He'd always told me that my eyes were the color of the stone that went by the same name. For my eighth birthday, he had given me a necklace with a tiger eye pendant hanging from it. I'd thought it was the most beautiful thing I'd ever seen, and I'd worn it every day until the clasp broke a few years later. Although it was still sitting with its broken chain in my jewelry box, it had been years since he'd called me by that name.

I shrugged at Reed. "Maybe a few people have mentioned it," I said nonchalantly, wanting to change the subject so badly that I burst right out with the issue that had been plaguing my mind for weeks. "So, what happens when we leave Green Island?" I asked, coming right out with it. My heart began racing as I anticipated how he would let me down gently.

"What do you mean?" he asked, his eyes becoming thoughtful.

"I mean, you're going off to college in Massachusetts and I'll be in high school in Michigan..." I trailed off, afraid I might cry, not wanting to voice my fear that he wouldn't want to begin college with a high school girlfriend several states away.

"Are you asking if I want to stay together?" he asked, his face unreadable.

"I guess so, yeah."

"Well, I do. For sure. Do you?" he asked, giving me a searching look.

I couldn't control the grin that burst across my face. "Yes, definitely."

"I love you, Brecken, really. I can't imagine breaking up. I can't imagine not talking to you every day."

"Me too," I agreed, nearly gleeful in my relief. "It won't be easy though," I said, mostly thinking out loud, but also hoping he would disagree and affirm that any effort would be worth it.

"I think it will," he said, running his pointer finger along the edge of my face – one of his weird habits that I loved.

"I don't know how cool my mom will be about me visiting you, staying in your dorm and all that," I said, wishing for the millionth time that I, too, was going to college in the fall.

"Then I'll come visit you," he said, making it seem as if there were a simple answer for each of the issues I had viewed as substantial roadblocks. "I'll stay at a hotel and just have chaperoned visits during the day, if that's all I can get," he said jokingly, his playful smirk on his lips.

"All right then, I guess that settles that," I said, still smiling as he started kissing me.

Chapter 42

I'd been holding off on telling my mom about Reed until after he and I had our talk about staying together in the fall. I knew she wouldn't be too enchanted with the idea of a college boyfriend, especially one of the Green Island variety, so I figured there was no point of getting into it with her if I was never going to see him again once I left the island. Now that I knew this was more than a summer romance, the time had come to tell her.

"Hi, Mom, it's me," I said, hearing her voice on the other end of the line.

"Hi, honey! How are you? Sorry I missed your call yesterday."

"I'm good, really good. How are things with you?"

"Oh, you know, things are pretty good." She always tried to keep a cheery tone these days, making every effort to avoid letting her issues with my dad impact me and Griffin, although, of course, that was completely impossible. "How are your lessons going? Did everything work out with little Eddie?" she asked, referencing one of my young students who had thrown his guitar into the wall the week before in a fit of anger over continuously messing up his B minor chord.

"Ha, yeah, that all worked out OK," I told her, trying to determine the best way to segue into my reason for calling. "Soo, um, have you been on any dates or anything," I asked, hoping this would provide me with the opportunity I'd been looking for.

My mom just laughed. "Uh, no, not really in that state of mind. At all. Why do you ask?"

"Oh I don't know..." I trailed off, and then realized I might be missing the window I'd created, however unsubtle it might have been. "Well, actually, I started dating a guy here..." I could feel my cheeks flushing a bit, having never really talked with my mom about this kind of thing too much before.

"Oh, really?" my mom said, sounding caught off-guard. "A guy from Green Island?"

"Yeah, his family has a house here. He's from New York though," I sputtered out quickly, unsure of why this conversation made me feel so awkward.

"What's his name?" she asked slowly, as if carefully considering each word exchanged between us.

"Reed. And, he's really great, Mom. I know you'll like him."

"So, is this serious?" she asked, and I felt a surge of warmth toward her as she did. I knew a lot of my friend's moms didn't think seventeen-year-olds were even capable of a serious relationship, writing it all off as melodramatic puppy love, and I appreciated that my mom wasn't like that.

"Yeah. It is," I said softly.

"Well, am I going to get to meet him?" she asked.

"Yeah, for sure. He wants to come visit some time soon."

"And stay with us?" she asked in a neutral tone, her voice not betraying how she felt about such a prospect.

"Uh, maybe. I'm not sure. I'll talk to you about it before we figure anything out, of course."

"OK..." she said, and I could tell she wanted more information.

"But, actually, I have to get going, unfortunately, because a bunch of us are going to Mackinac Island tomorrow morning and we have to get up super early. I still need to pack and everything, but I'll call you soon, OK?" I felt bad rushing to get off the phone, but describing Reed Whalen in minutiae to my mom just seemed too stressful — I knew I could never explain him in a way that would make him come off as he actually was. It would be much better for her to just meet him in person rather than have some pre-conceived idea of him.

"All right, well I don't want to keep you then," she said, sounding slightly annoyed.

"Love you, Mom."

"Mmhmm, you too," she said. As we hung up, I felt a slight hollow of loneliness in my chest and the urge to call her back, but I resisted and headed upstairs to get packed for my day on Mackinac Island with Lizzy, Greta and Charlotte. I knew I'd been letting my friendships fall by the wayside, and a day at Mackinac with the girls was the perfect way to remedy, or at least begin to remedy, my neglectful ways.

Chapter 43

"Please let me drive you," Reed insisted as we sat out on the dock at his house late at night, just three nights before I was heading back to Royal Oak.

I'd spent the whole day with Lizzy, lying out, swimming and just generally being lazy together as we had done nearly every day the summer before. Between my lessons and Reed, our time together had been minimal in the past month. I was here on Green Island with her, after all, and although she wouldn't say it, I knew sometimes the shift in our relationship was hurtful to her. It was hard for me too, but I was the one causing it and I wasn't sure how to make it right while still spending lots of time with Reed as well. Today had been different though, with Lizzy seeming calm and contented, bringing me up to speed on all the gossip that I'd been missing out on. It was a good day, and after hanging out at a beach party hosted by Todd Hamlin for a few hours, Lizzy had gone home to bed and I'd soon escaped to meet Reed on his dock as we'd planned.

"Are you really sure you want to?" I asked skeptically, and he quickly assured me that he did, in fact, want to drive me. Reed's family typically flew in and out of Cherry Capital Airport in nearby Traverse City when they came and went from Green Island. However, at the beginning of summer, they always drove one car out to Michigan from New York, filled with everything that hadn't been jammed into suitcases. Obviously, they could easily have afforded to leave a car at the Green Island and ship their stuff here, but I'd quickly learned that the Whalens weren't really into living lavishly just for the sake of it, so each summer they brought a car with them. Reed had proposed that this year he drive me home to Royal Oak and meet my mom before he continued on to Westchester to get ready to leave for orientation at Amherst, which began the following week.

I was protesting for a few reasons. First, I'd been feeling bad about neglecting Lizzy all summer, and I worried that bailing on our drive back home together would only magnify the extent to which I had been spending time with Reed rather than her. Also, I was nervous about Reed and my mom meeting, although I couldn't precisely explain why that was the case. Probably I just wanted them to hit it off and worried they might not, mainly because I feared my mom would be pretty closed-minded about him. On the other hand, if my mom got to meet Reed and she did like him, the chances of her letting me visit him in New York would drastically increase. A ride from him would also mean another day together, and at this point I was willing to do just about anything to stretch my time with him out in any way possible.

In the end, I agreed that he could drive me.

· · · · ·

"Oh...OK," Lizzy said with a rare flicker of anger in her eyes after I told her that I was going to catch a ride home with Reed.

"Are you mad?" I asked, sounding desperate. "Please don't be mad at me. I know I haven't been the best about hanging out this summer, but you know that your friendship is the most important thing to me." I wasn't used to Lizzy's anger, especially not anger directed my way, and it was incredibly upsetting.

"I'm not mad," she said curtly, as she continued going through the clothes in her closet and dresser in preparation for packing up her room, avoiding looking in the direction of the spot on her bed where I sat cross-legged.

"Well, obviously you are, and I feel awful. It's just that if my mom doesn't meet Reed in person now, I'm afraid there's no chance she'll let me go visit him any time soon, you know?"

"Mmhmm," Lizzy said, busying herself with folding a pile of about twenty sundresses, which she'd just, removed from hangers.

I sighed, knowing that she had every right to be annoyed with me. I'd been her guest for the summer and had spent most of my free time running around Green Island with Reed. More significantly, I had put someone else ahead of her, something she had never, ever done to me.

· · · · ·

By the time senior year began two weeks later, Lizzy and I were seemingly back to our old ways, virtually attached at the hip. I had apologized profusely to her, over and over, all the while guiltily knowing that I would probably act the same way if I had that summer to do over again. Maybe it was a necessary step toward establishing my own identity, separate from the friend who had been constantly beside me for the past ten years, the one whom I was afraid to do anything without. Maybe subconsciously I was pulling back from her before she left me for an east coast school, for what I expected would be a more glamorous life. Maybe. Or, as much as I hated to admit it, maybe I was just seventeen and selfish and too in love with Reed to care about anyone else.

PART V
SPRING – SUMMER 2009

Chapter 44

Despite the dim lighting in Inner Town Pub, I spot Reed immediately, sitting at a booth in the very back corner, looking down at his drink. I take him in for a moment as I slowly approach his table. His shirt is blue. For some reason, above all, I notice the blue shirt first. Probably because I am avoiding everything else. I let my eyes pass quickly over his face, and although he is more man now and less boy, it is very much the same face I remember, when I let myself remember. He spots me and I give a little wave, hating that I feel so incredibly self-conscious and awkward as I walk over to his table. He smiles in response, standing up as I near his table.

"Breck," he says, with more warmth and less shock than when he said my name a few nights before. His use of my nickname hurts, it's too personal given the distance I want to keep, the distance that exists, and it reminds me of too much.

"Hey Reed," I manage to say, as he wraps me in a quick hug, and for an instant I am absolutely, wholeheartedly overcome by the sameness of his smell, his feel.

"Can I grab you a drink?" Once again I am taken by the familiarity of his uniquely hoarse and amazingly appealing voice, which has grown even a bit deeper than it used to be, but nonetheless it is the same voice I know so well. Or, correction, the same voice I *knew* so well.

"Uhh," I mumble, my stellar first contribution to the conversation, as I'm caught in a wave of nostalgia so overwhelming that I could drown. "Jack and Coke I guess."

He saunters over to the bar as I slide into the other side of the booth he has staked out and try to pull myself together. Jack and Coke?! I scold myself silently. I had sworn that I would merely sip on one or two (at most!) beers to avoid unintentionally getting even slightly drunk and losing the composure I had been so committed to all day, so committed to for the past eight years. One beer, I'd told myself. And yet, one second after my arrival I have a liquor drink headed my way. So much for Plan A...

He sits down with a bottle of Bell's Two Hearted Ale in one hand and my drink in the other. As he slides my glass across the table to me, he is looking directly into my eyes without saying a word, which only serves to make our eye contact feel infinitely more intimate. The familiarity of it is terrifying. Everything is terrifying right now. But, I am determined to handle this well, to take this opportunity to fill in the gaps about what happened when he disappeared from my life and then be on my way. I look away, breaking free of his gaze.

"So," I start, desperate to regain some of my self respect after acting like a bumbling idiot on Saturday night, wanting to take control of the conversation. "That was quite a Houdini you pulled on me," I say, smirking, avoiding the pull of his eyes. These words just pop out of my mouth without a thought, and I immediately want to kick myself for referencing our old "Houdini" joke. This is not going to be a night about reliving the good old days and strolling down memory lane, I remind myself.

He cracks a smile, the tension in his eyes lifting slightly for an instant, before his face becomes serious and thoughtful again. I know all his expressions so well, and I cannot avoid the layers upon layers of memories that roll over me each second I spend in his presence, as much as I am trying to dodge them.

"I'm so sorry," he says, emphasizing each word, his eyes looking genuinely concerned. This catches me off-guard. I don't know what I expected, but apparently it wasn't a heartfelt apology right off the bat. I contemplate his words for a minute, taking a hearty sip, OK a gulp, of my drink as I decide how to respond and try to avoid dwelling on his painfully perfect face.

"Can you tell me what happened?" I ask slowly. "I guess not knowing where you were or why you cut off contact with me, that was the hardest thing for me. I mean, I talked to your sister a few times after you disappeared, but she was so distraught over everything that I didn't want to bother her with my questions.

"We talked on the phone that night, before you and your parents got in the car, and you said you would call me in the morning... and then, that was it." I had replayed it in my head so many times. It was as though it had happened yesterday, I remembered it so clearly, even all these years later. "I mean, Andrew Wells called Greta the next day to tell her about the accident, about your parents, and Greta called me... I guess all I would like at this point is to hear the whole story, from you." He looks down as I talk, and I wonder if the memory of that horrible night and all that followed is too much for him to discuss, even after so much time. I consider backtracking, but I don't want to be fake, not with him. I owe the memory of our relationship at least that much, and Reed owes me at least an explanation.

"Yeah, I wanted to tell you everything, to try to explain. That's one of the reasons I wanted to see you," he says, making me wonder, for just an instant, what the other reasons he wanted to see me might be.

We sit just looking at each other, once again, for what is probably only few seconds but feels much longer. Whether intentionally or out of self preservation, I'd forgotten the intensity of our looks. The brief thought that Will and I don't have these kinds of moments creeps into my mind before I immediately push it away and break from my eye contact with Reed, taking another sip, which prompts him to begin talking again.

"Right, so, that night. The Wellses were over for a Labor Day barbecue with my family before we left Green, and my parents and I ended up getting on the road to head back to New York later than planned. I thought we were heading out soon after I talked to you, but it ended up being another two hours or so before we were all packed up and headed to the ferry.

"My dad drove first, and my mom insisted that she wanted to drive next. When my dad needed a break it was about 2:00 A.M. and my mom was sleeping so soundly in the backseat that I decided I would just take the next shift. About two hours in, a truck swerved slightly into our lane, and I jerked the wheel to get out of the way, but I was so tired and startled that I swerved way more than I should have and hit the median. Swerving is the last thing I remember. I woke up in the hospital with a broken right arm and a concussion. My dad was killed on impact when our car flipped. My mom died from internal bleeding in the ambulance on the way to the hospital, about twenty minutes after the accident. She was conscious the whole time. The EMTs told me all that she kept asking was whether I was OK, and they had to keep telling her they didn't know. She died before they found out I was barely injured, so she never knew."

He pauses for a minute, and I want to tell him how deeply sorry I am about his parents' deaths but I cannot seem to find any words, even after eight years. The thought of Ellen Whalen in these agonizing dying moments is making me feel sick, and I can only imagine what Reed is feeling, what he has been feeling for so many years knowing that this was how his mom had died and probably blaming himself for it. I am softening to him as I listen to him recall that tragic night. I can feel it happening and can't seem to avoid it as I watch him focusing on his beer, his voice steady as he speaks. Deep inside, I feel the urge to hold him, to stroke his now buzzed hair and kiss his face, to tell him everything is OK, that he should not and cannot blame himself, as I would have done so many years ago, if he had let me. But, now I sit a table length and a different life away from him, knowing that I love a different man, that Reed is no longer mine to comfort, as he continues.

"So, I guess the only way to describe it is that I just kind of shut down when I came to and learned that that they were dead. That I had killed them. I just couldn't cope with it. As I was discharged from the hospital, I couldn't imagine going back to New York, to the funerals and the pity and blame. I couldn't put two words together, couldn't begin to believe that my parents were gone and that I was responsible. It wasn't the brave or respectable thing to do, I get that, obviously, but I just left. I rented a car and just started driving, ended up in Saranac Lake, at this bed and breakfast called The Point, and stayed there for about a week. I don't know where the days went, but I was basically catatonic. To some extent, my intention was to go home after that. To call you, to face Steph, to deal with what had happened. But then, while I was there, the planes crashed into the twin towers and I just felt like the world was honestly crumbling around me.

"I sent Steph an email because I knew she'd go crazy, that she had more than enough on her plate without worrying about me too, so I told her that I was going to be traveling and would keep in touch. It was so shitty of me to do that to her, but I wasn't thinking at all back then. As soon as planes were flying again, I booked a flight to Australia. I just wanted a few weeks away from everything and everyone, an escape from the devastation in New York, that was the only thing that sounded bearable. It was really weak of me, but it's what I did. I ended up staying in Australia for about a year, then I moved from place to place. I spent about two years in Thailand, a year in Japan, over two years in different parts of South America and some time in Europe, especially Spain.

I let that sink in for a minute. "What were you doing while you were in all these places?" I ask. This is just one of the many questions rapidly pulsing through my mind, but it's the first one that comes out of my mouth.

"All different things... I was actually in the Peace Corps for the two years that I was in Thailand, working mostly on Tsunami relief, and I taught English in Japan. In Australia and Spain I mostly just hung out and worked odd jobs while I focused on my writing. In South America, I traveled around a lot and also worked as a teacher for one school year in Guatemala."

I hadn't known any of these details and took a minute to absorb them. Other than knowing that he left for Australia shortly after 9/11, which Stephanie had told me when I'd eventually called her, I've had no idea where he's been all these years.

"Ready for another?" he asks, motioning to my empty glass after a few seconds of silence.

"Yeah," I say quietly, although I already feel buzzed from the first drink. I'm suspicious that it may have been a double. He makes a quick trip to the bar and then slides my new drink to me in the same way he did the first.

"I can't begin to tell you how sorry I am about your parents," I say. "They were such wonderful people," I add, at a loss for the right words to express the ocean of sadness I felt when I first learned his parents had died.

"Yeah. They were the best," he says, his voice melancholy and tight. "And, thanks, I really appreciate that."

We're silent for a minute, the topic making us both somber.

"So, what about you?" he asks, probably looking for more upbeat conversational terrain. "What've you been up to all this time?"

I wonder if I just missed my window for asking any more questions about his years away, but I roll with it for the time being. "Let's see," I start, "well, I graduated from U of M in 2005, majored in poli sci and violin. And I had no clue what I wanted to do when I graduated, so I just decided to apply to law schools. Somehow, I got swept up in that... I thought it would give me a lot of good options, to do meaningful work and have a decent income..." I pause for a minute, trying to recall how it was exactly that I'd ended up in law school. "So, I went to University of Chicago for law school and graduated last year. Lizzy moved to Chicago after college too, so I've been living with her and my best friend from college, Nevada, since I moved here."

"Her name's Nevada?"

I laugh. "Yep."

"I like it," he says, smiling. I'm not sure if he is referring to the way I've spent my last eight years or the name Nevada, but it seems like maybe it's both.

"Now I'm working for a law firm called Baron & Riehl, doing mostly corporate law stuff, mergers and acquisitions and that kind of thing."

"Yeah, I saw that on your firm's website, when I was trying to find your email address. How are you liking that?"

"Uh, not so much," I say, hearing a twinge of sadness in my voice. My drink is empty again, and he quickly goes to the bar and comes back with a fresh one for each of us. I see he has switched from beer to what appears to be whiskey on the rocks. I reach to grab my new drink with my left hand and am suddenly very conscious of my engagement ring. I resist my impulse to shove my left hand back under the table, and then hate myself for having that instinct to begin with. If Reed has noticed my ring, he hasn't said a word about it.

"So, why are you spending your life doing something you don't like?" he asks after taking a sip of his whiskey, his sexy voice making the simple question sound profound.

"Well, I'm not *spending my life* doing it. It's just a temporary situation. I need to pay off loans, get some experience, all that. It's a good starting point for me, even if I don't actually enjoy it."

"You're not going *Ya Mar* on me, are you?"

I shake my head at him and try not to look amused. "Don't be a dick," I tell him, our rapport becoming more familiar as I give him an annoyed look in response to this uncomplimentary reference to a Phish song we used to listen to together.

"Some of us aren't born with enormous trust funds. Some of us have to work at jobs that suck in order to get better jobs. Hard to believe, I know, but it's true," I say, mostly just giving him a hard time but also a little irritated by his comment.

"All right, all right, point taken," he says, giving me a smoldering smile.

I take the last sip of my third (extremely strong) drink and am officially on the verge of being drunk. The more I drink tonight, the more I feel myself slipping.

"So how's the writing coming along? Anything I should be looking for on the New York Times Bestseller list yet?" I ask.

He laughs. "Uh, not just yet. But, I have something that I've been working on for the past few years that I think is pretty much done, so I'm looking into finding an agent now, and I guess I'll see what happens."

"What's it called?"

"Hold that thought," he says, as he quickly heads to the bar to replenish both our drinks once again.

He's back a minute later. "Sorry about that. The book's called *Nomad in a Noose*." He shoots me what I recognize as his slightly self-conscious grin.

"Sounds upbeat," I say jokingly.

"Ha, yeah, I know, right? It's actually not too depressing, or at least I don't think it is. I meant for it to be an uplifting book overall, so hopefully it is. Maybe you could read it some time and give me your thoughts?"

I am not sure how to respond to this. I hadn't planned on keeping up a friendship with Reed, knowing it would be much too complicated, impossible really, so I try to dodge the question. "I'm sure there are plenty of other people who could give you much more valuable insight than I could," I say.

"No one's opinion would matter to me more than yours," he says matter-of-factly, the tone becoming intense once again.

After another pregnant pause, during which I say nothing, unsure of how to respond to his statement, he leads the conversation into safer territory. "I'm actually starting undergrad again in the fall. At Northwestern. My credits from Amherst don't transfer because of all the time that's passed, so I'm starting back at the very beginning. It's going to be me and a bunch of eighteen-year-olds... but I really want to have my degree, and I know it's what my parents would have wanted. Plus, they have a good writing program, so hopefully it will be a worthwhile experience. We'll see, I guess."

"I'm really glad to hear that," I say, now officially hammered, but making my best effort to sound somewhat sober. "Is that why you came back? To go back to school?"

{272}

"Well... it was a lot of reasons. For one, Steph's getting married in August and I wanted to be here for that. She wants me to walk her down the aisle," he says. "But mostly, I just felt like it was time to come home..."

I digest this information, feeling dizzy from all the whiskey, and the words come out of my mouth before I can stop myself.

"How could you leave me?" I ask, hearing my own sadness as I say it. "And without so much as a word, no goodbye, no explanation, nothing. How could you do that to me? Why?" I blurt it out suddenly, all in one breath. I had finally posed the question that has been weighing on me for almost eight years. As soon as I ask it, I know that this is the question that brought me to Inner Town Pub tonight.

Chapter 45

"Honestly, I don't know. I really don't," Reed replies after a moment, a hint of distress in his usually calm eyes. "At least, I don't know why I left like I did, other than that I was completely messed up back then. I think maybe I just didn't want to care about anyone anymore. By leaving everyone, I couldn't hurt anyone else or be hurt anyone, you know?

"And, obviously, I wasn't able to escape my problems by running away but somehow it felt like what I needed to do. As the weeks and months passed, I wanted to get in touch with you so many times, but I knew it would take a lot for you to forgive me, if you ever would, and I couldn't fix everything with an ocean between us. I knew I would need to see you in person, and I didn't want to make things worse by getting in touch with you before I had my life back together."

I was hoping for something more tangible than this, but the way he offers this explanation, it seems to make sense, at least a little bit, at least in my drunken head at this moment.

He starts again, "I'm so sorry that I hurt you. That's the last thing I would ever want to do... I hope you know that."

I want to believe him, I really do. I still don't say anything, and we exchange another meaningful look.

"And, I did send you that one email... I know that probably doesn't earn me many points, but I was thinking about you."

It takes me a minute to realize what he is even referring to with this comment. It had all started in the middle of October of my freshman year at U of M, a little over a month after Reed had disappeared. I was beginning to emerge from the deep depression that I had fallen into, and on that particular evening I'd decided to venture out of my dorm, which was called Couzens Hall, to take in a bit of the fall air. The truth was, I'd barely left my dorm other than to go to my classes, and I was feeling a little stir crazy. As I headed outside, I had grabbed one of the few, somewhat stale cigarettes that were crammed in the back of one of my drawers, just to give me something to do.

Outside, I found that the Hill area of campus – where Couzens and many of the other large dorms were located – was absolutely bustling. Apparently some sorority activity was going on, because packs of girls in matching t-shirts streamed past me on their way out of Couzens and the neighboring dorms. My mom had, at one point, suggested rushing a sorority as a way of getting out of my "funk," a proposal that I had immediately rejected. I couldn't think of anything that sounded less appealing or more anxiety-inducing in my current state. And so, having not rushed and having barely spoken to anyone in my dorm or my classes due to my Reed-induced depression, I had made exactly zero friends so far at college. My roommate, Sang-mi, was sweet enough, but she was an international student from Korea and didn't speak the best English, so it made it hard for us to get beyond small talk. She was rarely in our room anyway, having already made a group of other Korean friends during the international students' orientation. And, given the fact that I mostly just cried and laid in bed the first month she knew me, I can't exactly blame her for not being overwhelmingly excited to bond with me.

I perched on the stone wall outside the front doors of Couzens and lit a cigarette (sure enough, very stale, but I didn't mind) as the herd of matching girls thinned out. A pretty, willowy girl with long, dark curly hair strolled up and leaned against the same wall, just a few feet away from me. I'd seen her around the dorm cafeteria before and even in my trance-like state, I had noticed her bright, bold outfits, which always made her look uniquely cool. Something about her energy reminded me of Rayanne Graff from the episodes of *My So-Called Life* that I used to watch repeatedly on MTV, and for whatever reason, she always caught my eye. As I tried to discreetly observe her from my station on the stone wall, I became curious about the sweet-smelling, brown cigarette-like thing she was smoking.

"What is that?" I had asked her suddenly, motioning to her cigarette.

"A clove," she said, barely looking up at first. I'd never heard of a clove and wasn't sure if it was pot or something, or just a type of cigarette. A moment later she looked over as I put out my cigarette on the wall. "Want some?" she asked, stretching one of her dancer-like arms and the clove in my direction.

I had no idea who this girl was or what exactly she was offering me, but at that point neither of these factors really bothered me. "Sure," I said, slipping down off the wall and stepping over to where she stood. I figured that without the help of the knee-high brown leather high-heeled boots she was wearing, she was probably around 5'6", just like me.

"I'm Nevada. I've seen you around," she said, still looking serious and more than a little intimidating.

"Hey," I said, taking the clove from her hand, "I'm Brecken."

"Another unique name," she said simply, smiling for the first time. "You always look so sad... What's wrong, if you don't mind me asking?" This was my first introduction to Nevada Deague and her blunt ways. While I loved Lizzy and her sweet, subtle demeanor, Nevada's directness would turn out to be a kind of refreshing change of pace, just the slap in the face that I was desperately in need of to pull me out of my miserable isolation.

"Well, do you want the short story or the long story?" I asked, taking a small hit of the clove and listening with curiosity as it quietly crackled, the sweet aftertaste tempting me to lick my lips.

"How about the short version now, long version later?" she proposed. "What do you think of the clove, by the way?"

"It's sweet," I said, deciding I liked it. "Not bad. Can you buy them everywhere?"

"Yeah, I love these things. You can get them most places that sell cigarettes. I've heard they have fiberglass shards in them or something though. Not sure if that's true, but I try not to smoke them too often just in case."

"Oh..." I said, suddenly feeling a little wary of the clove and handing it back to her.

"So, let's hear the short story..." Nevada prodded.

"OK. So, the short story is my boyfriend broke up with me, I guess. I mean, the week that I moved into the dorms, his parents died in a car accident. He was driving but he was barely injured, and after talking to him earlier in the night before the accident, I just NEVER heard from him again."

"Seriously? Wow — that's brutal. How long were you together?"

"A little over a year... I guess that doesn't sound like *that* long, but... with him, everything was really intense. We just spent the whole summer backpacking around Europe together. And now, I haven't heard from him in over a month... I guess it's just so hard to accept that he would cut me off like this, no matter how horrible a time he's going through." It felt surprisingly refreshing to tell the story to a stranger, and I was struck by how easily these personal thoughts poured out of me that day.

"Yeah, that's terrible," she said, as she nodded empathetically. "Does he live in Michigan?"

"No, he goes to Amherst, in Massachusetts."

It was quiet for a minute, and I realized I didn't want the conversation to end. The truth was, it was the first real conversation I'd had with someone other than my mom or Lizzy since Reed left.

"What about you, are you from Michigan?" I asked, hoping to keep her engaged for a few more minutes, realizing how lonely my self-imposed exile had become.

"Well..." she grins. "I was born in Michigan, in Grand Rapids, which is where my mom grew up. But, she was a total hippie and hated Grand Rapids for the most part — it was waaay too conservative for her. She was just back there briefly when I was born because I guess she was pretty overwhelmed by the pregnancy and wanted my grandparents' help. My dad has never been in the picture too much. My mom and I moved all over the place though – Colorado, California, Maine, Canada, and lots of other places – we seriously never stayed in one city for more than two years. So, I'm kind of a patchwork quilt, I guess you could say."

I was liking my new friend more and more.

She was quiet for a second before changing the subject. "How about coming out with me tonight?" she asked, her voice now enthusiastic.

"Where to?" I asked, definitely not in the mood for a kegger frat party.

"I'm seeing this guy who's a bartender at one of the bars over on Main Street. Since undergrads don't really go over there that often, they don't ID at the door, and then he can hook us up with drinks. It's this really cool dive bar, with a great juke box and all these random characters who hang out there. Not sure if that sounds like your kind of thing, but we could go have a few beers and you could tell me the long version of your story."

"That actually sounds pretty good," I told her, surprising myself. "Although I won't force you to listen to me obsess over my ex-boyfriend all night, I promise."

"I like hearing about that kind of stuff. So, if you ever want to talk about it, I'm always up for listening." We started to walk toward the door to head back inside. "I'm in room 105, so come by around 8:00 or something like that, and we can get ready together in my room if you want."

"Well, I'm pretty terrible with makeup, so I usually end up barely wearing any, as you can probably tell...

but I'll definitely come hang out around 8:00 before we head out."

"Perfect, and I can help you with your makeup if you want," Nevada said with a grin.

That night, Nevada and I ended up having a ridiculous amount of fun at the bar, with her pulling me out of our booth to drunkenly dance around with her to "Ooh Ooh Child," by the Five Stairsteps, which she announced to the whole bar that she had dedicated to me. I laughed and let her twirl me around, even though it was not at all a dancing type of bar. Nonetheless, Nevada's bartender boyfriend and the other miscellaneous people at the bar, mostly old men, seemed to be enjoying our antics.

It was the first time I had been drunk since Reed went MIA, and despite all the fun I had, I felt incredibly lonely when I was back in my dorm room alone that night. I flipped through my CD case and located one of the few mix CDs we'd taken with us to Europe just a few months earlier – painstakingly burned on Reed's new CD burner. It was filled with our favorites, and we'd probably listened to it together a hundred times. I knew that for the rest of my life, every song on it would always remind me of him. Taken over by melancholy as I listened to our songs, I sat at my computer, opened a new email window and typed out a single sentence:

How was it so easy to forget about me?

In my drunken emotional state, this email struck me as especially poignant and I hoped it would tug at the heartstrings that I still believed he possessed. I'd previously emailed him several times in the weeks after his car accident, but when it became obvious that he wasn't writing back, I had promised myself that I would not write him again. Unfortunately, on this particular night, I had forgotten about my little promise to myself and went right ahead and sent this final email.

The next morning I had been furious with myself, first for writing Reed an email at all, and second for writing an email that now seemed extremely cheesy and stupid. I couldn't believe that the email had struck me as moving and meaningful the night before. Although I felt humiliated about it, I eventually consoled myself into believing that there was a pretty good chance he wasn't even reading my emails anyway.

Two years later, however, Reed had responded to that email. That's right, two YEARS later. It was the only email I got from him during his little eight year leave of absence, and all it said was, "It isn't easy at all, believe me." I had been so confused at first when it arrived in my Inbox, and it wasn't until I scrolled down and re-read my initial email that I realized he was apparently saying it wasn't easy to forget about me. The whole episode had enraged me. I hated that he'd sent such a cryptic response to the one stupid email I'd sent, yet totally disregarded the several long, heartfelt emails in which I'd poured out my feelings to him in the days following the car accident. I hated that my heart had practically stopped beating when I saw his name in my email Inbox after waiting in vain to hear from him for so long. I hated that I had sent that stupid melodramatic email in the first place. The entire incident had really upset me, sent me reeling.

All these memories race through my mind in the seconds after Reed makes the claim that he did, in fact, email me once.

"Are you talking about sending me one sentence in response to that sad email that I sent you when I was drunk?" I ask, my voice sounding slightly incredulous.

"Yeah..." he says, looking sheepish, and perhaps realizing he shouldn't have brought the email up at all.

"And you got around to writing me back after just two short years, no less. Yes, that was very nice of you," I say. "Not sure how I could have managed to let that one slip my mind." My voice sounds hurt, even I can hear it, and I hate myself for still caring, for still being sensitive about it after all these years.

"Shit, sorry I mentioned that. All I meant was, I *was* thinking of you. A lot." He sounds so apologetic that it's hard to stay irritated with him.

"Well, it's all water under the bridge now," I say, trying to downplay the whole conversation. I pull my phone out of my purse to check the time and see that I have missed about a million calls and texts from both Lizzy and Nevada. Although it's only just after ten o'clock, I know that I'm pretty drunk and, since I got the facts I came here tonight to get, I probably shouldn't stay with Reed any longer. "Anyway, I should probably get going. I have to be up early tomorrow," I say, thinking that it came out sounding pretty forced. I don't like to end things on an awkward note, but I know it's time for me to get out of here.

"Oh, OK," he says. I think for a second that he sounds disappointed but that might just be my imagination.

"So, I'm gonna grab a cab. Are you heading out now too?" I ask, unsure of how to say goodbye to him as I stand up from the table.

"Can I share a cab with you?" he asks, standing up as well, and I feel my heart skip a beat.

"Where do you live?" I ask, realizing we never covered some of the most basic questions.

He pauses for a second, then says, "Bucktown," hesitantly and tells me his address.

"Well, that's just north of here, and I'm way east," I mumble, feeling drunker by the minute.

"Yeah, but I want to make sure you get home all right."

"I'll be fine. After all, I've managed to get myself home for the past eight years without your help." I hate the bitterness in my voice, and I know I need to get out of here immediately.

"You're pretty drunk though," he protests, ignoring the accusation in my remark. "Just let me make sure you get home, and then I'll have the cab bring me back over this way."

"That's stupid," I say, unable to come up with a better response as we walk outside and I trip slightly on the sidewalk. "I'm not drunk, trust me."

Reed laughs. "I'm pretty good at telling when you're drunk. Lots of experience with it," he says winking, and I feel my heart race again. He flags a cab and pulls the door open, getting in after me without further debate. I tell the driver my address and lean back in the seat. Reed's chivalric manners are something I'd forgotten about, and although I would never admit it, I do think it's the tiniest bit sweet of him to take me home.

He asks me about my violin and guitar playing as the driver weaves his way through the city, letting me ramble on about Ishmael in response. We're still talking as we pull into the circle drive in front of my building.

I clumsily pull a twenty-dollar bill out of my wallet and hand it to Reed, who starts to object.

"Seriously, please take it," I say. "You paid for all my drinks, it's the least I can do."

"I'm not taking your money," he says.

"This wasn't a date, just take it." I put the money on the seat between us, completely unsure of what to say, unsure of if this is goodbye forever, which I know it should be. I am sure, however, that I do not want my last memory of him to be fighting over cab fare.

I scoot over toward him for a second, and we hug. I never knew a hug could be so emotional, and I'm fighting the sudden urge to cry.

"Bye, baby," he says quietly, and I know for certain that my tears will start if I say anything, so I squeeze him tighter for a second and then break from the hug and slide out of my door without another word as he turns back to the cab driver.

Chapter 46

Lizzy and Nevada pounce on me the second I walk into the apartment.

"Where were you? With Reed?" Nevada begins the interrogation.

I realize there is no hiding from them, and the truth is I'm feeling incredibly confused and emotional and wouldn't mind the chance to talk about it. I nod in response to Nevada's question.

"You were?!" Lizzy exclaims, clearly surprised. "Wait, you're really drunk, aren't you?"

"Uh, yeah I'm kind of drunk. It wasn't intentional, it kind of crept up on me." I mumble this explanation as I fill up a large glass of water and begin gulping it down.

"Well... tell us everything! How was it?" Lizzy asks, sounding both concerned and very curious.

I curl up next to her on the couch and give them the play-by-play as they both listen carefully. When I finish, I see a tear slide down Lizzy's cheek.

"Are you crying?" I ask.

"Well, it's just so sad," Lizzy says, now both crying and laughing at herself at the same time.

"I know..." I agree, once again feeling the urge to cry myself.

"So, I guess it's safe to assume that you still have feelings for him?" Nevada asks.

"No. Well, I don't even know. It's so complicated, and there's so much nostalgia and so many emotions from the past, that it's hard to separate those from whether I actually still, you know, love him or whatever," I explain, feeling more confused by the second.

Nevada looks skeptical. "I think you're just telling yourself that. Either you're still in love with him or you're not."

"It's not at all that simple," I insist, as I silently wonder if maybe it is. "I mean, just because maybe I'm still attracted to Reed and feel a connection with him, that doesn't wipe out the way he abandoned me or the way I feel about Will."

"This is *just* what I was afraid would happen," Lizzy says wistfully before Nevada can rebuff my explanation. "I knew everything would become a total mess if you let Reed back into your life."

"I know," I say softly, "but I had to see him. I had to."

"I know," Lizzy says, and I can tell she understands.

"Well, I guess this is just the age-old Brandon versus Dylan dilemma, now isn't it," Nevada says with a sly smile. "Think about it. The choice between a sexy, brooding, unreliable guy and the clean-cut, faithful do-gooder type is practically the basis of every romantic plot line ever. This is well-covered territory. I mean there's sexy Ethan Hawke or doting Ben Stiller in *Reality Bites*, there's doctor Jack or outlaw Sawyer in *Lost*, there's dorky Aidan Quinn or wild Brad Pitt, in *Legends of the Fall*, although who are we kidding with that one, not much of a debate there... There's Mr. Big or Aidan, I mean I could go on forever. True love always wins, and true love isn't usually with the reliable, safe option." Nevada seems very pleased with this analysis, and I just shake my head at her exasperatedly, which only makes me dizzy.

"Nevada," I say, stretching out each syllable in her name, "first off, those are fictional characters. This is my *real life* we're talking about here. And, those stories end when the girl chooses the guy who is more challenging and unpredictable or whatever you want to call it, and we never get to see if they are actually happy together. I mean, do you really think that Dylan McKay would be a better husband than Brandon Walsh, fifteen or twenty years down the line? No way."

"Actually, I think that in the new 90210 it turned out that Kelly picked Dylan and he left her with a baby and a broken heart," Lizzy tells Nevada in a mock know-it-all voice.

"I can't believe you watch that show," Nevada says with a smile. "But anyway, in *Legends of the Fall,* the girl does go with Aidan Quinn, the responsible option, although that's not really by her own choice, but regardless, Brad is always her true love and, as you probably recall, things do not end well," Nevada says, eager to back-up her theory.

"Well, I'm sure you can find some fictional plot line to prove any point, but one thing I learned from my parents' marriage is that just being in love isn't enough to make it work. They were madly in love when they got married. But then, they didn't want the same things out of life, and my dad wasn't the kind of husband my mom needed, and everything completely fell apart. Also, let's not forget that Reed hasn't even suggested that he's interested in me anymore."

"Plus, it's not like Will is some dweeby Ben Stiller figure," Lizzy says. "He's so charming, sweet, interesting AND good looking, and, Breck, you were totally happy with him and your relationship last week. The fact that Reed is back on the scene doesn't change anything about what you have with Will. Why would you risk what you already know is an amazing relationship for one that might not be."

All this talk is starting to become incredibly overwhelming, especially in my inebriated state. I sit up, thinking I should get to bed. "It's true that seeing Reed threw me a little," I agree, "but I love Will and I love what we have together. I'm definitely not going to risk losing all that for a guy who I barely even know anymore."

Lizzy smiles at me and Nevada continues to look skeptical. "I've got to head to bed," I add. "I'm drowning in work and need to go into the office early tomorrow."

"OK, well we'll be working on Crash for a while tonight," Nevada tells me. "So come hang out if you can't sleep."

I tell them both goodnight and head off to my bedroom, trying to keep my mind off our conversation. Thankfully, no doubt in large part due to the excessive amount of Jack Daniels I consumed, I fall right to sleep.

Chapter 47

Early Tuesday afternoon, I'm in my office working through the endless Project Aristotle due diligence when Stan walks in and settles himself in one of my chairs.

"I'm keeping busy with the due diligence, it's coming along," I tell him, hoping he won't stay long.

"Good, keep plugging away," he says. "Also, I'm going to need you to come to a cocktail party this evening. It's being hosted by Noah Cooney, and he wants the whole Project Aristotle team to come so he can meet everyone involved in the deal."

I'm beyond annoyed by this request, if I can call it that, but since Noah Cooney is the CEO of our client, I'm afraid I won't be able to get out of it.

"OK, well I would like to go, but I still have so much to get through with the due diligence," I say, trying not to sound frustrated.

"Well then you can come back to the office after the party. I really need you to be there."

"All right," I say, realizing there is no way out. "Are John and Matt going too?" I ask, referring to the other two associates on the deal.

"They are. We'll all meet in the lobby at 7:30 to head over. Oh, and you'll probably need to run home and change, this is the kind of thing where you should wear a dress."

The tone of his voice seems kind of lecherous when he makes this request, but it's hard to tell if it's all in my head. I'll lose another hour of time that I could spend getting caught up on work by going home to change. I'm tempted to just show up in the lobby at 7:30 still wearing my suit, which is what all the guys will be wearing and seems only fair, but I'm afraid that won't go over too well with Stan. And, as much as I might find him to be a little sleazy, in addition to being the head of the corporate practice group, he is also one of only six partners who are on the firm's Executive Committee, so it's definitely not a great idea to get on his bad side.

I call Lizzy, quickly explaining that I have to miss our Tuesday night Tiparo's dinner once again, which I know is going to rub Nevada the wrong way, and ask her if she would possibly be willing to bring me an unsexy dress that I can wear to this party. Without any questions, she agrees to bring the dress to me in the next hour and wishes me luck with all my work. I feel really bad asking this of Lizzy, especially given that it's pouring rain, but this morning she mentioned that she was going to be down in the Loop for an afternoon meeting anyway, so that eases my conscience a tiny bit at least. I send Hodge a text letting him know that I have to miss band practice tonight, feeling dejected that I am unintentionally becoming the kind of person who is constantly canceling on her friends because of work.

· · · · ·

Several hours later, I am sipping on espresso in the cap-sleeve navy Michael Kors dress that Lizzy dropped off, and chatting with Matt Nelson, another associate working on Project Aristotle. We are in

Noah Cooney's penthouse condo overlooking Lake Michigan, discussing Matt's newborn daughter Olivia, as I glance at a clock across the room.

"Itching to get out of here?" he asks, cracking a smile.

I laugh. "Oh no, am I that obvious? I'm glad we're getting a chance to catch up, but I'm just so swamped with the due diligence review. My mom's going to be in town later this week, so I really wanted to get ahead on work so I'd have more time to spend with her. But, instead, here I am..."

"I hear you, believe me," he says. "You already talked with Cooney for a while, so you should just take off. Seriously, you've been here for over an hour, I think that's enough face time."

"Really?" I ask, not wanting to upset Stan.

"Yeah, definitely. I'm taking off soon too."

Since Matt is a senior associate, as well as a pretty good friend, I trust his judgment more than my own when it comes to navigating this sort of thing.

"OK, do you think I should let Stan know I'm heading out?" I ask, hoping he'll say no, as I glance over at Stan schmoozing with some businessmen across the room.

"Nah. If he asks, I'll let him know you had to get back to work. Although, at the rate he's been slugging down Manhattans tonight, I doubt he'll even notice you're gone."

"Cool, thanks so much. And, don't forget to email me some new pictures of Olivia soon!"

He smiles at the mention of his baby's name. "Will do. See you tomorrow."

"See ya, Matt," I say with a little wave, and I head to the front hallway and into the coat closet to find the raincoat that I hung up on my way in.

I'm shuffling through the various identical Burberry raincoats when I feel a hand firmly grab my right butt cheek.

I instantly whip around and find myself face to face with Stan, who slowly lowers his hand off me, grinning.

"What the hell!" I hiss, startled and furious. "What are you doing?!"

Even in my heels, he is still more than a few inches taller than me, towering over me really. He slowly backs out of the closet as I stand there stunned.

"You must be imagining things, Ms. Pereira," he whispers, winking at me as he turns and rejoins the party.

In my daze, I look around. From what I can tell, no one else was in sight during the brief interaction with Stan. I'm beyond shaken up as I grab my coat and run out of the condo and into the elevator. I breathe deeply several times to pull myself together as the elevator makes the long trip down. During the cab ride back to the office, I replay it in my head, feeling disoriented and disgusted by the whole encounter. I decide that I'll just grab my laptop, rather than staying at the office to work. My productivity is inevitably cut in half when I work from home, but tonight I'm in no mood to stick around a largely deserted place where Stan could show up at any minute.

Chapter 48

It's 7:45 on Thursday evening, and after working more or less all day and all night since Tuesday, I have managed to get enough work done to make it feasible for me to spend a little much-needed time with my mom tonight. I'm treating her to dinner at one of my favorite restaurants – BOKA – which is a little pricey but definitely worth it.

Thankfully, I haven't seen Stan since I left the cocktail party. It turned out that he was heading to New York the next morning, and according to his "Out of Office" message on Outlook, he won't be back at work until Monday. We've been in contact over email regarding Project Aristotle, but there's been no mention of his impropriety or anything other than business matters.

So far I've only told Lizzy and Nevada about the ass-grabbing incident, and they both think I need to report him to someone higher up. While I agree with them in theory, in practice I'm not so sure what to do. In addition to Stan's powerful position at Baron & Riehl, he's also highly respected in the legal community. I'm sure he would deny that it happened, and he had been drinking quite a bit so who's to say if he would even remember it clearly. It would ultimately just be his word (a senior partner) versus mine (a measly first year associate). I hate to think that I could be the type of person who allows herself to be treated like that and says nothing, but realistically there are just so many factors to consider and I have no clue what to do.

I have no intention of mentioning it to my mom, who would undoubtedly be enraged to the point that she'd probably hunt down Baron & Riehl's managing partner tonight if she heard what had happened. I do my best to put Stan out of my mind as I step out of a cab at BOKA and make my way inside.

"Hi!" I cry as I approach the table where my mom is already sipping on a glass of red wine. Her dark curls have been blow-dried into a smooth bob, a new and unfamiliar style on her. She looks very sophisticated, wearing all black on her thin body, with stylish thick, dark-framed glasses, which are lined with green on the inside. Her soft features and fair skin make her look younger than her fifty-two years. With my darker complexion, which favors my Brazilian father, and my wavy blondish-brown hair, people rarely assume she is my mother.

"Hi, honey!" She stands up, and her thin arms enfold me in a big hug. "I ordered a bottle of red," she tells me, as she pours wine into the empty glass at my seat and hands it to me. "I'm sure you could use this after the crazy work week you've been having," she says as we sit.

"You have no idea!" I say with a laugh.

We cover all the basics first: work, Griffin and his latest girlfriend, and my mom's boyfriend, Ted, as we each munch on delicious beet salads.

"Have you and Will talked much about wedding plans yet?" she asks.

"No, not really. When he gets back we'll probably try to get a few basics figured out at least."

"Are you thinking Chicago?"

"I don't know really, we haven't even gotten that far..."

"It all seems overwhelming to me, and I'm sure with your work schedule and his hours at the hospital it must seem even more daunting to you," she says, squeezing my hand across the table supportively. "Once you have a basic idea of what you want, we can sit down and figure out how I can be most helpful. Your dad and I talked about the wedding briefly, and we both want to help with paying for it as much as we're able."

I feel my throat tighten with emotion, incredibly touched by this generous gesture and by the thought of my mom discussing my wedding with my dad, given that they have rarely spoken in the years since Griffin graduated from high school. "That's really generous, Mom. Thank you so much. I'll let you know as soon as Will and I have anything more concrete figured out."

"So how does it feel to be engaged, now that you've had some time to adjust to it?"

I feel a little pang of guilt thinking about how much more of my time has been spent focusing on work and Reed the past few weeks, rather than my fiancé. "It's been great. I mean, truthfully, other than the ring and calling Will my fiancé instead of my boyfriend, it hasn't actually felt very different."

She nods, considering this as our waitress circles back with our entrees.

I savor the first bite of my mahi mahi and then confess to my mom. "Actually, this week has been kind of crazy... You'll never believe this, but I ran into Reed Whalen last weekend and we ended up meeting for a drink the other night."

She lets her jaw hang down with intentional exaggeration, and I feel a sheepish smile spread across my face.

"*Reed Whalen*? Good lord, I never thought I'd hear that name again," she says eventually. "Let's hear the whole story," she prompts, as our waitress provides a much-needed top-off of our wine glasses.

Beginning with the Facebook photo spotting, I tell my mom everything.

"Wow, Breck," she says when I finish. "I don't know what to say. I can hardly believe it..."

"Oh I know. Seeing him walking down the street was completely surreal."

"Well, what did he say about you being engaged?"

"Umm, it didn't come up..." I say, feeling guilty once again.

"Brecken! Honey, why? Please don't tell me that you are going to let Reed interfere with your relationship with Will. Please." She looks at me sadly as she says this.

"No, Mom, of course I wouldn't. No way."

She sighs and takes a few bites of her risotto. "Truthfully, I've always worried about you in relationships," she says after a few seconds pass. This comment catches me off-guard – she's never said anything like this to me before – and she continues. "I know how hurt you were by the divorce and the way that your dad pulled away from you and Griffin after everything that happened. And, you relied so much on Reed back then, and then he abandoned you too. You were so head over heels about him, and I've always been concerned that between both him and your dad letting you down so significantly, you might never really feel that you could trust a man again. But,

Will is such a good person, and he loves you so much, that much is obvious. You seem like you finally feel secure in a relationship. The last thing you should do is let Reed or anyone else mess up what the two of you have. I'm worried that you're getting caught up in Reed's return because a part of you is afraid of committing, not just to Will, but to any guy who could let you down again."

I think about what she has said for a minute, having never really considered this idea before. Maybe it's possible that I *am* just afraid and using Reed as an excuse.

"Wow, I think maybe you missed your calling as a psychiatrist, Mama," I say, trying to lighten the mood a little. "I had never really linked Dad and Reed both letting me down and how it affected me, but I'm definitely going to give that some thought. And, don't worry, I won't let anything cloud what I have with Will," I say, giving her a reassuring smile, trying hard to convey a confidence that I'm not necessarily feeling. She returns a soft smile as I think how lucky I am that she is my mom.

"I just want you to be happy," she says gently, as she scoops up the last few bites of her meal.

"I know, Mom. I just want you to be happy, too. And, I feel like you actually are these days," I say, smiling at her. "Tell me about the seminar tomorrow."

And from there, the conversation turns away from my love life and we spend the next hour laughing and chatting over another bottle of wine and what we agree is the most incredible chocolate cake either of us has ever tasted.

Chapter 49

It's Saturday night, and I'm up on stage at the Double Door, waiting as Hodge and Pete discuss some issue with the sound engineer before we begin playing. Even though Ishmael is just the opener tonight, this is a big show for us. It's our first time playing at the Double Door, and the manager mentioned that if we're well received, they'll want us to headline a show in the near future.

While I'm typically not too nervous before shows, I'm feeling a little jittery tonight and have been sipping on a beer as we wait around in an effort to relax. Nevada and Lizzy are supposed to be here, and I scan the darkened room in search of them. It's always comforting to see their faces in the crowd before we play.

I'm in an especially good mood tonight, having sent the initial due diligence memo for Project Aristotle off to our client this afternoon, after having worked until 3:00 A.M. last night, so I'm hopeful that I'll be able to relax all day tomorrow and steer clear of the office.

My gaze stops on a face near the back of the bar, a face looking directly back at me. Reed. He smiles at me, and I return a quick smile before looking away.

What. The. Hell? I haven't heard a word from him since we parted ways on Monday, and I had kind of assumed that was goodbye forever. I've been trying not to think about him, and, after considering my mom's comments at dinner, I've been especially focused on how fortunate I am to be engaged to Will. I talked to Will for almost an hour on the phone last night, taking a break from work to make sure my priorities are where they should be. And now, here Reed is, at my show, staring up at me.

Hodge comes hustling back up the steps to the stage and winks at me. He exchanges a few words with Tim and then lets the rest of us know we're good to go. Hodge takes the mic and greets the crowd, getting everyone energized, and then we are off and running. As I play, I do my best to forget the crowd and immerse myself in the music. We play five songs, finishing to an uproar of applause, and I can't help but grin. I look out at the audience, avoiding the area to the back right where I spotted Reed, and see Nevada and Lizzy over to the left, jumping and cheering emphatically, with Nevada letting her trademark whistle loose.

The cheers die down as we pack up our instruments and equipment to make way for the headliner, The Nick Shaheen Band, and then I head down to say hi to Lizzy and Nevada, not at all sure how to deal with Reed. I move through the sea of congratulations and cheers and soon find my friends, who both hug me at once.

"You guys sounded phenomenal, as always," Lizzy says as she breaks away.

"Yeah, everyone was going crazy for you," Nevada agrees.

"Thanks, guys! I'm so glad you're here," I tell them, as Lizzy hands me a fresh Goose Island 312, my favorite beer.

And then, I see Lizzy's eyes widen in surprise as Nevada gets a flustered look on her face.

"Impressive, Pereira," says a familiar voice, as I feel my stomach drop for an instant and I whirl around.

"Hey Reed," I say uncertainly, and we quickly hug, my heart racing.

"Hey Lizzy," he says, and I hear the hesitance in his voice.

I watch as Lizzy's surprise quickly turns to anger.

"Hey," she says curtly, her lips pursed, which is about as mean as she is capable of being. He clearly gets the message.

"This is Nevada Deague," I say, gesturing toward Nevada, who still seems a little off balance. "Nevada, this is Reed." I watch as she processes this, looking slightly confused about how to act.

"Oh, sure, OK, nice to meet you," she says, giving an awkward little wave.

"Nice to meet you too," he says, and we all stand there uncomfortably for a moment.

"OK, well, Nevada and I are supposed to meet Jess and Lex at InnJoy now, before there gets to be a line. You coming, Breck?" Lizzy asks, her eyes pressing me to join them.

"Actually, Brecken," Reed says quietly, "would you mind sticking around and having a drink with me?" A part of me wants to stay there with him, but I know I shouldn't. Clearly I shouldn't. "Just one drink, then I'll make sure to get you to InnJoy," he says, flashing a ridiculously attractive smile at my friends.

"OK, yeah, I'll stick around here for one drink," I say. "I probably shouldn't take off on the guys so quickly anyway," I add for good measure. Lizzy's eyes are boring into me.

"All right, then," Lizzy says sharply, "Breck, can you walk us out?"

"Sure," I agree. "I'll be back in a sec," I say to Reed, with Lizzy nearly dragging me away mid-sentence.

Once we're near the door and out of Reed's view, Lizzy turns to face me. "What is he doing here?!" she cries.

"I have no idea. It's not like I invited him. He just showed up," I say. "I don't know what he wants."

"I know this probably isn't helping matters," Nevada pipes in, "but, Breck, I seriously had no idea he would look like that. I know you said he was really hot, but, I mean, I literally could barely speak around him."

Both Lizzy and I glare at her.

"OK, sorry, sorry. I mean, I know he's kind of a dick too, but I just wanted to let you know I was impressed..." She trails off as Lizzy continues giving her a death look. In a fit of anger or grief or the abyss in between, I had thrown away all my photos of Reed before I even met Nevada.

"I really don't want you to get hurt again, and I just think that having him in your life is a bad idea," Lizzy pleads. "Very bad."

"I won't get hurt, and he's not in my life, Liz. I'm just going to hang out with him for like half an hour, see what this is all about and say goodbye, for good this time. We left on a weird note the other night. Then I'll meet you guys. I promise. Thanks for looking out for me though," I say, giving her a hug.

She gives me another hard look before they head out the door and I turn back to the crowd to find Reed.

He's back sitting at the bar, having somehow sweet-talked two seats for us at an otherwise packed bar. I walk up to him and he smiles, spinning the bar chair away from the bar so I can sit down. My leg rubs momentarily against his as I swivel back around. I quietly take a deep breath and then look over at him.

He hands me a glass of whiskey on the rocks, which I accept without thinking about it. He has a glass of the same and clinks his against mine and takes a sip.

"I think I'm gonna have a beer actually," I say, sitting the whiskey back down on the bar.

"Breck... Just have one glass of whiskey with me, for old time's sake." He is virtually impossible to resist, but I look away, flagging down the bartender and ordering another pint of 312 before I turn back to him.

"So, what's up? How'd you end up here tonight?" I ask with a light tone.

"I was just curious to check out your band, so I looked you guys up online and decided to come see a show." His eyes are a little glazed over, which only makes their bright blue color more pronounced.

"How long have you been here?" I ask, thinking he seems like he might be slightly drunk.

"I don't know, a little while. Wasn't sure what time your band was going on."

I nod in understanding as I pay the bartender who has returned with my beer.

"Want to get out of here?" he asks suddenly, his face only inches from mine. "It's so loud, and I want to talk with you."

"I've got to stick around here for a little bit, to pack up the instruments and stuff," I lie, knowing the guys have definitely already loaded them into Hodge's Jeep by now. "And, I have to meet the girls soon anyway." A part of me wants to leave with him, to just let him sweep me right out the door, and yet... and, yet, of course, that is just the sentimental, nostalgic girl within me. Not the engaged woman who I have become in the past eight years.

I feel his firm yet gentle grasp on my left hand suddenly. "What's this?" he asks, looking down at my engagement ring for an instant and then into my eyes. "Who's it from?" he sounds both sad and hostile.

"I'm engaged," I say, yanking my hand away. "To the guy I've been dating for the past couple years, no one you would know." I look away from his penetrating eyes and drink my beer.

"You're in love with him?" Reed asks forcefully, his words ridden with emotion.

"Yes, of course," I say, feeling my nose burn and my eyes sting, knowing I will cry if I say much more.

"Is he here tonight?" Reed asks.

I shake my head, feeling the tears building up.

"Well, it's obvious he doesn't even know you, Brecken," Reed says, his use of my name making his sentence sound even more hostile. "That's the most generic ring I've ever seen. Who could think that was the right ring for you?" he asks, his voice becoming condescending and cutting in a way that I've never heard before.

And with that, I explode. "Fuck you, Reed!" I say loudly, causing a few people around us turn and look at me. "I'm not interested in your input on my ring or anything else about my life. You lost the right to have any say a long time ago. Why did you even come here tonight? Just to insult me? Just leave me the fuck alone!" And with that, I steer through the crowd, half-blinded by my tears, and find a cab to take me home.

Chapter 50

Once again, I am a blubbering mess escaping in a cab, thanks to Reed Whalen.

"You all right, ma'am?" the cab driver asks kindly as we whiz through the streets.

"Yeah," I say, smiling through my tears for a minute and feeling like an idiot. "Sorry! And, thanks for asking!"

"Boy troubles?" he asks.

"Uh, yeah, you could say that," I say, wiping my tears off my face.

"I figured as much. I see a lot of that," he says with a gentle chuckle.

I send Lizzy and Nevada a text message saying that I have a headache (which will probably be true soon anyway) and that I'm headed home, and I also text the guys in the band to ask them if they'll check to be sure my violin made it to Hodge's car before they leave.

I feel weak for letting Reed get to me, but there is something about him that causes me to come unhinged. And, what were all those comments about my ring anyway? I look down at the princess-cut diamond ring on my finger, complete with side stones. While it's true that I never saw myself as the big diamond engagement ring kind of girl, I love that this ring came from Will, and it certainly is beautiful.

When I arrive at my apartment building, I head inside feeling completely drained, even though it's barely 11:00.

I pull on sweatpants and a tank top and drink a big glass of ice water, feeling more awake. I then pour a glass of red wine, retrieve *City of Thieves* from my bedroom and turn on my iPod speakers, softly playing a mellow playlist, as I flop down on the couch and snuggle in my favorite Restoration Hardware blanket. As I read, my mind wanders to Reed's book, *Nomad in a Noose*, and I can't help but wonder if he will end up as a famous writer. Based on the bits and pieces of his writing that he let me read in the past, he is incredibly talented and it wouldn't surprise me in the least if he wrote a bestseller.

The ringing of our land line phone startles me from my thoughts, and I lift the phone from its cradle. It's the doorman calling, so I answer.

"Hey there, Brecken," Craig says, impressively able to distinguish my voice from my roommates'. "I have a visitor down here for you. A Reed Whalen."

"OK, uh, send him up," I say, thinking that I can't leave him standing in the lobby. An instant later, I realize that I obviously should have gone down there to talk to him, rather than having him in my apartment. Lizzy will literally kill me if she happens to come home while he is here. I'm still flustered from the call when I hear a knock on the door.

After pausing in the kitchen for a moment to collect myself, I pull the apartment door open. He is standing there, his hands in the pockets of his worn-in jeans.

"I'm so sorry, Breck," he says, his voice sounding incredibly sad. "The last thing I wanted was to upset you. It's just..."

He trails off and I wait expectantly, both of us still standing in the doorway.

Suddenly, he starts in again. "It's just, what I wanted to say was, I don't want you to marry this guy, whoever he is. I know I have no right to ask you for anything, but I have to say it, or I'll always regret it. Don't marry him, Brecken, please."

Tears are welling up in my eyes once again. I want to tell him that he's more than a day late and more than a dollar short, but I can't bring myself to say anything. He is staring into my eyes, looking as intense as I've ever seen him, and he very slowly moves closer to me. I actually begin shaking as he puts one of his warm hands on my face and the other hand on my lower back and presses me up against the wall, the door to the apartment falling shut behind him.

He is looking down on me, his tall, muscular body so different from Will's shorter, leaner frame. My heart is beating so wildly that I swear I can hear it. I don't push him away, and I know that for that I am already a cheater.

When he kisses me, my knees literally become weak. I am sent spiraling backward, remembering the first time we kissed, so many years before. Remembering being pressed up again the wall in the kitchen of his boat. This is, undoubtedly, the most passionate kiss of my life. In seconds, my betrayal of Will is gone from my mind, the fear of Lizzy walking in has vanished, and there is nothing left but me and Reed.

He kisses me furiously, pressing me harder against the wall, his hands all over me.

"I'm still in love with you," he says, stopping suddenly. "I've always loved you, since the day I met you." I am breathless, staring at him, wanting nothing more than for him to kiss me again. I take him by the hand and lead him into my bedroom, locking the handle behind us.

Even as I feel the lock click behind me, he is pulling off my shirt, lying me down on my bed. He is on top of me as I pull his shirt over his head. His body is still as flawless as his face, with his tan chest broad and muscular, his biceps literally bulging above me. We kiss for what might be seconds or hours, him taking off my bra, kissing my breasts, pressing against me, taking his time, the way he always did. It's startlingly familiar yet different as well, he is older, stronger and clearly more experienced.

I'd forgotten how intensely passionate he was, but it all comes back to me so quickly. I close my eyes, moaning in a voice I barely recognize as my own as I feel him deep inside me for the first time in so many years. I open my eyes for an instant, as we move back and forth together, and see that he is looking back at me. He kisses me sweetly, and I lose all control.

Chapter 51

I open my eyes Sunday morning and continue facing the wall for a minute, not sure what to say to Reed, uncertain as to how I feel about what happened last night, and overwhelmed by guilt. I roll over and find that he is gone.

I glance at the clock, which reads 9:37. Although I'm slightly afraid of crossing paths with Lizzy, I know I can't hide in my room forever, so I throw on a t-shirt and cotton shorts and walk out into the kitchen.

Nevada is standing there pouring coffee into a mug. She looks up with a mischievous grin when she sees me.

"So, spill," she says, and I know I'm busted.

"What do you mean?" I ask, curious to see what she heard and how much she knows.

She gives me a look that says *don't even bother*. "I saw your loverboy rushing out of here this morning," she says. "I got up to pee and saw him heading out the door, and I've been so curious to hear what happened with him that I haven't been able to fall back to sleep. So, come on, tell me everything," she says, handing me a mug of coffee as well.

"Does Lizzy know he was here?" I ask, my heart sinking.

"Uh, no. That's another interesting story... Lizzy didn't come home last night, but I'll let her tell you about that. So anyway, she has no idea Reed was here, as far as I know."

"What?! Who did she go home with?" I ask, extremely curious about this development despite all the chaos filling my head. We move into the TV room and sit on the couch, where I snuggle up a blanket.

Nevada just shrugs. "Like I said, I'll let her tell you. But, anyway, stop trying to change the subject. What happened after we left the Double Door?"

I don't want to lie to Nevada, and any attempt to do so would probably be pointless anyway, so I give her all the details of the previous night.

"Whoa, that's pretty intense," she says when I finish, sipping on her coffee as she appears to be digesting my story.

"Yeah, I know, right? And then I wake up and he's nowhere to be found. Did he say anything when you saw him this morning?" I ask, feeling a hint of desperation.

"No, I don't even think he saw me. I barely caught a glimpse of him as he headed out of here. So, I hate to even ask, but... where does this leave you and Will?"

I just shake my head, rubbing my eyes. "I have no clue. I love him, I really do. I mean, I thought I was ready to marry him but then Reed had to bust in here and make everything so... confusing." The reality of what happened last night, of my betrayal, continues to set in. "I feel like a total whore. Seriously. I cannot believe I'm the type of girl who would cheat on her fiancé." I feel sick.

"OK, now you just sound crazy. You are the absolute farthest thing from a whore," Nevada says, exasperated.

"Well I slept with someone other than my fiancé. So, ipso facto, I'm a whore," I say despondently.

"OK, first, enough with that ipso facto legal jargon shit, you know I hate that, and second, you slept with your long-lost love in a moment of weakness — that does not, I repeat does NOT, make you a whore. So, I don't want to hear any more about that, OK?" As Nevada looks at me sympathetically, I know she was the perfect person to confess to, not that I had any choice in the matter.

"OK," I agree. "At dinner the other night, my mom said that she had always been worried that I would never find a man I trusted enough to marry, because I would too afraid of being let down by him after what had happened with my dad cheating and then with Reed leaving me. Do you think this is some fucked up, subconscious way of me trying to push Will away?" I ask, wondering if I am grasping at straws.

"I don't know," Nevada says, pulling part of the blanket over her long legs. "Truthfully, I think you *do* love Reed, even if it is just a pent-up, passion-driven kind of love based on your dramatic past together. I'm not saying that's all it is, but it's clearly a different kind of love than what you have with Will, and maybe what you and Will have is more the kind of thing that a marriage should be based on. I don't know. Obviously the situation is anything but straightforward."

"Yeah, I'm just so confused. Really, seriously confused. I feel like the shittiest, most worthless human being for doing this to Will. And, do I tell him? Is there any way I could *not* tell him and live with myself? I can't bear the thought of losing him...He's only been gone a week but everything with him feels so distant, while everything with Reed feels so... I don't know... vivid, I guess."

"I don't know what to tell you, Brecks," Nevada says gently. "At least Will won't be home til next weekend, so you have a little time to get your bearings. And, if you can talk to Reed and get things more sorted out on that front, maybe that will help you figure out where you stand with Will?"

I sigh. "Well, that's assuming I even hear from Reed..."

"Oh stop," Nevada says. "I'm sure he went to get you bagels and coffee or something. You should have seen the way he was looking at you last night, it's unreal. And, he is ridiculously hot, so you can't really be expected to act that reasonably around him," she says with a wink, clearly trying to lighten my mood a little.

I roll my eyes at her but can't help smiling myself. "Not sure Will is gonna see it that way," I say, as I hear my BlackBerry buzz on the table.

It is only as I frantically reach to grab it that I realize how deeply stressed I have been about Reed's absence ever since I woke up. However, it is Will's name that I see illuminated on the screen. My heart races and I feel a sickening sensation setting in, but I answer anyway as Nevada looks on with intrigue.

"Hey babe," he says, his familiar accented voice somehow reassuring yet terrifying at the same time.

"Hey," I say as warmly as possible, trying to sound normal. "How are you? Sorry we didn't get to talk yesterday."

"No problemo. How was the show?"

"Great, actually. There was a really good turnout, and we didn't have any big mistakes or problems, so hopefully we'll get to headline there soon."

"Can't wait to see it. At this rate, you'll be able to ditch Baron & Riehl soon and make a full-time job out of being a rocker chick."

I can't help but laugh at this comment. "I wish. How was your grandma's birthday?" I ask, attempting to steer the conversation away from last night.

"Really nice. Most of my cousins, aunts and uncles and such on my mom's side of the family were there. I hadn't seen some of them in ten or more years, so it was great to catch up. Granny was very happy, so it was a nice day. And, no one could stop asking me about my beautiful fiancée whom my parents are always raving about," he says, and I can hear his smile through the phone. I feel sick with guilt, imagining Will's mom cheerfully discussing wedding plans as I am back here in America, cheating on her son the second he's out of the country.

"That's so sweet," I manage to say. "I'm really glad the party was a success."

"Yeah, the whole trip's been great, but I really miss you. I can't wait to come home to you."

"Me too," I say quietly, sitting back down on the couch and shooting Nevada a guilty look.

"Well, my dad and I have an afternoon tee time and we need to head out. Just wanted to try to catch you before we went. I'll call you tonight, all right?"

"Sounds good," I say, thankful to be ending the call.

"Love you, Breck."

"You too," I say, and I hang up the phone and curl back up on the couch, letting out an exaggerated moan.

"Well, that went well, from what I could hear," Nevada says, now munching on a bowl of Honey Bunches of Oats.

I shrug. "I guess," I say, feeling more confused than ever, as a new wave of angst continues to set in.

I hear my BlackBerry chirp, notifying me of a work email, and groan even louder. It's from Stan, telling me that I'm needed in the office by noon. So much for a break from work.

· · · · ·

By the time I head home from the office that evening, I still have not heard a word from Reed. No email, no call, no text. I even texted Nevada in the afternoon to double check that Reed hadn't come back to the apartment at any point after I left. Nothing.

The feeling is all too familiar, and yet, this time it is very different. This time there's no car accident, no tragic event to excuse his disappearance, no teenage innocence to blame for his blatant disregard for my feelings, and there is no way for me to erase last night and make things return to the way they were with Will. I am at a total loss as to how to feel — about Reed, about Will, about any of it. I was so preoccupied all day that I barely even noticed that this was the first time I'd seen Stan since the cocktail party. He was all business today, and I figured I would put off addressing the coat closet incident until my more pressing problems were under control.

As I walk down the hall to our apartment, I decide to stop in Hodge and Pete's place to grab my violin. I turn the door knob, which is unlocked as usual, and let myself in. Hodge, Pete and Sean are sitting around watching the Cubs game on TV, looking like they haven't moved in hours.

"Hey Breckenridge!" Hodge says enthusiastically, making me smile despite my dire emotional state.

"Hey, guys," I say. "Just wanted to grab my violin."

"It's over in the back of the hallway," Hodge says.

"Thanks for bringing it for me."

"Grab a beer and hang out with us," Pete offers, turning away from the game for a minute.

"Aw, thanks, but I can't really stay. Things are crazy at work, and I just got back from the office and need to get home."

"In the office on Sunday?" Pete asks, clearly appalled.

"I know, so awful," I agree.

"Hey, Breck, what was the deal with that dude last night?" Sean asks.

"What *dude*?" I ask innocently, wishing I hadn't bothered to grab my violin after all.

"Uh, I'm gonna go ahead and guess that he's talking about the dark and mysterious Abercrombie model looking guy that you were in some heated conversation with at the bar," Hodge offers in his good-natured yet mocking voice. I shoot him an exaggerated glare.

"Oh, him," I say. "Just an ex-boyfriend..."

"And?" Hodge asks, as both he and Sean look at me expectantly. Only Pete has remained engrossed in the game.

"You guys are such gossips," I say, with a combination of amusement and annoyance. "Seriously, you're huge dorks, you realize that, right? He's just this guy I dated in high school and the very beginning of college, and he recently kind of resurfaced out of the blue, that's all. It's no big deal."

"Ohhh, it all makes sense," Hodge says in his usual too-loud voice. "What we have here sounds like a classic case of First Lay Syndrome."

Sean nods knowingly, as he sneers.

"First what?" I ask.

"First Lay Syndrome," Hodge says, emphasizing each word and clearly enjoying this conversation a little too much. "See, every chick is permanently obsessed, some to a greater or lesser degree, with the guy she lost her virginity to. It's a fact, seriously, think about your friends. That's why girls are so obsessed with high school reunions." Clearly he is very proud of this theory.

"I went to an all-girls school," I say as I realize that this comment is pretty much irrelevant. The guys turn back to the game as I grab my violin and flee toward the door, realizing that maybe I am nothing but another pathetic girl fucking up her life due to nothing but a serious case of First Lay Syndrome.

Chapter 52

After I hightail it out of Hodge and Pete's place, I walk into my apartment. Seeing that no one is home, I remember a text from Nevada earlier in the day saying that she, Lizzy and our friends Alexa and Jess were going to see *The Proposal* at the Webster Theater. I begin heating water to make myself some pasta and then lie on the couch, my mind still stuck on Hodge's comments about First Lay Syndrome. Maybe it wasn't that far off base. Lizzy always seems nostalgic when she mentions Luke, her boyfriend freshman year at Dartmouth and the first guy she slept with, and even Nevada, not usually one to be overly sentimental, has spoken wistfully of Dakota Frisch, her first love, whom she lost her virginity to in his parents' basement at the ripe age of fifteen.

When Reed had brought up sex the first summer we dated, between my junior and senior years of high school, I'd been both terrified and intrigued at the prospect. The terror was probably the result of a combination of Catholic schooling, my insecurities and an excessive fear of teenage pregnancy, the last of which had been aggressively instilled in me by my mother.

I'd already known Reed wasn't a virgin. I'd asked him once about what the story was with him and Dalton Aldridge, having heard Sarah Sutter claim incessantly that Dalton and Reed were an on-again, off-again item. He'd looked completely uncomfortable as he said there was nothing between them, but of course I had pushed him on it. Eventually he told me their history. He said that one night, late in the summer the year before I first came to Green Island, he had been drinking a lot at a party at Shelby Rhode's house. Dalton had been coming on to him all summer, and that night she had asked him to walk her home. He'd agreed and as they'd walked along the beach, she'd starting kissing him. They'd ended up having sex right there on the sand. As he told me this, I'd felt like throwing up, but even so, I appreciated that he was being honest and tried my best to be relatively understanding about it. He said that after that night, Dalton had more or less assumed they were a couple, immediately telling all her friends that they were together. Reed claimed that he was never really interested in her, that he thought she was boring and he had just been drunk and stupid that night, but he didn't want to be the kind of asshole who slept with a friend and then blew her off. So, he'd just kind of gone along with the rumors and let people think they were together those last few weeks of summer, although he said he never hooked up with her again. Once that summer ended, he said he'd basically tried to avoid her, feeling bad about the whole situation.

After hearing this story, I didn't ask if that night with Dalton was his first time. I didn't think I could stomach his answer, because somehow I was pretty confident that it was not.

Although there had been a part of me that was worried that I might seem immature or unsophisticated due to my lack of experience, I was mostly hesitant because I knew that sex was a big deal, to me at least, and I just didn't feel ready. To my great relief, Reed had never pushed me on it at all.

As my high school graduation gift, Reed and his parents had given me an all-expenses-paid summer backpacking trip through Europe. Reed and I would fly into Lisbon in the middle of June, a few days after my graduation, and backpack around Europe for almost two solid months, flying home out of Rome in the middle of August. My mom had made her usual protests – I needed to work and earn money, the gift was much too lavish, she didn't think I was old enough to be traveling with my boyfriend for the summer, et cetera. But, she loved Reed and she loved Europe, and I think a pretty big part of her wanted to let me go, wished she'd had the opportunity at my age, so in the end she had given in. Reed, of course, had been to Europe a handful of times already, but it would be my first time. We'd spent hours planning all the cities we wanted to hit, researching hostels, train schedules, restaurants and museums, poring over *Lonely Planet* and *Let's Go*.

I can't remember ever feeling greater excitement or more pure, unabashed happiness than I felt as our plane prepared to take off from the runway at Detroit Metro Airport. Reed had flown in from New York a week earlier for my graduation, so we were on the same direct flight from Detroit to Lisbon. In typical Whalen fashion, we were flying first class, a luxury that I had never experienced before and a fact that had caused my mom to raise her eyebrow disapprovingly in more than one conversation. As the plane lifted into the air that day, a feeling that typically causes my stomach to clench for the minutes until we level off, I hadn't felt an ounce of my usual anxiety. I remember looking over at my incredible boyfriend in the spacious seat next to me as he squeezed my hand and smiled, knowing that the marvels of Europe would be waiting for us when we landed, and wondering what I had ever done to deserve such an amazing life.

It had been three weeks into the trip, when we were spending our second night at the insanely beautiful Grand Hotel Villa Serbelloni on Lake Como, that I had decided I was "ready." We'd gone for an evening kayaking trip, and with the Alps in the distance, we had watched a magnificent sunset as we glided along. We had mostly been going for the backpacking experience on this trip, but Reed had booked a few nights of luxury at the Villa Serbelloni in honor of our one-year anniversary. After a hot shower in our room's massive marble bathroom, I was sitting on the bed brushing through my long, wet hair, feeling blissfully happy, when Reed walked into the room, having returned from a quick mission to find us a few bottled waters.

"Thanks, baby," I'd said as he tossed me one, thinking how much I loved him.

"Anything for you," he'd said, planting a kiss on my lips. I'd pulled him onto the bed with me, not resisting as my towel fell off me. After a minute, I had pulled away.

"You all right?" he had asked, looking into my eyes with concern.

"I'm ready," I'd said simply, feeling drunk with love as I looked into his alarmingly beautiful face.

"You're sure?" he'd asked gently.

"Completely."

In truth, the first time had hurt a lot, despite all Reed's efforts to be gentle, but it had also been indescribably intense, and within a few more days, I was hooked. That summer had dissolved into day after endless day of unfamiliar and delectable foods, breathtaking views, historic museums, new friends, white beaches, dark tans, and making love. So, while it's true that he was my first lay, he was also my first love, and regardless of what Hodge might believe, I'm pretty sure it is the latter that I am having the hardest time letting go.

I stir the noodles in the boiling water as I let myself remember my summer abroad with Reed for the first time in a long time. Like everything else about our relationship, that summer was surreal and incredible. And then, just one month after we had returned from our summer in paradise, he'd broken my heart.

The fact that he ditched me this morning and has not so much as sent me an email has been continually stabbing at my heart throughout the day. Last night he told me that he loved me, that I'd been on his mind every day for the past eight years, and I was stupid enough to let myself get swept up in it. Once again. And now, my relationship, my *real* relationship with a guy who actually wants to be with me, might be destroyed because of my weakness. How could Reed be so selfish, so cruel?

I'm left eating my pasta, filled with a suffocating combination of anger and sadness, wondering if I ever even knew Reed at all.

Chapter 53

Monday mornings are always bad, but this one gets off to a particularly excruciating start. First, the L train that I am riding to work is delayed underground for twenty minutes, so I'm stuck sitting there without a signal on my BlackBerry, knowing Stan will be furious at me for my late arrival. Once I get to work (where I am greeted by about thirty new emails relating to Project Aristotle), Debbie comes flying into my office to ask if I have heard anything about layoffs (I haven't) and to tell me that rumors are flying to the effect that layoffs are taking place today (this information serving to intensify my stress level by a factor of about a hundred). I also find a gorgeous bouquet of flowers from Will waiting on my desk, which, according to the card, he sent just because he misses me. Talk about feeling like a truly shitty person.

As I sit in my chair, trying to avoid looking at my guilt-inducing flowers, trying to avoid thinking about Reed's disappearing act, trying to avoid considering a potential layoff, Stan saunters into my office.

"So glad you could join us this morning," he barks sarcastically, clearly in one of his more hostile moods. "Where are we with the ancillary docs? Specifically the Subordination Agreements?"

"They're coming along well. I sent the first set out to seller's counsel for review last night," I say, realizing it's not even worth the effort of explaining about the L delay.

"Well keep moving on the rest of them. Send me an updated closing checklist too. What's the status of the due diligence?"

"Finished reviewing the first batch of documents. Matt and I sent the memo to the client over the weekend. A few new documents were posted in the data room last night, so I'll review them today."

He nods. Then he points to my flowers.

"Your fiancé in the doghouse?" he asks, his gruff business tone softening slightly.

"Nope. Just being nice," I say, looking at my computer screen as I speak, my annoyance rising as I think about him grabbing my butt the other night. He nods again and then heads out.

With Stan out of sight, I pull my BlackBerry out of my purse, wanting to call Will to thank him for the flowers. He answers after a few rings and says he's in the middle of visiting with some old friends but didn't want to miss my call. We talk for a few minutes before I force myself to say goodbye and return to my work. I don't want to hang up. I'm so horribly afraid that the Will I know will be gone to me forever if and when I tell him about Reed, but I push that thought out of my mind and try to focus on my work.

Lizzy calls just after lunch. She and Nevada were still out when I went to bed last night, so I haven't spoken to her since she left the Double Door Saturday night, an unusually long time for the two of us to go without talking.

"Hey you!" I say, happy to talk to her, even if I can't break from my work for long.

"Hey! I feel like I haven't seen you in forever, and I have so much to tell you about. Will you be working late tonight?"

"Ugh, yeah, unfortunately. I doubt I'll get out of here before midnight. I need to hear about Saturday night though. Ney was being pretty illusive but sounds like you didn't come home that night? I've been dying to hear about it."

"I know, I've been dying to talk to you about it too, but I'd rather wait until we had a little time to hang out. Are you gonna make it to Tiparo's for Tuesday dinner?" Unlike Nevada, Lizzy is not a guilt-tripper, and although I know she will understand if I can't make it, I can't help but feel wrong about continually canceling on my friends because of work.

"Yeah, I'll be there," I say. Even though I'll probably have to come back to the office after dinner, I don't want to miss the chance to see my friends, even if it's only for an hour.

"Oh good! I didn't think you'd be able to...I can't wait to catch up on everything."

"Me too. I miss you," I say, realizing as I tell her this that I desperately need Lizzy's insight, that I feel a little bit like I'm coming undone, between my guilt about Will, my anger at Reed, my stress over work.

"Miss you too. See you tonight or tomorrow."

As I extend my arm to replace the phone in the cradle, I am startled by Debbie barreling into my office.

Her eyes are rimmed with red and her face looks utterly panicked as she quickly closes my office door behind her.

"Deb! Are you OK?" I ask, suddenly feeling panicky myself.

She shakes her head sadly. "The rumors were true. I just got a call from Sandra Simpson in HR to come to one of the conference rooms, and when I walked in, they told me they were letting me go." As she says the word "go," her face crumples slightly and her eyes begin to shine with tears. "I'm sixty-three and there are so many unemployed secretaries. How will I ever find another job? How will I pay my bills..."

My heart is breaking as I watch this sweet woman fall apart in my office. She slumps down in one of my chairs and I walk over to her and lean down to give her a hug.

"You're an incredible secretary," I tell her honestly, "and you *will* find another job. I promise."

"I can't believe they could do this to me. I've been here thirty-one years, you know?"

"I know..." I say sadly, unsure of what I can do to possibly make her feel better.

"Well, Sandra told me that I had to quickly box up my desk and be out of the office within an hour. She said I couldn't stop to talk to anyone because they don't want people getting upset. Can you believe she said that? But, I don't care. I'm saying goodbye to all my friends before I pack up. They can throw me out of here if they have a problem with that." A hint of a smile returns to her face.

"Yeah, that's completely ridiculous. I can't believe she would tell you that. I mean, I can, but, what a compassionless idiot. I'm so sorry that they're treating you like this. Really, I'm disgusted by this place," I say, feeling sad and powerless as I think of how Baron & Riehl is treating Deb after all her years of service, of how one of the heads of the firm felt entitled to grope me without any fear of consequences and continues to make millions of dollars a year while Debbie, who has done nothing but work extremely hard for this firm all her life, is about to literally be shoved out on the street.

"Well, I should get going, lots of goodbyes to say," she says, slowly rising from the chair. "Here's my personal email address," she says, handing me a little piece of paper. "You better keep in touch – I expect you to keep me in the loop with ALL the wedding details."

"Don't worry – I'll send you daily updates. Within a week you'll probably regret even giving me your email address," I say, trying to lighten her mood.

"Ha! Never," she says, giving me another quick hug and then reaching for the door.

"Oh, and Brecken," she adds, looking somber, "please don't ever forget that you're so much better than these heartless assholes you work for, OK? Don't ever let them change you," she says, and with that she is gone.

Chapter 54

Tuesday evening my cab is swerving through the later end of rush hour traffic as it heads toward Tiparo's. Although I am still buried in work, having left the office for only about four hours total last night to sleep, I refuse to miss dinner with my friends. I'll definitely be stuck in the office until close to sunrise again tonight, so I was thankful to have this little dinner break to look forward to all day. Debbie is just one of thirty support staff employees who were "let go" from our office yesterday, and an additional fifty staff members were laid off from Baron & Riehl's other offices around the country. No attorneys were included in this layoff, but the murmur around the office is that attorney layoffs will be coming next. Since the beginning of the whole subprime mortgage crisis, our real estate practice group has been especially slow, so it seems likely that the real estate attorneys might be the first group impacted. Then again, first year associates are always pretty expendable, and I've been feeling anxiety bubbling within me since the news hit yesterday, no matter how much I've been trying to keep it at bay.

Watching Debbie and the other secretaries pack their desks had been a painful experience. Of my neighboring squad, Rhoda had also been laid off, which she took even harder than Debbie, having an ill husband who is unable to work and relies on both her paycheck and her health insurance to get by. Tears had welled up in my eyes when she stopped in my office and said goodbye, her bottom lip quivering slightly as she tried to stoically tell me there was no need to worry about her, that she would be just fine.

Between my agony over Reed and Will and the depressing state of affairs in the office, I can't remember the last time I felt so abysmal. Wait, yes I can, it was the last time Reed abandoned me without a hint of an explanation. Fool me once shame on you, fool me twice... Yep, I'm an idiot. Really, I can't help but wonder what's wrong with me, how I allowed myself to end up here. How could I be stupid enough to get myself into this mess where my only options are lying to Will or risking losing him forever? How did I let myself become tangled up in Reed again?

While briefly escaping from the office for dinner with Lizzy and Nevada is the only bright spot in my day, I'm still not sure how to tell Lizzy about what happened with Reed, knowing how disappointed she will be in me. Almost as disappointed as I am in myself. I honestly don't know if I can bear it given my current emotional state. But, I also know that I just have to suffer through the conversation at some point, and I am in dire need of her insight. Thankfully Stan conveniently left the office before me because he had tickets to see Keith Jarrett in concert out in the suburbs at Ravinia tonight, so he'll be none the wiser about my little extended dinner break.

The cab pulls over just before we reach North Avenue, and I speed inside Tiparo's, knowing I'm already at least five minutes late. I spot Lizzy sitting alone in one of the tables near the back. She smiles when she sees me, and I slide into seat across from her.

"Sorry I'm late!"

"No prob — I'm so glad you could make it at all with all your work."

"Where's Ney?" I ask, surprised that I've beaten her to the restaurant.

"Not coming. She said to tell you she's sorry. Her dad is randomly in town though! He wanted to get dinner with her, so of course she wanted to go."

"Yeah, of course," I say, completely taken aback by this information. In the eight or so years that Nevada and I have been friends, she has only seen her dad one other time and rarely hears from him. I'm curious to hear about his visit and also concerned for my friend, who I know is hurt much more than she lets on by her dad's lack of interest in her life.

"So we'll see how that goes..." Lizzy says, clearly just as skeptical about Nevada's dad's visit as I am. The waiter arrives and I order a Coke, hoping a little caffeine burst will help perk me up for the long night ahead.

"OK, so, I need to hear about your Saturday night," I start in.

An awkward smile immediately creeps across her face, along with a flush of crimson that colors her cheeks. Lizzy is shy by nature, and even though we've been like sisters for pretty much our whole lives, I still often have to pry personal information out of her.

"Well, I already know you hooked up with someone, so come on, let's hear about it," I say.

"I feel weird telling you..." she says, still looking hesitant and awkward. While she is definitely more on the reserved side, this is a bit much even for her.

She is saved momentarily by the waiter, who has reappeared with my Coke and Lizzy's water and asks for our order. When he leaves the table, I give Lizzy a hard look. "Come on," I say, motioning with my hand for her to begin.

"OK... it was Pete," she spits the words out as if confessing some terrible crime. I have to admit I'm caught off-guard by this one. We've been friends with Pete Karaca for years now, and although I now vaguely recall her mentioning that he was cute when we first met him, back when he had a serious girlfriend, I've never had any inkling that she was still interested in him all these years later.

"Pete?! As in, Pete Karaca?" I ask, already knowing the answer before she nods in response.

"Was this just a drunken thing or more?" I ask, although I know full well that Lizzy isn't really one to do the drunken hook up thing.

"More I think," she stays, still looking timid.

"Well, tell me how it happened," I say, intrigued.

"All right, all right..." Lizzy says hesitantly, with a silly smile on her face once again. "Well, the other night at Map Room, he and I ended up talking for a while, just the two of us, after you left. And, it was just really natural and he's such an interesting, sweet guy. I had the best time with him, and I realized that I've never really hung out with him outside a big group, and Hodge is usually dominating the conversation, as you know."

I nod along supportively, wondering how I've never considered that the two of them might be a good fit.

"And I've always thought he was really good looking, but you know, he was dating Violet when we first met him and then by the time they broke up, it was so established that we were all just good friends that it seemed like he would never think of me as anything more than that, so I just kind of tried to forget about him."

I'm surprised that Lizzy has never mentioned her lingering feelings for Pete to me. Maybe she felt weird since he and I are such good friends, but it is really unlike her to keep something like this from me.

As if reading my mind, she says, "sorry that I never mentioned that I liked him to you...I guess I felt a little bit pathetic about it or something, because I didn't really think he'd be into me. He's so different from the guys I usually like and...I don't know, I guess I didn't want you and Ney always analyzing my interactions with him, even if you weren't doing it intentionally, you know?"

"I know what you mean, don't worry about it at all. So let's hear the rest, the suspense is killing me," I say with a smile.

She laughs, and I can tell she is genuinely happy. "OK," she says, "so Saturday night we left the Double Door to go to InnJoy, and by the way, we still need to talk about your night as well," she says, pausing to give me a look before she goes on. "But anyway, about an hour later, Hodge was texting Nevada saying that he, Pete and Tim wanted to meet up with us. The three of them met us at InnJoy, and Pete and I spent most of the night hanging out and talking. He's so funny, and I just feel like he really gets me..." She is smiling again as she trails off. "Anyway, a few hours later Pete and I were ready to head home and everyone else wanted to stay out. When the cab dropped us off, before going inside, he asked if I wanted to go for a walk. I thought it was pretty sweet, even though it was past 2 A.M. at this point and I was exhausted. But anyway, of course I wanted to go, and we walked around Old Town for a while, then sat outside the building on the benches by the fountain until the sun came up. When we finally headed back inside, he goes, 'I don't want you to go home yet.' So I slept at his place. We kissed a little bit, but mostly we just slept."

"Wow," I say, mostly taken by how happy Lizzy seems as she's telling me this story. Our food has arrived and I take my first bite of pad se euw as I ask her whether things between them still felt comfortable the next morning.

"Yeah, really comfortable," she says, ladling yellow curry over her rice. "I mean, it was maybe a tiny bit weird for a second when I woke up because, you know, it's *Pete* and I thought I might have to deal with Hodge hassling me if he saw me leaving. But for the most part, it was still really good between us. And, he called me just before I got here tonight to see if I'd want to go out to dinner with him Saturday night."

"Aww, this is so exciting," I say, considering Pete Karaca. While he certainly isn't Lizzy's usual cup of tea, which I think could be a good thing, he's a pretty great catch. Both his parents were born in Turkey and he has an exotic sexiness to him that Lizzy's past preppy all-American boyfriends have certainly lacked. Although he comes off as kind of quiet he has a really witty, dry sense of humor when you talk to him. He teaches middle school math at a public school on the south side of Chicago, and Hodge was once telling me that Pete's read every book ever written on Nelson Mandela. "Do you know where he's taking you for dinner?" I ask.

"Nah. He mentioned maybe going to get Turkish food somewhere though, since I was telling him I'd never tried it."

I smile at her in response, as I continue inhaling my food.

"Sooo..." she starts in, and I fear the conversation is headed my way. "Enough about me. I need to hear about the rest of *your* night. I was asking Nevada if she'd talked to you about it, but she said I had to ask you myself. So, let's hear it."

I sigh, not knowing where to start. "Well, essentially, after you left the Double Door, Reed started asking me all about Will and then made some rude remark about my ring not being the right ring for me, and I got really upset by the whole conversation and left. He showed up at our apartment a little while later, telling me that he has loved me all along. And for some unknown reason I succumbed to it and we ended up sleeping together." I look down at my food as I quickly mumble this last part then make sure to keep talking so as not to give Lizzy time to react. "He left in the morning before I woke up though, and I haven't heard a single word from him since. Absolutely nothing. I can barely carry on a normal conversation with Will because I feel so profoundly guilty and overwhelmed. I feel sick about the whole situation, and I have no idea what to do." Only now do I look up from my pad se euw to meet Lizzy's eyes.

"I know what you're thinking," I say. "You warned me that this would happen. It's so pathetic, I know, but I completely lose any ability to act sane when Reed is around." I am near tears again for the umpteenth time in the past week and a half.

"I know you do," she says gently, without a trace of judgment. "That's why I wanted you to stay away from him."

"But I didn't..." I say sadly. "And now, my whole life is a mess. Can you believe he would just leave me like that?"

"No. I honestly can't," Lizzy says. "Have you decided if you're going to tell Will? I mean, what do you plan to do?"

"I feel like I have to tell him," I say. "But I can't imagine that he could ever forgive me. And, I can't imagine losing him. Do you think there's any way I could act like it never happened?" I ask, hopeful that Lizzy will see this as a viable and not completely evil option.

"I don't think so, Breck. You're such a good person, and you have that guilty conscience of yours. You could never live with keeping a secret like that from Will."

"I know," I agree softly. "But then there's no way this can have a happy ending...At least not one I can see."

"Maybe he'll forgive you?" Lizzy suggests hopefully, although frankly she doesn't sound like she really believes this is possible.

"For sleeping with my ex-boyfriend the week after we got engaged? Do you really think he might?"

"Well, not right away. But, he really loves you, Breck, so you just never know. Maybe over time he could. I have no idea."

The waiter soon clears our plates and delivers our check. Somehow talking with Lizzy about what I've done has made the gravity of the situation infinitely more real. Not only could I lose Will, I most likely *will* lose him. And there doesn't really seem to be any way around it.

"I cannot believe I have to go back to the office right now," I mutter, feeling pretty despondent about my life in general at this particular moment.

"Yeah, that's horrible," Lizzy agrees. "I wish there was something I could do to help." She pays with her credit card as I give her money for my portion in cash.

"Why'd you do it?" Lizzy eventually asks, her voice gentle.

"I don't know, really," I say. But maybe I do, sort of, know why I did it, even if it's too depressing to admit. Because, when I saw Reed again, everything else melted away, just as it always has. And now, the life I've built in the years since he left is in jeopardy because I was foolish enough to believe that this time was different. I was stupid enough to think that this time when he said he loved me, he meant that he would stick around.

Chapter 55

It's been over three hours since I returned to the office from Tiparo's, and I'm still working through the obscene number of ancillary documents that need to be prepared for Project Aristotle. Deeply ensconced in my drafting and revising, Stan's voice causes me to nearly jump from my seat.

"Hope you're not mad at me for leaving you to work while I went to a concert," he says, his slightly leering voice making me uneasy.

"Just one of the joys of being an associate," I say, forcing a smile and feigning a lighthearted attitude. "Matt and John are still here working on Aristotle stuff too anyway, so I've had people to go to with questions that have come up."

"That's good..." he says, still milling near my doorway.

"How come you're back here?" I ask, hoping to find out if he will be leaving soon. "Weren't you all the way out at Ravinia?"

"I was..." he says, closing my office door behind him as he walks further into my office, making a little burst of anxious adrenaline shoot down my spine. "But, I realized I forgot my condo keys in my office, so I had to stop by here to grab them."

"Oh, OK," I say, desperately wanting him to leave. "I think Matt's coming by in a few minutes to talk about a few Aristotle items," I lie, hoping this information will prompt him to open my door and head out.

"Hmm, well he wasn't in his office when I just walked past," Stan says. The realization that he and I may be alone on the floor certainly does nothing to help me relax.

"I was sorry to hear that Debbie Stanzler was laid off," Stan says, and I'm not sure how to respond.

"Yeah, it was awful to watch her go through that," I say, not wanting to discuss the matter with him, knowing he was probably one of the decision-makers who had approved the layoff.

"Have you heard that attorney layoffs are expected to follow?" he asks, clearly knowing this will get a reaction out of me.

I try not to show my surprise that he is broaching this subject. "I've heard some rumors about that," I say, curious where he is going with this. "Are you saying there's truth to them?" I ask tentatively.

"Well, I assume I can trust you not to say anything about this, since only the Executive Committee members know the particulars," he pauses for a second as if re-considering.

I'm shocked that he would discuss a confidential Executive Committee matter like this with me and can't help but wonder how much he had to drink at the concert.

Before I respond in any way, he continues. "So, yes, unfortunately there will be attorney layoffs coming soon. Junior associates, especially in the transactional practice groups, are going to be hit the hardest." He glances around my office, as if intentionally forcing this last comment to hang in the air.

I am officially panicking, which is obviously what he had in mind, given that I'm a junior associate in a transactional practice group.

"So, are you trying to tell me that I'm going to be laid off?" I ask, desperately trying to stay calm but seeing no point in continuing to beat around the bush.

Stan looks away and rubs both his hands through his hair, as though he's trying out for a dandruff shampoo commercial, and waits a few seconds before responding.

"Well, the names aren't set in stone yet..." He gives me a penetrating look as he says it. "I could make sure you're not on the list."

"What?" I ask, instinctively looking down, afraid I already know what he is suggesting.

He walks a few steps closer to me. "Brecken," he begins slowly, each subsequent word then picking up momentum, "maybe I seem old to you, and I know you're engaged and all that... but I cannot even begin to fucking concentrate with you around. All I can think about when I see your long tan legs and that fucking perfect face is having you in my bed. What I'm saying is, just come home with me tonight, and I'll look after you, trust me. You won't regret it."

His face looks so earnest as he makes this disgusting proposition that there is a part of me that almost thinks I must have misheard him. I feel paralyzed, unable to react.

"You're too beautiful to be a lawyer. It's not fair to the rest of us who have to work with you," he says in a voice that suggests he is trying to be cute with this last comment.

My frozen state passes, and I spring to life, my pulse racing from a combination of fear and anger as I rush past Stan.

Without a word, I zoom out the door of my office, heading for the elevator bank. Thankfully, I do not hear footsteps behind me as I wait for an elevator. About fifteen seconds pass before I hear the bing letting me know that one has arrived, but it feels like an eternity as I stand there, anxious and awkward.

Once I hit the ground floor, I hurriedly jump into a cab waiting outside Baron & Riehl's building. As soon as the cab pulls out, I realize that I am sweating and my whole body begins to shake as I breathe deeply in an effort to calm myself.

Chapter 56

Never in my life have I longed to skip work as desperately as I did when I woke up this morning. I wanted nothing more than to stay in my cozy bed all day and hibernate, to escape the deluge of problems that has become my life in the past few weeks. Nonetheless, I couldn't stay home. I have something very important to tend to today.

When I walked into my apartment last night, I'd found Nevada on a high from her first completely positive interaction with her dad in years, especially from his seemingly heartfelt promise to be better about staying in touch with her. Although, of course, she knows by now to take his words with a grain of salt, or more like a whole salt shaker, she seems genuinely hopeful that he's turned over a new leaf, and this hope was evident in her every movement.

I hated to disrupt Nevada's buoyant mood, but I was still completely shaken when I arrived home, and I frantically filled her and Lizzy in on what had happened with Stan. They were horrified. Lizzy thought I should quit immediately and sue Baron & Riehl. Nevada, however, had a different take on the situation, and in the end we all agreed that her strategy was the best. After all, the messed up reality is that a lawyer who sues her law firm will never be hired by another firm. Filing a sexual harassment lawsuit would not only be an expensive, drawn-out, embarrassing and tedious process, it would also be a death sentence for any hope I had of working at a different firm in the future, and I'll have student loans hanging over me for the rest of my life if I don't have a big firm paycheck for at least two more years.

Instead of suing, Nevada had concocted what felt like an ingenious scheme to the three of us as we shared a late night bottle of wine.

Now, however, in the light of day, I worry that the plan is crazy, fear that I can't possibly pull it off. I consider calling Will for support, but I know that he will probably think jumping on a flight to Chicago and then murdering Stan is the best course of action, so I decide I'll stay calmer if I keep him out of it. And besides, everything with him is complicated enough as it is, even if he doesn't realize it yet. My mind floats to Reed for an instant before I reel it back, reminding myself that thoughts of Reed Whalen are no longer an option.

The work day passes in a flurry of Project Aristotle issues, with my anxiety mounting as the minutes tick by. Stan steers clear of my office all day, which doesn't surprise me and is exactly what I expected would happen.

By 9:00 P.M., most of the lawyers on my floor are gone for the evening, and I know that it's time to take action. I am trembling as I walk down the hall to Stan's office. The door is open a crack, through which I can only see a sliver of the adjacent wall. I knock gently, feeling lightheaded but determined.

"Come in," Stan says, and judging by his tone, he's in a decent mood.

I push the door open a bit further and slide into his large corner office without making eye contact. After pressing the door shut, I turn and face him. If he is surprised to see me, his face doesn't give him away.

"I've been thinking about what you said last night," I say, looking him in the eye without wavering, my voice sounding surprisingly steady despite the fact that my pulse is racing and my heart is beating rapidly. "I guess I was pretty overwhelmed when I ran out of here," I add.

"I apologize if I came on too strong," Stan says, his voice sounding as though he means it to be soothing. "Please, sit down. Let's talk."

I pull out a chair and sit across the desk from him. He stands up and moves from behind his desk to the other "visitor's chair" right next to me, his leg just inches from mine. I force myself not to flinch and immediately start in again with the lines I have been rehearsing in my head all day.

"Well, I guess I just want to make sure that I fully understand what you're proposing..." I trail off for a minute, forcing a shy smile. "If I sleep with you, then I definitely won't get laid off, right? I mean, I want to make sure that you're guaranteeing that for me."

He chuckles for an instant. "Well I hate to think of it as such a cut and dried business proposal. But, yes, I am offering to shield you from the impending layoffs, if you spend a night giving me a chance to win you over from that fiancé of yours in the bedroom. You might be surprised by all the experience that comes with age."

I resist the urge to throw up and try to keep a sweet look on my face in response to this comment. This is a man who has a daughter my age yet would treat me this way nonetheless.

"But if I weren't to give you a chance, then I may be included in the upcoming round of layoffs?" I ask.

He sniffs at this. "Well, as much as I hate to say it, I don't think I can go on being in such close proximity with you. You know, unless there is more going on between us. It's pure torture for me," he says with a wink. "So, you can probably go ahead and assume you will be included in the layoffs if you're not interested in my offer, as much as I would miss having you here. You might have been included anyway though, of course, so don't take it personally. You'd get severance and all the rest of the package that the others will get, so it's not all bad." He pauses, for a moment, before adding a final thought. "Of course, as you know, it's a pretty terrible job market out there for attorneys these days."

I am just standing there stupidly. "Well, I guess that's what they call an offer you can't refuse," I say, feeling hatred pulsing inside me yet fighting to keep an amicable look on my face. "I'm pretty much done with my work for tonight, would you want to grab dinner?"

"How about I treat you to dinner at Shaw's and then we can head back to my place."

"Sure, can I meet you back here in a few minutes?" I ask, my skin crawling. "I just need to change around my plans for tonight."

He is beaming. "Take your time, beautiful," he says in a voice I assume he intends to be sexy but which is simply very, very creepy, and I hightail it out of there. I rush down the hall to the women's bathroom, where I figure he won't be barging in, although maybe that's giving him too much credit.

Once I'm in a stall, I pull Lizzy's iPhone out of my pants pocket and hit "stop" on the voice recording app that we downloaded last night. Following the instructions Lizzy gave me, I save the file containing the recording of my conversation with Stan and email a copy to my own gmail address. I send a copy to Lizzy and Nevada as well.

Having ensured that multiple copies of the recording are safely stored, I turn the volume down low and play the conversation back to the empty bathroom, smiling at the confirmation that I have all the incriminating evidence I need. I send Nevada a text saying I will be ready for her and Lizzy to pick me up outside my office in about fifteen minutes.

Here goes, I think, as I head back towards Stan's office.

I walk in again and close the door.

"Ready to get out of here?" he asks, grinning at me.

"Actually, no, I'm not ready, you piece of shit," I say calmly and evenly, as I watch a stunned look of confusion wash over his face. I pull out the iPhone, click on the recorded conversation and press *play*.

His face becomes twisted in a sickened expression and then red with rage. "What is this?" he asks, nearly spitting out the words. "What the fuck is this?!"

"*This* is a recording of you sexually harassing me, Stan," I say coldly, surprised by the anger in my voice. "I already have several copies of it saved for safekeeping." I pause for a moment to let this sink in. "Remember how you gave me two options earlier this evening? The first was that I sleep with you and the second was that I lose my job?" I pause again, even though I know he won't respond. He continues to stare at me with pure hatred in his eyes.

Urging myself to stay calm, I try again. "Do you remember that, Stan? I can play it back for you again if you want."

"What do you want from me?" he hisses.

"Well, now I'm giving *you* two options," I say coldly, just wanting this conversation to be over with. "Your first option is that I send a copy of this recording to each member of the Executive Committee, the managing partner, abovethelaw.com, and so on. And then we'll let the chips fall as they may. If you succeed in finding a new job after that, I will send this on to your new employer as well. The second option is that I keep this recording to myself, which I will do only if you meet certain requirements. The first requirement is that my office be moved to the 32nd or 33rd floor with the litigation attorneys and that you personally see to it that I am added to enough litigation matters to fill my days. I know a well-respected partner like you has that kind of clout," I say, emphasizing the word *well-respected*. "And, since you know I actually am a good associate, you don't even have to worry that I'll make you look bad. I expect this full transition to litigation to be in effect by next week. In addition, effective now, I will never, ever be asked to work with you again. The last requirement of this option is that you will call each and every contact you have in Chicago until you find legal secretary jobs for both Debbie Stanzler and Rhoda Webster where they will be paid at least as much as they were making here. If you do not find both women a job within one month, the deal is off."

By this point, he is looking through me. It is clear that he is desperately thinking of a way to regain the upper-hand yet seems to realize there isn't one. My roommates and I spent all last night making sure there was no way he could turn this on me.

"So," I say, my voice firm with resolve, "which will it be?"

It's silent for a few seconds, and I am about to repeat my question when he clears his voice.

"Get the fuck out of here," he says. "Your office will be moved tomorrow. Consider yourself done on Aristotle. I'll have litigation partners contact you by Friday." His voice is venomous, and I cannot be out of there soon enough.

"Don't forget about Debbie and Rhoda," I say. "They need good jobs within a month."

"I heard you the first time," he barks.

"OK, so assuming they get jobs and all my other requirements are met within these time frames, consider your disgusting behavior to be our little secret."

And with that, I turn on my heel and walk confidently out of his office, leaving the door open behind me. Only then do I realize how tightly I am clenching Lizzy's iPhone. I loosen my grasp and quietly exhale. Once I'm out of his sight, I nearly run to my office, grab my purse and then scoot into the elevators. My personal life may be in ruins, but maybe there is hope for me as a lawyer yet.

I hurry out of the building into the unusually warm May night and see Lizzy's Range Rover waiting next to the curb.

Nevada rolls down the passenger window before I get close to the car. "You did it!" she squeals out the window, as I practically dive into the backseat.

"I've been freaking out!" Lizzy says as she shifts into drive. "We just got your emails and listened to the recording. It was perfect. What a skeaze!"

"I know! But, he agreed to get me out of the corporate group and into litigation, and he knows he has to find jobs for Debbie and Rhoda," I say, handing Lizzy's phone back to her.

"I wanted to bring champagne for the ride, but Lizzy said I couldn't," Nevada says, smiling her mischievous smile.

I laugh, relieved to feel that at least some of the weight that was bearing down on me all day has lifted. "Thanks for all your help, guys," I say.

"This was kind of exciting actually!" Nevada says. "I had a total adrenaline rush when you sent us the voice recording. I'm kind of sad it's over with, to be honest," she laughs.

"She does *not* mean that!" Lizzy says, and I just smile as the two of them dissolve into their affectionate bickering and I fall back into my seat and breathe a deep sigh of relief.

Chapter 57

I am a total and complete wreck, barely able to function as I drive toward O'Hare Airport to pick up Will. The sad truth is that I still don't know what to do, what to say, how to act. Nevada has been avidly advocating for me to hold off on telling Will about Reed. In her view, what happened was an understandable slip-up, rather than a complete betrayal, which is how it feels to me. Knowing Will, he's going to want to get home and shower after his long flight, so my current plan of action is to see how things feel on the ride to his apartment and then to collect my thoughts once we've made it to his place. I admit that it isn't much of a plan, but it's all I've got. It's difficult to believe that it has been only a week since the night Reed was in my bed. Once again he feels like a long-lost memory, a mirage of sorts, although unfortunately the damage he's done is real.

It isn't as though I haven't considered sending Reed an email. In my head, I've written a million emails – ranging from furious and seething to brokenhearted and deeply confused by his actions. But ultimately I've realized there isn't anything I can say that will change what happened. Whatever was going through his head when he left me there sleeping last weekend, disappearing once again without a trace, there is nothing that he could say to justify how he's acted, nothing that could ever make it right. And, so, I am left to pick up the pieces of my life once again.

The first piece being my relationship with my fiancé, which I desperately hope is not shattered beyond the possibility of repair. Hopefully everything will be clearer once I see him, it has to be.

As I pull into the pick-up waiting lane, a text message pops up from Will letting me know that he's landed and is nearly to baggage claim. My stomach begins to cramp with anxiety as I respond to say that I'm outside waiting for him. Maybe my timely arrival earns me one karmic point to begin offsetting my great betrayal? As I sit there contemplating how many considerate deeds it would take to counteract cheating a week after getting engaged, my shame and sadness continue to multiply.

Flipping on Lizzy's car radio, which is unsurprisingly tuned to 94.7, "Chicago's True Oldies" station, "Ooh Ooh Child" is just beginning, and I'm transported back to the night my friendship with Nevada began, years ago in Ann Arbor. I'm feeling the tiniest bit cheered by the song until I spot Will's blond head emerging from the airport, surveying the cars in search of Lizzy's Range Rover. I just sit there taking him in for a moment, the exuberant way that he is searching for me, and I wonder if maybe I could just put Reed and all that happened behind me, if I could believe that perhaps it was simply an inevitable misstep that was necessary for me to fully commit to Will. I am liking this thought and carry it with me as I honk lightly and wave to him, his face shifting to a full-blown smile as he spots me.

He opens the passenger door first, before going around back to load his suitcases.

"Babe!" he cries enthusiastically as he leans in the door. "God it's good to see you!"

"Hi!" I exclaim, and he leans over the middle compartment to kiss me.

I lean in as well, but when his lips touch mine, I feel nothing. In that moment, I realize that it is over with us, and a deep sensation of loss plants itself in my gut.

"Let me just throw these in the back and then let's get out of here!" As he says it, his British accent is as charming as ever. The lilting happiness of his voice makes it clear that whatever change has occurred is only within me.

Maybe the fact that I cheated at all should have been my clear sign that I do not love Will enough to marry him, but I so deeply wanted to believe it was just a misstep. However, I can no longer hide from the truth that was revealed when we kissed, after two weeks apart nonetheless, and I felt absolutely nothing. Nothing other than sadness, that is. And marriage is hard enough, from what I can tell, without such a lackluster launching pad.

As he climbs into shotgun, announcing how glad he is to be home and that he's craving a greasy American cheeseburger for dinner, possibly from Twisted Spoke, my face crumples and I begin to cry.

"Babe, oh, no, what's going on?" he asks urgently, clearly very distressed. I know I could tell him about Stan and explain the tears away, but I can't carry on this lie any longer. As much as I know I have to be honest, I hate that I have created such an awful situation, such an awful truth. I really, truly, absolutely hate it.

I can't look at him. "I... I slept with someone while you were away," I say, the words coming out in a choking stream. Will is silent, and all I hear is honking from the car behind me, awkwardly forcing me to pull the car up several yards and off to the side, out of the way of the other pick-ups, in the midst of my confession.

Finally he talks, and I can tell he is on the verge of crying. "How could you?" he asks, his voice sounding hollow and lost. "Really, Brecken, *how* could you do this to me? To us?"

"I'm so sorry. I know it doesn't mean much, but I've been sick over this, and I cannot even begin to tell you how sorry I am. I guess... I guess maybe I'm not ready to get married, I guess I got scared," I say lamely, my voice shaking through my tears.

"Well, that's a pretty fucking shitty way of letting me know," he says coldly.

I try to speak but only tears will come out, so I just hang my head. "I'm so ashamed of myself," I mumble quietly.

"You and I, we're done," he says somberly. "I'm taking a cab. Open the trunk."

"Let me drive you," I say, choking the words out between sobs.

"Open the trunk," he says, more forcefully this time, and I reach over and click the button to release the back hatch.

He doesn't look at me as he gets out of the car and slams the front door, nor when he opens the trunk to pull out his suitcases. I watch him go in the rearview mirror, rolling one of his bags as he works his way back toward the cab line.

As he becomes smaller and smaller, I am overcome by both devastation and relief. And then there's the fear. The fear that Reed has ruined me forever, that every man will eventually dim in comparison to that first unattainable boy, whom I seem unable to stop loving, no matter how many times he hurts me.

I wait until I see Will get into a cab before I drive away. A minute later, his cab speeds past me as we pull onto the expressway, but he doesn't so much as glance my way.

I drive back in silence, trying with limited success to clear my mind as I work my way back home through the Saturday evening traffic, numbly watching the buildings along the skyline increase in size as the sun sets behind me.

Chapter 58

"This is crazy," Nevada says, looking floored.

"Jesus, are you all right?" Lizzy asks, as I relay the break up to the two of them upon my return home from the airport.

"I don't know. Maybe not. I am a *terrible* person, I cheated on my *fiancé*..." I say, feeling completely forlorn.

"You are not a terrible person," Lizzy says emphatically. "What are you supposed to do? Marry someone you're not in love with anymore? I mean, you would be a terrible person if you *did* marry him. Sleeping with Reed wouldn't have obliterated your feelings for Will if they were real. In retrospect, I think you slept with Reed *because* deep down you must not have wanted to marry Will. Reed was just your way out, being with him again just made you realize that you and Will were lacking something," Lizzy says, now fully backing me up, as I can always count on her to do.

"Do you really believe that?" I ask skeptically. "Or are you just trying to make me feel better?"

"I really believe it," Lizzy says with conviction, and I can tell she's being honest. "You know what a big fan I am of Will, but you can't *marry* someone if you have doubts about him. You can't *marry* someone who you're not excited to kiss. Hopefully you weren't just feeding me bullshit all those times that you insisted to me that the world is full of incredible people – incredible guys – and that the challenge is just finding the one who is the perfect fit. It just turns out that Will wasn't your perfect fit, and you should be so thankful you realized that now, rather than when we were driving to the church on your wedding day or something. Geez, I probably would have had to be the one to tell the guests that there would be no wedding, so I really appreciate you sparing me that experience," she says, smiling.

"Yeah, right, you know you would have put that on me, Liz," Nevada yells from the kitchen. Lizzy ignores her.

"I'm supposed to be going to dinner with Pete tonight, but maybe I should cancel," Lizzy says.

"No way, please don't," I say. "Honestly, I kind of just feel like being alone anyway. I might borrow your bathtub though, if that's OK."

"Obviously. All right, well let me know if you want to meet up later..." She trails off, and I can tell she feels bad about leaving me.

"I'm staying in too," Nevada announces, returning to the TV room. "I need a break from going out, plus I have to prepare some stuff for our meetings with potential investors on Monday. So, I'll be around if you want some company," she says, squeezing my arm.

Feeling completely drained, I hug my friends and then head off to my room. Not bothering to turn on the bedroom lights, I slide my engagement ring off my finger and place it on my bedside table, feeling my way in the dark. I lie down on my bed, slipping off my jeans and bra, and curl up in my unmade bed. I lie there for hours, lost in my thoughts. Thoughts of Will, thoughts of Reed, thoughts of my parents, of my life in general. At some point I slip away into a night of restless dreams.

Chapter 59

I'm just settling in at work on Monday morning when two men from the file room and one woman from the IT department arrive at my door saying they have instructions to pack up my files and move everything to an office on the 33rd floor. I can't contain my smile.

A few hours later, as I am getting situated in my new office, both Henry Irwin and Jeannil Taylor, two of the top partners in the litigation practice group, call me to ask if I have availability to get involved in current cases. And, by that afternoon I am starting one document review project and assisting a senior associate in preparing a summary judgment motion for another case. While I know the litigation work will be just as tough as the corporate work I've been doing, at least I feel hopeful that I'll finally be gaining skills that will be useful to me when I am able to finally break free of Baron & Riehl.

While I still feel weepy and a significant sense of loss about Will, I also feel surprisingly OK for someone who just broke up with her fiancé. The fact that I'm not heartbroken about Will provides me some degree of comfort that breaking up was the right thing for us, although I clearly could have gotten to that realization in a less awful way.

After my emotional Saturday with Will, I'd spent all day Sunday lounging with my roommates – watching *When Harry Met Sally*, *Pretty Woman* and parts of other lighthearted romantic comedies that we found on TV while we ate Chinese food delivered from P.F. Chang's and pumped Lizzy for details about her date with Pete. That evening, I'd eventually forced myself to shower, dress and go to band practice down the hall, knowing that playing my violin always ends up being kind of therapeutic. Before I went to bed that night, I wrote an email to Will, saying once again how sorry I was. I considered going into more detail, but I decided to keep it simple instead. I told him that I would leave a box with his stuff and my ring down with the doorman on Monday for him to pick up, knowing he never has to be at the hospital during the day on Mondays.

• • • • •

Will didn't respond to my email, but when I get back to my building Monday, Craig informs me that Will came by to retrieve the box. With this, I realize that it is really and truly over with me and Will. Despite the pang of sadness that hits me at this thought, I am thankful that at least I'm able to head up to my apartment actually feeling good about my day at work, for the first time in a long while. At least it's something.

It's finally June, which means it's finally summer in Chicago, the time of year that every Chicagoan lives for, the season that makes trudging through January's sloppy slush and suffering through February's icy winds seem absolutely worth it. For me, the new month feels symbolic – a new direction for my career and a drastic change in the trajectory of my life.

· · · · ·

The days pass more quickly in the litigation group, and by the end of my first week on the 33rd floor, I am already involved in four different litigation matters and most of my corporate work has been transferred to other corporate associates. Although Matt Nelson and several other associates have inquired about my sudden transfer off the floor and the cessation of all my corporate work, I just shrug in response and say that the firm was shorthanded in litigation and I was shifted to focus on that practice group. They all seem skeptical at this explanation, but if Stan is keeping his end of the deal, I plan to keep silent on my end as well.

I've spent a few evenings on the phone with my family and the friends whom I'd told about the engagement, explaining that Will and I won't be getting married. My mom is clearly deeply worried about this development, especially given that she knows Reed was back in my life, however briefly. I've repeatedly assured her that the break up had nothing to do with Reed, but I can tell she doesn't really believe it. I'll tell her the real story down the line, but not now. I am not ready to share all of that just yet. It is all still too fresh.

Griffin initially seemed mildly concerned, but after I told him once that calling off the engagement was what I wanted, he seemed OK with letting the topic go. This was one of the times that I was thankful to have a brother rather than a sister. I tried to imagine how many conversations the Sutter girls would have if one of them called off an engagement. At least a hundred. At least. And if it was Sarah doing the calling off, then many, many more than that.

My dad only asked if I thought it was for the best. When I told him yes, he said that was all that mattered to him. Even though my relationship with my dad has never fully recovered from the way he distanced himself from me and my brother, I have never doubted his love. And, truthfully, sometimes his ability to skip the bullshit and only ask the questions that really matter is exactly what I need. Although I considered sending a note to Will's family, whom I really do adore, in the end I decided that it was best to let them be. And, truthfully, I wasn't exactly sure what I could have said that would have mattered to them at this point anyway.

Chapter 60

As I read through deposition transcripts on Friday afternoon of my second week on the 33rd floor, my office phone rings. I grab it before my new secretary, Janine, picks up on my behalf.

"Brecken Pereira," I answer.

"Aww, I miss that sound already," comes Debbie's chipper voice over the phone.

"Deb! So good to hear from you! How are you?" I ask, having trouble believing it's been just a few weeks since her layoff.

"Well, I'm good. I heard from Vickie that you moved off the 38th floor. Everything all right?"

"Yeah, actually, things are great. You know I always wanted to do more litigation work, and I got the chance to move to 33 and I thought I would have more access to the litigators that way," I say, feeling pretty bad lying to her, even though I don't really have a choice.

"Good for you, Brecken. You should go after what you want."

"Aww, thanks," I say, realizing how much I already miss her.

"I'm actually calling with good news."

"Oh yeah?" I ask, thinking I might know what it is.

"Yep. I just got a job offer at Evangelista & Jelinek!"

"Wow, seriously? That's awesome! Congrats!"

"Thanks! And, actually, it gets better. The offer is for their Schaumberg office, so my commute is going to be less than half as long, and the starting salary will be a little more than I was making at Baron."

"I'm so happy for you! You totally deserve it."

"Well, the craziest part is that I hadn't even applied there yet. *They* called *me*. Apparently Stan Dillingham is a friend of the managing partner of this office of Evangelista & Jelinek, and Stan called him to tell him that I was in the market for a job and that he highly recommended me. I went in for an interview yesterday and got the job. Can you believe it?"

"Wow – that's crazy! I'm so glad this is all working out so well," I say.

"I guess I shouldn't have been so hard on Stan," Debbie says, remorsefully. "Turns out he's a good guy after all..."

"Maybe it was just a random act of kindness or something."

"Maybe so. Anyway, I'm so thankful and just wanted to let you know things were working out for the best. Sorry that I was so upset the other day – the whole thing just pretty tough for me to swallow."

"Don't say that – you had every right to be upset."

"Thanks, sweetie."

"By the way, have you heard anything about how Rhoda's doing? I've been worried about her too."

"Yes! She's already got a job lined up at DeWitt Calice! I think she starts on Monday actually."

"That's great news," I say, smiling to myself.

"It certainly is," she agrees. "Well, you hang in there, kiddo, all right? Good luck in litigation. And, keep in touch!"

"You know I will."

We hang up, and I catch myself feeling genuinely happy for the first time in weeks, thankful that some good has come out of the Stan situation. No one deserves a little luck more than Debbie. Miraculously, for once Debbie didn't mention the wedding. I'll tell her about the break up eventually, but I'm glad it will be a different conversation. I decide to call it a day at work. Tonight is Hodge's birthday dinner at Adobo Grill, and tomorrow night Ishmael is playing at The Cubby Bear in Wrigleyville for the first time, so it should be a good weekend. I walk out into the beaming sunlight of the evening, feeling as peaceful as I have in as long as I can remember.

Chapter 61

"You guys were incredible," Lizzy cries as I come out into the tightly packed crowd at The Cubby Bear. She's standing with Alexa and Jess on one side of her and Pete, who hands me a bottle of 312, on her other side. "The crowd was going crazy – could you hear it? We could barely get up near the front," Lizzy continues, always my number one fan.

"Yeah, such a good show," Pete says enthusiastically. "The manager already found me and asked about booking your next show here."

"Awesome," I say, taking a huge refreshing sip of the beer. The bar seems to be a little stingy with the air conditioning tonight, and I was sweltering under the lights on stage. A few people from the crowd gather around to talk with me about the show and compliment the music, which is always a hugely flattering but somewhat uncomfortable situation for me, because I never really know what to say. I chat with them for a few minutes before escaping to rejoin my friends.

"Where's Nevada?" I ask Lizzy as I walk up next to her.

"She met some hot bar owner when she was getting us drinks and they've been talking ever since your set ended. She claims she's getting insight for Crash..." Lizzy points to the front of the bar area where I see Nevada talking to a tall, blond, muscular guy, and I can tell just from her stance that she's in full flirtation mode.

I smile. "Nice. Someday when I'm ready to start meeting guys again, I'm going to need to get some tips from that girl."

"Brecken, do you guys have a CD out?" Alexa asks from a few feet away. "I want one!"

"We're gonna be recording a new one soon," I tell her. "But Pete can get you a copy of our old CD, if you want."

"Cool," she says, turning to talk to Pete about it. Hodge, Tim and Sean join us once they're done backstage, bringing us shots of Jager, which, for reasons I'll never understand, they love.

I groan exaggeratedly when I see it.

"You know you love it, Breckenridge," Hodge says, wrapping his arm around my shoulder. "Jager warms the belly."

"I hate you," I tell him, as I take one of the shot glasses from him, cheers the group and drink it as quickly as possible, trying to minimize its contact with my tongue. Needing a new beer and wanting to get the Jager taste out of my mouth, I turn to head over to the bar. As I step away from my group, I nearly fall over. Watching me from the other end of the bar I spot the face that fills my dreams and let out a quiet gasp.

Chapter 62

I momentarily consider bolting out the door when my eyes lock with Reed's, but I change my mind and walk right up to him, adrenaline pulsing through my veins.

"Why are you here?" I ask, my voice sounding cold and angry, even though at this point I'm more sad than mad about the whole situation with him.

He looks slightly startled and seems to consider how to respond.

"I need to talk to you," he says, with a sadness permeating his big blue eyes.

"Oh, *now you* need to talk to *me*?" I practically spit out the words. "Now is a convenient time for you? Well too bad, Reed. I am completely done listening to you. I can't believe you have the audacity to show up here after the way you left me sleeping like that without so much as a word. Seriously, what have you become?"

I look away as he tries to make eye contact with me.

"I want to talk to you about what I said in the note," he says, with strain in his voice.

"You want to – wait, what?" Suddenly I'm very confused. "What note are you talking about?" I ask, the cutting tone of my voice suddenly softening unintentionally.

He looks confused now too. "The note I left you, on the bed, the morning... the morning I was at your place."

"You didn't leave a note," I say. Suddenly I'm fighting the urge to cry, and I don't even know why. The speakers in the bar are blasting "Your Love" by The Outfield, and people are pressing past us in both directions, leaving me with a claustrophobic sensation as he steps closer to me.

"Are you kidding me right now?" he asks. "Are you saying you *didn't get my note?*"

"Right," I say, feeling increasingly ill. "I didn't get any note from you. Ever. I woke up and you were gone, end of story." Unsurprisingly, the words come out sounding desperate as I try to comprehend the implications of what he is saying.

"Jesus," he says, running a hand through his short hair, the way he's always done when he's overwhelmed. "Well, I left you a note. I woke up early that morning, and I realized I didn't want to be there when you woke up and inevitably regretted what happened between us. So, I wrote you a note that said I wanted another chance to make things work with us, and to let me know if I had any shot at all." He's yelling now to be heard over the crowd. "It also said that if I didn't hear from you, then I would take that to mean you wanted to be with your fiancé, and that I'd respect that and leave you alone."

I rub my eyes as I take this in, not wanting to look at him, not trusting myself.

"But, the thing is, Breck, as the days went by and I didn't hear from you, I can't tell you how much I wished I'd never written that note. I realized I should have stuck around, stayed by your side regardless of if you regretted our night together, fought harder for you, even if I lost in the end. I'm not ready to give up on us, even if you are, and that's why I came here tonight. I was just waiting until you were away from your group to talk to you. I didn't know if one of those guys was your fiancé... I didn't want to cause trouble." His voice is gentle but filled with conviction. A part of me wants to collapse into his chest and believe what he is telling me, but I know I need to think.

"I didn't get your note," I say, finally looking him in the eye, my mind spinning. "I need to get out of here right now. I need a chance to think." For an instant I watch him studying my face, just as he's done since the first night we met. Then I turn and walk out the door before he can say anything more.

Chapter 63

After carefully sifting through the magazines and books piled on my night stand and rummaging around with a flashlight under my bed, no note has surfaced. I am not even sure if I want there to be a note. A part of me hopes he was lying back at the bar, trying to rectify his bad judgment with a concocted story. Then I could go on believing he was an asshole who'd let me down yet again. But, if I find the note, then what?

It's unlikely that the note is between the sheets and my comforter, given that I washed my sheets the day he left my bed and another time since then, so I'm beginning to run out of places to look. I start pulling my bed, which is unbelievably heavy, as it turns out, away from the wall a centimeter at a time. I move one front leg, then the other, slowly separating the bed from the wall. Once I've made a few inches of progress, I flip my flashlight back on and the beam illuminates the crevice. There, folded in half, I spot a lined sheet of paper now on the floor, apparently having fallen from the place where it had been nestled between the bed and the wall.

Sitting on the floor, I unfold it, seeing Reed's familiar handwriting scribbled across the lines.

> Breck – I hate to leave you like this, but I can't bear the thought of being here when you wake up and regret last night. The truth

is, you are the reason I came to Chicago. The thought of you is what kept me going all these years when I felt so completely lost. If there is any chance — any chance at all — that we can be together again, please let me know. I want that more than I have ever wanted anything. But, if there is no chance for us in your eyes, then I promise to respect that and leave you alone. I know that trying to be just your friend would be impossible, so I guess there can't be an in between, as much as I hate the thought of losing you completely. I love you, and hopefully I'll talk to you soon. R

How would I have felt if I'd read that the morning after we'd slept together? I know I read it differently now, almost a month after the fact, having a broken engagement under my belt, as well as weeks to accept that Reed left me once again.

I hear the sound of a key in the front door and stand up, the note still in hand.

"Breck?" I hear Lizzy calling my name.

"In here!" I say, just as Lizzy comes barreling into my room, Nevada and Pete in tow.

"Oh good, we were worried about you," Lizzy tells me as she takes off her high shoes. "You disappeared, and Pete said he saw you talking with the same guy who you were fighting with after the Double Door show, so I've been texting you and got worried when you weren't responding."

"Shit, sorry," I say, feeling terrible that I didn't say anything to them before I left The Cubby Bear. "Yeah, Reed showed up, and I just got distracted. I had to come back here to look for something." I hand the note over to her. Nevada quickly grabs one side of it and pulls it toward her so they can both read it at the same time.

"I'm sensing some girl talk is needed – I'm gonna head over to my place..." Pete says as the girls hungrily read the note. "Come by later if you want," he tells Lizzy, gently kissing her on the cheek and then slipping out of my bedroom.

"He left that for me the morning he was here," I tell them. "I never saw it though, obviously."

"Oh the drama," Nevada says with a smile, flopping on my bed. Lizzy and I follow suit, laying next to her.

"So, he thought you never contacted him because you'd chosen Will, meanwhile never knowing that you and Will were done and that you hadn't even gotten his letter!" Lizzy says, her eyes sparkling a little with what she undoubtedly views as the tragic romance of it all.

"You got it, Sherlock," I say playfully, although inside my stomach is in knots.

"So...?" Nevada says. "Then why was he at Cubby Bear tonight?"

"I guess he didn't want to give up, that's what he said at least. That he wished he'd stayed here that morning, not left this note, tried to win me back or whatever," I say. "But, of course, I didn't even know what the hell he was talking about, since I never got the note. So, I told him I needed to think and came back here to see if I could find the note. It was stuck between the bed and the wall, I guess it must have fallen off the pillow or something."

"Well, you need to go see him," Lizzy says matter-of-factly.

"Now? I don't even know how I feel about this," I say. "I need some time to digest it."

Lizzy gives me an incredulous look. "Oh please," she says, "you've loved Reed since you were sixteen years old. I know you've loved other guys since – Evan and Will – but with them, you were never the way you were with Reed. I know you, probably better than almost anyone, and I know you're still in love with him. You know it too, you're just afraid."

"Seriously, Brecks," Nevada agrees, lifting her head slightly from my pillow. "Enough already. You love him. We all know that. If you could just see how your face changes any time some one even says his name...It's obvious."

"Well, I guess I need to at least talk to him and see how that goes," I say, not sure that I'm quite ready to get on board with their belief that Reed is the love of my life. After all, I've spent so many years telling myself just the opposite.

The girls continue talking but suddenly all I want is to see his face. I head out the door a few minutes later, recalling the address he told me the other night.

Chapter 64

The building is an old brick three flat, with the name 'Whalen' written next to the buzzer for the third-floor unit. I'm feeling jittery as I raise my finger and press the button.

"Hello?" His voice comes through with a crackle of static.

"It's Brecken," I say. His response is muffled by the static but the door buzzes open and I enter. The stairwell is simple but nice, with fresh carpeting. I work my way up the flights of stairs, wondering what I will say when I reach the third floor.

He's there waiting in the hallway, smiling.

"You're back," he says, although it almost sounds like a question. Just being near him, hearing his voice, seeing that contemplative look of his that I know covers so much underneath, I know my friends are right. I love him now, just as I always have.

"I'm back," I say, returning his smile as he wraps his arms around me. "And so are you," I say.

He kisses my forehead and then pushes the door to his place open. "I never left," he says as we walk inside together, and I know exactly what he is trying to say.

EPILOGUE:

SUMMER OF 2011

As I breathe in the sandy scent of Green Island for the first time in more than ten years, I am overtaken by the memories of those two magical summers, which seem a lifetime away and yet remain as vividly etched in my mind as if they happened yesterday.

Since it's late August, the majority of the Greenies have already headed back home. A portion of them always return for Labor Day weekend, the official end of the season on Green, but for now there are people staying in only a small number of the houses, which is just how we knew it would be. We wanted a little peace and quiet, so we planned to come when we could re-open the Whalen house sans the well-meaning but nosy neighbors who were sure to surface when they saw that the lights were once again on in the long-vacant home.

Tonight and tomorrow, Reed and I will be opening up the old house, which has been sitting dormant for ten years, with the exception of a cleaning service that comes through now and again. Stephanie Whalen, her husband Mike, and their three-month-old son, Danny, are all going to be meeting us here tomorrow.

"You ready for this?" I ask Reed, curling my arm around his waist as we stand on the front porch of the house where he spent all his childhood summers.

"I suppose," he replies, a wistful tone in his voice. He wraps his strong arm around my shoulder for a minute, then reaches in the pocket of his worn Levi's and pulls out the key.

As he pushes the door open, the familiar scent of his house overtakes me, and I can see it hits him hard as well, even after all these years. We left our suitcases down in the front yard, where the carriage had dropped us off, but we're carrying in the groceries that we picked up in Charlevoix, needing to get them into the fridge. I reach to take the two bags of groceries he's carrying and then wind my way into the kitchen to unpack them, wanting to give him a minute on his own to take in the house.

As I unload the last of the groceries – corn on the cob, salmon and several bottles of wine – I resist the familiar urge to check my BlackBerry for work emails and can't help but smile to myself. I quit Baron & Riehl just over two weeks ago, and I'll be starting a new position with the ACLU in Chicago in three weeks. With my student loans paid off and two years of litigation experience to take with me, I am finally about to begin the career I had envisioned when I applied to law school in the first place. Not to mention that this weekend marks the beginning of the first vacation of more than a long weekend that I've had since I started working for Baron & Riehl almost three years ago. Reed doesn't start classes until late September, so we're planning to stay on Green through Labor Day.

Lizzy and Pete will be joining us on Green for the weekend, which will be Pete's first Green Island experience. I was hoping Nevada could come along as well, but she wanted to stay in Chicago over the long weekend to keep things running smoothly at Crash, which has been even more popular than usual after being voted Chicago's Best New Bar by *The RedEye* just last month.

"Hey baby," I hear Reed say, joining me in the kitchen. I see his eyes linger for an instant on the black and white photo of his parents on their sailboat that still hangs on the kitchen wall.

I smile sadly, thinking about how emotional this return must be for him. Even I feel consumed with memories, heavy with a sense of loss. I wrap my arms around him, and he gives me a long tight squeeze.

"You doing all right?" I ask, looking up at him.

"Yeah, I am," he says thoughtfully, as if considering this fact. "I really am."

• • • • •

After a few hours removing the covers from the furniture, putting fresh sheets on the beds, opening the window shades and reminiscing about the years gone by, Reed and I barbecue the salmon and corn on the cob, mix up a salad, uncork a bottle of pinot grigio and head out to balcony terrace to eat at the Whalens' black wrought iron table as we watch the sun set out over the lake. Reed seems distant, but I don't push him on it and let him lose himself in his thoughts without interruption. We drift from discussing bittersweet memories of his parents to lighter topics, such as our excitement about Steph's recent announcement that she, Mike and Danny are moving to Oak Park, Illinois, just outside Chicago, to be closer to Reed and to Mike's parents as well.

After dinner and a few glasses of wine, Reed seems increasingly present, though still more sentimental than usual.

I stand to begin clearing the dishes but Reed reaches his arm around my waist and pulls me into his lap.

"How about a walk on the beach?" he says, looking at me with the intensity that I know he can't help but exude.

"Sounds perfect," I say, rubbing his scruffy cheek with my hand as he moves in to kiss me.

Even after two years of being together again, I still literally feel weak when he kisses me. Somehow I don't think that will ever change.

He pulls away after a few minutes. "OK, let's get going or I'm pretty sure this walk on the beach might never happen," he says, giving me the same wry smirk that I instantly fell in love with so many years ago.

"All right, all right," I say laughing. "Shouldn't we wash these first?"

"Nah, let's just carry them down and leave them for later."

"Works for me," I say, picking up the dishes and silverware that I had been stacking before Reed sidetracked me.

He grabs the salad bowl, wine glasses and place mats and we head downstairs.

"I'm gonna grab a sweatshirt – you need anything?" he asks, as I set the plates in the sink.

"Um, sure. My purple hoodie would be great," I say.

He returns a minute later, and we head out.

"I always forget how many stars there are up here," I say, gazing at the deep blue sky that is literally covered with millions of stars that could never be seen amidst the lights of the city.

"Yeah, I love it," he agrees, taking my hand as we venture down the beach. "I'd forgotten how beautiful it is here. We should try to come here a few times next summer," he suggests, making me smile, and convincing me that he really is actually all right being back here.

"Definitely," I say, as we walk along and lapse into silence, our fingers intertwined.

"We should probably even get married here one of these days," he says, squeezing my hand playfully.

"Maybe one of these days," I say smiling, always giving him a hard time when he hints at marriage. We're just so content right now, and I don't need a diamond ring or a white dress to know that he and I will be together forever. I like the idea of celebrating with all our friends and family though, so I'm sure we'll go through with it soon enough, someday when the time feels right.

Eventually we come to the Sutters' house, which I know is empty for now. Mr. and Mrs. Sutter just left for a three week trip to Paris and the French Riviera and won't be returning to Green Island again until next summer.

"Let's go sit out there," I say, motioning to the Sutters' dock.

"Hmm, you read my mind," Reed says, and from beneath the sweatshirt he's been carrying, he pulls a bottle of Booker's Bourbon, making me laugh.

"I hope that bottle's cold," I say. "I'm not sure I can handle warm whiskey right now."

"Don't worry, it is. My hand's fucking freezing from holding it though," he says, putting his icy hand to my face as I squeal and dash ahead of him onto the dock.

• • • • •

We're returning from our walk with a slight buzz, laughing over memories of his Fourth of July boat party years ago, when Reed suggests we swing by the cluster of mailboxes a few houses from his to see if there's any mail.

"Didn't Steph cut off the mail service years ago?" I ask.

"Yeah, but I started it up again a few days ago. Sam said that the first copies of my book might be ready this week, said he'd send me a copy if they were."

"Seriously?" I ask excitedly. "You didn't tell me that!"

He laughs. "Calm down, it's no big deal..."

"Yes it is! *Your* book is being published – you told me that was your dream the very first night I met you. It's going to be sold all over the world. People will be discussing *your* ideas, experiencing sadness and joy from *your* story. It's a *huge* deal, Reed," I say enthusiastically.

"Whatever you say," he says, smirking at me. Sure enough, a padded envelope addressed to Reed sits amongst a few pieces of junk mail in the mailbox marked "Whalen".

I shriek, unable to help myself. "Open it!" I can see that he's excited, despite his efforts to appear nonchalant.

He tears open the package and holds the hardcover book out to me, before he even looks at it himself.

"It's beautiful," I say, feeling overwhelmed with emotion. "*Nomad in a Noose*," I read aloud. "A novel by Reed Whalen." I'm beaming as I say it, and I can see his smile breaking through. I admire the cover art and then reach to hand it to Reed but he shakes his head.

"It's dedicated to you," he says, putting his hand gently on the small of my back, and I hear a catch in his scratchy voice. I'm taken aback. Although I've seen the manuscript and cover art in their final form before, I've never seen a dedication page included.

I crack the crisp book open and read the first page:

For Brecken,

My muse, my rock
My heart, my life
You are everything that is anything to me.

Made in the USA
Lexington, KY
06 December 2012